I0788450

clash of HEROES

special edition

NATH DRAGON MEETS THE DARKSLAYER
BOOKS 1 -3
THE COMPLETE SERIES

CRAIG HALLORAN

CLASH OF HEROES
BOOKS 1-3
Copyright © July 2018 by Craig Halloran
Print Edition

TWO-TEN BOOK PRESS
P.O. Box 4215, Charleston, WV 25364

ISBN eBook: 978-1-946218-53-7
ISBN Paperback: 978-1-723479-58-8
ISBN Hardback: 978-1-946218-54-4

THE DARKSLAYER is a registered trademark, #77670850
http://www.thedarkslayer.com

All rights reserved. No part of this publication may be reproduced, stored in a retrieval system
or transmitted, in any form, or by any means, electronic, mechanical, recorded, photocopied, or
otherwise, without the prior permission of the copyright owner, except by a reviewer who may
quote brief passages in a review.

Publisher's Note
This book is a work of fiction. Names, characters, places, and incidents either are the product of
the author's imagination or are used fictitiously, and any resemblance to actual persons, living
or dead, events, or locales is entirely coincidental.

TABLE OF CONTENTS

Quintuklen
Thraag
Pool of the Dragons
Narnum
Shale Hills
Elome
Valley of Bones
Ruins of Barnabus
Morgdon
The Settlement
Mountain of Doom
Lost City of Borgash
Nalzambor
Key Location Guide

THE WORLD OF BISH
KEY LOCATION GUIDE
Hohm City
City of Three
The Mist
Hohm Marsh
Dwarven Hole
City of Bone
Red Clay Forest
The Warfield
Great Forest
of Bish
Two-Ten City
Nameless Mountains
Outpost
Thirty-One
Outlaw's Hide
Caves
of the
Underland
Lush Lakes
Outer Outlands
The Mist
N
W
E
S

INTRODUCTION

This crossover is based off my two bestselling book series, The Darkslayer and the Chronicles of Dragon. It's purpose is to have fun with my main characters while at the same time introducing them to new readers. You don't need to have read my other books to read this. It's a clean start for all. Think of it as Portal Fantasy where anything can happen.

Before diving into this one-of-a-kind adventure, I wanted to cover a few things. First, you'll be bouncing between two worlds, Bish and Nalzambor. Second, you will be dealing with two different time lines from each series. Nath Dragon begins this journey at some point in his series 2, Claws of the Dragon. Venir, the Darkslayer, is in part of his life that occurs before his series 1 begins. This is after he gets the armament, but before book 1, *Wrath of the Royals*, begins. Third, well, there isn't really a third, but be prepared to be reacquainted with some familiar faces. My, my, my, what will happen when Brool and Fang clash?

Fight or Die,

Craig

BOOK ONE

HEROES COLLIDE

CHAPTER 1

NALZAMBOR

REACHING DOWN, NATH EXTENDED HIS scaled arm, clasped Brenwar's thick wrist, and hauled him up onto the rock.

"I could have handled it," Brenwar said.

"Oh, I know, I just wanted to move a little faster," Nath replied.

"You don't need to hold up on my account." Brenwar, built like an anvil, stood proud in his dwarven breastplate, combing his powerful, meaty fingers through his black and grey-peppered beard. "I'll catch up. I always do."

Nath took a swig of wizard water from his flask and offered it to Brenwar. "That's only because I let you."

"Har." With his skeleton hand, Brenwar snatched the flask from Nath and guzzled it down. "Ah!"

"You might want to save some, just in case the journey turns out to be longer—"

"Don't you go and worry about me!" The dwarf stuffed the flask into Nath's chest and resumed his climb. "I'm fine."

Shaking his head, Nath watched Brenwar march up the hillside.

They were in a peculiar area of Nalzambor, several miles south of the Shale Hills, where the landscape was still green and coated in spring flowers. In was a nice sunny day in the beautiful land, the kind Nath was most fond of. The critters scurried in play and searched for food. The birds chirped. The river rapids cascaded over the rocks in the canyons far below.

Nath rubbed his forearm. His black scales glinted, seeming to soak up the sun with vibrant energy. Energized, Nath followed after Brenwar.

The pair had been tracking for days.

Weeks ago, a caravan of elves and dwarves had been attacked while moving the mystic Thunderstones from the home of the elves, Elome, to the home of the dwarves, Morgdon. After using them in the final battle of the last great Dragon War, the two races—after months of heated debate—had agreed to exchange custody of the Thunderstones on designated years. The first transport year had turned into a total calamity. The heavily armed envoy had been taken by a superior force of gnolls, goblins, ogres, orcs, bugbears, and even giants. The elven and dwarven forces were wiped out, and by the time the message of the fallen troops and lost stones reached the leaders' ears, the enemy was long gone, their tracks scattered in all directions.

Nath sighed.

Many of his and Brenwar's friends had died that day. The loss was heavy. Jolting. Deflating. The funerals lasted more than a week in celebration of the brave dwarves and elves who had died in a valiant battle.

As soon as Nath arrived on the scene, he had been able to picture what happened. The caravan had been outnumbered ten to one. Heavy footsteps were all over the bloodstained road and grass, the wagons toppled and torn apart.

As they all gathered there, the elves and dwarves had formed search parties, assigning Nath and Brenwar their own: a trail of goblins. Over a dozen had scurried through the highlands and hills. It seemed unlikely that goblins had put anything this big together, but he and Brenwar had reluctantly agreed.

"They leave their stink on everything, don't they?" Brenwar stood on a bed of pine needles, inspecting a tree. A small broken branch was pinched between his fingers, and his nose was crinkled.

"I haven't gone a moment without a whiff of them yet." Nath kneeled down. The goblin trail was getting more recent. They were closing in. "We should catch up with them in another day or so, don't you think?"

"Aye, but it seems like a lost cause. Goblins couldn't have pulled off that raid. I think they were just paid to hit and run. Cheap hired hands.

Probably paid in sandstone coins. Stupid, smelly things." Brenwar kicked the tree, rustling the branches. "They'll pay. All of them."

"We're after the stones, not blood."

"If we were after the stones, we wouldn't be hunting the goblins. I can't figure why we were given this task. It makes me want to spit through my beard."

"The goblins are just as clever as the others. Truth be told, I can't figure any of them being able to harness the stones' power. They aren't capable. Someone else is behind this."

"Who else could it be other than the titans?" Hefting his war hammer, Mortuun the Crusher, up onto his shoulder, Brenwar started moving on.

"The titans are trying to run things, but they can't run everything. No, not at all. There's plenty of other forces that would want those stones." Nath ducked under the branches and headed after Brenwar. "Humans, perhaps."

"Men couldn't control those ugly goons. Not in a century or a millennium."

"We can at least eliminate the possibility that they have them. Who knows, it's possible they don't even understand what they have."

Waving his war hammer over his head, Brenwar replied, "Well, they aren't going to be ready for what they are going to get. I'll tell you that much."

Nath chuckled. It didn't help the grim feeling that had set in, though. When he'd been younger, the unknown had been exciting, but the older he got, the more danger filled it became. People died. Friends were lost. And now, great power was in the hands of another unknown enemy.

Let's just eliminate the goblins as suspects and move on. Hopefully the others will have tracked down the perpetrators when we return.

After a short night of rest and another half day of travel, their trek led them across a broad stream that was very familiar.

"Say, Brenwar, do you remember the last time we passed through here?"

Stomping through the knee-deep waters, his friend said, "No."

"Aw, of course you do. Sansla Libor. You know, the winged ape? He chucked you through those trees. Ha! Now *that* was astonishing."

"Are you going to talk, or are you going to track?"

Nath didn't reply. Instead, he resumed the lead.

The goblins, though crafty, weren't too hard to follow. They were bold and often traveled in heavy numbers so it wasn't likely anyone would mess with them. It was past midday, just when the sun crested and started to dip, when Nath's boots landed on the edge of the Shale Hills. Aptly named, they were covered in black fragments of stone from one massive hillside to the other. Still, underneath was fertile soil, and trees burst out of the ground like flowers.

Standing beside him and staring up the hill, Brenwar said, "Odd."

Nath nodded and kept on the trail. By the end of the day, he found himself staring at a very familiar cliff face lined with caves and crisscrossed with stone footholds. The rows of openings made out a pattern of skulls with vines and ivy oozing down the sides. He glanced over and found Brenwar's eyes on his. "You thinking what I'm thinking?"

"Aye, we should have killed him."

CHAPTER 2

I T WAS CLEAR. THE GOBLIN trail led straight for the cliff face full of caves. Nath led the way, traversing the narrow trails, following the signs to the bottom of the ancient and abandoned mountain city. It had been here, decades ago, where they had crossed paths with a vile necromancer named Corzan. Nath's memory was as clear as yesterday. He'd bound the mage up in *Elotween*, the elven twine, and left him to his own fate. Perhaps that had come back to haunt him. Perhaps he'd come back to haunt Corzan, assuming the man was still alive.

"Do you want to take the other way in?" Brenwar was facing a valley where the mountain waters crashed into a lake below. It was there they had slipped in undetected the last time.

"No doubt they'll be expecting someone." Nath hooked his clawed hands into one of the footholds in the rock. "And I didn't even see any guards posted. It's possible this was just a pass-through. Or hideout." He started his climb. "Maybe they moved on."

"Moved on or not, I don't care. I'm taking them down. Just go."

One foothold at a time, Nath made his way up the sheer cliff. There were staircases, narrow and busted, that could have been taken, but Nath liked to climb. He liked to outdistance Brenwar and get a clear look at things before the dwarf got there. He'd never say so, but it was for Brenwar's safety. The battle-hardened dwarf had lost a fraction of a step over the years. Forty feet up Nath went until his head almost crested the top of the wall. Brenwar was huffing it twenty feet below him. "I'm gonna take a peek," Nath said.

"Don't you dare!"

With the ease of a lizard, Nath slipped over the wall and looked down. Bones of a dead goblin lay on the broad landing, but nothing else was present. Just a long, narrow roadway and several cave openings. There were two more levels above, and those stairs looked far easier to climb, though they were smooth and eroded. His nose twitched. The oily stench of goblin sweat and death lingered near. Reaching over his shoulder, he slid Fang from his sheath.

"I heard that!" Brenwar yelled from below.

Nath peered back over the wall. "Do you want them to know we're coming?"

"Yes."

Nath reached down to help Brenwar up over the wall.

The dwarf pushed him away. "I don't need your help." He unslung his war hammer and took a big whiff through his nose, narrowed his eyes, and said with a fierce grin, "They're in there, all right. I can smell the fear in them."

"That's not fear. It's just stink."

"No, it's fear. They know Brenwar's coming."

Nath slapped him on the shoulder. "You've made your point." He gazed upward. "So, do you want to start bottom up or top down?"

Brenwar pointed his axe toward the nearest cave. "There."

Nath shrugged. "Fair enough." In stride and sword ready, he headed toward the nearest entrance. The last time they'd been here, there had been goblin guards posted everywhere, but now, both the mouths of the caves and the roads from one cave to the next were abandoned. Other than the rotten smell and the stiff wind, they had no company.

Eyes narrowed, Nath eased his way inside the shadowy mouth of the first cave. In moments, his eyes adjusted. "Doesn't seem like they've done much decorating since the last time I was here."

Brenwar grunted.

There was still enough light outside to show the outlines of the inner city within. Nath had been in dozens of places like this in his two hundred and some years of life. Grand cities carved out of the heart of a mountain. Rooms. Roadways. Throne rooms and cathedrals. Just like a castle, but only cut out from within. The dwarven city of Morgdon was much like this, but according to Brenwar, this here was a cruder work from long, long ago. Where they stood now was a wide-open expanse, probably an old courtyard or marketplace. Its makings were timeless and abandoned.

"Follow the stink, I guess," said Nath.

Brenwar agreed, "Aye."

Tracking goblins on stone wasn't easy if they got too far of a lead. Eventually their scent, like that of most things, would fade. Following his nose, Nath ventured deeper into the mountain city, peeking through one opening and another, until they were standing in the pitch black and Brenwar bumped into him. His sight was strong in the blackness, and Brenwar's dwarven senses weren't half bad either, but Nath didn't want to overlook anything.

"How about a little light, Fang?" he asked.

The great blade glimmered with a very faint light.

"Thank you."

They ventured deeper into the city. Little had changed in the decades since Nath had been there. Far from a marvel, the inner sanctum was one dreary room after the other. Alcoves abandoned. Wooden tables and chairs rotting. The strange thing was that it had been abandoned at all. It was livable. Cold, dreary, but livable. But that was common in Nalzambor. There were fallen cities and temples throughout the land, places that time and war forgot for whatever reason.

Spending little more than an hour, they finished checking the rooms.

Brenwar started into one of the passages that led deeper into the city. "I'm thinking there's another side to this city. We never went that far last time."

Something ate at Nath. He said to Brenwar, "Let's go back. We didn't even check the throne room."

"We got a good enough look at it when we passed. I say we keep going."

Nath was already moving, however, traversing the rough-hewn corridors. Fang's soft light led him to the throne room. The giant urns where fire had burned were still on either side of the throne made from large blocks of stone. He scanned the balconies above, but there was only darkness. Not even the slightest scuffle caught his ear, only Brenwar's breathing and the soft squeak of the leather that held the buckle on his breastplate armor.

"Still nothing," Brenwar said.

Nath approached the metal cage that was big enough to hold a small dragon. A blue streak dragon had been imprisoned there, and last time, Nath had come to rescue it. Now, the empty cage sat there as a silent reminder of the evil in the world. Nath had thought he defeated it, but he knew in his heart there were still people that would poach dragons. Kill them. Sell them. Enslave them.

Brenwar eyed the cage and turned to Nath. "Nothing here. Let's go."

"I suppose."

Suddenly, the nape hairs on Nath's neck stood up. Fang's blade brightened. He whirled toward the throne just as all of the urns burst into a new fiery light.

A formidable figure appeared on the throne, tall and long, in dark-grey robes that hid his feet. Hairy fingers clutched the arms of the great chair. Long fingernails emanated arcane power. The man's face was lean, strong chinned, and hairy.

"Corzan!"

CHAPTER 3

CORZAN SAT UNFAZED, WITH A look of delight in his large dark eyes. He bounced his fingertips together. "I assume you are looking for the Thunderstones, eh?"

"No, we're tracking down a bunch of murderers!" Brenwar blurted out.

The necromancer rolled his eyes. "Oh my, I shouldn't be surprised you brought that two-legged goat with you. Really, Nath Dragon, or should I say Dragon Prince? Shouldn't you be keeping a better class of company by now?"

Brenwar started to storm forward.

Nath caught him by the arm and held his friend back.

Corzan was way too poised, a game master waiting to make his move. And there was an air about him that hadn't been there decades ago. Power radiated from him.

"Stand down, Brenwar." Nath stuck Fang in the stone. "Let's find out what this is all about."

"I don't want to stand down. I want to take it to him!"

"Me?" Corzan eased back into his chair. "Well, I didn't say I had the Thunderstones, now did I? Perhaps I was going to lead you to them. Certainly things have changed over the years. Why, I'm a new man, thanks to you showing such mercy on me."

"You hardly look new," Nath joked.

Corzan stiffened in his chair, and his eyes narrowed.

"Aye, he's still the ugliest goblin I've ever seen."

Corzan leaned forward with a sneer. "I'm no goblin. Heh. But there are plenty close by that you can get acquainted with, you bearded tree stump."

That's when the rustling came. The scuffle of feet and shifting armor. Metal scraping out of scabbards.

Nath wrapped his fingers around his sword Fang's hilt.

A goblin horde filed into the room. They emerged on the balconies above and hooted. Yellow eyes gleamed with murder.

"I'll take the ones below. You take the ones above," Brenwar suggested. "We'll knock the stink off all of them."

"There's no need for violence, dwarf. My, aside from battle and engineering, your race is far from interesting. Perhaps, for your own safety, you'd be better off in a cage." Corzan snapped his fingers. A bright mystic spark popped. Brenwar vanished and reappeared in the cage with a confounded look on his face. "That's better."

"You dirty wizard!" Brenwar drew back his war hammer.

"No, don't!" Nath yelled.

It was too late. The war hammer slammed into the metal.

Krang! Zap!

The cage bars struck like lightning and knocked Brenwar clear off his feet and slammed him into the bars. He lay shuddering on the floor with his fuzzy beard smoking and then went still.

Nath ripped Fang out of the floor. "No more games, Corzan. I can easily cut you down before your men can save you. Now free him."

"I'll do no such thing. And as you recall, I've not been found guilty of anything. It was your hard-headed friend who was posing danger. My, I thought you would be wiser than you are by now. What have you been doing all these years, getting slower?"

"We tracked the goblins here, so I'm confident this raid has your fingers all over it. And you proved to be quite obsessed with the last Thunderstone."

"I was a much younger sorcerer then."

Nath scanned his surroundings.

The goblins, at least a hundred, hung back behind the flickering shadows of the fiery urns. The throne room was vast, however. Even with so many goblins, they'd be hard pressed to hem Nath in, not to mention containing the power he had with Fang.

"Older or younger, it's not going to change your fate." Nath gave Fang a twirl. "Just like the last time, you're going to lose again today."

Corzan rose up off of his throne. The gaunt sorcerer pushed up his sleeves, revealing his hairy arms. He was a man, but he had the scary looks of a fiendish goblin about him. His eyes were stones of black power. He took a couple of steps toward Nath and stopped. "You know, it's hardly a coincidence that you are here. I've been planning this day for a very long time."

"Ah, I see. I spared your life, and it's vengeance you seek. Well, I've been around long enough to know that compassion and mercy don't work on everybody." Nath laughed and tossed his long red hair. "So, please share. Um, let me guess. You want to sell my scales to the titans."

"Oh no, that's tempting, but far too simple. I have much grander plans for the likes of you." The sorcerer eased closer and stood within a sword swing of Nath. Suddenly, two stones now filled his very large hands. Thunderstones. Each was a different shade of colorful marble, with arcane symbols engraved in the middle. They pulsated with a life of their own. "I just want vengeance, well, and more power."

Nath's scales shuddered.

Corzan's presence was pure power. Awesome, building-shaking power.

Be wary, Nath. But be quick!

Nath was fast. But he knew the sorcerer's thoughts, and therefore his spells, were even faster. He lowered his sword. "It seems clear that I was right all along. You have the stones. Your goblins are the killers. Or at least some of them. I'm sure the elves and dwarves have avenged the rest by now. So what is it going to be, Corzan? Are you going to try and kill me? I must warn you, it's very, very hard to do."

"Let me share something with you."

"Please, talk," Nath said.

Yes, let him tell me his plans. Evil loves to boast.

CHAPTER 4

A S NATH'S MIND RACED, TRYING to get a handle on how to deal with the situation, Corzan prattled on.

"I've always been obsessed with the Thunderstones, ever since the first day I observed one's power in my enclave long ago. Of course, each was a prized treasure and heavily guarded, and as you well remember, you fetched the first one for me." Corzan's eyes flashed. "Ah, to have it in my clutches, only to lose it. That day, Nath Dragon, you'd have been better off killing me. But you didn't. And instead of cowering into the unknown with my proverbial tail between my legs, I focused more on my craft." He paced around Nath as he spoke. "I devoted months, years, decades to particular disciplines. I sought deeper, darker ancient knowledge, and do you know what my efforts revealed?"

"Long, thinning grey hair?"

Corzan cackled. The two Thunderstones he carried floated out of his hands and around him like moons. He slipped another one out of his sleeve, and it joined the others. "No, I learned there were many more stones." His brightly painted fingernails clasped the air. "And I could have them all if I could find them. And I did find many. And my, aren't they quite powerful. And the more you add, the more powerful they become. Of course, you know that, having seen Quintuklen for yourself. Such power can destroy an entire city."

As Nath watched the stones circle the man, a sliver of worry crawled down his spine.

This isn't good. Not good at all. I had better act fast. How to act is the question.

"Oh Nath, please. There's nothing you can do at this point. Act fast? Huh! You aren't fast enough."

Nath swallowed.

He can read my thoughts!

"Yes, I can read your thoughts. You see, that is what the Stone of Thought does. Fantastic, isn't it. Oh, how I marvel at these divine objects." Corzan made his way back to his throne and sat down. The stones formed a floating arc over his head. From his robes, he filled his hands with two more. He radiated power, magnificent, perverted power.

Nath looked over at Brenwar, but his friend was still out cold.

"Oh, and I like that one thought you had, 'Evil likes to boast.' Truly, truly it does, especially when it can. Now, where was I before your pathetic little thoughts interrupted me? Ah yes, as you can see, I have five stones, and each has a special function in addition to lending me its power."

Each Thunderstone twinkled as he named it.

"The Stone of Thought, so grand it is. The Stone of Command. Yes, that one I used to convince you to follow the goblins here. Yes, Nath, I was there, well, near enough to influence the direction of those prissy elves and dullard dwarves. Pah, so predictable. Then, I used the Stone of Transport to come back here in the twinkling of an eye. The Stone of Sight lets me see many things far and near, and the Stone of Power harnesses them all together. But to think, there are even more of them to be had, and I will have them all, especially once you are gone."

Scratching the back of his neck, Nath yawned. "If it were me, I would have gotten all of the stones first. After all, I was—"

Corzan finished his sentence. "Very distracted. Oh yes, yes, I know. These musings between the dragons and the Clerics of Barnabus, Gorn Grattack, and the Great Dragon War have been highly beneficial to me. Everyone was so concerned with that, they overlooked the likes of me. Oh, how I delighted in it." He licked his lips. "Why, I snatched one stone from those overly keen elves themselves. Now, that was something. I bet they didn't share that loss with you, did they? No, no, of course not."

Nath tried not to think. To blot out his thoughts. It wasn't one bit easy at all. Instead, he let his instincts take over. He started to spring. But then his body lifted from the ground and he was suspended in the air! He could move, but he couldn't go anywhere.

"Honestly, Nath Dragon." Corzan shook his head. "You won't be able to get within a hundred yards of me unless I will it. Why, I could tell you how many birds are in the trees for ten miles around, if I so wanted. As a matter of fact, I can sense how many dragons are in the area as well. Not that I need them now. I don't need anything now."

"Then why fool with me, Corzan?"

"Why indeed. Well, let's just say you have a way of spoiling things. And also, I really, really don't like you."

Nath crossed his arms over his chest and raised his chin so that his long red hair swayed around him. "It's because I'm so handsome, isn't it? I get that a lot, and I can certainly understand that, coming from a man in your unfavorable condition."

"Be silent!"

The entire room shook with the words. The goblins oohed and ahhed.

Nath fastened his tongue inside his mouth. The power that Corzan wielded was impressive. Extraordinary. And he had it mastered, too. Scary.

The adversaries locked eyes.

Nath could feel Corzan's vile mind picking around inside his head. A tiny hammer tapping. Probing. Attacking. Finally, Nath unleashed his tongue. "Whatever you do to me, release my friend from harm."

Corzan rose from his throne and spat out his words. "Such nobility! No! No, I won't. He'll be as dead as the stone where he lies."

"How wonderful it must be to be evil," Nath said with a sneer. He'd had it now. Still floating in the air, he connected his thoughts to Fang and summoned the sword's power.

The blade ripped free of his grasp and clattered on the floor.

Corzan laughed. "Ha ha ha! Feeble. Very feeble. Do you not understand that I am omnipotent now?" The mystic stones began to swirl above both of them, forming a colorful vortex above Nath's head.

"Is this where you kill me?" Nath asked.

"Kill you? No, no, I don't want your blood on my hands. That will bring out too many unwanted enemies. And as you were merciful to me, so I will be merciful to you. Death, no. But banishment? Yes." Corzan chanted some ancient words in a language Nath didn't know.

The Thunderstones turned into a bright ring of sparkling fire with a sparkling starlit hole in the middle of it.

"I don't know where this goes, Nath Dragon, but I do know this portal goes to another world far, far away. You can be their problem now."

Fear seized Nath. His hair was standing on end, stretching toward the portal.

Guzan! This is serious!

"Corzan, don't do this!"

"What in Morgdon is going on?" Brenwar yelled. He was on his feet again, his brown eyes filled with worry. "Let my friend down!"

With a subtle wave, Corzan said, "Goodbye, Nath Dragon. May your journey be miserable and your death in the next world swift."

"No, Corzan! No!"

The portal started sucking Nath in. His boots flipped over his head. Up, up he went, into the star-filled darkness. His golden eyes locked on the dragon hilt of his sword.

Fang, I need you. Come!

The great blade lifted off the ground and soared into his hand.

He heard Brenwar screaming, "NAAAAAATH!"

Suh-loop!

Nath's body turned icy cold. Everything went black. Nalzambor was gone.

CHAPTER 5

BISH

A SMALL WOODEN BARGE GLIDED OVER the dark and stagnant waters. There was little to see in the tunnel. It was pitch black aside from the glow of a small lantern that lit up the front end of the craft with a faded illumination. Below, in the waters, glowing minnows darted underneath the craft, feeding on the algae on the bottom before darting away again. A lone figure sat on the back of the craft. Black robes covered his small body. His violet eyes, like gemstones, smoldered.

"A meeting," he grumbled. "Nothing I detest more than a meeting with my fellow underlings." He let out an aggravated chitter. "And with those two, no less. I've been cursed only to be cursed over and over again."

In front of him sat a chest made from wood, strapped and hinged in iron. He ran his fingers over the cool metal. From this, perhaps, he could give his masters what they sought and then be gone. He didn't care to fool with his kind much anymore. No, he had other interests. Experiments. He enjoyed toying with the world above far more than the world below. Not that he didn't find comfort in the caves, but he just didn't find much comfort among the underlings. And his fellow underlings didn't find too much comfort with him. He was odd like that. A loner.

"Oh well, I suppose I might as well make the most of the journey." He shifted on his bench and reached down with his furry grey hand into a small open crate nestled between the planks behind him. His nimble fingers grabbed a bottle by its neck, and with his sharp teeth he pulled the cork out of the bottle, only to spit it into the crate and take a long drink.

"Ah. There's nothing quite like a fine bottle of underling port." He guzzled down another drink. "And how it eases the senses, yet doesn't dull them too much." He thought of who he was about to face and shrugged. "On second thought, I don't think I could dull them enough."

Without looking, the underling rummaged through the crate and took out a jar big enough to fill both hands. Small insects crawled within. He removed the cap and ate several crunchy bugs one by one, washing them down with port. Satisfied, he replaced the lid, dropped the jar in the crate, finished off the bottle, and with a tap of his chest, let out a long but somewhat polite burp.

Bwurp!

Picking his catlike teeth with his long black pinky fingernail, he said, "That makes things a little better."

Traveling the Current waters that spanned like black veins beneath the surface of the world of Bish, he meditated on his upcoming meeting. Rubbing the light-grey, rat-like fur on top of his hands, he said to himself, "Don't worry. Know full well that it will be far worse than the last time. It always is."

The small barge banked itself on the soft sands of the inner-world beach. With a groan, the underling shuffled to its end and hopped onto the dry land. With a wave of his fingers and a mystic glow in his eyes, the chest lifted up and out of the barge and followed him onto the land. Head down and shoulders slumped, he trudged away from the comfort of the lantern and into one of many tunnels that seemed waiting to devour him.

"Here we go. No fear. No fear."

He entered the mouth of the nearest cave with the chest gliding behind him inches above the ground. It was pitch black, but the path was far from confusing. This was his home, after all. The Underland. Darkness was a comforting blanket for him and all of his kind, but there was still a peculiarity about it. He was no longer welcome here. He had been banished.

Rubbing his palms together, he stopped at the last bend.

Be arrogant or be humble, they're never pleased either way. Oh, I'll just let them do the talking.

He emerged into a cave created from carved stone.

The soft bluish underlight illuminated the edges of the walls. Two more underlings, dressed similar to him, sat at the back of the room in large, ornate, high-backed pewter chairs. Four massive mangy dogs bigger than him lay at their feet. The underlings didn't speak. The one's silver eyes and the other's golden eyes burned right into him.

Oh great. It's both of them. Why must they always be together? They're insufferable with each other.

He swallowed the lump in his throat, approached, bowed, and took a knee. His voice almost cracked when he said, "Lords Catten and Verbard, I am here, as you requested."

Silence followed.

Minute after agonizing minute, he remained on one knee until he trembled. His brow beaded in sweat. His body ached.

The four cave dogs walked over and sniffed him. One growled in his ear and licked its hairy lips before sauntering back again and lying down.

It was miserable. It always was miserable here.

Catten, the golden-eyed one, spoke. "Oran, must you grovel all the time? Get up!"

Oran rose on his aching legs, fought the urge to shake the numbness out, and said with his eyes down, "As you command."

"Oh, come now, Oran. You know you are most welcome among us," Catten continued.

No, not true. Never true. Last time, you let the urchlings scourge me.

"Yes," Verbard said with a silvery smile, "please, tell us how you have been."

"How I have been?"

"No, how I have been," Verbard said with sarcasm.

"You are most excellent as always."

"Don't be a suck-up, Oran!" Verbard formed a fist and punched forward.

An unseen force knocked Oran off his feet onto his chest.

Gasping for breath, he crawled forward on his hands and knees, croaking out the word, "Apologies."

"I hate apologies," Catten said with an evil flicker in his eye. "They imply failure."

"Yes," Verbard agreed. "Oran is a failure, and we know what happens to failures around here, don't we?"

Without even looking, Oran could feel Catten nodding.

The underling master then said, "Yes, we turn one's apologies into successes by tormenting them night in and night out until they get things right."

CHAPTER 6

ORAN'S VIOLET-SAPPHIRE EYES TURNED RED. He bounced to his feet and said in a fit of rage, "Oh, will you two stop! Have I not faced all of your whimsies? Done your vile deeds? And yet you continue treating me like one of the demented urchlings! I am here on your request. I didn't have to come, but I did." He rolled up his sleeves, and his fingertips glowed with yellow light. "Either kill me or do business with me. What will it be?"

"Well now, it seems Oran the Outcast has a spine in his back after all," Verbard said. His eyes turned into storms of silver. "But no underling dares talk to me like that." He cocked back his elbow and let loose the first jolt of lightning from his hand.

The bolt slammed into a citrine shield of energy that Oran had summoned at the last second. His sandaled feet scooted backward through the sand.

If I die, I die. So be it then. At least I'll never have to listen to these two again.

"Enough, Brother, enough," said Catten, the voice of reason, to Verbard. "Oran is our ally, not our enemy. And he is right. We did summon him here, did we not?"

Tiny streams of lightning danced on Verbard's fingertips and winked out. Nodding, he said, "We'll see."

Huffing for breath, Oran wiped the sweat dripping down his cheek with his sleeve. He turned to the chest and flipped open the lid.

Catten and Verbard, robes dragging over the ground, floated over. The lithe underlings were already taller than him, but hovering over the ground made them seem like giants. Flanking him, they peered into the chest.

Oran cleared his throat and spoke. "Here it is."

Catten tilted his head. "Here what is?"

"Yes, I thought you'd brought us the corpse of our enemy." Without a crease in his inquisitive face, Verbard frowned. "Instead, you bring this? A chest with an urn in it? Do tell me it is filled with the ashes of our enemy."

"You summoned me here to help you catch him," Oran objected. He reached inside the chest and removed the urn from its packing. It was bigger than his head and heavy. With a grunt, he teetered over and set it down on the ground.

Fool of a cleric! I suppose I could have lifted it with a spell, but I'll need my energy.

He cleared his throat again. "This will help you catch him."

"Are you jesting?" Catten's eyes were slits. "You catch the enemy, not us. We have better things to do. That is why we summoned you, fool!"

The two underling lords glared at the urn with suspicion. It was crude but majestic in its own way. Its arcane markings were vibrant, deep and spacy.

"I don't know this thing," Verbard remarked. "Where did you get it?"

"As things in the world of men go: one of the Royals with sorcerous ways was betrayed. Cut down. I bartered for it in a trade."

Catten and Verbard hissed and chittered. Anger filled their eyes. "You are a fool to dally with the humans above. That is why you were banished. A trickster. Deceiver. Traitor, they call you. Dabbling with our sworn enemy."

"They are easily duped," Oran argued back. "So steeped in greed, they even kill one another. I serve our cause, the underling cause, not my own. Our leadership is too blind to see that. Making an example out of me." He spat on the ground. "Pah! I am Oran. Every castle, every cave knows that."

"Knew that," Verbard corrected. He stared down at Oran. "But they know our names now, don't they? Don't make me finish you, Oran. I will, you know."

With effort, Oran kept his anger in check. "I can't operate this object without your help."

"Surely you jest. You come for our help?" Catten said.

Oran reached back into the chest and withdrew an ancient scroll. It was a dusky brown parchment, fastened with leather cords and wider than his very shoulders. "This is power from a millennium ago, maybe longer. I can read it, but I cannot summon the power of the urn at the same time. I need someone to harness my words, turn them to energy, and ignite the urn."

"And then what?"

"Then, as it says, it will summon a monster to do anything we want."

"All of this trouble on account of one lone slayer," Verbard said. "This butcher should have been dispatched already."

"This butcher slays us in our own night. Our blood feeds the soil above. It makes men's spirits fertile. I dare not face this menace of slaughter alone. I'll need help."

Catten and Verbard drifted away and conferred, leaving Oran alone in his thoughts.

Such a waste of my precious time this is, but whatever I can do to get them out of my business, I will. As the humans would say, 'Slat, let's get this over with.'

The brothers returned.

Lord Catten spoke for both. "You read. I'll channel. Verbard will ignite." He extended his hand and took the scroll from Oran. As he unrolled the parchment, his brows lifted. He showed a row of straight pin-needle teeth to his brother. "Let's pluck this thorn, cast it in the fire, and go home."

CHAPTER 7

NATH CRASHED HARD INTO THE ground. His head was pounding. Limbs shaken, he forced himself up into a sitting position. He was in a cave, he knew that much. It was dimly lit by a faint blue light, and the walls were slick and wet. Rubbing his neck, he tried to remember what he'd been doing before. As he searched his memories, he was seized by panic. He didn't recall anything. Not a single moment from before, just nothing.

A rustle caught his ear. He twisted around.

Three ugly, hairy humanoids were there in robes, one standing and two floating a foot above the ground. They had bright eyes. Nothing at all was familiar about them. They spoke a strange chitter, none of which made any sense.

A growl caught his ears.

Four huge dogs, mangy beasts and ugly, snuck toward him with their heads low. Their jaws slavered with drool that dripped from teeth that looked like they could chew stone. The beasts surrounded him, closed in, and snorted.

"Easy," Nath said, holding out his hand.

A glint of metal caught his eye. A sword, grand and exquisite. It seemed familiar, but it was too far away.

On instinct, he locked eyes with the biggest of the four dogs. He knew them for what they were and could name the normal objects that he'd seen, but aside from that, he had no memories whatsoever. No idea who he was or how he got here. "Easy," he repeated.

The dogs' mostly white eyes narrowed. All together they pounced. Nath balled up.

Wet snouts probed his body, sniffed. Rough tongues licked him.

With his head cocked to one side, Verbard said, "What is this? They lick him like a pup?"

"Bizarre," Catten replied. "Oran, what sort of demon is this? No doubt, he is a hideous beast, but he's taken command of our dogs. Is that a smile on his lips? Pah! You have summoned no monster but a human."

Breathless, Oran argued, "That is no human." His breathing was ragged. The spell had taken quite a toll on him. He could barely stand. It didn't help that the monster he'd worked so hard to get and paid so much for in trade looked like a man with a mane of wild red hair. And the cave dogs bathed him like an old friend. Quickly, Oran's master plan had become a disaster. "Cave dogs have quirky natures. You know that. No, look at this thing. Look at those arms. They are scaled. And those claws could tear through a Vicious!"

"You fool!" Catten yelled. "This creature you have summoned shows glee. Name me any demon that shows such an expression. Where did you summon this man from, one of the Royal brothels?"

Oran was speechless. The ... thing he'd summoned was a far cry from anything he could ever imagine. At first, he fought to find something to say, and then instead, he watched the man rise to his feet.

The ... thing was a towering figure. Human perfection. Strong chinned, his chiseled frame was covered in powerful supine muscle. He wore well-crafted breastplate armor, breeches, and nothing else. The red-haired stranger scratched a dog behind the ears with his yellow claws. In every way, the summoned being was as graceful and fluid as a cat. And unlike Catten's cold, metallic golden eyes, this being's eyes were as captivating, warm, and golden as the dreaded sunrise.

"Just send it back," Catten said.

"You know that's not possible." Oran's violet-sapphire eyes were fixed on the marvelous being. Surely this was the answer to his call. The very presence of the man, thing, or demon he had summoned dominated the room. With tongues hanging out of their mouths, Verbard and Catten's protective cave dogs looked like playful pups. "We have not even communicated with it."

Catten and Verbard's metallic eyes found his and prodded him on.

Oran approached the creature inside the charred circle that still smoked. "What is your name, demon?"

The scaled stranger tilted his head and lifted a brow.

Oran asked again, this time in Common, "What is your name?"

The demon creature shrugged his shoulders. Pushing through the dogs, he made his way over to the great sword and bent over to pick it up.

The sword slid across the cave floor and stopped at Lord Catten's floating feet. The blade was every bit as long as them standing.

The demon gave them a curious look.

"Well," Catten said, "Not only is this pet of yours hideous, but it's also stupid. We can't have it playing with sharp objects, now can we?"

"I'd say not." Verbard's feet touched the ground. His silver eyes studied the sword. His fingers rubbed his chin. "This is a fascinating blade. Are those dragon heads on the pommels? That is not of Bish. If only I had a soldier big enough to wield it." He reached down and touched the hilt.

Zzzt!

Verbard jerked his hand away and screamed. "Argh!"

Oran backed away.

Verbard looked furious.

Heh, they always find a way to make things worse. He had it coming.

"It seems it is a demon after all." Catten chuckled. "The blade is possessed. Either that, or it's an excellent judge of character."

"This is a farce! I'm ending it." Lightning flashed in Verbard's silver eyes and erupted from his fingers. Streams of fiery light blasted the demon full in the chest and knocked him off his feet. He stopped at the edge of the cave, unmoving. Verbard dusted off his hands and turned to Oran. "It's time to turn your banishment into a funeral."

CHAPTER 8

"Look," Catten said. He was pointing at the corner of the cave. "It lives."

The demon rose to his feet. His scorched chest plate was smoking. The expression on his face was grim. Anger surged in his golden eyes.

"I think you made it mad," Catten added. "Perhaps you should apologize to it. Make amends."

"Oran, do something with your transgressor," Verbard ordered. The underling lord and his brother glided backward. "Quickly."

Fascinating!

Oran couldn't believe his fortune. It seemed the portal spell he and the brothers had cast had drained them quite a bit. They were vulnerable. If there was ever a time to strike them down, now would be the time.

If I weren't also so weak, I'd be done with the both of you!

The demon approached, one cautious step at a time. Less than a dozen feet away, he coiled down, ready to spring.

"Oran! Get this thing under control!"

No, I'd rather see you die.

Oran had read the scroll. He had the connection with the demon, and he should be able to control it. He felt its mind in his. It was angry. Confused. Lost.

Oh, I should let it pick up that blade and strike both of them down.

That would be the end of their foul words. But unlike me, they'd be missed. Avenged. And it … fascinates me.

Oran cut in between the demon and the lords. "Halt."

The redheaded creature stopped and stared at him with gold lava in his eyes. His huge, clawed hands clutched in and out. The sharp nails looked like spikes. Cords of muscle rippled underneath the black-scaled forearms. No doubt those arms were as powerful as a squeezing python.

Oran held his palms up and out, bowed, sat down and said, "Sit."

The strange man eyed Verbard and shook his head.

"You have no control over it," Verbard hissed. "None at all, you failure."

"Give him a moment, will you, Brother?" Catten laughed at Verbard. "You are the source of all this agitation, and all because that little sword stung you."

"Shut your mouth, Catten. This monster is dangerous and too hard to control. Look at him. That's no ally to us. It's an enemy. I tell you, it must be destroyed."

"I can control it, Verbard," Oran said. He pushed his sleeves up over his knobby elbows. "Just give me a moment."

"Nay." Verbard snapped his fingers.

Pop!

A small band of urchlings poured out of the nearest tunnel. They were smaller than Oran, barely four feet tall. Their bare backs were hunched over, and their limbs were filled with corded muscles. Teeth and claws were sharp as knives, and their black eyes underneath their thick and protruding brows were filled with hunger and evil.

"Urchlings?" Oran said with shock. "What kind of game are you playing, bringing along those savage little monsters?

Catten, to Oran's surprise, spoke this time. "Perhaps we thought your monster would need feeding."

"Give me a moment before you destroy all trust," Oran argued.

But the lords would have none of it. This was obviously entertainment for them. Their eyes were filled with an avid and bloodthirsty curiosity.

He sprang to his feet. "End this now."

"Mind your tongue, Oran. Or once this is over, I might have the urchlings tear it out." Verbard fixed his eyes on the prize, the stranger from another world. "Besides, we need to see if this grotesque demon is worthy of this quest. If he lives, glory to you. If he dies, gory to me."

"Oh, that was witty, Brother," Catten said with a bob of his head. "'Gory to me.' How enchanting."

Verbard pointed at Nath and let out a commanding chitter. "Kill."

A dozen urchlings charged in a frenzied horde. Nath stretched out toward his sword that lay on the ground.

The blade flew straight into his hand.

Like a striking cobra, he swung.

Slice!

The first rank of urchlings died, torsos severed mid-section. The great blade struck hard and fast. The little monsters fell in ones and twos. They latched onto his arms and bit at his scales. Their teeth broke off, and they howled. Claws tore at his skin and tried to rip his red hair from his scalp.

He more than matched their fury with his own ferocity. Quicker. Stronger. Deadlier. He stomped them, cut them, pummeled them into submission. The floor was wet with their dark blood as well as his own, but less than a minute later, it was all over. He stood tall and easy.

The urchlings were cave-dog food.

Marveling at what he'd just seen, Oran rubbed his jaw and turned to Catten and Verbard.

They were gone.

His heart fluttered in his chest. It was just him and the demon holding the great sword coated in greasy urchling blood. Dry throat cracking, he said with command, "You must come with me."

Uncertain of anything, but with his senses full of alarm, Nath surveyed the carnage. The creatures lay dead at his feet. Cruel and vile things. Evil. He didn't understand it, but he knew it. The silver-eyed fiend that had attacked him was gone, along with the other. His shoulder muscles eased. The lone living person in the room seemed to be trying to befriend him somehow, and Nath was drawn to his words. The tones of the foreign words of the smallish rat-man, a child in comparison to him, were convincing.

What do I do?

Scanning the cave, he found no place to go. Instead, he stood and watched the odd little person gather an urn and scroll and place them in a chest. The chest rose from the dirt and floated after the jewel-eyed rat-man into the cave.

Toting his bloody sword, Nath, having no idea where to go or who to trust, followed Oran onto the small barge. Two total strangers from different worlds sailed the Current together.

CHAPTER 9

"Y OU ARE QUITE ADEPT, QUITE adept indeed," Oran said to Nath.

The old pair were sitting at a table inside the underling's cave lair, leagues away from the Underland. Oran had been working with Nath, teaching him the common language of Bish. Nath had found just about everything within the lair disturbing and odd—the glass jars, huge and small, with heads from many races in them, on deep shelves. Potions and odd decanters. Oran, however, had little trouble explaining his experimentation. He just said, when asked, "That's what I was created to do."

"I can understand losing my memory," Nath said to Oran, "but I don't understand why I would lose my speech."

Gaping, Oran said to him, "Marvelous. You spoke that so well. Why, I've never had such an apt pupil. Of course, it's only natural that your common language would return so quickly.

My, this creature is smart. He memorizes everything I show him. If I could only somehow duplicate him. Oh, an army of him! Now that would be something.

He pushed a burning candle toward Nath, looked at Nath's arm, and said, "Do you mind?"

"Mind what?"

"Eh, holding your hand over the flame? For experimental purposes. I need to see how these scales hold up."

Nath held his scaled hands over the flames. The orange-yellow glow licked around his fingers. He shrugged.

"That is marvelous, just marvelous." Oran scurried away and returned with a small scalpel-like knife. "Take your hand out of the flame."

Nath withdrew his arm. "What are you going to do with that?"

"Just be still." Oran leaned over and sliced the scales on the summoned creature's forearm. The fine blade didn't make a mark. "Did you feel that?"

"I felt it, but there was no discomfort."

"I see. Let me try something else." He held the scalpel up to Nath's cheek and cut a straight line.

"What was that for?" Nath said.

Oran wiped the laceration with his finger. The wound closed before his eyes. "Fascinating. My, you are a quick healer. Astounding." He wiped the blood from his fingertip into a small vial and stowed it away on a nearby shelf.

"I don't follow why you are surprised by these things. Did we not know each other before?" Nath got up from his stool and stretched his long limbs. "And how much longer do we need to be stuck inside this cave? I'm curious. Is there nothing to see other than the black water of this abyss?"

Oran made his way over to a rack of bottles stacked against the wall. He withdrew one, a wine bottle from the world of the races above. He found some metal goblets and poured two glasses of wine. He handed one to Nath. "Have a drink. Now that you've grasped the language, I'll try to make this clear to you."

Nath took the wine, sniffed it, and handed it back.

Oran set the goblets aside. He took Nath by the arm and led him over to a large sofa. It was plush and covered in soft red-and-purple patterns, with a fine view of the stagnant Current. "Please, sit."

Nath obliged.

Oran felt another moment of triumph. He didn't have complete control over the creature that sat beside him, but he had enough. Unlike most summoned creatures, this one operated with a will of its own. Very, very unique and otherworldly. But it was clear: Oran hadn't summoned some mindless monster but rather a person from elsewhere. Still, it was going to be difficult to earn the dragon man's trust. Oran had his work cut out for him. Turning him into a weapon would take some convincing. He chose the thoughts he shared carefully.

"You are a hunter. A champion of our kind. The ultimate fighting machine," he said.

Nath straightened up a little. "Really?"

"Yes." Oran nodded solemnly. "We underlings live below the ground, hiding ourselves from the slaughter that awaits above." He filled his voice with despair and sorrow. "We used to live above, in peace, but the world above forced us beneath the ground. It was the only way our race could survive. So here, in this black pit, we live like rodents. I've lost so many of my family. Dozens over the years. Wives. Children." He made a strange sob. "Butchered. Pleas for mercy fell on deaf ears."

"Women and children? That's horrible." Nath patted Oran on the shoulder. "Tell me more."

Oran produced a handkerchief and blew his nose. "I will. I will … friend." He looked up into Nath's eyes, and with a pleading face, he said, "That is why you came. To bring us justice. Vengeance. Not all are bad in the world above. There are others." He rubbed the scales on Nath's arms. "Like you."

"Like me!"

"Oh, but don't get so excited, my comrade. Your kind are rare, and your brethren allied with us against the men above." Oran sighed. "And I fear that most of your kindred are dead. They hunted them down and killed them. It's quite possible that you are the last."

"But I thought I was summoned with magic?" Nath said.

"It was to our benefit that one of your kind came. Fortune is finally in our favor."

Nath turned to him. "Then why did the other underlings try to kill me?"

Oran lifted his eyes. "Alas, this is our problem. You have served us for quite some time. You had a mission to hunt down and destroy a man. He cuts our kind down with bloodthirsty barbaric cruelty. Turning us into crow food!" He smacked his hand on the couch's arm. "We are peaceful! Yet he slaughters us like sheep!"

"Easy now, Oran."

Rubbing his temples, Oran said, "I'm sorry. I didn't answer your question. It seems I got caught up with myself. Where was I? Ah yes, old silver eyes, Verbard. Indeed, he wanted to kill you because you failed."

"Failed?"

"You were sent to take out this slayer. Months ago. We lost track of you; hence, I summoned you back. Somehow, Lords Verbard and Catten knew this Darkslayer still lived." Oran patted Nath on the knee. "Those two don't take failure well, but I fought for you. Hence, I summoned you back, and you didn't recollect anything. Tell me, do you not remember anything? Anything at all?"

Nath shook his head.

"Oh, it's going to be difficult to pick up where you left off then, but I'm certain we can put the trail back together. We must. You are all the hope we have to stop this Outland butcher."

"Oran, you knew me before, so tell me, what is my name? It escapes me."

"Uh, er …" Oran fumbled over the words. He needed to come up with something quick. This man was too keen, so he needed to be convincing. He knew Nath's real name because just before the man had dropped out of the portal, he'd heard a gruff voice screaming it from the other side. Oh, why not just tell him. "Nath. Yes, Nath. I should have thought of that. I think that might help you."

But I hope not. Risky Oran, risky.

"Is it helping?"

Nath's face was a mask of concentration. He repeated the name over and over. "Nath. Nath. Nath. It seems familiar enough." He sighed and clutched his head. "But no."

Thank the evil Current!

Oran rubbed Nath's back. "Don't fret, comrade. Perhaps some of the air above will restore your thoughts. But we must be careful."

"We're leaving?"

Oran got up, found the goblets of wine on the nearby table, and drank them both. "Ah! Now, get in the barge. We have an ugly world to see."

CHAPTER 10

"THIS LOOKS A LOT MORE accommodating," Nath said, shielding his eyes with his hand. He stared over a rugged, dirt-coated landscape where the trees had no leaves. In the distance, a bright burning sun sank over the rocky hillsides with another, smaller yellow sun behind it. "I can see why you'd rather live above than below. It's hot but incredible."

With his back turned to the hot blaze, Oran said, "Indeed. Come, we need to go."

Nath followed, taking in the landscape as he strolled. Little spiny lizards darted over the sunbaked ground. Green-brown cacti seemed to burst from it. Ahead, facing the sun's burning light, Nath's keen eyes could make out the details of a large stagnant marsh filled with vines and willow trees. A gentle breeze drifted in the foul sulphur-like smell. "We are going in there?"

"Yes." Oran replied.

"You seem a little quiet. Why is that?"

"It's places like this where that butcher thrives. We never know when he may strike, but we often find sanctuary in these marshes. The smell keeps men away. Often we have survivors hiding there. Come."

Nath found himself slowing down from time to time because Oran struggled to keep up with his long strides. Judging by the ugly grimace on the underling's face, Oran was either scared or out of his element. Or both. His face had been drawn tight since they left the caves.

It took about an hour, but finally they entered the swamp, just as the last ray of sunlight dimmed.

Ankle deep in murky waters, Nath covered his nose with the back of his hand and pushed through the thickets. Small creatures with big white eyes hopped from tree to tree. Ugly birds cawed. Something snaked through the waters past his ankles. Unable to help himself, Nath said, "And your people live here? I think the caves are better."

Oran grumbled a chitter. "It's not ideal, but many prefer the lands above ground. Underlings are fearless and often live on the edge, Darkslayer or no. We will not cower forever. That's why you're here."

"I see."

After venturing deeper into the dark swamp, Nath came to a stop. He reached forward and grabbed Oran by his robes. The scales on his neck tingled. His hand reached behind his back and locked around the pommel of his sword.

The soft breath of a nearby predator pricked his ears, and then the sound of metal slipping from leather sheaths.

Peering in the dimness, Nath found himself surrounded by dozens of gemstone eyes, dark colors: red, blue, and green that gave off the faintest twinkle of light in the dimness.

"Be still," Oran warned.

On cat's feet, smallish and intent figures revealed themselves and closed in. They were stout and wiry underlings, with various razor-sharp blades that filled their hands. Some carried small crossbows, and others had blowguns pressed to their lips. They moved with deadly intent, wiry bodies corded in muscle, ready and poised to strike.

"Friends of yours?" Nath said through his teeth.

Palms up, Oran started speaking Underling in strange chitters. Their weapons remained poised at his and Nath's chests. The underling cleric spoke fast, with authority behind it.

Nath tried to put together bits and pieces of the odd language. He hadn't had any trouble with the one Oran had taught him, but this one was more complicated. He wasn't exactly sure why Oran hadn't bothered to teach it to him, but for now he'd just have to accept it.

Finally, the underlings lowered their weapons and put them away. One of them approached, a shirtless little brute with two curved swords strapped on his hips. The emerald-eyed underling ran his finger over Nath's forearm and let out an excited chitter.

"What's going on, Oran?" Nath asked.

"They are inspecting you. Just give them a moment and they'll soon be through."

Nath wasn't sure why, but he had the urge to recoil from the pressing throng of hard-faced underlings. Finally, after about a minute or so, they broke off and vanished back into the marsh. "Where are they going?"

"To the grave."

"The grave?" Nath said, eyeing the lone underling fighter that remained. It was the one with emerald eyes and two fine blades. "Whose grave?"

"Our graves."

Corpses. Underling corpses. More than a dozen of them cut down in their prime. Some were jammed in the murk with their legs tethered up with sticks. A bald one's face was split open. Another one was cut in half.

Nath covered his nose and fanned away the flies and gnats.

"Do you not bury them? How can you leave them exposed like that?"

"It keeps that fiend away. He'll not hunt again where he's already passed. It's a sanctuary." Oran was gazing up at one of his dead brethren that hung in a tree. He'd been scalped. "The monster even takes trophies. How sick is that? Twisted and diabolical, is it not?"

Nath hacked a cough and spat the foul taste from his mouth. Indeed, the carnage was a grisly scene. The underlings, a well-armed and trained fighting force judging by the look of them, had been massacred. He picked his way between the bodies, inspecting them with his eyes. "What in the world does this monster fight with?"

"He carries an axe. Like your sword, it's almost as big as a man. They say he strikes like a snake. Twirls it with the ease of a stick." Oran nodded his head at one of the underlings from the small force that accompanied them. He was rough looking, and his right arm was missing. Oran took him by the good arm and said to Nath, "He saw the Darkslayer and lived."

The ruby-eyed underling fighter nodded.

"He is a Badoon," Oran said. "One of our finest hunters and soldiers. He is cherished and he is vengeful. He'll stop at nothing to kill this slayer."

Nath studied an underling that looked to be pinned to a tree with his own spear. "Was this slayer even wounded?"

Oran chittered back and forth with the wounded underling and said back to Nath, "He falls and then he rises, they say."

By Nath's best guess, the corpses were weeks old, maybe longer. It seemed the marsh's sulfur and salty waters had a way of preserving bodies from decay. He pinched some brown tree moss between his fingers. Even it smelled bad. Everything stank, and it seemed a shame that these underlings were forced to live here. He eyed an underling filling up a canteen with the foul marsh waters and said with a sour face, "You drink this?"

"We've adapted. It's a unique capability of our race. Perhaps some of these waters will quench your own palate." Oran took the canteen from the underling who had just filled it. He offered it to Nath. "Drink and replenish yourself."

Nath pushed out his hand as if to push the canteen away. "No, thank you. I'm not thirsty."

"And you've eaten very little at all. You need to fill yourself. Be strong for the hunt."

Jaw set like a stone, Nath balled up his fist. "I've seen enough, Oran. And the only thing I hunger for is revenge for your and my people." He smacked his fist into his hand. "It's time this slayer was slain."

CHAPTER 11

Back in Oran's lair, Nath stood on the sandy beach staring down at the black waters. He was convinced the underlings needed his aid, and that that was what he was here for. Besides, it was the only way he could learn about himself and others like him.

"You're a hunter, are you not?" Oran said, hooking a rucksack over Nath's shoulders. "Yes, yes, of course you are. Fine hunters your kind are. The best. This food will preserve you if needed. And you may need to cover yourself. It's possible you will have to venture into the cities to track this miscreant down. He's a man by day, we believe, and demon by night. We'll see. Rather, you'll see."

Even with his memories gone, Nath didn't have any trouble feeling comfortable about hunting. He wouldn't go hungry, if that was what the underling was worried about. No, he'd be fine. Staring down into the black waters, he watched the ghostly fish go by. He had an urge to catch them. Scale them. Eat them. "Look, I'm ready, Oran. I have my sword and my instincts. I say let's go."

"Oh, well, there is no 'let's'. The Badoon underlings will lead you from here." Oran approached. He had a solid necklace of twisted metal in his hand. "Put this on."

Nath took it in hand. "Is it a gift?"

"It's for your protection. I won't be accompanying you, Nath. But, with the aid of this, I can keep track of your location. If you are in danger, all you need to do is call my name." Oran placed a metal band on his head that was of a similar makeup in dark metal material. "See?"

The underling's words were convincing. As a matter of fact, every time the underling spoke, Nath felt compelled to obey, and as strange and unpleasant as the underlings seemed, for some reason he wanted to help them in their time of need. He clasped the band around his neck and immediately felt the urge to tug on it with his clawed finger. "It's a bit snug."

"You'll get used to it."

"I suppose I can take it off if it bothers me," Nath said. He tried to unclasp it, but the hasp would not loosen. "Oran, what treachery is this?"

"You cannot take it off," Oran said, "but I can. Listen, Nath, I cannot risk losing you again. You were summoned by me and need to trust me." He pressed his fingers to his head and closed his eyes.

You can hear me, can you not?

"Yes, yes I can."

"Then trust me. It's for your safety, and you'll get used to it. Before long, it will be like a second skin to you." Oran escorted him onto the barge, where several of the underling Badoon fighters stood ready. "Nath, do not fail me. You must kill this slayer once and for all. If you fail, I fear all will be lost in this world. Not to mention, my lords Catten and Verbard will certainly skin both of us alive."

"I'll find this fiend that strikes in the night."

"And on your journey, I'll give you plenty to think about." With his foot, Oran pushed the barge into the Current.

The windless tunnels swept the craft away and took Nath into the darkness.

Oran sat on the sofa, wringing his hands. The dragon man Nath that he had summoned was unlike any creature he'd ever dealt with before. Unlike the other monsters he'd toyed with, this one, he was certain, was good natured. He guzzled down some human-made wine and wiped his mouth across his sleeve.

"Oh, if it weren't for Verbard and Catten, this could be so much more interesting."

He poured another glass, sat back, and took the metal headband off. Eyeing it, he was pleased. He could keep an eye on the man without putting himself in any danger. He could do other things as well, such as change the man's perception of things. The man would need to be tougher, meaner. Day by day, hour by hour, the collar Nath wore should turn him away from any noble deeds. Oran grinned.

I'll turn that good nature dark.

"And it should strengthen my grip on him." He stretched out his arms and yawned. "Oh, how I would delight in going on this journey, but why endanger myself? The Badoon have their orders: find the slayer and help my new champion kill him. And if he fails, he fails. It wouldn't surprise me one bit if Catten and Verbard had forgotten all about this already." He rubbed his lips with his finger. "And if he wins, then my, what a weapon I will have at my disposal."

CHAPTER 12

NATH'S JOURNEY WITH THE UNDERLINGS took him through some wild country, wasteland, and marshes. Finally, they led him into a jungle-like terrain thick in vines and narrow ravines. The underlings said little. If anything, they were all business. Skilled. Tactful. They crept through the rugged foliage like a band of slithering snakes. They were nothing short of an impressive knot of people.

Nath thumbed sweat from his eyes. In addition to its vibrant sounds of wildlife, the jungle was dripping wet with humidity. The dampness dripped from the grey faces of the underlings. They were a hard little people, the same in size and build, but each different. Some wore black-dyed leather armor. Others were shirtless or had tattoos, branding, or scars. Hairstyles were various: braided, long, short, and bald, one just as intimidating as the other. Nath found it hard to believe that anything could push them around.

He kneeled down on a soft bank of mud and drank from the creek that trickled by. The fresh water cooled his throat and eased his senses. They'd been walking for days, daylight and dark. Nath didn't rest easy when he needed to either. He tugged at his necklace. Ever since he'd put it on, something had been tugging at him, probing at him. It gave him a slight headache.

The underling with dark-green eyes and two blades on his hips poked him in the back and chittered at him.

Nath refilled his canteen and fell back in step. Even though he didn't understand their tongue and they spoke little, he was picking up bits and pieces. *Come.* That chittered word was simple enough.

"How are you?" asked a voice inside Nath's mind. The voice of Oran.

Ducking underneath some brush, Nath replied in thought. "Fine."

"Any bloodshed?"

"Not yet."

Oran had been communicating with him daily and filling him in. He spoke about the other races and described them. He sent images as well. Dwarves and halflings. Gnolls, kobolds, and orcs. The sweaty-nosed orcs bothered Nath most for some reason. And then the men. Oran and the underlings truly despised men. The underling cleric said most men were worse than the other races, and they couldn't even trust themselves. "Be wary of them," Oran said. "After all, this journey may take some time."

The underling Badoon came to a stop. Quickly, they dashed off the path and burrowed into the thickets.

Nath did the same. He sent his thoughts to Oran. "We have action on the way."

"Keep me posted." Oran's connection was gone.

As he hunkered back in the foliage, the sound of hooves caught Nath's ear. Riders were coming up the path. With hushed breath, he waited alongside the Badoon leader, who squatted in the brush ready to spring.

Three riders appeared, men adorned in heavy armor from the shoulder down. One carried a banner of white and blue stripes. Each had a heavy sword strapped to the saddle. Their faces were weathered and formidable.

The wildlife chirped and hooted. The day winds rustled the leaves. The underlings started cawing on their own. It was a unique birdlike sound. The Badoon leader snaked his swords from his sheaths.

Nath felt the underling's heartbeat speed up.

They're going to attack.

The lead rider came to a stop and held his gauntleted hand up. His eyes narrowed, and quickly his hand went to his sword. Scanning the trees, he cried out, "Ambush!"

Clatch zip! Clatch zip! Clatch zip!

Small crossbow bolts rocketed into the horse's hind quarters. The mare reared up and threw her rider to the ground. In an instant, the underlings filled the path and pinned the riders in. Four underlings pounced on the fallen rider, cutting him open where he stood. His blood was the first to feed the ground.

With astonishment, Nath watched the battle ensue. With the surprise over, the riders rode hard and trampled a handful of underlings under the hooves of the well-trained beasts. Long swords were out and started to strike, keeping the fierce knot of jewel-eyed fighters at bay. Quick and deadly, the underlings chopped away at the battling steeds, dropping them to the ground.

Still concealed, Nath's neck tightened. A conflict within arose.

Metal banging against metal, the swift hunters whittled away at the men. The taller warriors chopped with well-placed ferocity. Back and forth they went.

Glitch! Stab! Hack! Slash!

One underling lost his arm. Another clutched at a bleeding hole in his neck. The heavy armor of the bloodied second rider slowed him down. His chops became sluggish. The underlings, in quick, accurate flashes, overwhelmed the man with quick-striking steel. The lights went out in his eyes, and he sagged to the ground.

That left the lead rider and his blood-coated longsword.

The Badoon leader faced off with the man and chittered a command to the other underlings. The throng of wiry fighters stayed their weapons and encircled the two.

The man, stern and short bearded, filled his free hand with a dagger. "I might die, you black fiend, but you'll die with me."

Spitting on the ground, the underling charged.

Sword poised, the man parried. *Clang! Clang!*

Fast and relentless, the underling struck blow after blow. The seasoned fighter slapped away every blow. With the ease of a cat toying with a mouse, the underling kept striking. It wasn't long before the defending warrior's breath labored and his shoulders drooped.

Nath could see the end coming, but he was torn. What merited the men getting ambushed? And the slaughter of horses seemed to be a tactic that was uncalled for. It formed a knot in his stomach.

The underling's fine curved blade bit deep into the man's wrist. His dagger fell to the ground.

Grimacing, the man said, "Fool of a fiend! You may take me, but you will not take what is coming. Hear that, underling? Hear that?"

Nath lurched in the bushes. A rumble came. The leaves on the trees started to shake. The thunder of hooves roared.

Riders!

The underling leader's blades darted in and skewered the man in the chest. He ripped them out again and turned. Riders, a dozen, galloped down the path. Spears were lowered. Elbows locked in place.

The ambush wasn't over. It had just begun.

CHAPTER 13

Horse hooves thundered down the path. Fighting men in heavy steel plowed into the underlings and skewered them with their long spears. Fearless, the underlings heaved themselves up on horse and rider and fought with wild fury. One warrior was dragged to the ground and overwhelmed by two of the stabbing little rat-men. It was far from enough.

What are these underlings doing? They should retreat.

Faces filled with hatred and rage, the underlings fought on with well-trained ferocity. Using everything at their disposal, they cut down the men from the horses.

On their feet, the human fighters, superior in strength and armor, unloaded on the underlings with a heavy clash of steel.

Quick as cats, the underlings jabbed sharp steel and drew blood. One underling cut open a man's leg, only to overlook the man closing in on him. A sword split his face right between his ruby-red eyes.

Something made Nath's temper flare. He sprang into action. After bursting out of the foliage, he charged down into the ravine. With Fang in hand, he rushed the closest man. The man in battle-ravaged plate armor locked eyes with him and seemed to smile. Nath cut him down.

The battle raged all around him. Nath carved a path through the men, trying to save underling after underling. Every fighter was in a frenzy, battle lust in every face. There was hatred in the air. Deep, fathomless hatred. Underlings screamed in fearless defiance as they fell under bloody steel.

Nath cut. Slashed. Hacked. He found himself facing a bewildered human warrior, who said to him, "What kind of man defends these fiends?" The human, covered in blood and sweat, hefted his straight blade with two hands. "You have a black heart, you red-haired demon!"

With Nath's blood fueled from what he assumed was battle, the man's words didn't register. Sword arcing high, he pounced. Fang collided with the man's fine steel with jarring effect. The man's blade smacked into his own eyes. Dazed, the warrior let loose a wild swing. The blow should have been lethal, but on Nath it just clipped his scaled side as he spun away.

After days of irritation, Nath turned loose his frustration. With a savage swing, he cut down the durable human fighter and charged the next.

Slash! Rip! Hack!

In a sea of black blood, everything became a blur. The cries of battle and the clamor of steel crested and fell silent. Nath stood, chest heaving in a field of death. Fang burned hot in his grip. When he released the blood-stained blade, he snapped out of the battle haze and came back to his senses. The scene before him was ghastly. All were dead: man, underling, and beast.

A ragged breath caught Nath's ear. He turned.

Behind him, gasping his last breath, was the emerald-eyed underling.

Nath kneeled down at his side.

Wide eyed, the underling looked up at Nath, pointed at him, said, "Kill ssslayer," and died.

Nath sat on his knees with a numb feeling all over him. Something was wrong. He clutched his scaled hands in and out. They were sore. His sword had burned him!

What is going on?

Glancing all around, he surveyed the carnage. Everything became louder: the buzzing of insects, the scurry of creatures. His heart pounded in his ears. His stomach turned. He clutched at the burning wound in his side and stared at the blood on his hand. He rubbed his head and said, over and over, "This is not right. This is not right."

On hands and knees, he crawled over to his sword, which lay still on the dusty path. He grabbed the pommel. It was no longer hot. He dragged the great blade behind him as he looked for survivors. Men were dead, and Nath didn't remember killing them. He didn't remember a lot. He couldn't ignore the sick feeling in his stomach either.

Did I do this?

He stared at the dead man who had spoken to him just before his battle lust consumed him. The man's appalled face had said it all when he'd said to Nath, "What kind of man defends these fiends?"

Stomach in knots, Nath ran as far and as fast as he could.

CHAPTER 14

"HO!" VENIR PULLED HIS HORSE to a halt and held up his hand. Eyeing the steep valley below, he spied several unmanned horses drinking from a stream. "Do you see what I see, Billip?"

"I already saw it," Billip replied. Atop his saddle, he popped his knuckles then unhitched his bow. "I was waiting to see if you saw before I said anything."

"I saw it first," said the man riding in behind Billip. He was a big black man, short haired, heavy in muscle. He rode a big chestnut horse and had a broad smile. He placed a steel cap on his head. "It's my claim."

"You didn't see anything," Billip said. The wiry archer, black haired and dark eyed, wore leather armor over his chest. His eyes were sharp and penetrating like an eagle's. Nocking an arrow, he scanned the jungle valley. "Bats have better eyes than you, Mikkel."

"We'll see," said the brawny warrior as he unhitched a heavy crossbow from his saddle. Covered in sweat, his muscle and sinew bulged when he pulled back the string and loaded a long bolt. "I bet I kill a fiend before you do."

"I don't think we'll be killing anybody if you two keep broadcasting our whereabouts to every living thing in the jungle." Venir slipped off his saddle. Wide shouldered, powerfully built, and rangy, the tawny-headed, long-haired warrior crept over the pathway's rim. He drew his long hunting knife. "Cover me."

Shaking his head, Mikkel said, "And he's worried about us making noise? Maybe you and your little pointed sticks, Billip. But not me."

"Oh, shut your jolly hole," Billip replied. "And I killed five to your three the last time."

"That fifth didn't count," Mikkel argued. "He was already dying from a Skull Basher wound, and you shot him in the neck."

"He had the drop on you, and it was the back of the head, to be specific …"

Venir ignored their words and eased toward the abandoned horses. Daylight still crept through the leaves on the heavy trees, but the thick greenery still coated the sweltering landscape in an eerie dimness. Hair caught in some hanging briars, he pulled his head free and placed a section of his braided locks in his mouth. Gentle as a breeze, he traversed the landscape and snuck up behind the horses.

By his side with his tongue hanging out of his mouth was Venir's dog, Chongo. He was a huge dog, big enough for children to ride, with a bull mastiff face and a soft coat of chestnut hair. His tail was sharp and flipped back and forth.

The saddled mounts were loaded down with gear common to Royal soldiers. Their tails flapped away at their backs, and their ears twitched. The horse nearest Venir nickered.

Chongo's head lowered and his tail stiffened. A growl rumbled from his throat.

"Easy," whispered his master. He placed his hands on the horse's neck and rubbed it. "Easy."

The horse nickered again and stared at Venir with an unblinking eye. The horse was calm. Well trained. Venir checked the area again. His keen eyes and ears didn't pick up anything out of the ordinary. He raised his long arm over his head and waved. "All right, let's see what's going on here." He dismounted and said, "Chongo, let's go."

He tethered the three horses together one by one and led them upstream. The horses' hoof prints were pressed in the soft bank, and the ferns that lined the stream were pressed down as well. Venir led them up the valley, straight through a path of broken branches for another half mile. It was there he happened upon another path he'd traveled before.

It was more common, wider, and often used by Royals traveling from outpost to outpost.

His nostrils flared. "Hmmm." The wind stirred the golden leaves, and a howl ripped through the ravine below. He came to a stop and rested his hand on a mossy boulder. He sniffed then took the lead horse's reins and stuck them in a tree and moved forward. His brow crinkled, and he covered his nose.

Death. Nothing on Bish smelled quite like it.

Venir picked up the pace and trotted down the mud-packed path. Rounding the bend, he came face to face with the scene of a horrific battle. Crows scattered into the trees. Royal soldiers, over a dozen, lay dead. Many of their mounts were dead too. Knife ready, he investigated the graveyard. His eyes enlarged on the body of the first underling. It lay dead with a spear sticking out of its chest. Its dark sapphire eyes glared unblinking at the leaf-laden sky.

"I'll be." Venir stuffed his long bone-handled knife into its sheath. "Hah! It seems we are not the only ones who have had a good day feasting on these grey-skinned fiends." He ripped a spear out of another dead underling and picked his way through the dead. He poked at the underling corpses, but no more black blood ran. He spat the foul taste from his mouth and took a swig from his canteen. "Sorry I missed it."

Billip and Mikkel, on horseback, rounded the bend. Mikkel had his nose tucked inside his elbow and said to Venir, "When did you do all this?"

"Hah," Venir said with a fierce smile. "I wish. No, they're more than a day dead. Maybe two. It's a sad thing, however, that the varmints won't feast on the underlings. But they will eat the men, so someone's got to bury them."

Stroking his goatee, Billip said, "We could get a lot of money for all of these horses and hardware, and all of this underling steel is worth its weight in silver. It seems the sands of the Outlands have smiled on us today. Mikkel, get out your shovel."

"Shovel my arse! Let the crows eat those soldiers. I don't owe those Royals. If anything, it's the other way around."

Venir picked up a blood-tainted sky-blue and white banner. "This is a good house, Mikkel. The Jakkens of Outpost Fourteen. We'll have to make this right with them."

Mikkel folded his arms over his chest, shook his head, and said, "Nuh-uh. Not after the last time they stiffed us. Almost got us killed, and they laughed. I say we take this steel and leave them."

Venir turned his back. Mikkel had bigger issues with the Royals than he did, and not without cause, but sometimes you just had to move on. Checking the dead, his eyes popped wide. "Bish! Look at this wound!"

Billip and Mikkel slipped alongside him. They gaped at the dead man that was split asunder. Mikkel said, "Are you sure you didn't do this?"

Scratching the back of his head, Venir said, "I know I didn't, but even worse, I know an underling didn't do that either." He noticed another dead Royal with a leg missing and another missing his head. "Underling weapons aren't big enough to do that."

Leaning on his bow and looking down at the corpse, Billip said, "Maybe the underlings are getting bigger." He glanced up at Venir. "Whoever it was I say is quite a warrior."

Venir eyed him and shook his head. Scanning the ground, he tried to make sense of what had happened. The scuffling footwork of battle revealed a few things. With his fingers in the impressions in the dirt, it was clear to Venir that the battle had been man against underling and nothing else. But there looked to be one man, a big one, in particular. Looking up at his bewildered friends, he said, "Looks like a sword wound. A big one. And it sliced clean through the flesh and plate armor. I've never known another blade to do that."

"Aside from yours, you mean?' Mikkel said.

"Aye," Billip added. "Methinks our comrade Venir is a wee bit jealous. Perhaps there is some other indiscriminate slayer out there, eh?"

Rising up to full height, Venir replied, "Whoever it was didn't kill any underlings, so he must be their ally."

"I bet it's the brigands, Venir." Mikkel took off his skullcap. "A gnoll, orc, or ogre could swing a sword that big."

"Agreed," Billip said, popping his knuckles. He gave Venir a stern look. "That doesn't mean it has to be our problem, Venir. I say we take what we can of this gear, and if you like, I'll escort you to one of the outposts to tell the Royals about the slaughter of their kind. But this underling steel I'm taking back to Two-Ten City. I know a smithy who will pay good coin for it."

Grim faced, Venir nodded.

He unslung the rucksack from his broad back and dropped it on the ground.

"Oh no you don't," Mikkel said. He picked up the pack and shoved it into Venir's chest. "We've been out for weeks, and I'm ready to do some drinking. You're just going to have to wait!"

"You go," Venir said, "I'll stay."

"Business first, Venir," Billip chimed in. "Let the Royals handle this. And don't go running off again, either. You put us both in a bind the last time."

Venir's face darkened. "Don't tell me what to do."

In silence, Billip and Mikkel backed away and started gathering up the horses and their gear. Finally, Mikkel said, "You need some civilization. You get too wild out here."

With a frown and a nod, Venir slung his pack over his shoulder. "Fine. But I'm still going to hunt down and kill whoever did this."

"We know, Billip said, "but let's fill our bellies with rotten food, our tongues with lousy grog, and our laps with generous hips first."

CHAPTER 15

NATH SAT IN THE WOODS, clutching his head. He couldn't erase the scene of the battle from his mind. Men were dead by his hand, and for what reason he did not know. Something wasn't right. It wasn't right at all.

Clutching at the necklace that dug into his neck, he said, "Oran!"

"What is it, Nath?"

"They're dead. All of them."

Oran's voice in his head was an agitated hiss. "What do you mean? Who is dead?"

Nath told him everything. The underling attack on the soldiers. The ambush the soldiers had brought. The slaughter. The mayhem. His own memory loss.

"You did well, not wrong, Nath," Oran reassured him. "Those were Royals, a sworn enemy. Great deceivers. Surely they would have hunted you down and killed you first if they had the chance."

"But they did not seek my death," Nath said, standing up and trembling with anger. "They sought your kind. And it was your kind that instigated this."

"Listen to me!"

Nath froze.

"I tell you this: we strike when it suits us. It's part of our survival. Take them down before they take us down. We had the numbers. Underlings do as underlings do."

Nath pulled at his collar. The more he tugged, the more it tightened. Shaking his head, he said, "I don't like this."

"Then end this!" Oran urged.

"How?"

"Hunt down and kill the Darkslayer. He is the one behind it all. He leads the hunt. Inspires these men. Kill him."

An image formed in Nath's mind. Powerful and sharp, a huge man in a dark helmet with burning eyes slaughtered defenseless underlings like sheep. A mighty axe smote them like the strike of lightning. His throat tightened. Jaws clenched. The monster of a man needed to be stopped.

"You want peace? Then find this savage and tear him to pieces," Oran suggested. "That's an order."

Nath's blood stirred. His mind darkened. Oran was right. He just needed to find this slayer and kill him.

"I sense your anger, Nath," Oran said. "You can use that to avenge your allies. Defeat this enemy, and all of underling kind will revere you. We'll make every effort to find your own kindred and protect them as well. You must trust me. You must obey me. Do that, and everything will resolve."

Nath rubbed his temples. "I have no guide. I don't even know where to start."

"Go to the nearest city. Be discreet. Blend in. A keen ear will always discover something, and it wouldn't hurt for you to learn more about the ways of this world. In the meantime, I'll send help from my Badoon. Just let me know where you are when you get there."

Nath grabbed his sword and ventured through the woods with a stony expression on his handsome face. "I will."

Oran slung his headband across the room. It bounced off a big glass jar with a man's head in it and clattered on the hard cave floor. Fingers contorted over his head, he screamed.

"Gaaaaaaaaaaaaaaaaaaah!"

An entire underling Badoon was dead, and no doubt Lords Catten and Verbard wouldn't be happy about that. Someone would have to pay for it. The only bright side was that Nath lived. It seemed the man had a fiery disposition that tore through the humans like a whirlwind. Still, controlling the man was not easy.

Oran needed to poison the well even further.

Hands behind his back, he paced around his experiment table. In a flash of anger, he wiped the jars, vials, and candlesticks off. "I hate this!"

For decades, Oran had been outcast from the Underland. He had been found guilty of meddling and conspiracy with the other races. His experiments were considered detrimental, and now his life was spent in solitude, doing devious deeds with little underling support. But he knew what he was doing. He was subverting the ways of the world above. Learning. Probing. Exposing weakness. One day he would further the underling cause, he was certain of it, but now he had to play lackey to the likes of hallowed Verbard and Catten. He had to do their dirty work for them. Get his nails dirty where they wouldn't.

He grabbed a bottle of underling port from his wine shelf and sank into his sofa. Staring at the face of a dwarf's head pickled in a thick jar on the table, he drank. He thought. He planned. He fussed. He drank.

If this fails, I'm dog meat.

CHAPTER 16

L IKE THE UNDERLINGS, NATH SKULKED through the jungles, avoiding the winding paths. Hours into the trek, he hunkered down and waited. A deer with black horns and a black tail pounded right past his location, and two more, smaller ones, followed.

Alert, Nath coiled up behind a fallen rotting tree and bent his ear. Someone came up the path. The lively sounds of the woodland dulled but did not fully descend. Shifting in his position, he found an opening through the vines and branches that gave him a better look at the trail.

The soft clomping of shod horses became more distinct through the brush. A jangle of metal rattled against the bodies of the horses. There were three riders. Two towering men, one in front and another in the rear, with a stout, black-eyed man in the middle. They were unlike the men he had slain. They didn't wear heavy armor, preferring a lighter protection. Their voices were rugged and somewhat jolly when they spoke. The chatter was constant when without warning, the one in the lead, a powerful, light-headed man, halted.

Nath sank deeper into the brush. His keen eyes caught a steely blue glimmer in the hard eyes of the lead man, who scanned the forest.

"What do you see?" said the man in the middle—who loaded his bow.

"I don't see. I sense," the brawny warrior replied.

Nath was far away, well beyond the line of sight of the underlings he'd banded with. His own senses were uncanny compared to those of the others. He'd figured that much out in his travels. Now, far down the hillside, he was certain the warrior's stern gaze was right on him. It sent a shiver up his scales.

He can't see me. I know he can't see me.

Holding his breath and not blinking, Nath didn't shuffle in the slightest.

Finally, after several long moments, a black-tailed deer burst out of the foliage and bounded through Nath's view.

"Did you see that?" the archer said. "A black horn! I want that black horn!"

"You aren't going to get it before me!" said the black warrior.

With a whip of their reins, the two men in the rear galloped up the hillside after the deer. That left the leader alone with a large dog. His eyes glided over Nath's spot once more. With a snap of his reins, he moved on up the trail and out of sight.

The dog looked right at Nath, shook its tail, and went off after its master.

Nath unloaded his breath. He wasn't certain why his heart had almost frozen in his chest, but it had. Perhaps he was uneasy, being a stranger in such a strange land. From his spot, he waited until the night fell hours later before he ventured forth again. Picking his way through the forest, he found the trail in the bush where they had chased after the deer. About a mile into it, he found a grove where the black-horned deer had fallen.

Reaching down, Nath touched the blood with his fingertips and rubbed them together. *Impressive.* He hadn't figured the men capable of hunting down the incredibly swift deer. Not in such rugged terrain. They had proved him wrong. They had proven themselves formidable, and formidable men know things.

Tracking them, he cruised through the black jungle like a great lurking cat until the glow of a fire caught his eyes. He sniffed the air. The scent of cooked meat watered his mouth. Laughter and joking caught his ear.

Who are these men? I must know.

Like a shadow, Nath followed the men on their short journey. They made their way to a fort made from tall trees, and he heard them call it Outpost Fourteen. The establishment was big enough to hold a garrison of about a hundred men, and Nath could hear every conversation in the place if he chose to.

The travelers returned the horses and gear here and told a tale of fallen men and underlings a day's walk away. Their leader, called Venir, grumbled and argued with the soldiers in the fort. He pressed them for help, but the soldiers seemed desperate and had nothing to offer.

According to the conversations Nath overheard, times were becoming grim for the men. The underlings had the upper hand on things. Not so long ago, the underlings had had a major victory at another fort called Outpost Thirty-One.

After parting ways in a gruff manner, the party of three men headed east several leagues, out of the jungle into a flat plain of high grasses and crooked trees. Deep down in the belly of the valley stood a shamble for living that the men he followed called Two-Ten City.

CHAPTER 17

IT WAS DUSK WHEN NATH waded through the loose livestock and ventured into Two-Ten City. He stowed away his sword high in the trees and donned a traveling cloak that Oran had packed for him. He also stuffed on a pair of leather gloves. The tips of his nails poked through, and he shrugged. Hooded, he traipsed into the city, stooping a little low and moving slower than normal. There was a half built wall of stone that only surrounded parts of the city. There were watchtowers, too, three-stories tall, scattered about. Some had men in them; others had no one at all. People hustled about, paying Nath no mind at all and hassling one another over this and that.

A boy bumped into him, tipped a burlap cap at him, and said, "Excuse me." He was an ugly half-orcen boy with devious eyes and a sweaty, piggish nose. He had his free hand behind his back, and there was nothing Nath liked about him. The boy backed away and had started to turn his back when Nath said, "Stop."

The boy, with Nath's coin purse in his hand, took off at a dead run.

Nath closed in on the boy in two strides, seized him by the collar, and lifted him up from his feet.

The boy fidgeted and squealed. A small crowd gathered. Nath clamped his hand over the boy's mouth and said into his ear with a dangerous tone, "Be silent."

"Mrph!" the boy said. He bit Nath's hand hard. His beady eyes widened.

Nath didn't feel a thing. He snatched his purse out of the boy's grip, stared into the boy's eyes, and offered a stern warning. "Don't steal."

The orcen boy rolled his eyes.

After setting the struggling boy down, Nath shoved him away.

The boy turned, spat at him, and ran off, saying over his shoulder, "You'll pay, golden eyes! You'll pay."

Shaking his head, Nath shoved himself through the crowd of onlookers. They were a mixed lot of men and women, poorly dressed and grimy. Teeth were missing. A few were of the orcen breed, at least in part. Most of the others were human: durable farmers, tradesmen, and merchants in colorful robes with tassels on the hems. There were some smaller people too, cheerful and curious, trying to get a peek at his face behind his hood.

Coin purse tight in his grip, Nath made long strides for the heart of the city. Before long, he found himself with his back against a barn.

Night had fallen.

Aside from the livestock that had moved on, the dusty streets were still busy. The people milled about from building to building, conducting as much business at night as they did in the day. Surly characters walked about with wine bottles to their lips. Greasy-headed men in long robes chanted strange songs. Women pushed carts filled with pouches of snuff. There was a lot of cursing and spitting.

Nath's nose crinkled. There were bad attitudes and smells and plenty of colorful conversations as he waded through the streets for a couple of hours. He picked up a lot about the people, but while still a bit familiar to the extent he could surmise what was going on, everything was foreign to him. There was not a doubt in his clouded mind that he'd never been here before. And nothing the people talked about jostled his memory, either. He was as alone and in the dark as ever.

He tracked down the sound of a hammer banging on metal, and before long, the wide-open layout of the city led him to a black smithy. Thick-thewed men stood inside, pounding hot iron on an anvil. One person in particular was startling in size. His head almost hit the rafters and was the size of a barrel.

That must be one of those ogres Oran was talking about.

From across the street, leaning on a porch post of the general store,

Nath fixed his eyes on the molten metal and the flying sparks in the haze. There was something familiar, comforting about it that set his senses at ease.

But the rumbling of his stomach snapped him out of his thoughts.

A woman passed by carrying a tray full of little sticks with morsels of meat on them. He rubbed his stomach and smacked his lips. His throat was dry. It was time to dive into something. The underling food that Oran served was tasteless and unfulfilling. Walking the dirt-packed streets again, Nath searched for a tavern where it would be easy to be inconspicuous.

It wasn't long before he came across a loud and bawdy place. On the porch, a sign dangling on chains swung in the brisk winds. Nath couldn't read it. Beneath the sign, an old woman in a rocker beckoned for him with a crooked finger and a lusty glimmer in her bright eyes. She sipped from a clay jug on her lap and wiped her mouth with her bony hand.

Nath averted his eyes and headed up the stairs and onto the porch that wrapped around the disheveled building with uneven planks.

Men with tankards milled about. They smoked from pipes and on sticks made from wrapped-up tobacco leaves. He fanned his face and started for the front door then stopped, turned, and laid his hands on the nearest rail. Facing the bustling city, something became more apparent to Nath. Many faces were concealed. Footsteps soft. Some were in groups and pairs, but there were many loners. Then it became abundantly clear why so many places weren't locked up for the night and the people worked all the time.

It wasn't safe to ever leave your store untended.

When do these people rest?

He glanced up at the yellow moons in the sky. An unsettling and eerie feeling came over him.

One thing is for certain: this is not my home.

Shoulders slumped, he pushed through the swinging doors and went inside.

CHAPTER 18

THE TAVERN WAS SMOKY AND filled with the rank odors of sweat and bad wine. Fires burned in metal cauldrons throughout the torchlit room, and a bar stretched from one side of the misshapen tavern to the other. People of all shapes and sizes—soldiers, merchants, cutthroats, and drifters—huddled, chatted, and argued together. Several more were all alone, heads down and destitute. Everyone was oily with sweat.

A buxom woman in cheap and skimpy clothes sat on Venir's lap and poured him another tumbler full of grog. It brought a broad smile to his lips, revealing his strong white teeth. He tickled her ribs, bringing forth a giggle. She kissed his neck. "Tell me more about your adventures."

"I'd be glad to." Clasping the clay tumbler between his thumb and fingers, he drank it down. "Ah!" He clomped the tumbler on the table, rattling the nest of empty jugs and glasses. One bottle teetered off the table and smashed on the floor. "Oops."

"Do you mind?" said an irritated, rail-thin man who also sat at the table. He was pale, with more pepper than salt in his hair. Even though he wore long sleeves and a vest that was very contrary to the weather, he was the only one who didn't show a drop of sweat from the humid room. He eyed the busted jug on the floor. "There was still plenty of lousy wine in there."

Venir plunked a silver coin on the table. "This is for your wine." He plopped down another coin. "And this is for your whining, Melegal."

The coins disappeared in the thief's slender hands. "So you're going to pay me for my whining? Excellent! I'll be a wealthy man before the night is through." He started counting on his fingers and folding them down one by one. "Let's see. This place stinks. The people stink. The women are a far cry from comely—"

"That's not what I meant," Venir said.

The woman sitting on his lap asked of him, "What does *comely*, mean?"

"Er," Venir said, eyeing Melegal's curious eyes, "unpleasant. Yes, you are far from unpleasant."

She smiled at him, pinched his chin, and said with a purring voice in his ear, "Well, I can't wait to show you how pleasant I can be."

Venir patted her on the rump. "You could start by grabbing us another round of drinks."

She popped up out of his lap. "I'll be right back."

Venir watched the sway of her hips all the way to the bar, eyed Melegal, and said, "You thought you had me with that one."

"Well played for a lout." Melegal started cleaning his nails with a tiny razor-sharp thumb knife. "But judging by the current company in this room, it falls far short of astonishment. And your bouncing woman, I don't think she can even count all the digits on her fingers."

"Don't you mean the digits on her hand?"

Melegal frowned.

Venir continued, "Besides, I don't need her to count."

"Simple favors for simple minds."

"Hah! Don't give me that, Melegal. Where's the woman you've been keeping company with? Is she out howling at the moons tonight?"

Melegal slumped over the table. "I'd rather not talk about it."

"Oh, don't pout. You're just mad that Billip and Mikkel and I made a nice score."

"In what, underling metal? That's hardly a catch. Besides, I'll wager Billip's share right out of him sooner than later." Melegal's eyes glided over the room. "Where are your bumpkins, anyway?"

"They needed a nap. Ha."

"And you don't? You look like you haven't slept in days." Melegal's eyes made a closer study. "Make that months."

"I get plenty of winks. Those two whiners are the ones who dragged me back into this city. I was quite at home in the bush."

"It must be wonderful being so restless all the time."

Venir tilted his head toward Melegal. "Restless? I'm as at ease as I ever was."

"Which would be never."

"You jest." Yawning, Venir stretched his long sinewy arms out and put them behind his head. "See what you made me do? Bone, everything was fine until you showed up and began your griping. You spoil the mood."

"Speaking of Bone, I think it's time we returned back there." An orc bumped into Melegal's shoulder, and a dram of ale splashed on his tunic. The wry rogue gave a shove back. "Watch it, pig swill!"

The orc, brazen and hairy, turned, glared down at Melegal with yellow in his eyes. "What was that, human?"

"He said, 'Watch it, pig swill,'" Venir replied.

The orc caught Venir's deadly gaze, blinked a few times, turned, and walked away.

Melegal rested his elbows on the table. "We need to get back to the City of Bone, Venir. I've had all the stink I can handle. No matter where I go here, it's like living in a stable. I can't stand another day of a place where the people stink worse than the animals."

"I've got unfinished business still. And my blood still boils at the thought of those bloodsucking Royals," Venir said. He craned his neck. "Say, where is that woman and our ale?"

Melegal shrugged his scrawny shoulders. His steely eyes surveyed the room. "I can't imagine she abandoned you to consort with more favorable company."

The bubbling woman was nowhere to be found. Not at the bar. Not anywhere that could be seen from where Venir sat with this back to the wall. A few minutes passed. "By Bish, do I have to fetch my own swill in this place?"

"Says the man who cannot stand the Royals," Melegal said. "Please, Venir, don't exert those tender muscles and strain that fragile mind. Allow me to fetch the swill for you." Melegal scooted his chair away from the table and departed.

"Such a wisearse," Venir said.

The grump returned with a pair of jugs and set them down on the table. He had a rare grin on his face and twisted delight in his eyes.

"What is it?" Venir asked.

Sitting down, the thief touched his chest. "It seems that I was wrong."

"Wrong about what?'

Pouring himself a goblet of purple wine, Melegal said, "It seems there is more favorable company after all."

Venir's eyes narrowed. "What do you mean by that?"

"Your woman, that hefty wench that filled your lap, she consorts with another as we speak. Seems it's a good thing you have good old Melegal the Rat around to fetch your drinks."

Venir got up. "Where?"

"Back against the wall, where the deep cauldron burns." Melegal took a sip. "He's quite fetching."

A head taller than most, Venir rose up on his tiptoes. On the other side of a crowd sat a man with flame-red hair. And Venir's woman, one of many, hung on his every word.

CHAPTER 19

SURROUNDED BY WOMEN, NATH CHEWED on a mouthful of juicy turkey. A pretty woman in fine silken linens tilted a goblet to his lips while another one dabbed his chin with a cloth napkin.

"Thank you," he said, unable to contain his smile. He winked at one. "Thank you." His belly was full of meat, cheese, and hard bread. The strong drinks lifted his spirits up, and the company, full of compliments and flattery, had him brimming out of his boots. He lapped it all up.

Maybe this place isn't so horrible after all.

"Stranger, what is your name?" a woman asked, batting her extremely long lashes at him. Her honey-brown hair was up in a bun, and her outfit accented every curve. Her voice was sweet but forceful as she hugged his arm.

"Nath," he said, "and yours?"

"My name is Naydeen." She squeezed his arm. "Your arm is firm like the limbs of a mighty tree," she said with a purr in her voice. "I bet you're strong."

There was a hungry look in the eyes of every woman who surrounded him at the table. One had slipped behind him and began to massage his shoulders. Another continued to stuff chunks of food into his mouth. Probing hands pawed at him, and a surly redhead tried to remove the long leather gloves from his hands.

"No," he said, forming a fist. "Let's leave the gloves on for now."

"Aw," the woman said, sticking out her lower lip. "Please, let me do something else?"

"You could fetch more of that stew. It was quite satisfying."

"And lose my seat?" She shook her head. "No, I don't think so."

All of the women peppered him with questions—and demands.

"Where did you get those golden eyes, stranger?"

"Are they from your father's or mother's side?'

"You must be a Royal from the north. What city do you hail from?"

"Make me your bride. I will do anything you ask."

Naydeen tangled her fingers in Nath's hair. "It's softer than a baby's and yet glimmers like fire. My, you are the most ravishing man I ever saw."

"You don't have tabs on him, Naydeen!" argued a buxom gal.

"And you think you do, Rosewynn?"

"I'm far fairer than you, oily skank!"

The women started arguing, pushing and shoving. They pulled, pinched, and punched.

Nath interjected, "Ladies!"

Every one of them went still and glued their softened eyes on him.

"Ahem, that's better," he said. "We have plenty of time. Let's just sit here and get to know each other better, shall we?"

"We only want to know about you, Nath. Tell us everything!"

Disappointed that he didn't have anything to say, he dodged the subject. It wasn't difficult. He ate, drank, and offered vague answers to their questions.

"I bet he can play!" one of the women said.

"Play, play what?" Nath replied.

"Yes, yes, you are a handsome troubadour, aren't you? One that travels the world."

He shrugged his shoulders and said with a wink, "Perhaps."

One of the waitresses returned with an ebony three-stringed lute.

"Play it!" they urged. "Play it."

Nath took the lute in hand and plucked at the strings. "Seems a little difficult with these gloves on."

He plucked away some more, turned the tuning pegs on the upper neck, and said, "I think I have it." Not knowing why or how, his fingers danced over the strings, and beautiful music poured out, never heard before in all of Bish. The tavern fell silent. When Nath finished, the women's eyes were wet with tears, and he caught an old bald orc thumbing water from its drooping eyes. The place erupted in applause.

Astonished, Naydeen said, "There are no words for you and what you do."

"Thanks," said Nath, setting the lute down on the table. "I must admit, I don't have any words for that either."

A scuffle erupted in the room. Pushing through the crowd came the young orcen boy he'd dealt with earlier. He wasn't alone this time. This time he had friends, big ones. Full-blooded orcs with coarse black hair, armored and with weapons all over. The orcen boy pointed at Nath and said, "That's him!"

The biggest of the four orcs stared at him with his nostrils flared wide. "You're ugly."

"Says you with more hair in his nose than grass in the meadows," Nath replied easily, surprising himself.

The women all giggled, drawing the lead orc's perturbed eye. He reached down with his grubby yellow-skinned hand and picked up the lute. "Is this yours? You play like slat."

"No," Nath said, glancing around, "I think it belongs to that fellow over—"

The orc took the lute and cracked him upside the head with it.

Smash!

Red faced, Nath turned on the orc. All of the women scrambled. One by one, orcs weighted down in armor and leather piled on top of him.

CHAPTER 20

THE TAVERN EXPLODED INTO JOVIAL shouts. The excited people frolicked with glee. They chanted. They screamed.

"Brawl! Brawl! Brawl!"

"Cut his eyes out!"

"I want his hair!"

"Break his fancy quick fingers!"

Venir headed straight for the melee. He felt a firm tug on his arm.

"What do you think you're doing?" Melegal said.

"I'm going to break it up."

"No, you're not going to break it up. Those are some of those inhuman Royals's guards. You stay put. We don't need any more trouble around here."

"But they're orcs," Venir argued.

"It's not like that's Mikkel or Billip over there. That man with the furious fingers must be a Royal." Melegal wedged himself between Venir and the wild crowd. "He probably has it coming."

"I don't like those odds. Three on one."

"Why, you've handled more than that before. He looked to be a big fella. I wouldn't worry. I doubt a few lumps will kill him." He patted Venir's chest. "You get steamed up too easily. Save it for the underlings."

Venir grunted. The taunting crowd fired the blood in his veins and reddened his ears. There was a fight happening. He wanted in on it.

Melegal pushed him toward the door, "Let's go. Now. Find your plush little harlot, and we'll drag her out as well."

It wasn't uncommon for a fight to break out on any given night in Two-Ten City. Venir had been in the middle of plenty of them. Soldiers, frontiersmen, brigands—they all had a wild side to them that brought their worst qualities out. And there was nothing Venir would rather do than pummel a handful of orcs. He'd had his fill of them of late.

"Let's just stick around and see how this thing turns out," he said. "Besides, shouldn't you be placing a wager? This is the type of action you thrive on."

"And bet on who? The man being pummeled under the tables? I like long odds but not that long."

"Perhaps he can tickle his way out with those fingers," Venir said.

"How do you know orcs are ticklish?"

Crack!

"What was that?" Venir said, snapping his head around toward the fight.

An orc teetered out of the fray with his neck bent over and collapsed to the floor. A sound of heavy punching followed. *Whop! Whop! Whop! Whop!*

The crowed oohed and ahhed.

The flame-headed stranger had an orc pinned down and was delivering strike after strike. The biggest orc of all scrambled for a chair, snatched it up, and shattered it on the golden-eyed man's head. The chair broke. The stranger's fighting spirit didn't. His golden eyes were flashing when he stood up and glowered at the orc leader, snatched the broken chair from the orc's grip, and smacked him in the face with it. The orc staggered back into the crowd. They shoved him back into the melee.

"Get in there and finish what you started!" they said.

The orc drew a blade. The stranger struck like a cobra, wrenched the blade free, snatched the big orc up like a giant sack of potatoes, and hurled him through the glass window.

Crash!

"By Bish!" Venir nudged Melegal. "I knew you should have taken those odds."

"Agreed. One never knows about these things." Melegal needled his chin. "I don't know of many men that can toss an orc like a stone."

"Aye. Me either."

The flame-headed stranger huffed for breath and scanned the crowd. The fires in his eyes were far from dim. Finally, they settled on the orcen boy, who sneered at him and said, "This isn't over yet! You'll see!" He turned and ran.

"That man will be marked for death now. That one orc isn't even breathing, and that boy, he's one of the Royals's little loudmouthed mongrels," Melegal said. "We might want to clear out of here."

"I say we stick around," Venir replied.

"Fine. Enjoy your time in the stockade."

"Look!" a man cried out in a loud voice, "He's got scales on his arms!"

Melegal's brows perched.

Venir cocked a brow himself. He'd seen many strange things but nothing quite like that. The stranger's arms were layered with black scales that had a dull sheen to them.

Quickly, the crowd's affection for the red-haired stranger turned sour.

"He's a fiend!" one of the women cried.

Another man, one-eyed and gutsy, spoke above them all. "The underlings sent this thing to deceive us! Grab steel, everyone. He'll have naught of me." He ripped his blade clean free of the scabbard. "Kill him!"

CHAPTER 21

NATH COVERED UP HIS ARMS. It did little good. Part of the cloak was torn and one arm was exposed. *The secret is out.* On feet ready to spring, he scanned the faces of the crowd. Moments ago they'd been cheerful and light. Now, darkened expressions filled all of them. The temperature in the room started to rise. He could feel their heartbeats. See the tension in their faces. The very word "underling" had ignited something in them.

He eased back toward the wall with his hands up and palms out. "I'm not a threat."

"Hah!" the gutsy one-eyed man said. "And with scales like that, what are we to take you for, a fish?"

More metal appeared in everyone's hands, aside from a few observers. One of them, the straw-locked tracker from the forest, stood tall behind the rest. An intent observer.

Nath decided to try reason once more. "I'm only passing through. I'll be gone." He waved his finger at them. "I've not brought harm to a single one of you."

"So you say! But you killed him." The brash warrior said, pointing at the corpse on the floor. "And you tried to kill the others!"

"I was defending myself," Nath argued. "It was them or me."

"Nay! You'll bring all of the Royals down on us for your trespassing. No, you did this because you serve the underlings!"

The crowd stirred and grumbled. Eyes blinking and shifting back and forth, a handful of them crept forward. The man with the eye patch got an encouraging shove in the back and found himself only a few steps from Nath. Eyes like saucers, he said, "Stop shoving."

"Kill him, Garth! We're behind you. Kill him!"

Garth the one-eye summoned his courage and stabbed his longsword at Nath's chest. The blade skipped off the metal breastplate. Aghast, Garth cried out, "He *is* one of those black fiends!"

"I'm not a fiend!" Nath argued.

The people, most drunk and unruly, became bolder. Louder.

"His tongue is deceitful! Don't believe him!"

"Did you see how he deceived our women?"

"And that lute! I've never seen the best play so fine as that!"

Nath ducked. A wine jug crashed on the wall behind him. He snatched one jug out of the air, then another, and pleaded, "Stop throwing things. I am not your enemy!"

"Garth is right!" said the honey-blond woman who'd sat with him earlier. "No man's tongue could be so polished if he wasn't a serpent. And I've never seen a man so handsome. It's wizardry! Dark, underling wizardry." She chucked a plate at him. "I'm with Garth. We must kill him, pretty or not!"

There was no dodging the next wave of tableware. Nath was pelted with food, drink, and pottery. He swatted away what he could and tried to head for the door. His path was blocked at every turn. He screamed, "If I was an underling, wouldn't I be trying to kill you people?"

"Did you hear that? He's trying to kill us people!"

The frenzied and disorganized mob pressed with their blades and started to strike. With quick and powerful hands, Nath disarmed them one by one. The throng, sensing that he wasn't fighting back, became bolder. Sluggish sword swings became arcs of death.

Nath couldn't tamp down his agitation any longer. Side-stepping the blades, swing after swing, he started dropping the foolish men with hard punches. Men fell to their knees, holding their guts. Others lay on the floor, out cold. Heading for the exit, Nath yelled, "Get out of my way!"

It wasn't just words that came out either.

It was words and fire.

Oh my!

Flames streaming from his mouth and unable to shut them off, Nath started fanning his arms and tried to say, "Get out of the way! Get out of the way!"

The bright orange flames clung to the walls and crawled up to the ceiling. Finally, the flames in his mouth ceased. The damage was done. The tavern roared from the uncontrollable fire. Smoke filled the room. People were hacking, screaming, and coughing. Others were being dragged outside, on fire. Through the haze and chaos, Nath turned to run.

Something hard as an anvil smote the back of his head.

Chok!

Dazed, he turned to see his attacker. Another fierce blow struck again.

Chok!

Surrounded by a raging fire, he sank to the floor, and all of the bright flaming lights went dim.

Splash!

Nath's eyes popped open, and he sat up with his head ringing. A guard—part man, part orc—held an empty water bucket on the other side of steel bars. The guard sneered and walked away.

Grunting, he heard a rattle of chains. His arms were behind his back, his legs in tight shackles. A tight cord of leather tethered his mouth shut. All he could do was sit there and breathe. He was in a dungeon or jail. His nostrils flared. The place reeked. It was filled with dampness and stink.

Great!

His neck was burning too, under the metal collar. An agitated voice was screaming in his mind.

Nath! Where are you? Nath! Report in!

Speaking in thought, he said to Oran, "I am here."

"Here as in where?" Oran replied.

"A cell in a place called Two-Ten City."

"You've been captured!"

"Yes."

There was no reply for the longest time, and then finally Oran said, "Farewell to you then, fool. Now you will see what it's like when those villainous surface dwellers try to kill you. Now you will understand our suffering."

CHAPTER 22

THERE WAS LITTLE LIGHT IN the dungeon that hosted Nath aside from a lone torch on the wall where the last guard who had woken him departed. Sitting in the dank dimness, he was alone aside from some rats bigger than his feet, hungry, and in deep thought. The only things he wore were his boots and trousers. The air wasn't cold, but he still shivered.

Fire. Fire from my mouth. How did I do that?

Things weren't adding up for Nath, but something familiar about himself seemed to be trying to claw its way to the surface. Something deeper about who he was? Those flames that had gushed from his mouth. He could still see the people's panic-stricken faces. Some of them had caught fire. An entire building had burned, and it was all because of him.

Perhaps I am a fiend? Perhaps those vile, drunken sots had it coming?

Nath might not have had a clue about who he was, but he wasn't stupid. If he was from some other local race as told by Oran, someone there should have understood that. The scales should have at least been normal. Familiar.

No, these people have never seen a person like me. What an indecent bunch. It probably would have been best if this entire city burned down.

He tried to reach Oran. The thick metal collar only seemed to constrict even tighter. He gave up on the thought. Stomach growling, he wrestled with his chains. Rats nipped at his toes and elbows. He kicked at them.

I bet this is what captured underlings go through. Torment. Suffering. And all at the hands of dirty debauchers. What a foolish thing of me to do.

Leaning against a moldy, slime-coated wall, he reflected on where he'd been. The tavern had given up some helpful information. So keen were his senses that he'd picked up on conversations held in low voices. There was talk of underlings. Men paid for their scalps. Their colorful eyes. There was fear and reverence in the hard voices. Some men wouldn't talk about the underlings and left the table. But it was clear: men—bold men, fierce fighters—hunted the underlings for money.

Nothing but madness in this violent world.

The main dungeon door creaked on its hinges, and new light spilled into the room. Orcen guards in heavy armor escorted another. The man, or creature rather, towered over his guards, firm in build with a head big enough for two. He wore a vest that half covered his broad, hairy chest, and his trousers had seen too many days.

Nath's nose twitched.

He stinks like manure. Not sure, but I think he's part ogre.

An orc guard banged his battle axe on the bars to Nath's cell. "Stand in the presence of Royalty."

Unsure why he obeyed, Nath pushed up against the wall and into a standing position. He blew the hair out of his eyes. "Can I help you?"

A second orc guard jammed his spear butt through the bars and stuck him in the ribs. Nath doubled over and took a knee.

Sultans of Sulfur! Don't forget you don't have that breastplate on anymore!

Coughing, he rose again. "Sorry, I was just trying to be helpful."

The orc struck again.

Nath twisted away. Still shackled, he dodged the next few attempts.

"Stop," the ogre growled. "You, be still." The ogre's big yellow eyes were glued on Nath's ebony-scaled arms. Finally, the ogre said, "Why did you burn my tavern down? Why did you kill my people?"

Nath could have been reasonable, but something about these people just stuck in his craw. "I was doing you a favor."

The ogre clutched the bars with his huge hands. "You owe me a tavern. You owe me new guards. How do you intend to pay?"

"Well, in case you haven't heard, I'm an excellent lute player. Funny, but that's kinda what started the whole thing. You see, I was playing the lute, to the delight of the crowd, when—"

"Silence! Farc does not like humor. Farc does not like you!"

"Who is Farc?" Nath asked.

Glaring at Nath, the half ogre said, "I am Farc, the Pit Master."

"Oh, so this is your pit?"

"This is not the Pit."

Looking around, Nath said, "Are you sure?"

Farc's canine teeth popped out from his jutting lip, and he shook his bullish head. "You have a clever mouth like the humans. Scales like underling spawn or black lizards. And you make fire, they say, with your mouth. What are you?"

There it was again. Oran said Nath was from a race of men who were being hunted down. This half ogre, Farc, had no idea what he was.

But Nath had a question of his own. "What do you think I am?"

The coarse-haired orc showed a cruel smile. "Tonight's entertainment." He stuck his hand through the bars, turned his fist over, and dropped something. He and the orcs covered their mouths with rags. A little ball of glass shattered on the floor, and colorful blue mist with many shades puffed out.

Hands bound behind his back, Nath was helpless against the mystic smoke that enveloped him. He choked and coughed, yet the vapor raced into his lungs. His eyes became heavy, his taunt limbs loosened, and he sagged onto the dungeon stones like a slumbering child with a head full of nightmares.

CHAPTER 23

THE PIT. BRUTAL. HOSTILE. FINAL.

Venir and company stood inside the arena, crammed in with rank and sweaty bodies. The underground battle yard was packed full of all the races, mixed and full, that Two-Ten City had to offer. Wooden bench seats circled a great iron cage made from crisscrossed bars. The cage rose thirty feet in height, and inside was a pit carved from stone ten feet deep and thirty feet in width and girth. It was Two-Ten City's precious gem, where fighters of all kinds came from all over Bish to battle, some of their own free will and others without a choice.

"Oooooh!" the crowd shouted. "Ahhhhh!"

The bloodthirsty thrill seekers watched with hungry gleams in their eyes as a rangy warrior in robes and a long brown ponytail chased some desperate and gimpy orcs around the arena. The orcs attacked. The man, fluid as water, locked up their arms and shattered their elbows. His fast feet busted their knees, and a hard chop busted their throats. The orcs pleaded for mercy but got death instead. Within seconds, the orcs lay dead at the man's feet and the crowd started chanting.

"Gaul! Gaul! Gaul!"

The man raised his long arms, turned to a particular group of individuals in their own section of seats, and bowed. It was the Royals of Two-Ten City, a dozen men and women, part orc and part ogre—a foul mixed breed that ran things in the destitute and southern city. One of them in fanciful robes, layered in heavy jewels and gold, gave a nod. Two orc guards opened up a gate at the top of the pit, and the warrior, Gaul, climbed out, smiled, waved, and departed to the chants of the crowd.

"Gaul! Gaul! Gaul!"

"Do we really need to be here?" Melegal said to Venir.

"Say what?" said Mikkel. "Are you telling me you've soured to the Pit fights too, Melegal?"

"I'm tired of all of it."

Brawny arms crossed, Venir said, "Then you shouldn't have clocked that stranger over the head if you didn't want to get involved."

"Surely you jest. If I hadn't acted, the blame for that entire incident would have fallen on us," Melegal argued. "The Royals—"

"They aren't Royals," Venir said. "They're anything but."

"Yeah," Mikkel agreed.

"No, but they run the show around here, and it wouldn't kill us to be in better favor while we're here. It's their coin that feeds our vices now, and face it, Venir. They don't like you. They don't like most humans. We're tolerated at best."

Billip squeezed his way into the discussion. "They seem to like Gaul. He's one of the finest fighters I ever saw."

"Gaul the Tormentor?" Mikkel said. "Are you jesting, Billip? He fights the walking wounded. The fallen out of favor. He's just an entertainer."

"Then *you* challenge him," Billip said.

"Why would I do that?"

Cracking his knuckles, Billip replied, "So Melegal and I can make some money off you."

"Aw," Mikkel smiled, "so you're going to bet on me."

"Bet against ya," Melegal said.

Shaking his head, Mikkel said, "You are cold, Melegal. And here I always thought you had my back."

Shrugging his narrow shoulders, Melegal said, "I'm a businessman first and a friend somewhere further down the ladder."

As the men bantered back and forth, Venir kept his eyes fixed on the Pit. The dead bodies were hauled out and another body was lowered in.

It was a man, covered from head to toe in sackcloth. A pair of halflings, one with brown hair and the other black, accompanied the big body inside. They tore the sackcloth away and then climbed out of the cage like monkeys. On the hard, bloodstained floor lay the man with black scales and flamelike hair. Slowly, the raucous crowd fell silent.

"That's him," Mikkel said in Venir's ear with mild astonishment. "He really does have scales. I've never seen anything like it. You two jokers weren't lying."

The murmurings and whispers started among the crowd.

"Fiend."

"Demon."

"Underling."

"Mage."

"And you took that big fella down, Melegal?" Mikkel said with perched brows, "I'd better be a little more careful around you."

"Yes, you should be."

Venir shook his head. "I'm far from convinced that he did the right thing. So what if the scaled man killed an orc and burnt a half built tavern down? Many of these denizens are former brigands."

"Sometimes, I think you just like to disagree with me," Melegal said.

Venir looked down at him. "Says a thief shaming the pickpocket."

A monstrous half ogre stood up from the seats where all of the Royals sat. He was powerfully built, covered in coarse black hair, and wearing a dark-blue vest that looked too small for his huge chest. He raised his arms and spoke in a thunderous voice over the crowd.

"Two-Ten City! We have a reaver. A deceiver. A murderer. An arsonist. A trickster." He pointed at the man in the cage. "He must be dealt with!"

The pack of thrill seekers erupted into deafening cheers.

"Silence!"

Mikkel nudged Venir in the ribs. "Old Farc ought to get in there," he said about the talking part-ogre. "I bet that would be a fight. I can't wait to see who he puts in there. We know it won't be Gaul though. Now, are you sure he breathes fire? Because I want to see some fire."

Venir nodded. He was just as curious as anyone. A large, fire-breathing, cat-quick fighter with scales on his arms was in the Pit.

Farc glowered down at his guards. "Wake him up."

Taking a long metal rod out of a fiery cauldron, an orc in a leather chestplate blew on the hot, glowing orange end. He stretched it into the cage and poked the stranger in the back of his ribs. He jumped wildly in the air. Clutching at the burn in his side, he spun slowly around the Pit with his golden eyes wide.

Farc then said, "Send in the scrappers!"

From one of the tunnels, a knot of bare-chested brutes emerged, pumping crude clubs into the air, elating the crowd. Like hungry apes, they climbed up the bars of the cage, moseyed over the irons, and climbed down a rope lowered into the Pit through the trap door. There were five in all, mix blooded, long haired, with tattoos and brands all over. The guards slammed the door shut. The arena became a frenzy.

"Time to make some wagers," Melegal said to Venir. "Time to make plenty."

CHAPTER 24

NATH FINGERED THE NASTY BURN in his side. He smelled the stink of his own singed flesh. His shock from the loud gathering behind the iron bars dissipated and turned into a smoldering fury within. The unruly gathering wanted his blood, and for what? He pushed his hair out of his eyes and watched the men crawling down the rope. As the last one dropped to the ground, the rope was hauled up, and the cage's trap door closed. The chanting began.

"Scrappers! Scrappers! Scrappers!"

Overlooking the cage, a balcony sprouted out that held a host of colossal onlookers. One of them was the part ogre that had spoken to him in the dungeon cell. The rest of them were pretty much one and the same, but dressed in exquisite clothes that did nothing to enhance their uncomely faces. The half ogre, Farc, pointed across the room, where a black-bearded dwarf held a leather-headed mallet in front of a man-sized gong.

That dwarf seems familiar somehow, for some reason.

Farc stretched his mighty arms over his head. The scrappers circled around Nath: sweaty, oily men who moved more like beasts, smacking their clubs into their hands. Farc's hands came down.

BONG!

Every scrapper converged and swung at Nath. Knees bent, he leapt high above the fray. The crowd gasped as he came down again and stuffed one man into the ground. A club found his back. His legs. His arms. *Smack! Smack! Smack!* The brawny, tattooed men were relentless. Savage. Murderous.

"I'm not a baby," Nath said. He spun away from one blow and backhanded another man in the face. Moving faster than the scrappers were thinking, he twisted club after club away and smote their onrushing bodies square in the face.

Clok! Clok! Clok!

Skulls cracked. Hardened men fell. Nath didn't let up until he prevailed. Temper ignited, he stuffed their clubs and his fists into their bellies until they were down. One struggled to rise. Nath clocked him hard in the back of the head. The scrapper fell face first with a *thud*.

The arena was silent. Eyes were wide. Jaws dropped open. Nath tossed the club away and said up to Farc, "Who wants to dance next?" He pointed at Farc. "How about you, big man?"

Farc yelled down in the cage. "You dare call me man!"

"Apologies," Nath smiled, "let me rephrase. How about you, big woman?"

The arena burst out in laughter.

Glaring at the audience, Farc let out a loud grunt, and the horde fell silent. Somewhere, someone giggled. "You taunt me! No more games! You pay!" He clapped his hands. "Bring out the cutters!"

"Hold on a moment, your grand ugliness!" Nath shouted over the throng. "If this is some sort of contest, what do I get if I am victorious?"

"You will not be victorious!" Farc said. "You will die!"

Nath lifted his brows a few times. "What if I don't die? Freedom?"

Sneering, Farc motioned to the ilk behind him. "We will decide."

"I say let the crowd de—"

"We will decide! Where in Bish are my cutters?"

From down in the tunnel, a murmuring arose. Two ogres strolled down the walkway, one after the other. They both looked like the one from the smithy, standing nearly eight feet tall. They wore chain-mail armor that covered their knees, and they moved like two men in one. To the thrill of the crowd, the lumbering brutes with heavy eyes climbed up the cage. The first one hopped in and landed flat on the back of a scrapper.

Crack!

The second cutter did the same.

Crack!

With the callousness of hungry wolves, they kicked the broken bodies aside and leered at Nath.

Throat tightening, Nath swallowed. Oft times, great size negated speed, but though the ogres seemed to move slowly, they were agile even with the armor. He eyed their weapons. Each ogre had one good hand and fingers, and on the other hand there was a big razor-sharp blade. The ogre on the left picked up a dead man by the neck, gutted him, and tossed him away.

Shaking his head, Nath turned his nose away. "You can toss down my weapon anytime now."

"You can use your fire!" Farc said. He pointed at the black-bearded dwarf.

BONG!

CHAPTER 25

"I HAVE TO SAY, I LIKE that red-haired man, or whatever he is." Mikkel rested his hand on Venir's shoulder. "He reminds me of myself, just not quite as handsome."

Venir huffed a chuckle. "Lap it all up. I don't think he's going to last very long against those cutters." His grip was tight on his long knife. "He needs a weapon."

"Keep your mouth shut, Venir." Melegal was stuffing coins into his pocket. "I made good on that last fight. Really good. What does your gut tell you on this one?"

"A weaponless man against two ogres with blades? I like his spirit, but it's hard to fight with your belly slit open." He shook his head. "I wouldn't wager on this one."

Melegal slunk away muttering, "Perfect."

Venir shoved an orc aside that had jostled into him. "Watch it." For some unknown reason, he was irritated about the battle that was ready to transpire. So far as he could tell, the stranger hadn't done anything but defend himself. He was out of place. Really out of place. But likeable. It would be a shame to see a good fighting man go down to the ogres. But this wouldn't be the first time an unfair battle stuck in his craw. He'd seen plenty of decent men fall before. That was their way, the Royal way in Two-Ten City. The thug ogres, gnolls, and orcs controlled everything.

"What do you think, Vee?" Mikkel said. "I think Me's betting on how long this stranger lasts. That's what I would do. He's quick, so I'd give him thirty, no forty seconds. What do you say?"

"For a pitcher of grog, I'll take fifty."

"It's a wager!"

BONG!

CHAPTER 26

THE LARGE AND HIDEOUS OGRES circled Nath, cutting and jabbing. He shifted left and right. Earlier when he'd battled the scrappers, much smaller people, they'd given him plenty of room to move. The two ogres practically filled the cage. Their arms stretched out from one side of the bars to the other.

I need a weapon. Anything.

He spied one of the clubs on the floor, ducked under an ogre's jab, and dove for it. He snatched it up, rolled away from another strike, and cracked the nearest ogre in the knuckle.

"Ahrooh!" it cried out.

Nath spun the club, a shaft of wood with a metal head, danced in again, and popped its knee.

The ogre delivered a downward body-splitting chop.

Slash!

Nath hopped out of the way.

The second ogre struck, its blade skinning a piece of Nath's leg. Blood dripped from the wound.

A new fire lit in Nath's eyes.

This is real.

To the thunderous roar of the crowd, the three contestants danced round and round. Nath attacked one; the other countered with deadly jabs. Nath hopped from spot to spot, fending them off with the club as best he could. They were big but quick as a man their own size. Every time they swung, it was to kill. Lathered up from battle, the brutes swung hard. Their blades skipped off the stone wall. Pierced the rock.

Nath's wary eyes probed for weakness.

Go for the jaw, Nath. Maybe you can knock one out.

He was stepping side to side with blades whisking by his ears when a glowering ogre lunged in. Nath cranked back and unleashed a mighty swing. At the last second, the ogre's head snaked back.

Swish!

Nath missed. The momentum of the club spun him off balance.

The second ogre pounced and drove him hard to the floor and knocked the club out of his grip.

Amid the salivating shouts and wild cries of elation, Nath found himself fighting for his life.

Both ogres were on top of him. One wrapped around his legs. The other had him by the hair. Its bladed hand started stabbing.

Nath seized its wrist and held it back inches from his belly. Muscles straining, he pushed back against the ogres' great size and power. "No!" he said, spitting and pushing. "No!"

The ogre drew back and shoved its blade forward again.

Nath held fast and locked his arms as the ogre shoved back.

It roared in Nath's face.

"Raaaahhhhhhhhhh!"

On impulse, Nath lunged his forehead forward and flattened its nose.

It staggered back, nose bleeding and eyes watering.

Nath turned his attention to the second ogre, the one locked on his legs. He started jabbing it in the head. "Get off me!"

Pop! Pop! Pop!

It was like hitting a wall.

The ogre increased its fierce grip that would crack a normal man's bones.

Wiping the blood running from its nose and mouth, the standing ogre said, "You pay!" It took a short run, jumped high, and elbow first, dropped its entire weight on Nath.

The crowd squealed with delight.

"Eeeeeew!"

Somehow, struggling with all of his might, Nath twisted out from under the assaulting bulk and raked his claws over the eyes of the ogre locked on his legs.

It let out a roar and loosened its grip the slightest bit.

Nath ripped his legs free and sprinted away. He stood with his back against the bars, laboring for breath, bleeding from chest and legs.

The feverish arena chanted for his death as the ogres rose to their feet with angry eyes. They came in slow, heads low, flanking him. One had an eye closed, the other a busted nose, but it was cosmetic damage at best. He could have torn one of their arms off and it wouldn't have slowed them down. They were full-blown natural killers.

Back pinned against the rock, Nath looked left and right. There was nowhere to go. He tried to summon fire, but there was nothing there. Just him looking silly by blowing imaginary smoke.

The ogres tapped their steel together, and one of them said, "We gonna skin them scales off you and eat you."

Still puffing for breath, Nath replied, "I'm sure I taste better than chicken." His laughter that followed was shallow. He narrowed his eyes. "Fine. Have at me, then."

The monstrous pair closed in with their blade hands slashing.

Hemmed in, Nath shifted from side to side. He blocked.

They grabbed. Stabbed. Punched. Tripped.

He found himself flat on his back and rolled away from one strike only to find another blade bearing down on his throat. In a split second, Nath's forearm shot up and blocked the blow.

The blade skipped off his scales.

He didn't feel a thing.

"Did you see that?" an onlooker cried out.

"His hide is like iron!"

"A fiend of fiends!"

"A demon of demons!"

"Aim for the heart!"

"Kill him!"

Quick as a cobra, Nath parried away the powerful, lethal strikes with his arms and hands.

The ogres pumped with fury.

Jab! Jab jab!

Nath skipped away.

I can't do this forever. Scaled arms or not, soon enough, they'll skewer me.

He ducked underneath a devastating chop that sheared off a lock of his hair.

That's it! Time to fight dirty!

He flopped to his back underneath two swings and with all of his might launched his booted heel into the nearest ogre's groin.

It doubled over. "Urk!"

Seizing the borrowed time, Nath taunted the other ogre with his claws while standing in front of the doubled-up ogre. "Come on! Come on then, Ugly!" He stuck his chin out and stood flat footed. "See if you can skin my scales!"

In a bull rush, the ogre charged in, lowered its shoulder, and delivered a tremendous life-ending uppercut.

Nath sidestepped.

The blow caught the bent-over ogre right in the neck.

Glitch!

The monster dropped back to its knees, clutching its neck. Blood dripped down its chest.

The other ogre's eyes widened with horror, watching its brother collapse face-first on the floor and die. Its horrified eyes turned to fury. Letting out a tremendous bellow that filled the room, it stomped up and down.

"RRRRAAAAHHHHHHHHHHH!" Seething, it searched for Nath.

Having slipped out of its sight, Nath snuck behind it and hopped on its back. He locked his arms around its great neck and squeezed with all of his strength.

The beastly creature clutched at him. Stabbed at him. Its bladed hands sliced at Nath's legs. Gashed him.

Hold on, Nath! Hold on!

He cranked back.

The ogre slammed his back into the wall.

Woomph! Woomph! Woomph!

Pain exploded in Nath's back. His body was jarred again and again. He held on, squeezing the ogre's windpipe harder and harder.

It drifted through the Pit. Stutter stepped, tripped over a broken body, bounced off the blood-stained wall, and fell. It twitched. Kicked. Groaned.

Agonizing second after second, Nath held on.

The ogre gave a final body-juddering lurch and moved no more.

Nath rolled out from under the beast soaked in blood and sweat and sucking for his breath. The crowd murmured and grumbled. Shock and bewilderment filled their dirty faces. Finally, a cry came from among the crowd.

"Victory to the dragon man!"

Farc answered back, "NO!"

CHAPTER 27

"THAT WAS SOMETHING I'VE NEVER seen before," Mikkel said, shaking his head. "One man, two ogres with weapons? That ain't normal."

"No, that was something," Venir replied. He caught Melegal snaking through the conflux of people and said, "How did *we* do?"

"*I* cleaned up. Now, let's get out. Too many of these people are of the impression they've been taken. It's about to get ugly."

"You mean to tell me you don't want to see how this plays out?" Mikkel said.

Melegal's grey eyes glided toward the cage. Guards with crossbows roosted on the bars, their deadly contraptions pointed at the man in the cage. "I have a pretty good idea how this freak's adventure is going to end. Quick!" He scurried away.

"Dragon man," Venir said, uncrossing his arms. "Huh."

The crowd's attitude started to shift in favor of the scaly-armed stranger. More people, particularly the women, amped up their protest. "Dragon Man! Dragon Man! Dragon Man!"

Farc spoke over their voices and silenced them all. "This slayer is a murderer. First my friends and now my family, nephews of my own blood, have been killed by this lizard's deceit. Nay!" He pointed his finger into the cage. "It must die!"

Venir couldn't stand the fouler races any more than Melegal could, but this was where he meant to be right now. Still, the Royals, the current misbegotten ilk, ran his blood hot through his veins. In a voice full of thunder, he blurted out, "Why don't you fight him yourself then, Farc?"

The simmering horde hushed.

"Are you a fool?" Billip hissed at Venir. He slunk away a little. "You'll get all of our hides skinned. Let's get out of here. Now!"

"Who dares?" Farc asked.

The group of people closest to Venir increased their distance from him. Billip, back turned, stood a half step behind him. His knuckles were popping. Mikkel stood firm at his side, pointed at Venir and said, "He did ... er, and I'm with him." He muttered under his breath. "I think."

"Humans. Hah." Farc straightened his vest and spat a glob of snot into the cage. "That's what I think of you."

"And I think," Venir said, "you and your almighty stink are cowards."

Eyes filling with rage, Farc replied, "Cross words for me, Venir? Cross words for you. You and your puny ilk can fight him." He spread out his arms wide and pointed to his guards. "Block the exits and bring them forth and throw them in the Pit!"

"See what you've done, you fool!" Billip admonished. "You'll get us all killed."

The arena was full of Royal guards, stout men in full helmets and light metal armor. Without hesitation, they shoved through the throng and closed in with swords and clubs ready.

"Now you've done it," Billip said. "We're going to have to fight that thing."

Melegal slid into the mix, glared at Venir, and said, "You owe me."

"What do you mean?"

The thief revealed a purse full of coins. "I mean, you're really going to owe me!" Gritting his teeth, he flung the coins all over the room. The people went into a frenzy, running roughshod over each other—including the guards. "Now get your arses out of here!"

Catching his breath for the next battle, Nath watched the entire scene unfold. People trampled people and let chaos loose. Without hesitation,

Nath scaled the iron bars like a spider, reached the trap door, and jerked one of the guards down into the cage. The orc's head bounced off the bars, knocking it out cold. The second guard stabbed Nath in the shoulder.

"Argh!"

Dangling by one hand, the orc chopped and stomped his fingers. With a tremendous heave, Nath pulled himself up, grabbed the orc by the leg, and jerked him down. The orc's legs split the bars, and it groaned in pain. Nath fidgeted with the pins that locked the trap door tight, shoved the door open, and climbed out.

"Get him! Get him!" Farc screamed when Nath emerged.

A bolt ripped past his face. Nath ran the bars like a tightrope and knocked the shooter over. In one great leap, he made it to the edge of the arena, bounded up the steps, and rushed the crowded tunnel. Pushing through the knot of screaming people, he emerged in the belly of a tavern, skinned up and bloody. A handful of women screamed. Two more guards with heavy swords blocked the exit. Nath ran straight for them, juked right, and jumped through the nearest window. In long, painful strides, he ran until the black forest swallowed him up again. The cries of pursuit fell away. Only the whistling wind in his ears remained.

CHAPTER 28

THREE STOCKS. THREE MEN LOCKED in them. The rising suns beat on their bare backs. Many of the people of Two-Ten City gathered around them all. Venir, Billip, and Mikkel had been fighting their way out of the arena when Mikkel got hemmed in by halberds. He had given himself up. Venir and Billip had then given themselves up. It was that or see their friend die.

"It's no surprise Melegal wormed his way out of this," Billip said, squirming in his prison. "He's probably sleeping right now, with Chongo and the horses, and my back is killing me already."

Shaking his head with heaviness in his voice, Mikkel said, "I'm sorry."

"Don't apologize," Venir said, "I'll take the blame if any."

"Fine by me. After all, you're the one whose big mouth intervened for that stranger. If you would have kept it shut, we wouldn't be in this situation."

"Yes, keep reminding me, Billip." Venir craned his neck and tried to flick the numbness from his fingers. "I'm sure you will. I deserve it."

"You do deserve it, you numbskull. Every time you crawl out of the woods, you hit the town and become too rowdy. There's always some price we pay for it." Billip cracked his thumbs. "Bish, my back hurts!"

"Maybe we can get one of the guards to rub it for you," Mikkel said with a smile in his voice. "Excuse me, Orc Face is it? Could you take those strong hairy hands of yours and rub my comrade's back?"

"Will you shut up!" Billip yelled.

Venir and Mikkel started laughing. Finally, Billip joined in as well. The three men had roamed together for years, and this wasn't their first time in the stocks. It probably wouldn't be their last time, either. Now, in misery, backs to the rising heat, they stood amid the town criers, unable to block out the mockery. There were two orcen guards laden in chain and helm that poked at them from time to time too. It went on all day. Rotten food. Vile jokes. Venir had a lump from where a rock had hit his head.

Mikkel smacked his lips. The guards were sharing a canteen of water. Another man, old, bearded, and wearing ragged clothes, had a bucket of water and a ladle. He sat on a stool in front of them, sipping and cackling.

Venir kept his split and parched lips shut until Farc and company finally showed up. The giant ogre, ugly in nature, had a troupe of hard-looking warriors in tow. One, a pale-skinned half orc, had a lash in his hand.

Suddenly, the people of Two-Ten City started to gather.

Lifting his head that felt heavier than an anvil, Venir said, "Farc, what an unpleasant surprise. But I'm glad you showed up. We were just arguing about what that bad smell was. I thought it was us, but now that you've shown up, I am convinced it's not."

"Will you shut up?" Billip said.

Farc took the old man's bucket and crashed it into Venir's head.

Stars exploded in Venir's eyes.

The ogre tossed the bucket away. "You know I can't stand humans."

Bleeding from a gash in his scalp, Venir looked back at him. "And you know I don't like your ilk either. But we aren't here to be friends, are we? We're men of business."

"You're trouble, Venir. Talk too much. Cause problems. We don't like you in our city."

"I thought it was a free city and that so long as we traded in good faith, which we do, we were welcome. And so far as I can tell, we didn't do anything wrong. I only offered a suggestion in the arena. You got all temperamental about it."

"My prisoner escaped because of you."

"Me? We turned him in to you. You let him escape."

Face to face, and breath foul as sludge, Farc said to Venir, "You're a trickster. You make us look bad. You pay for your deception."

Venir knew there wasn't going to be any reasoning with the ogre. Whether he had a hand in it or not, it didn't matter. Just like the Royals everywhere else, they did what they did for their own sick pleasure and made others suffer for it. It was their way. Always was. Always would be.

Farc gave a nod. The orc with the lash disappeared from sight. The sound of his whip cut the air and cracked behind them.

Venir, Billip, and Mikkel's jaws were clenched. Sweat dripped from their brows.

The whip snapped.

Crack!

Billip cried out a curse.

The lash snapped again.

Pain shot through Venir's toes and fingertips.

Mikkel was hit next. He grunted and shuddered.

One by one, the lash cracked over their backs, agonizing minute after minute. Dripping with sweat and back soaked in blood, Venir still couldn't hold his tongue. "Is your arm getting tired yet? I never realized how big your ears were, Farc. Now hear this, you're one ugly bast—"

Crack!

After what seemed to be an eon, Farc gave a wave of his hand and said, "Enough."

The lash handler stepped back into view. The lash's leather tails were soaked in blood. Drops dripped on the dry ground. Sagging in the stocks, Venir gulped for air and said in a cracked voice, "Now what, Farc?"

"You leave. Never come back."

"And if I do?"

"I will kill you myself, in the Pit."

"Is that a challenge?" Venir said.

"It is."

"I accept."

CHAPTER 29

HUNGRY AND HURTING, NATH CUT through the dark brush, retrieved Fang, and went deep into the forest. Hours into his journey, he came across a stream and lay Fang down by his side, scooped up the cool water, and drank. Nothing seemed to quench his thirst. He waded in where the water burbled over the rock, sat down in a nook, and let the falls rush over him. He reflected on Two-Ten City.

These people are madmen.

It seemed pretty clear that the underlings had a point. The people above had little character at all. They were cutthroats. Cruel. Without mercy. The pain and suffering of others brought them profit.

It's a wonder that men survive very long at all.

Soaking in the hair-drenching stream, he tugged at the strange chunk of metal harnessed at his neck.

Should I contact him or not?

His stomach moaned so loud he could hear it from underneath the waters. Rinsing the blood from his wounds, he eyed salmon shooting up the stream. Something about the fish triggered his memories. A flash of a different land, bright and filled with lush colors. Nath smacked the waters with his hands.

"Something is wrong! Everything about this place is wrong!"

A salmon shot out of the water, sailing over the rocks. Nath snatched it out of the air. By instinct he gutted the fish with his sharp nails and ate. He must have eaten ten of the fish before he finished, leaned back, closed his eyes, and let the water rush over his shoulders. Within seconds he was asleep.

He awoke hours later in the pitch-black comfort of the jungle and crawled out of the water. Retrieving Fang from the bank where the great sword rested, he followed the water upstream. Refreshed but sore, he tugged at the collar and called out for Oran. He made it another half mile along the green banks before the underling cleric replied.

"You live?" Oran said in his mind.

"If you can call it that," Nath replied. "If this is how life is, I'm not so sure it's worth living, Oran."

"Tell me everything."

Nath spent more than an hour describing even the minutest details. The more he recalled, the more confirmed he was in his thoughts. The people in the world were bad. Ornery. Loathsome. Despicable.

Without hesitation, Oran confirmed everything he was thinking. "Yes. Yes, Nath. Now you know. Now you see. Perhaps your memories are coming back to you after all. These men, orcs, gnolls—all of that foul ilk—are nothing but merciless and cruel. There is no dignity among them. They hunger for power and vile entertainment. They have no value for life at all. And Two-Ten City? Why, though it is small, it is one of the better places in Bish."

"Really?"

"Oh, you have no idea," Oran continued. "There are bigger cities. They appear to be fair but are filled with even more wickedness and despair. I often wonder how their kind even survive at all."

Nath's blood stirred with conflict. "Oran, what do I do now?"

"Your purpose is still simple, Nath. Kill the Darkslayer."

"I don't even know where to start," he said.

"He haunts the woods you are in. We are certain of that. You will pick up his trail soon enough. Listen to me, Nath. My lords Catten and Verbard are quite serious about this endeavor. They want his blood. You must bring it!" Oran hissed. "And they have told me that if you fulfill this honorable duty, then they can restore your memories."

Nath stopped in his tracks and stared at his faint reflection in the dark water. His own face wasn't familiar to him at all. At best, it was someone he might have passed in the crowd. A shade but not a memory. "Do you really think they can restore my thoughts?"

"I am great in magic, and I would do it myself if I could, but they, Nath, are far, far greater than I. Else I would not be carrying out this quest. Why, I'd be in the Underland, soaking in milk, with my hands and toes being massaged by the ladies. Those days are gone, but Nath, you can help me restore my honor. Save the underlings. Save all of their good kind. Can you do it?"

Nath nodded to himself and said, "Yes."

"Will you do it?"

"You have my word."

Oran chittered with confirmation. "Many underling soldiers hide in the jungles, Nath. One group, Badoon fighters, are gathering. There are many outposts run by men like you have seen. We have striven to take them back, but this slayer in the night has thwarted our plans. Spilled blood. Split heads. Defiled our eyes. Seek out these places. Find him. Kill him."

Nath felt a wave of thoughts rushing through his mind. Underlings running in terror. A great shadow hunted them down. Slaughtered them. His thoughts became darker and darker. Nostrils flaring and jaw clenched, like a hungry panther he vanished into the woods.

"Yes!" Oran jumped up high, came down, and tripped over his robes. He knocked over an empty wine bottle and laughed. "Yes, this is most excellent!"

He'd been sulking. Loathing. Tormenting and pickling heads. Now he had hope. Options. Perhaps Nath could pull off this irritating feat. He pecked on a glass jar that was big enough for two heads. A distorted orc's head hung suspended, somewhat lifelike, in a pale green goo. "Ah, perhaps I can have the slayer's head in one of these when I return to the Underland." He chittered with delight. "Then I will no longer be considered a parasite."

On one of the many tables inside his cave sat the skull of an underling. Two gemstone eyes hovered in its sockets, deep, dark blue. Oran took off the headband that was linked to Nath's collar and placed it on the skull. Violet eyes aglow with dark energy, he chittered some mystic words. The skull's eyes filled with radiant, eerier light.

"Yes," Oran said with a wave of his hand. "Irritate. Inspire. Ignite the man. Let him show no mercy to any who cross him."

CHAPTER 30

WITH A GROAN, VENIR SLUNG his legs off of his horse and hopped down to the ground, where immediately Chongo licked his hand. Having ridden for the better part of a day, his back was stiff, and the wounds from the lash still burned hot as fire. Behind him were Billip and Mikkel on horseback. Their eyes were bleary, and the cotton shirts on their backs had been stained red.

Mikkel slid out of his saddle and led his horse to the stream and lumbered into the water. He took his shirt off, revealing several layers of bulging muscle and a back coated in sore and bloody wounds. He sank neck deep into the water. Grimacing, the sound he made was pain, not pleasure "Ack!"

"Yes, yes, please bathe all that you want, the three of you," Melegal said. He rode on a grey pony with a shaggy black belly. It better resembled a donkey than a horse. "Your scent can only draw in more trouble. After all, I would much rather be stuck in the belly of a forest filled with brigands and underlings than in my cozy cot inside the city."

Venir pulled off his shirt and waded knee deep into the water. "Quit complaining. You said you wanted out of the city, and now you are out of the city. No one made you come along anyway. It was your choice."

Swatting a buzzing insect from his frowning face, Melegal replied, "I didn't have a choice, and you know it. They'd have flogged me if they caught me."

"I didn't think you could be caught if you didn't want to be," Venir said, sinking into the water, clenching his teeth. "And I doubt they would flog you. There's nothing to flog off. They'd probably stick you in a cell and let the rats nibble that thick layer of skin off."

"Ha ha," Melegal said. His grey eyes scanned for the source of the hooting and odd chirping sounds beyond the tree line. "You know I hate this bug-infested greenery. Why couldn't we just stay on the trails? Why don't we just go back to Bone?"

"You can go. There are plenty of caravans that you can latch onto. And I'm sure they'd enjoy your company," said Venir, stretching out his arms, formed like mighty tree trunks. "I know we certainly do."

The slender man slapped flying bugs from his black-and-grey clothes. He plucked a huge mosquito from his neck and crushed the blood out of it. "Uck!" He cleaned his hands off with a rag.

Billip, not as primordial and towering as Venir or Mikkel, jumped off of his saddle and grabbed his bow. "While you men soothe yourselves with such colorful and seedless banter, I think I'll fetch myself some dinner." He grabbed a handful of arrows from his saddle quiver and eyed Melegal. "Care to join?"

"I'll pay you a fair wage."

"You'll pay what I say you pay," Billip said. "And you still owe me for that pony you're riding on."

"Quickster is mine," Melegal retorted. His hand slid inside his vest. "You lost the bet. Really lost the bet bad."

In one fluid motion, Billip nocked an arrow and fired.

Twang!

The arrow zinged past Melegal's face and embedded itself in a nearby tree. A grey squirrel was pinned to the tree. "There's your dinner," Billip said. "Three silver plus two to skin it, one more to cook it for you. That's five."

Mikkel busted out in laughter. His face seized up. "Five? Don't, don't make me laugh right now, Billip. It hurts too much."

"Agreed," Venir said, trying to contain his chuckles. The burning in his back was just beginning to subside when his eruptions set it on fire again. The jungle stream water was refreshing and soothing. It would help clean and heal the wounds. "Relax, Melegal. You're as safe here as anywhere else."

"I don't want any part of this blood hunt, Venir. I'm not a tracker. Not a bounty hunter." He pointed at Venir. "You need to take me back to Bone."

"I'm not stopping you from going." Venir submerged his stalwart frame in the water, popped up, and wrung out his blond head of neck-length hair. "Just give it a few days. It will do you some good. My business is here. You know that."

"Let the Royals fight their own battles, Venir." Melegal smashed a bigger mosquito between his hands and cleaned them with a handkerchief. "Back in Bone, you'll make more money brawling than you make here skinning underling scalps."

"I've got business. I like what I do, and the Royals pay well for our services. Besides, the setback in Two-Ten will pass."

"My arse it will. Farc will break your neck if you go back in there. He'll break all of our necks."

Venir stiffened. "You don't think I can take Farc?"

Mikkel stopped rinsing himself off. "You're thinking about going back, aren't you? I see that look in your eye. That blue-wild fire. Don't do it."

"That's your home, Mikkel, and Billip's too. You have to go back at some point. And if fighting Farc is what I have to do, then that's what I'll do."

"You're crazy." Melegal threw a bedroll down on the ground. Chongo promptly lay down on it. Melegal pushed the huge dog aside and lay with him as a pillow. Chongo licked the skinny man's face, and he tried his best to stay grumpy. "Now hurry up. Finish your bath and make a fire. If I'm going to be here, then you goons need to see to my comfort." He lifted a clay jug, pulled the cork out, and drank. "And stay away from my wine."

"Oh, we can stay away from your wine, but I don't think there's any avoiding your whining," Billip said. On deft feet and soft steps, he vanished into the forest.

Melegal made himself comfortable on his bedroll, and so did Chongo. "Seriously speaking, Venir, you aren't really considering going back to Two-Ten anytime soon are you? We all know you're tough, you battle-damaged lout. No need to prove it … again."

Thinking of Farc and his Brood, Venir wasn't about to let anyone tell him what he could or couldn't do. Where he could be and couldn't be. He'd had his fill of that in the City of Bone already. No, he wanted Farc. He wanted to teach those misbegotten Royal behemoths a lesson. Even if it got him killed. "We'll see."

CHAPTER 31

ENIR AND COMPANY SNAKED THROUGH the jungle on faint paths that few knew about or ever trod. They were a full day into the trek, pushing through brush and dangling vines, avoiding civilization.

Melegal rode in the middle of the rugged men, face concealed in a dark-grey cowl. Speaking through the garment, he said, "Venir, we need to get on a road. This is ridiculous."

"It's a shortcut." Venir wiped the heavy sweat from his eyes. "You like shortcuts, don't you?"

"I like seeing ten feet in front of me. The bush out here is as bad as in the Outlands, and the horses can barely push through it." He eyed a big spotted cat perched in one of the trees. "We don't belong here, Venir. This is another one of your quests. I know it."

"It's not a quest. I told you, it's a shortcut."

Melegal and his pony Quickster drifted back alongside Billip. "This isn't a shortcut, is it?"

"Can't say," Billip replied with a grim face. "I've never been this way."

Melegal's hands, covered in leather gloves, squeezed the reins. Venir had been wearing over the past few months. He'd changed from a boisterous young man full of life and loaded in muscle and bravado into a restless and wild hunter. He came and went from the city, sometimes with Billip and Mikkel and sometimes without. He was after underlings. The little fiends drove Venir like he'd never been driven before.

If there isn't trouble where we're going, there will be trouble when we get there. Wherever that is. Bish, I should have gone with a caravan.

"Venir, let the Royals handle this mess with the underlings," Melegal said. "They have their armies. You are only one man. The odds will catch up with you."

"This is more than that, Melegal. They took Outpost Thirty-One. Now the entire South is exposed to their treacherous ways." Venir shook his head. "No, I'm going to fight whether the Royals pay me or not. You've seen what they've done to our people."

"Our people? I don't think I have any people. And I don't think you do either. I haven't seen that many underlings, and I like it that way too. I see what they do." Hiding inside his cowl, he shook his chin. "No thank you. And where is this shortcut taking us anyway?"

Venir didn't reply. His eyes were intent on everything around him. Seeking. Probing.

Ugh! I hate it when he gets like this.

Melegal had had his fill of Venir's adventures. His longtime friend had taken him far out of his home in Bone and had promised to take him back. And though the times in Two-Ten were enjoyable, things had gotten old really fast. Especially after Venir went sideways with the Brigand Army.

Why do Billip and Mikkel put up with this?

"Ah." Venir brought his horse to a halt. His blue eyes were bright fires under his long tawny locks. He got off his horse, took a few steps into the brush, and knelt down. His eyes ran up and down some nearby trees. He pointed. "See it?"

Layered in with the vines were some well-concealed robes. Some of the smaller trees were bent over. Melegal knew what it was. A snare. Great. "I'm sure it's set for animals, not people."

Venir rose up, cracking his back. "No, that's not some vermin trap. It's a people snatcher. I've seen them before. Underling work."

No! No! No!

Melegal locked his fingers on his head and squeezed a little. With a bite in his voice, he said, "This is what you've been looking for all this time."

"No, just good fortune." Venir reached into a pack hitched on his saddle and opened it up. He pulled out a large, stitched-up leather sack.

An uneasy feeling settled in Melegal's stomach, and he scowled. "Why would underlings set traps out in the middle of nowhere? No one is around for miles, except us."

"Heh," Venir replied with a gleam in his eye. "It's just one of their little tricks that keeps any strangers from wandering into their camps. A precaution."

"Then I suggest that we go another way." Melegal eyed his other comrades. Billip and Mikkel dismounted. The archer slung his quiver over his shoulder with a grimace. Mikkel put his steel cap on and cranked back the string on his heavy crossbow. "I don't suppose you brought an extra one of those along for me?" he said to Mikkel.

"Don't worry. I'll protect you." With his mighty arm, the huge black warrior held out a massive studded club. "You can use this if you like."

Melegal eyed the battered wood coated in dark stains. "I think you can make better use of it than I, but feel free to crack a few skulls in my name."

"No problem," Mikkel hoisted it over his shoulder.

Melegal fixed his gaze on Venir. The man, like Mikkel, was one of tremendous girth and packed with thick muscle. He held a battle axe in his hands. Bigger than two normal axes, it had two long blades, razor-sharp cleavers. A steel, icicle-shaped spike jutted from the middle.

Venir twirled the awesome weapon around his body. He chopped and stabbed at imaginary enemies. A hungry grin started on his face.

"You shouldn't have any trouble scaring underlings with that."

"Scare them?" Venir removed a round metal shield from the sack. It was ornate, hammered like black iron, with odd markings engraved in the metal. Venir slung it over his shoulder. "They won't live long enough to be scared once I find them."

"Lucky them."

Venir removed the final item, a helmet of dark metal with hammered iron outlining the trim. It was crafted the same as the shield and war axe, finely honed and unique. The eyelets seemed to burn with a life of their own. Venir slid the great helmet over his head. His scarred hands buckled the leather chinstrap.

And just like that, the robust man Melegal knew was gone, enhanced into something greater. An uneasy feeling came over him when Mikkel said, "Here we go."

"What's that supposed to mean?" he said to the other two men.

Mikkel pointed.

Melegal turned back just in time to see Venir, moving like an armored ghost, merge into the forest. "Is he just leaving us here?"

Mikkel, lathered in new sweat, eased along Melegal's side. "You might want to stay with Chongo and the horses. Are you sure you don't want Skull Basher?"

"You aren't leaving me too."

"Come then," Billip said. The archer's eyes were charged with new energy. He popped the last cracks of his knuckles. "You don't want to miss the show, do you?"

"You mean Venir dancing with underlings in that terrifying getup? I think I'll pass."

Billip handed Melegal a knife. "If any underlings squeeze through, you know what to do."

"I have my own blades, Billip. I don't need something that skins goats and cuts fishing lines." Melegal watched the men slip deeper into the forest with big smiles on their faces. "How long do you think you'll be, eh?"

"We'll be back as soon as the underlings stop screaming," Mikkel said.

"I thought they didn't scream." Melegal said.

The stiff wind rustling the leaves in the branches was his answer. Stiff in the saddle, he slid out a pair of long daggers and scratched his pony Quickster behind the ears. "If it comes right down to it, I hope you can get us out of here. If not, I guess I'm screwed."

CHAPTER 32

As soon as Venir buckled on Helm, life exploded around him. His blood rushed like a great river. His senses tingled. Everything he could see, hear, and smell was so much more distinct. The scented flowers. A distant flow of water. His friends' heavy breathing. A new hunger was in his mind. His thoughts intermingled with Helm's, and they fed each other.

Run! Kill! Slaughter the underlings! Kill till there are no more!

Surefooted, he raced into the forest, outdistancing his pursuing friends in seconds.

Yes!

He glided through the heavy brush with Helm, a dangerous beacon. If there were underlings near, it would find them. Venir and his axe would carve them down. Most men in the world hated the underlings, but not like him. Their vile nature was the opposite of everything he knew. They killed. Tormented. No discrimination among men, women, and children. The horrors Venir had seen fueled fires in his mind.

I want them all. Dead.

His feet sank into the soft mud of the jungle where a marsh filled with willows cropped up. The little grey-skinned fiends thrived in the dampest spots on Bish. Venir slipped underneath the gentle greenery hanging from the crooked branches. The sinking daylight subsided into the heavy natural darkness. Helm pulsated and throbbed. Venir's heart pounded in his ears.

I can't see you vermin, but I know you're here. Helm says so.

His knuckles whitened on the axe's dark oak shaft. His nostrils widened. There was sulfur in the air. The vile, distinct scent of the skin of underlings. Like men, they perspired. Unlike men, it wasn't ever from fear. They feared nothing. Each and every one that Venir had ever encountered was a stone-cold killer. Hatred was their strength. Fear was their friend. They fed on the weak hearts and feelings of men.

Close. So close.

He zoned in on an underling pressed against the trees. It faced away from Venir, but its huddled form was quite distinct. A long, jagged blade filled its hands. Its head scanned from side to side.

Venir fought Helm's pleading impulse.

Rush in. Cut it down. Run to the next. Cut them all down. Now. Now. Now.

Fighting his own urges that merged with Helm's, he crept forward in the darkness. Twice, the underling's ruby eyes glided over him, through him, until Venir was almost on top of it. Looking right at Venir, it cocked its head to the side and squinted its eyes.

How does it not see me? Am I toying with it, or is it toying with me?

It took everything Venir had to not strike it down immediately. The armament had powers he did not yet understand. He wanted to master it. He stood like a ready statue, dying to reanimate at every moment.

The underling in its black leathers and pinned-back hair came closer with the look of a dangerous predator. Sword ready, it cocked its elbows back to strike into the unknown.

Towering over the fiend, Venir unleashed his axe.

Slice!

The underling's head popped off of its shoulders. The body and head hit the murky ground at the same time.

Helm still throbbed with urgent life, sending Venir in every direction at once.

"Chitter. Chitter. Chitter."

The underlings appeared in all directions. Fearless and vengeful, they came.

Setting his feet, Venir faced the onslaught with unbridled power.

The first underling rushed in with two blades, striking like a snake. In a single lethal strike, the axe's spike gouged it in the neck.

Glitch!

Too-Wah! Too-Wah! Too-Wah!

Darts shot through the air.

Clatch! Clatch! Clatch! Zip! Zip! Zip!

Small crossbow bolts ripped through the leaves. Like violent insect stingers, the projectiles buried themselves deep in Venir's legs. He exploded into a whirlwind of fury. "You think that will stop me?" He bore down on two underlings.

The wicked pair hurled javelins at his chest.

He swatted them aside with the flat of his axe, and with a single whistling swing, he cleaved the both of them in half. "Let the jungle have your blood!"

The underlings were everywhere. They came in twos and threes. Stabbing, cutting, screaming with vile resentment, they tried to tear the human juggernaut down. Lethal strikes bit at Venir's skin.

Constantly in motion and guided by Helm, he dodged, twisted at the last instant. Venir's awareness was beyond instinct. His hardened muscles functioned beyond normal limits. The underlings—their evil, treacherous ways—fed his battle-honed skills. Brool, his axe, arced overhead with bone-jarring impact.

Slice!

An underling lost its hand.

Chop!

Another lost an arm.

Chop!

Its leg.

Chop!

Legs.

Coated from the gore of battle, Venir tore through the forest like a gale of fury. His axe shattered bones. Cleaved skulls. Hearts and throats were punctured. Although he bled from lacerations and burned from the poison of darts, his fury did not stop. His will and Helm urged him forward.

Kill them. Kill them all!

Ranks decimated, the hive of underlings fought on. They shot. Jabbed. Chittered. Screeched. They attacked with the fearless ferocity of hungry wolverines. Skilled and deadly, one dashed in and carved a hunk out of Venir's leg. Darts skipped off Helm.

A javelin pierced his side.

Venir roared. He snatched an underling by the neck in his mighty grip and yanked it up from the ground. He slung the fiend into another and hacked them both down. He zeroed in on the nearest thinning batch of heat and charged. A throng of three five-foot-tall terrors loosed another attack. Flanking Venir, one ducked under his swing. The others latched onto his legs like black ticks. Sharp teeth bit. Steel-hard nails clawed.

"To Bish with you fiends!"

Locked on his legs, the underlings bore him down to the ground. They ripped and tore at his skin.

Letting the axe go, he locked his forearm around one's throat and squeezed until its eyes bulged. With his free hand he slipped out his long hunting knife and plunged it into the second underling's side. It wilted as the underling in the nook of his arm suffocated and its windpipe cracked. He tucked the knife back into its sheath. Two more were dead, and Helm told him the third enemy lurked somewhere nearby. Venir could feel its presence. His calloused hands found the shaft of his axe again. His senses zeroed in.

Keeping to the brush, the underling loaded another crossbow bolt.

Venir closed the gap in two great strides and swung.

Metal rang off metal with jarring impact, sending a ringing shockwave through the forest.

CLANGGGGGGG!

Venir found himself face to face with a powerful figure as tall as he. The flame-headed stranger.

CHAPTER 33

"YOUR DAYS ARE OVER, SLAYER," the stranger said.

Deep in his battle-hazed mind, Venir recognized the man. Buried in his blood hunt, it didn't matter. Nothing living or dead would stand between him and the slaughter of the foul underlings. Brool uncoiled like a steel spring and jabbed into the scales of the stranger's dipping shoulder.

"Auhg!" the man yelled. And then without hesitation, the stranger slipped out of Brool's reach and countered with size-defying speed. The great sword flicked out like a striking snake.

The metal of Brool crashed into the metal of Fang once more.

CLANGGGGGG!

The master warriors battled back and forth.

Venir cut, stabbed, and chopped.

The stranger parried, deflected, and countered. The man with scales on his arms swung his great blade with the ease of a stick, fencing like a true swordsman. The man staggered back against Venir's relentless press.

Chest to chest, steel scraping on steel, they locked up head to head.

"You shouldn't prey on underlings, slayer!" the stranger growled.

The statement only fueled Venir's temper. The man was out of his mind. No one on Bish ever fought for the underlings. Face to face, he could see the deep anger in the man's golden eyes. Resentment. Hatred. There was no doubt this man was here to kill him. He drove a knee into the man's ribs a few times. Drawing his head back, he busted the rim of Helm into the man's perfect nose. *Crunch!*

A powerful shove sent Venir tripping over the vines. Down on the ground he went. As he scrambled to his knees, his keen eyes caught the gleam of steel baring down on him. His arms snapped up the axe, catching the oncoming sword.

CLANGGGGGG!

The jarring blow shook his elbows. Venir twisted his axe, caught the sword between the blades, and held it fast. He kicked the man in the gut, doubling him over. With a surge of his legs, he charged the man back into a tree.

Thud!

The man shoved Venir's chin back with his clawed hand. The stranger was muttering to himself, "Yes. Yes. Yes. I will kill him. Die, Darkslayer. Die!" With the strength of an ogre, he shoved Venir and broke the grappling off.

The two muscle-bound behemoths squared off again.

Venir held Brool tight in his bloody grip, ready to strike. His lungs burned. The boundless energy that usually fueled him ebbed.

Before him, the stranger stood, bloody nosed and wild eyed, his movements fluid and at ease.

Billip and Mikkel appeared from the brush, ranged weapons poised to attack. Billip let an arrow fly.

Twang!

The stranger easily slipped out of the arrow's path.

"Impossible!" Billip said, nocking another shaft.

Mikkel aimed his heavy crossbow at the man and said, "I won't miss."

"Stay out of this!" Venir ordered. Chest and shoulders heaving, he added with a growl, "He's mine!"

Mikkel pegged an underling squirming through the brush.

Clatch-Zip!

The bolt rocketed through its skull. "We have your back. Do your thing!"

Venir slid his shield from his shoulders, strapped it to his arm, and hunkered down. He eyed the foreigner and said, "Let's dance."

"It's him! Kill him! Kill him!" Oran's voice said in Nath's head. "Kill the slayer!"

Fueled by constant thoughts of destruction, Nath waded in toward the warrior. He'd watched the slayer carve down the underlings like a cold-blooded killing machine. It was just as Oran had said. All of the horrific details had come to life.

Embedded in his thoughts, Oran urged him on, "Put an end to this man! End all of this madness! Bring me his head!"

Fang ready, Nath struck. Hard and fast, the sword hammered away at the Darkslayer's shield. The warrior in the dark helmet—fierce, cunning, and crafty—jabbed at his eyes. His belly. His legs. The rangy man was quick and powerful. His axe was an arc of death. Nath matched everything the man had and then some.

Time to end this. Time to free this world from this disease.

He turned loose his own savagery.

Bang! Bang! Bang!

The powerful blade Fang pounded into the warrior like the striking rain of a thunderstorm.

The great axe chopped at his legs.

Nath leapt high.

Swish!

Striking from mid-air, he poked the slayer in his metal head.

The man staggered back, reset his jaw, and marched back forward.

Matching weapon length for weapon length, Nath aimed high for the shield, stopped in mid-swing, pulled Fang back around, and chopped at the man's legs.

The man's axe, a living thing in his hands, banged the sword away at the last second. Off balance, the surefooted fighter stumbled through the tall grass.

Nath smote.

Bang!

Sparks flew like fire.

Bang! Bang! Bang!

"Yes! Yes! Yes!" Oran said. "I can feel it! You have him! Kill him!"

Venir's iron limbs gave way to the thunderous strikes of the lightning-quick man. With tremendous effort, he fought on. His will would not break or bend. But now, with all the nearby underlings dead, the armament no longer fueled his blood. It was him against the foreigner, who moved unlike any creature he'd ever known.

This is it.

With the sword hammering away at his shield, Venir summoned everything he had left and counterattacked. He lowered Brool and clipped the man's thigh with the spike. The pounding of the sword ceased, and the attacker eased back. Arms feeling like lead, huffing for breath, his boundless energy gone, Venir tossed the shield aside.

To the end.

He locked both hands around Brool's shaft. It was going to be a fight to the finish. A fight to the death. To match the stranger's speed, he'd need both hands and all the strength he had left. Jaw set, he advanced again.

Fight or die, Venir! Fight or die!

Blocking out all doubt, he took the man. The great axe slammed into the brilliant metal of the outsider's blade and drove it downward. He hacked. Chopped. Sliced.

The stranger sidestepped, parried, and countered.

Brool's razor edge clipped the man. Cut the scales on his sinewy arms. Drew blood from his legs and chest.

Inches away from death, the man escaped again and again.

Venir poured everything he had into it. The axe rose and fell. His strikes became sluggish and clumsy compared to the finesse and weaving of the sword.

Keep swinging! Keep swinging!

Putting everything he had into it, Venir unleashed a side swing that would have split an ox in half.

Slice!

The stranger flattened in a fraction of a second and popped up again.

Venir's heavy axe and tired frame shuffled out of balance. He started to recover his swing. Out of the corner of his eye, he saw the stranger's sword coming back.

With a golden fire in his eyes, the stranger rammed his sword to the hilt into Venir's chest.

Venir's head snapped back, "Urk!" Brool slipped from his fingers.

The gasps of his comrades resonated in the deep recesses of Venir's mind. Melegal's ashen face appeared through the branches in the forest.

Venir felt life slip out of his body, from his fingers down to his toes. His eyes fixed on the sword plunged into his chest. The pain burned like a hundred fires. Raising his stare, he found the eyes of his opponent.

The bright eyes were filled with victory and a twisted confusion.

Spitting blood and racked with pain, Venir managed to say, "Well fought." The last of his fires dimmed. His inner furnace of molten fury cooled. Somehow, Venir held on to the last thread of life. His bloody fingers clutched at the warrior's red locks of hair and held them fast.

The fighter's golden eyes enlarged.

Holding the man fast, Venir snaked out his hunting knife and drove it hilt deep in the stranger's exposed chest. Dying, he said, "But you're coming to the grave with me."

CHAPTER 34

Led by Chongo to his friend's aid, Melegal shouted at the others. "Why did you two idiots just stand there? You let him get killed!"

Venir's body fell backward, sliding off the sword and toppling to the ground. The man with red hair collapsed as well.

"It was his choice," Billip said, kneeling by Venir's side. "Not ours."

"He isn't very competent in his reasoning! You know that!" Melegal looked at his friend. His strapping frame was broken and bloody, unmoving. The skin on his arms was clammy. "Bloodthirsty fools!" Melegal rarely raised his voice over anything, but today had been enough. Surrounded by piles of dead underlings, he'd reached his breaking point.

Kneeling alongside the other man, Billip pulled Venir's knife from the stranger's chest. "This one's still breathing, I think." He held his hand over the stranger's mouth. "His breath has fire behind it. What manner of man breathes flame and survives a gash like that?"

"Finish him off," Melegal suggested.

Blast my skinny hide, I'll never get back to Bone. Fool of a man, Venir! Just had to get yourself killed, didn't you?

"I hope you goons packed a shovel, because I'm not burying him. My back hurts just thinking about digging a hole that big."

"Watch your mouth, Melegal," Mikkel said. His jovial smile and tone were far gone. "That was as honorable a fight as I ever saw. Never seen two men fight like that. Never."

"So what do we do with this one?" Billip asked. "Why would he battle alongside underlings? No one does that."

"Maybe it's like Farc said, he's something their dark mysticism summoned." Mikkel tilted his head and added, "But it doesn't feel right. None of it does."

"It doesn't matter now, either way," Melegal said. He thumbed what looked to be sweat from the corners of his eyes. "Vee is dead."

The warrior lay still as a stone with wounds all over his body, slick in grime and blood. It seemed a fitting end to the robust warrior, but the helmet still had a strange life of its own, even with the eyes within closed.

The jungle fell silent.

The hairs stood up on the nape of Melegal's neck. Goosebumps rose on his skinny arms. He glanced down at Venir.

The man's eyes snapped open. His hands lashed out and snatched Melegal by his shirt.

Melegal fought against the iron grip that seized him, but his voice was calm and matter-of-fact when he said, "Get your bloody mitts off me, you incorrigible ape."

Venir's fingers popped open.

Melegal hopped to his feet.

A lock of red hair was trapped between Venir's fingers. He cast it away, unbuckled his helmet, and peeled it off his head. His hair was damp with sweat, but his face was clean from the nose up. A wary look was in his eyes. He said, "What happened?"

"This man fed you his sword through the chest," Billip said, motioning to the stranger. He pitched Venir's knife to him. "You bladed him. Somehow, like you, he still breathes but shouldn't."

Melegal rubbed the bumps from his bony arms, shaking his head. Bish didn't offer explanations. Life moved on.

Venir's color had returned, and so had the brightness in his eyes. He shrugged his broad shoulders and gave him an explanation: "Bish happens."

Melegal set his steely gaze on the other man who lay near death on the ground. Chongo sniffed the man and licked his face and wounds.

"Chongo, get away from there," Venir said with a groan. He got up to his feet. "Come."

The muscular beast lay on top of the man. Billip reached for his collar. The dog snapped at his fingers and growled.

"Seems he likes the stranger, Venir," Billip said, backing away. "Strange, strange indeed. He just eats the underlings."

Venir picked up his knife. "That's no underling." He reached down and scratched the dog behind the ears. The waist-high beast had a few wounds of his own. He still licked at the wounded man on the ground. "I've never seen Chongo act like this for a stranger. And this man seemed confused."

"And who wouldn't be? Clearly he doesn't belong in this armpit of the world," Melegal said. He smashed a mosquito sucking on his neck. "Bone! I don't belong here either. Venir, it's time to get out of here."

"Take a moment and catch your breath."

"I'm not out of breath."

"That's because you didn't fight anybody," Mikkel said with a slight return of his smile. He shook some gore from his club. "Not that you wouldn't have, given the opportunity."

"I say I'd fare better than Venir did and not wake up with a wound the breadth of a canoe in my chest. Now, I mean it, it's high time we departed."

Billip began stacking underling weapons in a pile. There was a gleam in his dark eyes. "Underling steel by the bushel. Hah. Even you should be thrilled about this, Melegal. It's quite a haul, it is."

"The only thing I want to haul is my skinny arse out of here!"

Mikkel picked up a huge sword that lay on the ground and swished it around. "Bish! What a thing this is! The balance, the weight. I'm no swordsman, but even I know perfection."

Melegal eased toward the magnificent blade, along with Billip. He had an eye for detail and had seen his fair share of weaponry in the world. The Royals lusted and boasted over such weaponry in their world. But the dragons with twinkling gemstone eyes built into the crossguard were entirely an unseen thing.

"We'll get a fortune for it." He nudged Melegal with his elbow. "What do you think? Split it four ways?"

"It's Venir's to decide," said Melegal.

Venir, chin sagging on his chest, flipped his hand. "Have at it … but this man's heart hasn't stopped yet. Billip, Mikkel, why don't you take your leave with Melegal if you wish? Chongo and I will stay with this man."

Incredulous, Melegal replied, "Oh, so now we can leave? Now that you've had your fill of the underlings, we can suddenly go?" He wanted to spit. "Fine! You two burly brigands take me to Bone, and I'll fetch a price so high for that sword that you'll be sleeping in gold."

"Now you're talking," Mikkel said. His big smile returned. "I like how you think, skinny man!" He took a few steps away from Venir and the crowd, whistled for his horse, and suddenly dropped the sword. "Ow! It burned me!"

"What do you mean, it burned you?" Billip asked.

Rubbing his palm, Mikkel blew on it. "I mean that hilt heated up like an iron. Don't believe me? *You* try it."

"You're crazy." Billip strolled over and picked it up. "See? It's fine. Cool as a cucumber—Ow!" He dropped it and kicked it away. "Cursed thing!"

"Told you." Mikkel shook his head and said back to Venir, "We'll let you decide what to do with it."

"Just wrap it up in some cloth or something," Melegal argued.

"If you want to take it, you take it then." Billip poured a canteen of water on his hand. "I've got a blister from it!"

"Venir, are you really going to stick with that dead man?" asked Melegal.

Massaging Chongo's neck, Venir replied, "We'll catch up."

CHAPTER 35

CRACKLE. CRACKLE. POP.

Nath's senses came to life. Surrounding sounds filled his ears.

Chop. Split. Clonk.

Unable to command his limbs to move, he somehow forced his eyes open. A figure moved behind the shadows of a glowing fire, splitting wood and tossing logs on. Staring into the flame, Nath gathered his thoughts. The fight. The blade sinking into his chest.

All of a sudden his lost memories resurfaced. All of them.

Sultans of Sulfur! I'm not in Nalzambor. I'm in a world called Bish!

His heart raced and pounded in his temples. Like all that had happened in his whole 200-plus years of life, Nath remembered everything that had happened since he arrived on this world, in crystal-clear detail. The underling lords Catten and Verbard. The cleric Oran. Their nature was so vile and deceitful. Killing came as easily as breathing to them.

I fought for them! What have I done?

He sensed a presence by his side. A huge dog rested its head on his lap. Its brown eyes gazed up and into his. Chest filled with pain, he summoned his strength and moved.

The dog's throat rumbled.

The figure beyond the fire approached with the great axe in hand. His helmet was gone. His face was haggard and tired. "What is it,

Chongo?' He squatted down and fixed his eyes on Nath's. "Ah, so he does live?"

Nath couldn't speak yet, but he could think.

I *live? How do* you *live? I skewered you like a pig!*

Venir put a canteen to Nath's lips and trickled water into his half-open mouth. "You know, I don't question much, stranger. But you, my friend, are a mystery. I would have buried you, or at least what was still living of you, but for my dog, Chongo. He likes you." He rubbed his dog. "And if he likes you despite your affiliation with the underlings, I'll have to like you enough to spare you. But if you ever have at me again, I'll peel that fire top from your shoulders."

Nath groaned. He could still feel the hole in his chest. A steady, burning sensation. His limbs were weak and aching. But his body, as tired and as in agony as it might be, was intact and healing.

Lie low. See what this man has to say.

The man called Venir huddled by the fire, picked up a large slab of rabbit meat, and skewered it with a stick. He took another hunk of raw meat and tossed it at Nath's feet. With a nod of the man's head, the dog, Chongo, devoured it.

Nath's belly moaned.

The dog lifted its ears and sniffed his stomach.

Venir dusted off his hands. "Trying to kill people works up quite the appetite, doesn't it?" He fastened his eyes on Nath. "Once you get your strength back, I'll be interested to know where you hail from and why you aided the underlings. And don't play possum with me, either. I've no doubt that a warrior such as you has played many games. Chongo will alert me to any tricks. So if you can speak, I say the sooner the better."

Unblinking, Nath studied the man's cold blue eyes. There was a fire in them. A purpose. Something direct and honest. A big-framed youth by Nath's standards, Venir seemed to carry a great deal of responsibility on his shoulders. Now that Nath had his memories back and a sense of who he was had returned, he could see things as they were more clearly. He forced his parched lips open and spoke, "Nath."

Venir nodded at him. "Sounds like a Bish name." He rubbed the dog behind the ears and said, "I'm—"

"Venir."

The burly warrior cocked an eyebrow at him. "Are you an assassin sent to kill me?"

Finding his strength and grimacing, Nath pushed himself up to his elbows. "Assassin, no. Sent to kill you, yes."

"I'd say that makes you an assassin."

"Assassins get paid. My motivation came from deception." He managed to tug at the collar that squeezed his throat. "An underling named Oran harnessed me with this. Tricked me, one might say, but that's just the beginning of my worries."

"What do you mean?"

"This is not my world. My home is Nalzambor, and this clearly isn't it. Anything but this place is."

"Never heard of it, but I haven't been everywhere in this world either. I'd like to think I'm savvy to most places, those worth mentioning, that is."

Nath stretched his hand over and petted Chongo. "He's a fine friend. I suppose I owe him a thank you."

The dog panted with his big pink tongue hanging out of his mouth.

"Food will do. Old Chongo will eat about anything." Venir eyed Nath's arms. "I've never see the likes of that before. It's real?"

"Venir, are there dragons in this world?"

"I've heard the name, but never seen. They coat banners, paintings, and such. But never such a sight on this side of the Mist. Perhaps that is where you come from? Do you remember how you got here?"

Nath's head sagged down into his hand. Brenwar had been trapped when he left Nalzambor, thanks to Corzan's trickery. "Oh no."

"You sound like a man who just fell underneath another avalanche of trouble," Venir said. "This rabbit's cooked. Perhaps you should eat."

Nath started forcing himself to his feet, but Chongo had his legs pinned down. "May I get up?"

Venir gave the dog a nod, and he moved along Venir's side. He extended his hand and helped Nath to his feet.

Nath nodded. "Thanks." He moseyed over to the fire and warmed his hands. Nearby, underlings were stacked up in a pile, and a stench was growing. He spied his sword lying in the grass and Venir's axe stuck spike first in the ground nearby with the helmet and shield right beside it. "That's quite an assortment."

"That's quite a sword. Brool has shattered many."

"I could say the same about Fang."

Venir edged up to the fire. "You breathed fire in the tavern. You wield magic?"

It was a funny question. Back in Nalzambor, Nath had lost that ability, along with many others. Perhaps now he could recall it again. "In a manner of speaking yes. Urk!"

Venir's eyes filled with alarm as Nath clutched at his throat and dropped to his knees. "What is it?"

The collar choked him, and Oran's voice was inside his head. "Kill him!"

CHAPTER 36

VENIR WATCHED WITH UNEASE AS Nath writhed on the ground, pulling at the collar around his neck. It squirmed and convulsed like a living thing. Tiny barbs sank into the meat of Nath's neck like teeth. It seemed that the harder the stranger pulled, the tighter the dark magic contracted, making his face turn first red and then a deep purple. His fingers clutched at the air. His lips tried to speak.

"What is it, man? Tell me!" Venir pulled his knife and aimed for the neck. "Let me slice that thing from you!"

"No," Nath choked out. "Sword. Get sword."

Wary, Venir hopped over to the sword and snatched it up. The hilt was cool in his hand. He put it in the writhing man's free hand.

Fighting for his life, Nath clawed at the sword and drew out a dagger from the pommel. Pulling at the living collar, he tried to get the knife under it.

Venir reached down, wrapped his fingers around the collar, and gave it a pull himself. "Give me that dagger."

Nath stuffed it in his hand.

Venir sawed at the dark coil.

It screeched like a living thing before it finally broke.

Snap!

Venir ripped the collar off Nath's bleeding neck. It squirmed like a headless snake. Venir bashed it on the ground. Stomped it. Kicked it. It slithered toward the woods. "The cursed thing lives!"

Nath's scaled hand lashed out and seized the collar. It coiled around his wrist tighter than a wound spring. He crawled over to the fire and stuck his entire hand in it.

"Are you mad?" Venir objected.

The collar caught fire, burned a bright green, and sizzled out in a bright, screeching flash.

Oran ripped off his headset and screamed. "I had him! I had him! Now my weapon allies itself with him!" He floated up toward the cave ceiling, hovered to his shelves, and started throwing books and glass jars on the floor. "Catten and Verbard will have my head for this!"

He needed a plan. An explanation for his superiors. He threw up his arms. "I don't know why I want to go back to the Underland anyway!"

Huffing for breath, Nath said, "Great Guzan! Does everything in this world have the stench of death?"

"Aye, but it reminds one he's alive." Venir nodded. "You sound worried for a man that breathes fire and is not harmed by it. Are there others such as you?"

"Not here on Bish." Nath climbed up to his feet again. His stomach knotted. Perspiration ran down his face. He didn't remember the last time he'd ever felt so bad before. Now, with his faculties restored, he felt more lost than ever. He stuffed Dragon Claw back into the pommel and picked up Fang.

Venir eased toward his axe.

"I'm far from ready for a rematch, and I would prefer that the contest never came again. You're quite a fighter. You'd be quite renowned if you were in my lands."

"You fare pretty well yourself. You fought two ogres and won. That's an extraordinary feat. Those bumpkins in Two-Ten City will be talking about it for years." Venir picked the stick of roasted meat up off the fire and held it toward Nath. "Can you eat?"

Ravenous, Nath picked the bones clean while Venir skinned another pair of rabbits and cooked them. The wounds he suffered didn't feel quite as bad as the one deep inside his chest. His dragon heart was wounded—not from the blade but from being far from home.

How will I get back to Nalzambor?

On the other side of the fire, hunkered over like an ape, Venir gnawed the meat off the bones and sucked his fingers. The warrior seemed at ease in a jungle that seeped with treachery. "Mmmm ... these rabbits are good like chicken and make for excellent stew. What meat do you prefer?"

"Fish."

Venir nodded. "There's plenty of fish in the streams around here. Things on the bank won't be so vile as near the dead underlings. This is rich land, here below the Outland borders, but the underlings are poisoning it as well as everything else." He chucked the bones to Chongo. The big dog's iron jaws crunched right through them. "Why don't you tell me about this land of yours?" He lifted a brow. "Are the women pretty?"

Nath huffed a laugh, paining his chest and watering his eyes. Thinking of the women he'd encountered in Two-Ten City, he politely said, "A good bit fairer than the ones in your city. No offense."

"Hah!" Venir picked up his knife and started wiping it clean with a rag. "Those hags! Two-Ten isn't known for the prettiest of things. It's a place of despicable people. It's also a place to get away from things. No, there are women a far bit more fair than what you have seen." His face darkened a little. "But oft times, the most beautiful can be the most deadly."

"Sounds like you have a wounded heart."

"Wounded pride is more like it." His eyes drifted to his axe. "But at least I've got something to show for it."

Taken aback, Nath said, "You killed her."

"No," Venir frowned and changed the subject. "So, tell me about your sword. Fang, you called it? It sizzled my friends."

"Did they try to take it?"

"Aye?"

Nath smiled, "Well, like your Chongo, Fang won't leave my side unless I tell him it's all right to. At least sometimes. He can be a fickle thing."

"Your steel can think?" Venir didn't seem surprised, more like interested.

"Let's just say it has innate magic qualities." Nath pointed at Venir's armament. "And I'm thinking you're familiar with something like that."

The corners of Venir's lips came up over his strong chin, forming a smile. "I suppose. It helps me hunt these underlings. Perhaps when I'm through with them, I'll come and visit this Nalzambor of yours."

"You're going to kill all of them?"

Venir got up and pointed at the pile of bodies. "As many as I can. Are you finished eating?"

"Sure."

The warrior ventured to his horse and took a flask of oil that hung from the saddle. "You think it smells bad now, wait until I burn these things."

Watching the man sprinkle oil over the underling corpses, Nath said, "Is there no reconciliation among your peoples?"

"Underlings? Hah! Killing men comes as easy as breathing to them. No chance of that if you want to live."

"We don't cut people down like a new harvest in our world," Nath said.

"Perhaps you should," Venir replied. He pointed to the fire. "Do you mind?"

Nath picked up a log from the fire and tossed it on the oiled dead. "This is not a practice I take pleasure in."

"Stick around long enough and you will," Venir said.

CHAPTER 37

THEY RODE FOR MILES, NATH on horseback, resting his healing body, while Venir and Chongo led the way. The thick brush of the jungles merged with steep hills, where they came across an overgrown pathway that led to a place of desolation. Near the top were the remains of a village that was nothing but fallen stones and charred huts.

Brown vermin and ravens scattered on his approach. Nath's chest tightened. Terror had torn through the area months ago, maybe a year. Bodies were buried in holes head first with the legs still sticking out. Animals had picked the bones clean. Bodies of men and women were impaled and hanging in trees. Ash piles were filled with bone.

"What do you think?" Venir said to Nath.

"Underlings, huh?"

"Not even the orcs or gnolls act like this. No, this is the underling way of striking terror in the heart of everyone who comes across their work. I found this a while back. I was too late to save them." Venir wiped the sweat from his brow with his forearm. "That's why I hunt them down and do the same to them. Come on, there's more up the hill."

I think I've seen enough.

But Nath dug his heels into the horse and followed after the man. As they trekked through the day, the giant leaves did nothing to shield them from the heat of the two suns. It was sweltering. Miserable. And the buzz of insects was annoying. Nath loved the sun, but in this world, the kind of warmth it gave was punishing.

It's no wonder the underlings prefer caves.

Where the hill crested, a wooden garrison stood. Squarely built of logs jutting from the ground, it looked to hold about one hundred people. The walls were damaged and burned. The front gate hung wide open, with half of the establishment covered in overgrowth. There were bodies. Skeletons in armor lying in metal shells on the ground. Others were draped over the wall. One man's body was hoisted up high on a flag pole.

Venir removed his backpack and took out his helmet. "They're getting bolder now. They've been directly attacking Royal outposts such as this. And right now, the Royals of the north seem to be leaving them to die." He buckled the helmet on. "It's sick. Men can't even trust men in this day and age."

Groaning, Nath dismounted. Fang in hand, he approached the fort. "Are you expecting company?"

Venir rapped his knuckles on the helmet. "Not if I greet them first. Stay back if you want."

Sword resting on his shoulder, Nath followed the man and dog into the abandoned fort. The interior was nothing more than the busted remains of what had been. Dead men. No dead underlings. There were even horses picked clean to the hooves. He shielded his nose with the back of his hand. With his sword's tip, he lifted up the remnant of a charred purple-and-silver banner with leaves in the stitching.

"A decent house," Venir said with a shrug. "The Royals keep the trade routes clear toward the north and south with posts such as this. It was a tight network until the underlings took over Outpost Thirty-One. Now the Royals, high in their castles, have all but abandoned their men. Some still stay and fight, however. This was them. The brave."

"We have our fair share of problems like this where I come from, but nothing quite like these underlings." Nath slapped at a fly the size of his thumb on his neck. "And I swear there aren't so many insects!"

"It's not as bad in the Outlands. Just hotter. I prefer that climate."

Nath's nose crinkled. Bish had a gamut of foreign smells, but this one was new. He tightened his grip on his sword. Venir's stride through the fort came to a halt, and he cocked his head to one side and poised his axe to swing. The breeze stopped. Chongo's tail went stiff, and his large head hung low.

The ground shifted beneath Nath's feet. Vibrations shuffled the loose dirt and pebbles. A green mist drifted up from the ground, covering his feet. The hair on his neck stood on end.

"Venir, what do you know of this?"

"Sorcery," the warrior said, "with the stench of the underlings."

The mist rose higher, like the rotting stench of the dead.

Nath started to cough.

Chongo began to howl.

In a moment, Nath's eyes were covered and he couldn't see his hand in front of his face. While he was stumbling forward and fighting for breath, tentacles erupted from the ground and seized his legs. "Guzan!"

CHAPTER 38

H ANDS BEHIND HIS BACK, THUMBS digging into his palms, Oran stood on the small black craft that skimmed quickly over the black waters of the Current. Aided by magic, the craft moved quicker than usual. Underlings had more time than most, living hundreds and in some cases more than a thousand years. Now time was pressing, and he wanted to get as far away from the likes of Lords Catten and Verbard as he could. He'd never hear the end of it. Not from them. Now he'd failed at the minute task of killing the pest called the Darkslayer.

"I hate my life, I hate my life, I hate my life."

Moving faster than a thundering horse, the craft cruised beyond the great forest and toward the jungles near Two-Ten City. Unlike most underlings, Oran had allies outside the Underland realm.

The craft came to a halt on a soft bank in the darkness. Cloak dragging, Oran wound through a long network of caves until he emerged outside beneath the light of the moons above. He made his way through the shadow-filled black, pushing aside branches through thickets and trudging into a deep ravine. Just as he hit bottom, a knot of people far bigger than he surrounded him. One, a gnoll packed with muscle in his neck and shoulders, carried a sword big enough for two men to hold.

The underling held up his hand, filled with red, glowing fingernails, and spoke in the common tongue. "It is I, Oran. I need a great service performed."

The gnoll stuck his sword in the ground. "Speak it."

"Recently," *you dog-faced fool*, "in Two-Ten City there was a red-haired menace called Nath. His arms had black scales like those on a snake. Find him. Kill him and everyone he is with. I want his head. I want all of their heads." Oran tossed a bag into the gnoll's chest.

The gnoll poured out the contents in his hand. The others, orcs and men, gasped. Gemstones twinkled like color-filled stars in his hands.

"There is more than that to come if you can follow through. Use that as a bounty."

"Bounty?"

"I'm not toying around with this!" The tips of Oran's fingers glowed with a deep-red fire. "You will do as I say or I will bury you. All of you!"

Wide eyed, the gnoll and company took a half step back. "It will be as you say, Oran. A bounty."

"Yes," he hissed. "A bounty. I want every rogue and cutthroat from Two-Ten and beyond hunting this man down!"

The gnoll nodded. "It will be done as you say."

Oran's hand flashed with red light, and a bolt of fire shot from his hand into the heavily armored half-orc guard, who was missing half his arm. The body shook and trembled. The hair sizzled and decayed. A smoking corpse in red-hot metal was all that remained.

Snarling, Oran said, "It had better be."

CHAPTER 39

SPIDERS! BIGGER THAN CHONGO, HAIRY black arachnids erupted from the ground and latched onto Nath's legs. He pierced one in the body, drawing forth an eerie screech. In a flash of steel, he hacked into another, splitting through its fang-filled face. Dark green gobbets splattered all over and burned through his clothes and into his skin.

"Argh!" Nath cried out.

"Sand spiders!" roared a thunderous voice above the charge of the scurrying masses. "Their venom is lethal!" Heavy chopping sounds cut through the hovering mist. A spider's leg whizzed by Nath's head. "Don't just stand there. Kill them!"

Lungs filled with choking gas, eyes stinging, Nath fought on. The spiders surged from all directions, erupting from the mist and spitting poison at his legs. He stuck Fang in one's face, ripped out Dragon Claw from the pommel, and gored another.

Zzzlip!

Webbing tangled up his feet, and a hard tug dropped him to the ground. "Sultans of Sulfur!"

Zzzlip!

More strands of webbing pinned his arms to his sides, cutting off his chopping motion. A spider scurried up and sank its teeth into his arm. Ahead, another spider, bigger than two, was hauling Nath toward its mouth. It was a big, black-haired thing, its bulk ghastly. Red insect eyes had a hungry glow in them, and the chopping teeth that filled its mouth sizzled with dripping venom.

Nath kicked it as best he could. The webbing held his efforts at bay. "Get off me, scary thing!"

Venir emerged from the mist, axe high in the air and coming down fast.

Chop! Chop! Chop!

The blade splattered the insect into twitching legs and goo.

"I forgot to mention the silk they spin." Venir sliced the webs that tethered Nath's legs with one of the razor edges of his huge axe. He gored the smaller spider with the axe's spike and flicked it off Nath's arm. "At least now you know."

Using Dragon Claw, Nath started sawing the webbing from his arm.

"I wouldn't try that, it will stick." Venir hacked down a charging spider.

Coughing, Nath continued to cut. His blade's keen edge sliced the webbing away. "Seems my steel's as sharp as yours, eh?"

Venir pushed out his palm and said in a low voice, "This is underling magic. The fiends are near."

Climbing back to his feet, blades ready to fight, Nath replied, "Then what are we waiting for?"

A bright bolt of lightning ripped through the mist and slammed into Nath's chest.

Sssraz!

Nath was lifted from his feet and knocked back into the leftover goo from a spider Venir had just killed. Chest burning and teeth tasting like metal, Nath said with a groan, "I need to get that breastplate back, Venir."

The fierce warrior was gone, but angry chitters and battle cries erupted from beyond. Covered in spider goo and wracked with pain, Nath forced himself to his feet, braining an oncoming spider with his sword on his way to the sounds of battle.

Chop! Hack! Slice! Urk!

As he staggered through the dilapidated fort, the mist started to lift.

"Over here," said a rugged voice.

Turning his head and shoulders, Nath found Venir nearby. Three underling fighters lay dead at his feet. The fourth was impaled to the ground by Brool.

"That's the last of them," said Venir. "This one here in the robes called the lightning. Stings like a hive of bees, doesn't it?"

"I've been stung worse," Nath replied. He rolled his neck and sighed. "I need to get out of here."

Holding the underling corpse fast with his boot, Venir tore his axe from the body and wiped the blades on its robes. "And go where?"

It was a good question that Nath didn't have an answer to. His best bet was to track down the underling Oran. After all, he was the one who had cast the spell that brought him in on the Bish side. Corzan had cast the other portion, on the Nalzambor side.

But Nath's gut told him that what he needed was improbable at best. He needed help. "We know these underlings use magic. Are there others aside from them that do?"

"There are, but most of them are Royals that hole up in the bigger cities. I can't say I know many. Strange they are. Aloof and creepy, at least the ones I've met."

Nath scratched below his eye with his pinky nail and stared up at the bright sky with a sigh. The bright-orange suns hung like brilliant sunflowers in the foreign sky. His heart sank. "You know, there is only one sun and one moon where I am from."

Venir peered above. "Sounds cold. One would think you'd have fur on your arms instead of scales."

"It's a fertile land with harsh winters and mild summers. The mountain peaks are always frozen. But sunrises and sunsets aren't so devastating to the skin. Most of the land is lush and full of less temperamental greenery."

Venir slung his axe over his shoulder. "Sounds like you need a trip to the Red Clay Forest. Plenty of pretty plants in there, and I suppose that place would take to you." He reached down and rubbed Chongo's neck. "Look, Nath. I don't know where to tell you to start on this journey, but if you want to seek out the underlings that voodooed you, I can help."

"I appreciate it. Just give me a moment, eh? I need time to think." He glanced at the spider grime coated on his arms. "Yech."

"Sand spiders. Pretty nasty, eh?" Venir eyed one of the eight-legged fiends. "Your friends the underlings sometimes ride on them."

"They ride on the backs of bugs?" Nath said, not hiding his disgust.

"Just like horses. Up walls and under bridges. It's a creepy sight that chills your bones."

"I guess I shouldn't be surprised. It's different, but there are plenty of enemies such as this where I come from."

"Tell me."

"Wurmers. Eh, I guess to you they'd be giant black lizards. Some have wings and fly through the air. Many breathe fire, too." He didn't go on about it. There just didn't seem to be much of a point. "That's just one of many frightening things." He limped toward the deteriorating fort's exit. The spider venom on his leg still burned, and his body was far from healed up from the chest wound he had suffered. His eyes landed on Venir's horse. "Great Guzan!"

The horse lay dead on the ground with a sand spider sucking on its neck.

Nath stormed over and hacked the spider into goo. Covered in sweat, he dropped his sword and bent over with his hands on his knees, panting for breath. He turned his chin toward the approaching Venir.

"You look frustrated," said the younger warrior. "Don't be. Bish happens all the time."

"Do you ever get used to it?" Nath asked.

"You don't have a choice."

BOOK TWO

HEROES UNITE

CHAPTER 1

DRIPPING IN SWEAT, NATH TOOK a knee alongside a brook and scooped up a handful of water. He sipped it out of his hands and then dabbed the sweat from his brow with his sleeve. In all of his two hundred twenty years, he never remembered sweating so much before, not in Nalzambor. Compared to Bish, the weather in Nalzambor was moderate and pleasant.

This place is despicable.

The large green leaves in the trees draped down toward the ground. The branches were all twists and knots and overgrowth. Vines as thick as his arms constricted the trees as if they were trying to choke the life out of the limbs. Everything from the vermin that crawled and scurried to the bugs that crunched under his toes moved with desperate intent and dissatisfaction. Life was not easy here.

A small waterfall about three rock slabs high cascaded into the brook. Green and red ferns fanned out like leafy ears on his side of the stream, adding a touch of serenity. Nath rubbed his chest. His heart ached for home.

A scar in his chest still burned a little, where Venir had buried a hunting knife in him. If the warrior had been a little closer to the mark, it would have been the end of Nath.

He splashed more water on his face and rubbed it in. His limbs were still a little woozy from the spider that had bitten him, and his vision had a haze which hadn't drifted from his sight as of yet. He rubbed his temples and closed his eyes.

I need to shed this.

Over the sounds of the babbling stream, he heard something splash into the water. When he opened his eyes, Chongo was on the other bank, paws deep in the stream, lapping up big gulps of water. The red-brown dog was almost as big as a man, maybe two hundred pounds, with two heads and necks like bulls have. All four of his eyes were soft, and the wrinkles in both of his mastiff-like faces made the giant dog seem a little slow, but he had proven to be a loyal and fierce friend.

"Greetings, Chongo."

One of the dwarven setter's mouths expanded into a yawn that could swallow a melon. The other gave a nod and focused back on the water, its huge pink and black tongue spooning in gulps at a time.

A breeze picked up in the ravine, rustling the red locks of Nath's hair. The mist from the splashing falls had a cooling effect. Nath sighed and sat back down. Eyeing the ferns and the falls, he thought of home in Nalzambor. This was the closest he'd felt to home since he'd been in Bish.

Hang onto your memories, Nath. They're all you have. Hang on.

With Chongo slurping up the water and the falls crashing over the rocks in the background, Nath eased back onto his elbows with his chest aching. He took in the beautiful display of the ferns among the flowers and thought about home. Selene. Brenwar. Balzurth. Grahleyna. Bayzog. He missed them all. It hurt.

At least I'll have moments like this to remember them.

Venir emerged. His soot-covered boots crushed the ferns, and the grime from them muddied the crystal-clear stream. He stood there glowering down at Nath, a man among men. In his two-plus centuries, Nath had never encountered one so grizzled and restless.

A fire burned in Venir's blue eyes, one the seas could not quench.

Sweat dripping off his nose, Venir said in his gusty voice, "Feeling at home, are we?"

"I had a moment." Nath sat back up and crossed his hands over his knees. "At least things aren't so bad right now."

Not wearing his helmet, Venir swept his flaxen locks over his shoulder. "I don't know about that." He looked at Nath, slipped out his hunting knife, and flicked it between Nath's legs. "You spoke too soon."

Puzzled, Nath checked his surroundings. At first he didn't see anything, but then he caught a glimpse of something clinging to the scales of his arms. He jumped up. "Sultans of Sulfur!"

Chongo barked.

Slimy leeches were sucking on his scales. They weren't little things like the finger-sized ones in Nalzambor. Instead, they were fist sized, and they had teeth like fish hooks, wiggling and wriggling their way toward his flesh in the cracks between his scales.

Nath snatched up Venir's knife and skinned them off one by one.

They writhed on the muddy bank and flopped back toward the water.

"Yuck!" Nath checked over his shoulders and spun around. "Did I get them all?"

"Yes. I don't think they'll trifle with you ever again, Nath." Venir hopped off the rocks onto the bank and skewered a leech with the spike on the end of his huge battle axe. "But it's best we make sure."

Chongo splashed over the water and gobbled up the leeches.

"Ew," said Nath. "He really does eat anything." Eyeing the blade that almost killed him, he handed it back to Venir. "That's an excellent piece of work. What kind of bone makes up its handle?"

Taking his knife, Venir replied, "When I was a boy, my grandfather said it was from the finger of a giant. I never believed him. If I were to guess, I'd say it was made from an elk. They were ample on our land."

"So, you think your grandfather lied?"

"My grandfather was a grand storyteller, and I was just a child. Perhaps it was a story to keep us in our beds at night." Venir stuffed the knife back into his belt. "Are there giants in your world?"

"Why do you think I carry such a big sword?"

Venir leaned over to where Fang was stuck tip first in the ground and gave Nath's sword further study. "Perhaps there are giant leeches?"

Nath laughed. "No, our leeches are quite normal, but we have men of renown, evil men who stand thirty feet tall. They use axes like yours for toothpicks."

"That's tall." Venir stuck his axe in the dirt, squatted down, and scooped water into his hands. "The trick is to not dip in too deep, but I think those leeches liked the skin under your scales. They aren't common things. You found a nest." He rinsed his face off and refilled his water skin. "Are you able to continue into nightfall?"

"Aside from being a little achy, I'm ready."

"Achy?"

Nath shut up. One thing he'd learned from Venir was the man didn't complain. He was used to this harsh environment, used to pain. A real hunter and survivor. And whereas Nath's gifts were natural, Venir's had obviously come through tests and trials. The strapping man was young, yet his skin was crisscrossed with scar upon scar. Most of the people Nath had met here on Bish were like this, but this one more so than any.

Venir gathered up his things and stood face to face with Nath. "Time to move."

Nath's gaze fell on a spot where Venir's chainmail was sliced clean open. Over his heart. "Forgive me for being curious, Venir, but I can't help but ponder why you aren't dead. And your comrades weren't shocked about it—aside from Melegal, who was aghast. Do the dead often revive in this world?"

Venir started walking. "I don't ponder such things. The sages and royals do, and they get nothing done. And like you, perhaps I was not fully dead." He smirked. "It was just a flesh wound."

Keeping pace, Nath shook his head. "I thoroughly gored you."

"I don't understand the ways of this world, but what happened has happened before. I don't know if it will happen again, but when my time comes, it'll be my time."

"But you're healed."

"Aye." Venir crossed the stream and pushed through the brush. "My body might have been dead, but my mind was alive. It felt like thousands of tiny burning needles stitched my flesh and bone together. It's this get-up I wield. I'm a vessel. It's the fuel."

"You sound as if you don't like it." Nath shoved aside some branches scraping over his back.

"It's a price I'm willing to pay to finish off the underlings."

CHAPTER 2

"I'M AS ACCURATE AS ANY man with any blade who ever lived," said Billip. The well-knit archer drank down a slug of ale and wiped his sleeve across his mouth. After setting the goblet down, he cracked his knuckles, and his busy eyes landed on Melegal.

Inside the tavern, the slender thief sat at a table, frowning at a goblet of wine. "Anyone?"

"Not this again," Billip said.

Mikkel's black hands were filled with two tankards of ale. He sucked the foam off of both of them and sat down at Melegal's table with a smile. "You aren't going to take that from Billip, are you?"

"I want to get my arse back to Bone." Melegal gave his wine a try and pushed it away. "What is this, orcen made?"

"It's all they had." Mikkel gulped down a tankardful. "Ah!"

The group of men were on the outskirts of Two-Ten City, waiting for Venir to return. Knowing the royals of the humanoid city would still be searching them out, they were lying low.

It had been three days since Venir departed, and Melegal was as uneasy as he'd ever been. The warrior had been taking him back to the City of Bone, until trouble got in the way. Now, the thief was stuck in one of the foulest, most corrupt places he'd ever been. The small tavern—barely big enough to host them and the other dozen people who lurked in the corners—was little more than an old storage shed. There was even a loft in the top where birds roosted.

A strand of straw landed on the table. Melegal dusted it off with his hand and sneezed. "Achoo! That's it! I'm leaving!"

Mikkel's big hand landed on his shoulder and settled him down into his seat. "You aren't going anywhere."

Scowling, Melegal replied, "Fine. Nowhere suits me just fine. May I rot in this slat-hole."

Facing Melegal, Billip scraped a pair of daggers against each other. "Come on, rogue. Give it a toss."

Tucking his hands under his armpits, the thief replied, "I'm not in the mood."

Billip, still dressed in his outdoor leathers, gave a friendly shrug. "Now now, think of all that underling steel we scored, and you want to pass up on an opportunity to earn more? I've even got a flask of mead soaking in my belly." He winked at Melegal. "Your chances are greater than ever."

Melegal looked away. "No."

Nuzzled in one of the corners, a young flabby orcen woman was kissing a man as old as he'd ever seen.

Melegal sneered. "Just hurts the eyes."

Billip dropped ten silver coins on the table. "What do you say now?"

Melegal sat up. "Fine, I'll take your money, then." He removed himself from the table, approached Billip, and took the blade from his hand. "What's your challenge?"

"I'm going to make it an easy one, but you need to put up first."

Melegal opened up his purse and poured out the coins. He set eight coins down next to Billip's, then rolled the other two coins back and forth on the backs of his slender fingers, making the silver twinkle. He said to Billip, "Are you sure you want to do this?"

"Your little parlor trick may impress the ladies in Bone, but it's worthless salt to me." Producing a piece of chalk from his trousers, Billip marched up to the wall and drew a pair of circles about the size of eyeballs. Rapping his knuckle on the wall, he said, "There's one mark for me and one for you. We'll start at five paces." He stepped them off.

"I should take you up on this." Mikkel clonked down an empty tankard. "I'm a better aim than the both of you."

Billip and Melegal looked at each other and burst out laughing.

"That's it!" Mikkel dug into his purse and slapped ten coins on the table. "I'm in. Make a third mark."

Standing a full head shorter than Mikkel, Billip looked up at him. "I didn't challenge you, I challenged him."

"Just give me the chalk."

With a shake of his head, Billip marched back to the wall and drew a circle that could swallow the other two. "There! And you'll still lose!"

Mikkel rolled his shoulders and cracked his neck from side to side. "We'll see. Now give me a blade."

Hands filled with glimmering steel, the three men lined up in the dimness of the lantern-illuminated room, standing shortest to tallest.

Billip tossed first.

Thunk!

His blade smacked dead center in his circle.

With a flick of his wrist, Melegal aimed dead on.

Thunk!

Mikkel made a toss barely inside his big circle.

Thunk!

He glared at both Melegal and Billip. "I'm just warming up."

They pulled their blades from the wall and stretched the distance back two steps.

Thunk!

Thunk!

Thunk!

All of them hit the mark.

Billip backed up to the other side of the tiny room. "Let's get at it again. Do you want to go first this time, Mikkel?"

Mikkel shrugged his heavy shoulders, squinted an eye, and took aim. With a flick of his wrist, he once more hit just inside the mark. "Bull's-eye!"

"Bull's-eye? You barely made it in there, and your mark is thrice ours." Billip cracked his knuckles. "You're next, Melegal."

Smooth as silk, the rogue released an underhanded throw and buried his dagger in the dead center of the target. Melegal shrugged his brows. "Now you, archer."

With his face a mask of concentration, Billip wound back and gave the blade a flip.

Thunk!

"Now that's a bull's-eye! Let's take it all the way across the room diagonally!"

Mikkel bumped up against a table of patrons who had just sat down in the way, a pair of surly, greasy-necked men—out of shape, but as big as him. "You two oafs need to move."

With slurred speech and one eye closed, one of the men said, "We're not going anywhere. Move your game."

Towering over the man, Mikkel said, "I asked nicely."

"I don't care. Take your game out—hey, what are you doing?" The fat man's mead-glazed eyes popped open. His mouthful of missing teeth gaped.

Mikkel stepped behind the man and picked him and the chair up and carried him to the side of the shed. He set him down with a grunt, saying, "Stay put." He marched back to the table, but the second man waddled away and left the tavern. Mikkel scooted the table aside. "Let's get back at it."

Everyone retrieved their blades and lined up again. Melegal's ears caught a jangle of heavy steel.

A gnoll and a pair of orcs entered. The gnoll was a monster, even for his kind. A bastard sword built for his two huge hands was strapped across his broad back. The orcs' fingers were on their weapons with narrowed stares fixed on Melegal and his comrades. There was a dark intent behind him.

Slat. What have we done now?

CHAPTER 3

PUSHING HIS WAY THROUGH THE jungle overgrowth, Nath noticed a snake thicker than his leg hanging in the tree tops. Its body was at least thirty feet long and drooping between the heavy branches. Its scales were white and egg yolk yellow. A forked tongue flickered in and out of its mouth.

Venir followed his stare. "A big snake. We call them 'orc eaters.' They fill their bellies with sleeping orcs all the time. Hmm. It hasn't eaten recently. We'd best keep moving. Once the night sets into this jungle, one can barely see at all."

"I'm used to big snakes," Nath said. He shoved a branch out of the way and followed Venir, thinking it best not to mention his ability to see in the dark.

The first sun was down and the second sun wasn't far behind as its hot red light bled through the branches. Venir was right. The jungle was dark, almost like a vegetable cave, but he didn't have any trouble seeing at night. At least normally he didn't. The haze from the spider bite still hung with him, but he might be getting better. "Much bigger than that."

"Is everything so big in your world?" Venir asked.

"Hard to say. I've not spent much time in yours." Nath kept pace as Venir followed Chongo through the brush. They were heading back to Two-Ten City by a different way, but if he had to guess, he'd say they were getting close.

Venir moved through the thickets like a natural predator. His footfalls were soft, and his lengthy frame ducked in and out of the vines with no trouble at all. They'd been at this for a couple of miles when the world turned pitch dark. Up ahead, Venir came to a stop.

"What?" Nath asked.

Catching up to the warrior, Nath saw where a green plant, much like a fern with larger leaves, wavered in the glade. Something from above was dripping on the leaves, but there wasn't any rain. It was dark and sticky. The coppery smell told him what it was an instant before Venir explained.

"Blood," Venir said.

At the same time, the pair of men turned their gaze upward.

A dead body, a man, was hanging in a tree by webbing.

Nath's chest tightened. He said, "More spiders?"

Venir took a knee and slid his rucksack from his shoulders and fished out the mystic sack. "Worse. Underlings."

Chongo returned to Venir's side and was panting.

"But spiders make webs," Nath said, looking around. He didn't hear any movement crawling in the trees.

"Yes, but the underlings can, too. They have a dark magic. Bone! I was afraid of this."

"Afraid of what?"

"There are plenty of small settlements stretched through the forest surrounding Two-Ten City. The underlings terrorize them. I thought I'd rustled them out, but they're up to the same old tricks again."

"So we weren't really going back to the city. We were making your rounds." Nath wasn't agitated, more curious.

Rising to his full height, Venir said, "That's what I do." He stuffed his head inside the helmet and buckled the chinstrap. Shield on arm, axe in hand, the iron warrior was back. Without a word, he took off through the forest like a black phantom possessed.

CHAPTER 4

THE GNOLL—DOG FACED AND HARD eyed—lifted its long finger and pointed at them. "You. We have questions for you." Billip, Mikkel, and Melegal all faced the gnoll.

Billip spoke up first. "We don't care. We're in the middle of a game, here. Now go gnaw at your fleas elsewhere." With a hard throw, he slung his dagger right past the gnoll, hitting the mark dead center. "Gnoll's-eye!"

Mikkel unleashed his blade in a powerful motion and skewered the wall with a louder...

Thunk!

"Orc's eye!"

Melegal held his blade as he watched the bravado soften in the gnolls' and orcs' eyes. Their grubby fingers fidgeting on the hilts of their weapons didn't make him feel any easier.

Whatever questions they had, they looked intent on getting answers. A couple more orcs slipped into the shed from the other entrance, and the other patrons left the now very crowded room.

"Throw, Melegal, throw," Billip said, shaking his head at the gnoll. "They're just looking for trouble."

No, the company of the thugs that had emerged in their midst ate at him. Melegal faced the gnoll. Holding the tip of his blade, he tapped the hilt in his hand. "What's your question?"

"We seek a law breaker," the gnoll said. "The man with hair of flame. He was last seen with you and your friends. Where is he?"

Mikkel went and pulled his blade out of the wall. "We don't keep track of troublemakers. If you want to find the man, then find him yourself."

"Aye." Billip retrieved his own blade. Scratching it over his whiskers, he said, "But if we did know something, how much would it be worth to you?"

"Billip!" Mikkel said.

"What?" Billip shrugged. "I've no interest in this stranger, and if it keeps trouble off my back, then perhaps I can oblige."

Melegal drifted back out of the conversation and took a peek outside through a knothole in the wall. The shed was surrounded by goons.

Well over a dozen. Bish! It looks like they have a garrison of stink out there. This is Venir's fault. He should be back here by now, and I should be long gone.

Mikkel shoved Billip. "You always were too greedy for your own good."

"I've got a spending habit I like to feed." Billip sauntered over to their table, pointed to the stacks of silver, and said, "If you want information, you'll have to match this."

The gnoll laughed. "Let me hear your information."

Billip put his foot on the seat of a chair and leaned on his knee. "What do you want with the troublemaker?"

"That's our concern, not yours." The gnoll walked up to Billip and leered down at him. As more orcs slipped into the crowded room, it darkened and the tension built. This gang of thugs wouldn't be leaving without answers. "What do you know?"

Billip peered among the new faces in the room and said back to the gnoll, "What do you have to offer?"

With a sneer, the gnoll dug his long-nailed fingers into a pouch and produced a small ruby with a twinkle of fire in the middle.

Melegal eased forward. It was a beautiful thing, easily worth ten times the coins on the table.

What's a gnoll doing with this kind of treasure? Who's paying him?

Swallowing and with his eyes full of the stone, Billip said, "You must want this stranger awfully bad."

"I do."

Billip reached for the ruby.

The gnoll closed his hand around the gem, dousing its brilliant light. Leaning his oversized head into Billip's face, he said, "Where is this man?"

"We gave him a place to hole up. The village at Crumple Creek. It's long abandoned, but now it's his home."

"Billip!" Mikkel slammed both of his fists down on the bar. "You betrayer!"

Holding out his hand to the gnoll, Billip said, "The stone, please?"

The gnoll pulled his fist back to his chest. "We'll check it out first."

"No, we had a deal," Billip said.

"And if what you say is true, you shall be paid," the gnoll said. "But I'm no fool. My men will check it out first, and when they confirm what you said, you shall be paid. Until then, you wait."

Melegal slipped over to the table and sat down. "Well done, Billip. I see you've managed to sell us out again."

Mikkel hit the bar again, turning everyone's heads.

Melegal scooped the coins off the table and tucked them away. "I don't want to be around you when Mikkel finally gets his paws on you. He's going to rip you apart."

"Oh? Well, the angry bear is just going to have to settle down!" Billip said in a loud voice. "It's not like we owe this stranger anything!" He shoved the table. "I'm tired of always getting blamed."

"Be still," the gnoll warned. He gave a quick motion with his thumb and spoke in Orcen. Several of the orcs for hire hustled out the door. Six more orcs came inside with weapons bared. "I go. If any of these men try to leave, kill them."

"Great! Just great!" Mikkel cried out, clutching his head. "Do you see what you've done, Billip? You're a fool!"

"Pitch your weapons." The gnoll pointed to the wall where they'd been hitting targets with their knives. "Bind their hands and sit them down over there."

After Melegal, Billip, and Mikkel tossed down their blades, the black-haired orcs made quick work with the bonds and shoved them all down against the wall.

"What are we, children?" Billip scoffed.

Melegal made a head count. There were still ten orcs left inside the room. He scooted up alongside Billip, and before long all three of them were sitting against the wall.

With a grunt, the gnoll leader departed. The whinny of horses was followed by the galloping of hooves.

Melegal peeked outside through a knothole in the wall. There were still orcs standing guard, but most of them had left. Under his breath, the thief said, "They'll be back in two hours, maybe less. We need to get out of here, and out of here now."

Mikkel shouldered Billip, knocking him into Melegal.

Through clenched teeth, Billip said, "Will you quit overselling it?"

"No. I'm mad." Mikkel lifted his bound hands. "This is stupid."

"You think everything is stupid," Billip said.

"No, I think you are." Mikkel shoved him again. "All you had to do was keep your mouth shut. Now, we're in this mess. They didn't have anything."

"There are thirty of them with murder in their eyes. I had to try and bluff them. I thought I did, but the gnoll, he's no fool."

"He outplayed you," Melegal said, shaking his head. "Next time, let me do the talking."

An orc tossed a tankard of ale against the wall, and it splattered all over them. He stuck his machete-like sword, an orcen-made blade, in their faces. "Silence, or I'll cut your tongues out."

CHAPTER 5

W EAVING THROUGH THE WOODS, NATH lost sight of Venir and Chongo as they both glided under the heavy branches and vanished. Nath came to a stop.

They lost me. I can't believe they lost me.

Slowing his breath, he pressed on. His keen eyes saw their tracks even on hard-packed dirt, and his dragon ears picked up the strange twirling sounds of birds and critters nestled in for the night. The crickets and tree frogs were loud. Annoying. They drowned out anything else. In fact, now that he thought about it, they had gotten louder upon his arrival, which was strange.

Are the bugs trying to warn someone about me?

Moving on with additional caution, he slunk through the heavy vines and oversized leaves. A rustle erupted from a nearby thicket. An underling busted out of the woodland, crossbow in hand, with his head twisted over his shoulder. The small humanoid crashed right into Nath and fell down. Its dark ruby eyes gave him a glance and a hiss. There was blood on its leather armor. It wasn't concerned one bit about Nath but about something else. It sprang to its feet and darted away, slipping free of Nath's clutching grasp.

Perhaps I should have stopped it.

From out of nowhere, Venir's mighty frame cut into the underling's path. The great axe Brool's song of death had begun. There was a sharp whistle in the air, a biting strike, followed by the underling's head being peeled instantly from its shoulders. Its body collapsed on the forest floor. The next thing Nath knew, Venir was gone.

Sultans of Sulfur, where did he go?

Nath gave chase. The jungle had erupted now. The chitter of

underlings had exploded in cries and howls. The little black fiends were angry. Confused. He hurled one fallen tree after another, rushing after the skirmish.

There they stood. Two underlings were back to back in a small clearing, circling around. Eyeing Nath, one chittered to the other. The underling steel that filled their hands came to life. Sharp blades were rushing cat quick at Nath Dragon's throat.

To kill or not to kill, that is the question.

With a single swipe, Nath's sword knocked into both of theirs.

Steel rang off steel, and one of the underlings lost control of its weapon. It dove for it.

The other underling slipped under Nath's next swing and jabbed the point of its blade at Nath's arm. The pinprick skipped off his scales.

Nath launched his fist hard into the underling's jaw.

Its limbs went limber. It staggered back and fell.

Moving quickly, Nath pinned the other underling down with the tip of his sword. "Surrender, underling."

The bright citrine eyes of the fiend narrowed. Its sharp teeth gnashed. Clearly it had no intention of surrendering to anything or anyone, ever. Its fingers stretched out for its blade.

Nath pressed his sword closer to its neck. "I'm warning you, underling."

Eyeing Nath, the fiend sized him up in a moment. Ignoring the sword lined up with its throat, it snatched up its sword again and advanced.

Something shot through the air and buried itself in the underling's side. Spike first, Brool, Venir's weapon, was sticking out of the now-dead underling.

Venir was colossal and foreboding in his helmet. He marched up to Nath and tore the axe from the underling's body, saying to Nath, "Stop talking and start killing." He eyed the second underling, still breathing on the ground. "Well?"

"I'm not going to kill a prone thing," Nath replied.

Venir gored its heart. "Then stay out of my way."

"You can't just..." Nath started, but Venir was already on the move, slipping between the trees and out of sight again. Nath glanced down at the dead underlings, watching as the light in their eyes dimmed.

There was something different about them. Unlike any of the races in Nalzambor, all of the underlings were... Cold. Lifeless. Their demeanor wasn't much more animated living than dead. Their corpses were more like dead animals.

Underlings are not people! Then what are they?

Above, something whooshed through the air above the clearing and was gone. Nath's spine chilled. He picked his way through the foliage, eyes up, searching. Chops and scrapes of steel drifted farther away the closer he got. Before he knew what had happened, he was held fast by something. Face down, he was stuck in a giant web, much like the one the man from earlier had been caught in.

Great Guzan!

He wriggled. The strands were as strong as steel, and they held him tighter the more he moved. "This is bad," he murmured as his lips were partially stuck to the web. Nath felt like a fool. Angry. The last thing he ever expected was to be snared in a spider's web. But this wasn't just any type of web. It was something different. Using his clawed fingertips, he tried to saw at the silky, steel-like cords. His claws stuck.

With his face and lips stuck in the webbing, Nath half yelled, "I hate this world!"

Wait, Fang's steel should be able to cut anything.

Hands still locked around the grip of his sword, he squirmed and struggled, fighting to get the blade to angle into the web. Without being able to see what he was doing, he strained and pressed, hoping the cords would give.

But the more he sawed, the more constricted he became.

A rustling stirred above in the branches. Through the jungle murk, a dark-robed figure lowered. An underling hovered a foot off the ground, eye to eye with Nath. Its eyes were deep see blue and filled with fathomless hate. It drew its clawed hands out in front of Nath's eyes. The fingers glimmered like rods of lightning. Through the webbing, the sinister underling grabbed Nath by the neck and squeezed.

Nath's head snapped back. He screamed. "Gaaaaaaaaaaaaaaaah!"

Jolts of painful energy stabbed through his eyes and limbs. His body convulsed and sputtered. The stubble on his chin sizzled with a foul aroma.

The underling floated back and away. It made a puzzled chittering sound and rubbed its chin.

In a voice as dry as a desert riverbed, Nath said, "Is that your best?"

The underling's brows buckled. The long fingertips on its hands glowed with new fire and, stretching forth its hands, it blasted a ray of power straight into Nath.

Zap!

CHAPTER 6

B ILLIP AND MIKKEL FINALLY MANAGED to quiet their tongues, which proved to be a bigger test of their mettle than Melegal had imagined.

The orcs chucked scraps of food at them and poured ale over their heads.

Melegal, unlike his comrades, was unscathed.

Speaking low when the orcs weren't looking, Billip said, "How is it you escaped these wretched things and we didn't?" He brushed a chicken bone off his shoulder with his chin. "I hate orcs."

"Perhaps that's why they pick on you," Melegal said.

"And you don't hate orcs?"

"Not as bad as I hate bad negotiations."

"I did fine. That gnoll was sold. If not for my clever sell, we'd be dead already." Billip got a nudge from Mikkel.

An orc with a lazy eye approached.

Billip dropped his head down.

Melegal looked away. He'd managed to avoid trouble from the orcs by looking weaker than his friends. Orcs were bullies. Burly and covered in coarse hair, they poked and prodded at his more formidable companions. They had nothing to fear from a sickly-looking man like him. They wanted a challenge. They often got it through provocation.

The orc slapped them all on the top of the head and backed away. Huddling together, the orcs were drinking more and more. Their attention to the men was fading, but time was running out.

Melegal figured the gnoll commander would be back within minutes. Once he returned with nothing to show for his trouble, he'd cut all their throats.

It's time to get out of here. These two sandbags are just going to have to make do on their own.

"What are you doing?" Billip said.

Melegal had wriggled his hands free. "I'm getting out of here."

"Not without us you aren't!"

Mikkel leaned over, peering by Billip. "You'd do that? Leave us? You have a heart of ice, Melegal. I'm disappointed. I can understand you leaving Billip, but me?"

Melegal leaned forward and shrugged. "Sorry." He didn't mean it entirely. If it came right down to it, he'd have to help them.

It's a shame I need these louts.

The last thing Melegal wanted was to be stuck in Two-Ten City all by himself. He was a fish out of water, and he wanted to get back to Bone. He'd considered going with some other travelers before, but the lands between this city and Bone were too risky. He needed men he could trust, and Venir had given his word. "Just be still while I think."

"I'll figure a way out of here," Billip said, struggling with the cords on his wrists. "Just give me a moment." Before long his cheeks were red, and he bumped his head back into the wall. "Bloody orcs can't take a bath, but they can tie a knot, can't they!"

"Shush!" Mikkel said.

It was too late. Billip's voice had caught the orcs' attention. Talking in Orcen, the brood huddled together, and in moments they had their sharp knives at the ready. They pointed at the circles above the men's heads.

"Oh no," Mikkel said. "You don't think they're going to play that same little game of ours, do you?"

Billip scooted down. "I'm afraid so. Blast my hide, if there's one thing an orc is worse at than taking a bath, it's aiming. A long bow's nothing but a bent spear to the likes of them."

An orc with a scuffed-up and scarred face pushed some of the other orcs back. Knife in hand, he closed one eye. He was about ten paces back, and he swayed a little. Cocking his arm back, he threw.

Melegal watched the projectile sail end over end as if it was in slow motion. Everything was wrong with the throw. It tumbled—not over the top, but from side to side. It was coming right at him. He hop-

scooted away out of the blade's path. The metal bounced off the wall and clattered on the rotted wood floor.

The orcs erupted in laughter.

Scowling, Melegal said, "That's it. We're getting our arses out of here!"

"Oh, so now you're coming to our rescue?" Mikkel said. "I can't wait to see this."

"If we can't take out a few drunken orcs, then we're not worth our salt," Melegal said.

"Aw, look who's gotten all spirited all of a sudden," Billip said. "So what's the plan?"

"Once I make my move, we split up and go," Melegal replied.

"You know, there's a lot of steel out there," Billip warned. "It's going to be hard to get out of here without some nicks."

"Maybe for you two."

Another orc lined up, set his feet, and prepared to throw. He chucked the knife. The butt of the hilt bounced off Mikkel's skull.

"That's it! Let's go!"

CHAPTER 7

NATH'S ENTIRE BODY JUDDERED IN the webbing. All of his limbs shook like leaves. Groaning, he lifted his aching lids and stared at his attacker with blurry eyes.

The underling mage slipped a jagged knife out of its belt and floated closer.

"Get away from me, you fiend," Nath managed to spit out. He'd never imagined himself being slaughtered in such a helpless position—at worst, taken captive and made a prisoner. But this lithe humanoid of the caves came with the murderous intent to kill him. Nath took in a deep breath, concentrated on summoning his inner fire, and blew as hard as he could. No fire came, only despair.

The underling let out a wicked chitter. His blade closed in on Nath's throat.

Glitch!

Something from behind the underling pierced it through the chest. The dagger fell from the underling's grip as it rose higher into the air. It was not the power of the underling lifting it. It was Venir.

The Darkslayer hefted the underling on the tip of Brool's spike with one arm like meat on a stick and slung the dead mage aside. "I thought I smelled something cooking," Venir said to Nath.

Sagging in his sticky bonds, Nath tried to straighten himself. Painful fire raced through his jolted limbs. A veil of smoke burned his eyes. His clothes were smoking. He sniffed. "What is that foul smell?"

Using his axe, Venir cut at the webbing. The sticky strands peeled away on the keen edge. "That's your hair. It stinks."

"My hair!" Nath exclaimed, combing through his red locks as he landed on his feet. He gaped at Venir and his gory axe, Brool. "I'm indebted."

"If you insist on showing mercy to these monsters, then we're going to have to part ways, Nath." Venir hefted the axe over his shoulder. "You're too good a fighter to go down without a fight."

"I was raised not to kill," Nath replied as he peeled away the webbing from his body. The stickiness was gone. It was more like dew of the morning.

Shaking his head, Venir said, "Even in war?"

"This isn't war."

"Bish if it isn't!" Venir growled.

Nath wasn't going to argue with the young warrior. This was his world. Things were different here, and to get back home, he might have to consider doing things he wouldn't normally. Eyeing Brool he said, "So, it cuts anything?"

"Anything underling."

"Interesting." Nath noticed that everything in the jungle had become odd and quiet compared to before. The loudness of the tree frogs and crickets had softened. "Are all the underlings dead?"

Venir took a deep breath and let it out as if his world stood on his shoulders. "Not by a long shot."

Nath tensed.

Venir put a calming hand on Nath's shoulder. "But I don't sense any live ones nearby. Come."

Feeling like he'd just inhaled a lightning bolt, Nath forced his stiff, burning limbs forward. Webbing gripped his boot to the ground, and he tore it away.

Venir led him through the dark until they emerged beyond the trees and found themselves inside a hamlet. There were people, many of them sobbing. By the look of it, no more than a hundred people lived there. The homes were huts made from clay bricks and straw. It was just a small hunting and fishing village like so many back home. In the center, a campfire burned, and the bodies of people were lined up on the ground.

Removing his helmet, Venir said to Nath, "The underlings do this to the innocent. Simple people. I'm from simple people. When the underlings shed our blood, I shed theirs. But them?" He looked at the people huddled, crying with one another. "They're not fighters. That's why I fight for them. Now you tell me this isn't war."

With a heavy heart, Nath asked, "Don't the Royals offer protection?"

"They used to, but they've lost their spines to the highest bidder. If people don't have enough to offer, then the Royals don't care. That shouldn't make these people sheep for slaughter. Stay here."

Venir walked away, leaving Nath to himself. He watched as Venir wiped the tears from a sobbing woman's eyes, then took a knee with the others around the bodies and joined hands. Chongo lay on his belly at the people's feet. They knew who Venir was and treated him like one of them. A brother. A protector. Nath saw something different in the young warrior's eyes. The man was a fierce fighter, a killer, but there was compassion in his core. Pain, too.

One can only suppose the underlings laid waste to his village. How sad.

When Venir came back, Nath was sitting against a tree with his sword in his lap. He said to Venir, "I'd like to help any way I can."

"No, it's too late for that." Venir took a drink from his water skin. "They don't take to strangers well. Five dead. Two of them children. They say a fog came. Then the underlings slipped right inside and dragged them out of their huts into the night." He capped the water skin. "Only monsters kill children. They're fiends, I tell you. Do you have anything so wicked in your world, where women and children are terrorized and slaughtered?"

"I guess there's a different code, even with the worst from my home. I've never seen anything like this before." Nath's fingertips clawed at the ground. "And to think I was fighting with them."

"At least you know better now. I'm going to fetch the other body. Come if you want."

Nath went. He was eager to see if Fang's blade could penetrate the webs, but when they got there, the man's body was gone. Only torn wisps of webbing remained.

Venir put on his helmet.

Nath went numb. "Well?"

"I don't sense any underlings."

"Then what did this?"

"I don't know."

Somewhere in the village, Chongo was barking.

CHAPTER 8

Tossing away the loose strands on his wrists, Melegal snatched up the dagger on the floor and slit the cords around Billip's waiting wrists.

Billip grabbed the blade that had bounced off of Mikkel's bleeding skull and cut the third man's cords away.

The orcs, though a little slow and inebriated, were quick to respond. Advancing toward the men, all their hands went to draw swords and knives.

On his feet, Mikkel picked up a chair and barreled right into the orcs at the forefront. "Go! Go!" he yelled to the others.

The back doorway was blocked. Melegal snaked up into the rafters above with Billip on his tail, scattering the roosting birds. The archer's bow and quiver were stowed up in the loft, and quick as a snake, he nocked and fired arrow after arrow. "Get out of there, Mikkel!"

The orcs let out a clamor. One clutched at an arrow buried in its side while another hopped up and down on one leg. The orcs dove for cover.

Billip kept firing at the gnoll guarding the open exit until he nailed it in the chest. "What are you waiting for, Mikkel? Go!"

Mikkel bolted for the front door and was gone.

Melegal peeked outside and caught a glimpse of the orcs giving chase after the long-legged warrior. Mikkel was fast for a big man. He spread the distance and disappeared. "We'd better go."

Billip tossed him Mikkel's club.

Melegal scowled. "I'm not carrying this. It'll slow me down."

Throwing Mikkel's crossbow over his shoulder, Billip replied, "This contraption isn't going to make me any faster, but I'm taking it—and you're taking that." He peered over the side of the loft and jumped.

Melegal landed right beside him. Orcs were spilling out of the tavern. He said to Billip, "See you at the meeting place." He took off at a dead sprint and split right between two pursuing orcs. He clipped one in the knee with the heavy club, sending it sprawling to the ground.

Bone, this thing's heavy. But it's effective.

Taking full advantage of the night, the thief dashed back into the city, wandering the streets in the shadows until any sounds of pursuit were gone. With his back to an alley wall, hands on his knees, he huffed for breath.

Losing the orcs hadn't been difficult. They were slow and not very good trackers. They also weren't the most organized people. With their forces divided in their search, Melegal highly doubted the orcs would be able to find any of them. No, the orcs would give up within a few hours. Sticking to the shadows, Melegal held his position for a couple of hours, then headed to the place of meeting. It was in a tent city on the western side of Two-Ten City, where many of the local workers lived. He entered the ten-man canvas tent and found Billip and Mikkel inside.

"Ah, you do have Skull Basher," Mikkel said with a smile. He took his club from Melegal and pointed at him. "I won't forget this."

"How could anyone forget carrying around a tree stump?" Melegal said, twisting from side to side. "My back aches from it."

Mikkel flipped the club around. "A strong back is a good thing."

"A strong mind is better," Melegal replied. He sauntered a little deeper into the tent and took a seat on one of the cots. There wasn't much of anything else inside other than some bedrolls. The cots were barely big enough to hold Melegal, and when Venir or Mikkel slept here, they looked like bears in them. There were also some empty wine bottles and a clay jug. He kicked at it. "So, do we wait or get out there after Venir? The lout's probably in a mix. He's nothing but trouble."

Mikkel perked up. "He's saved all of our hides more than a hundred times."

"Sure, after he preps us for skinning," Billip replied. The oldest of the group stroked his goatee. "He's got a direct way of going about things. It's trouble, but I can't blame him for what he does. Takes guts."

Melegal produced a thumb knife and cleaned his nails while they talked. "Will the two of you just take me to Bone, for the lust of Bish? I need to get home. We're finished in Two-Ten City, are we not?"

"We need to warn Venir," Mikkel replied.

"Aye," said Billip. "He and Nath have an entire host after them. We need to warn them." He shook his head. "Did you see the stone that gnoll had? Where does a gnoll come across a ruby? You tell me. These mixed-breed Royals don't dally with treasure around here."

"I wouldn't claim to know about it." Melegal put his knife away and lay down on the cot, envisioning the jewel. It was a spectacular little thing, and judging by the gnoll's bulging purse, there were many more of them.

If there was one reason I'd spend more time in Two-Ten, it would be to deprive that giant varmint of those jewels.

He could see himself catching up with the gnoll in a crowded place, sliding in behind him, and cutting the purse strings. He'd done it plenty of times before.

Simple as my dimple.

"Who was that gnoll, anyway? I suspect he was part of the brigand army."

"Never seen him," Mikkel said.

"Nope," added Billip.

"Well, I don't know my way around this strange woodland. I'd just as soon avoid it altogether. And Venir can take care of himself. Son of a Bish, we just saw him die and come back to life. I say we go. He knows where the next rendezvous is."

"Red Clay," Billip said, shaking his head. "I'm not going into Red Clay. It's spooky."

"No, I'm not going in there either, but there's a village south of it. We can leave word," Melegal added.

Billip and Mikkel both shrugged.

"I don't suppose we have much of an alternative. Let's sleep on it." Billip stretched out his arms and yawned. "Besides, I'm tired. I had a good drinking going on, and now my head hurts." He pointed at Melegal. "And don't you think I didn't see you scrape our coins off the table, you little rat."

"Oh, I forgot about that." Mikkel sat up and leaned forward, "Hand them over."

Melegal fished in his vest pocket, but he was saved by a fracas somewhere in the tent city. Billip was the first to his feet, and he stuck his head out the flap. Sitting up, Melegal heard the turmoil increase. Men and women were arguing with someone and yelling.

Billip brought his head back in, grim faced. "Time to go."

"What?" Mikkel replied. "Why?"

Grabbing his gear, Billip replied, "Because that big-arsed gnoll is here."

CHAPTER 9

EAPONS BARED, NATH AND VENIR rushed back into the camp and came upon a startling sight. Chongo's heads were down low, and he was barking at a weird creature that had invaded the camp. It had long, hairy legs like a tarantula, but there were dozens of legs, and it had the body of a centipede. Tall as a horse, half of its barrel body was reared up, revealing a bug face with many eyes and antenna. A cocoon was on its back, and its front legs spun a web like tiny fingers.

"What is that?" Nath exclaimed.

"A night crawler. They feed on the dead." Venir slowly made his way toward Chongo.

Nath flanked the giant insect from the other side. He thought he'd seen enough for one night, but apparently Bish had a few surprises left for him.

That's the biggest, creepiest thing I've ever seen!

He lifted his sword overhead.

The night crawler skittered back and forth. Whichever way it went, the men and dog cut it off.

"Yah!" Venir cried, waving his axe. "Yah! Be gone, vermin!"

One of the villagers stuck a spear in the fire, lighting its end, and then waved it back and forth. "Yah! Yah!" he said.

The night crawler backed away. Its nasty legs neared the edge of the forest.

A woman let out an ear-splitting scream.

From behind one of the huts, another night crawler swept through the camp and plowed into the villager with the flaming spear. A sharp tongue shot from the giant bug's mouth and struck the man in the head. He screamed.

Nath pounced. In two great strides he closed within sword length of the night crawler and swung. Fang whistled through the air and bit into the monster's shell. A bright blue light burst from the blade. The monster wriggled and squealed. Frozen strands spread out from the blade's tip, changing the giant insect from head to toe into an ice sculpture. Twinkling in the camp, the night crawler moved no more.

Nath tugged his sword free and turned his attention to the other creature.

Helmetless, Venir hacked at the other insect's body with his axe. The chops came fast and furious. The oversized bug didn't stand a chance. Its lengthy sections twitched in the dirt and dust. It was over. Venir managed to peel open the night crawler's body. Brool's edge sliced it, revealing a man inside.

Nath glanced down at the villager he'd tried to save. His eyes were open and blinking, but nothing else was moving. A pair of villagers rushed over and dragged him away.

"Poison," Venir said. "He won't make it." He marveled at the second night crawler turned into an ice sculpture. "First fire, now ice?"

"I can't take credit for this. My sword Fang did it."

Venir laid his hand on the frozen face of the ugly thing. Many of the villagers did the same. "Is it dead?"

"It's ice." Nath chipped away at it with his sword. "It will melt before the day is over."

"Well, my axe certainly can't do that, ha!" Venir stuck his axe in the ground. He was running his hands over the ice as if he'd never seen ice before. Chongo was licking it. "And the sword does this on your command?"

"I can't lay claim to that. It, well, surprises me."

"It thinks," Venir said, "like a man?"

"It has magic that I command but can't always control. Well, can't ever control." He rubbed the blade with his fingers. "Its powers will be different in this world. I'm surprised it works at all."

Venir nodded. "Well, the danger is gone. The night crawlers tried to feast and failed. But we'd better go."

"Why?" Nath asked.

The villagers—not primitive by any means but dressed as ordinarily as any common folk he'd seen—were beginning to murmur and stare at him.

"They don't trust strangers, and they trust magic even less. They associate it with evil. You're a bad omen. Before long, they'll blame this entire incident on you." Venir kneeled down and whispered something to Chongo. The big dog looked up at Nath and then walked away with his easy sway. "Follow him. I'll catch up."

Nath gave the people a nod and moved on. He expected some thanks from them, but it was clear that wasn't coming. They'd had a rough night, and the grumbling had begun. Following Chongo's lead, he vanished into the forest and waited for Venir about a mile away.

Chongo sat back on his haunches with his tongues hanging out of his mouths and panting. Nath scratched him behind the ears, and the dog leaned into him. Before long, his leg was kicking. Nath never had a dog back in Nalzambor, but many people did. Being around Chongo gave him a better sense of the kinship people shared with their dogs.

"Venir has a good friend in you, doesn't he, Chongo, huh? And you in him."

Nath gazed up into the trees, trying to locate a hoot owl burrowed in the branches. He was hanging onto whatever made him think of home. Seeing the people in the village had made him miss Nalzambor and his own kin even more. "Chongo, no offense, but I hope I can get my scales out of here."

The dog lay down and gave a big yawn. The beast was at ease, the same as Venir. The people of Bish, Nath assumed, were just used to all the danger and didn't know any better.

"Brenwar would love it here."

An hour later, a scuffle in the brush caught his attention. His hand fell on his sword, and Chongo's ears perked up.

Venir came. His white teeth were showing. He said, "Who is Brenwar?"

"My friend, a dwarf. What are you all smiles about?"

"The underlings are dead and we're alive."

"And?" Nath asked.

"And," Venir replied, easing down to pet Chongo, "one of my village lady friends was very grateful."

"So that's why Chongo and I have been keeping company with the bugs? That's a bit inconsiderate."

"Oh, what do you expect when a man's blood is up and a scrumptious gal comes his way?" He stretched back up. "Besides, it would have been an insult if I hadn't. Her father offered."

Shaking his head in disbelief, Nath replied, "So, it's not all about being a hero then, is it? There are other less noble benefits."

"Think what you want, but I think you're jealous."

Nath blustered. "Jealous! Of you?" He crossed his arms over his chest and lifted his chin. "Hardly."

Venir slapped him on the shoulder and gave it a squeeze. "It's understandable. You're away from home and lonely, but I'm certain we can find you someone willing. There's another little town north of Two-Ten where the orcen gals are more palatable."

"Now you're being crude."

Venir laughed. "You think that's crude?"

Nath nodded.

Venir resumed his trek through the jungle, poking at Nath with light conversation. "So, do you have a woman back in your world? Tell me about her."

Nath's thoughts immediately went to Selene. Before he even realized it, he was filling Venir's ears with details. He told him about her looks, her raven hair. How they met.

Venir's mood became cloudy. His brows buckled and his stride lengthened.

"What is it, Venir?"

"The woman you describe. I've known one such as her. A raven-haired witch. A traitor of men. I've sworn to kill her."

Nath got ahold of Venir's arm and turned him back toward him. "You'd really kill a woman?"

"This one I would. She has it coming."

"They do such a thing in this world?"

"They do if the woman cavorts with underlings."

In silence, they continued until they landed on an overgrown path which took them just outside of Two-Ten City. Taking their time, they walked toward some establishments about a mile away. Nath could make out torchlight in the distant windows and some other strange lights. The green goo they used glowed inside jars.

"Wait here," Venir said, stripping off all of his gear except his knife. He tied his hair back in a ponytail. He pointed at a shack. Light glimmered through knotholes in the walls. "We're supposed to meet up with Billip and Mikkel in there, but something stinks. I'll be back."

Nath watched Venir take off like a deer and slip into the building. His claws dug into his palms as he waited.

What's taking so long now? Did he find another woman?

Fifteen minutes later, Venir reappeared and trotted right back at them. "Time to go," he said, looking over his shoulder. "And go now."

"Care to explain?"

Grabbing his axe and rucksack, Venir replied, "We're upwind and they're after us, and if we don't get going now, we're going to be up to our armpits in orcs and gnolls."

Looking around, Nath said, "I don't see any orcs or—"

From inside the shack, a sharp whistle erupted, loud enough to wake the town. Somewhere in the loft of the shack, a man with a thunderous voice yelled out, "Collo! Collo! They are here, Collo!"

Nath turned to ask who Collo was, but Venir and Chongo were off and running.

CHAPTER 10

JETTING THROUGH THE JUNGLE, VENIR pushed himself to the limits. His lungs were burning and he labored for breath. Up front, Chongo led. The dwarven setter anticipated exactly where he wanted to go: deep into the brush where the hardiest of men did not even venture. The bush. The Outlands. This was his home. His territory.

He cast a glance over his shoulder. Nath was on his heels, running with the ease of a stag. They'd been running through rugged terrain for miles, and the strange warrior hadn't even asked to slow. Not even Billip and Mikkel could keep up with Venir when he got going, only Chongo could.

What is this man made of?

He slowed his pace where the jungle terrain began to take on another shape. The hard dirt below his feet softened and even got squishy. A rank odor built in the air as he ran through one nest of mosquitos after the other. He slogged through it a few dozen yards before he came to a stop under an oversized willow tree of the marsh.

Holding his nose, Nath said to him, "What is this abyss you have brought me to?"

"Keep your voice down," Venir replied.

"Shouldn't be a problem. I can barely breathe enough to talk," Nath muttered.

Venir rubbed one of Chongo's necks and said, "Go."

The big dog lurched through the muck, back into the jungle.

"Where's he going?" Nath asked.

"I thought I told you to be silent." Venir waded deeper into the marsh and hunkered down in the thick muck to his chin. "Get back here, Nath. Do as I do."

Hand over his nose, the scaly man backed into the foul waters and sank in beside Venir, making his best effort to keep his hair from getting wet. "I could have kept pace with Chongo, even if you couldn't."

"Quiet," Venir said.

The nicker of a horse caught his ears. Trail dogs sniffed the air. Somewhere in the black leaves of the forest, his pursuers neared. Nath's head tilted and his eyes narrowed. He looked at Venir and nodded. A host of hunters and several trail dogs traversed the brush. Stirrups and reins jangled. Many of the pursuers carried lanterns. The tight-knit band moved in a single column, and their efforts slowed. Thirty yards away from their location, the dogs and their orcen handlers waded into the waters of the marsh. The dogs sniffed and snorted. They shook themselves.

A huge figure on horseback led his horse up to the edge of the marsh. In the dimness, Venir could tell by the shape of the figure's head that it was a gnoll. Orcs did nothing quietly. Everything they did was rough handed. The gnolls weren't much different, but they were smarter and taller. Their wolfish faces were very wide, too. The leader was talking in Orcen to a pair of the others.

Must be the one called Collo.

Collo barked out an order in Orcen: "Get in there. Search!"

The gnoll-led orcs dismounted and fanned out in a search line, advancing into the marsh. The glow of the lanterns shimmered on top of the murky waters and fuzzy lily pads.

Venir caught Nath glancing back at him. Under the waters, he had Brool in his grip. Nath readied his sword, hilt out but blade deep in the water.

I hope he's going to use that thing for what it's meant for.

The orcs were ten yards away when a set of the trail dogs bayed. Everyone in the search party turned. The orcs just outside of the marsh led the dogs in pursuit.

They must have picked up Chongo's trail.

Collo backed his horse away from the edge of the marsh, leered once more into it, and said, "Mount up, brethren! The scent has surfaced again."

With knees jumping out of the water and lanterns shaking, the small knot of orcs trudged out of the marsh and climbed back into their saddles. Within seconds, they were galloping back into the jungle, and then they were gone.

Venir rose up out of the grimy water.

Nath did the same, raking the nasty water from his hair. "Close call. I feared Fang might have to feast on them."

"Wouldn't be such a bad thing, assuming you do know how to skin the enemy."

"Well, I really hate orcs, no matter what world. There's just something so irritating about them." He ran his eyes up and down the length of his sword's muck-coated edge. "Sorry, Fang."

"You talk to it?" Venir eyed his axe. "I don't think I'd want to risk my axe talking back, but he always has a fine message for the underlings."

"And what's that?"

"Goodbye."

"So," Nath said, "Do you care to fill me in, now that we're no longer running?" He fanned his face. "And why do you keep insisting on leading me into one nasty place after another? Can't we just climb a tree next time?"

"It would still smell. Besides, the dogs can't track us in the marsh, and the orcs wouldn't want to. You saw the yellow in their eyes. This is underling territory. They're just as scared of underlings as everyone else is, even though they probably like the smell." Venir caught Nath by the elbow as he started to walk away. "Just give it a few more minutes."

"But Chongo?" Nath said.

"He'll be fine. No orc or gnoll will ever catch him. Just try to enjoy the stink a few moments longer. You need to get used to it."

Shivering, Nath said, "I don't know which is worse, the stink or the slime. So tell me, what in Bish is going on?"

"The gnoll is called Collo, and he's after you."

"Me?"

"You've been here long enough to make some enemies. Well, the tavern dwellers filled me in with plenty of details. Billip, Mikkel, and Melegal were there and raced out in a scuffle. I'm sure they are long out of Two-Ten City by now."

"So the tavernkeeper gave you all of this information willingly?"

"I didn't give him much of a choice, but like most of the slobs in that foul city, he tends to side with the more villainous people." Venir made a little chuckle. "I was surprised I made it out the door before he started his yelling. Fat slob. I even gave him a pair of silvers."

Nath scratched his head. "So the Royals back there are going to all this trouble after me?"

"They have their vendetta, but Collo and his brood are of another kind. They are a different breed. Hunters. They are well equipped. My guess is they're working for someone else." Venir eyed Nath. "Or something else."

"It's the underlings, isn't it."

CHAPTER 11

The Current was an underground river. A barge with a tiny green lantern cruised over the black waters, stirring the black locks of hair on the underling that sat alone in the middle. It was the cleric, Oran. He nibbled on his fingernails and grumbled.

"Catten and Verbard again? Why must I meet them? I have not been gone so long." He hissed. "I hate this mission."

Oran hoped he'd have more time before he reported to the underling brothers again. After all, he'd just loosed the gnoll Collo, a formidable asset he'd utilized before. Certainly the gnoll could dispatch the man he'd summoned known as Nath. The newcomer of Bish was unfamiliar with the world's ways. But the man he fought, the Darkslayer, wasn't. He only hoped the unlikely pair didn't team up. He wanted control of the dragon man again.

After hours of endless travel, the mystically propelled barge pulled up on a soft underground beach, sending ripples of stagnant water onto the shore. Oran hopped off the barge, caught his foot on the hem of his robes, and stumbled into the sand. He let out a chitter full of underling curses, stood up, and dusted the palms of his hands off on his robes. Looking ahead, he sighed.

A temple-like structure, thirty feet tall and twice as wide, was carved out of the cavern walls where many caves opened like mouths. The blue underlight illuminated the temple's outlines with haunting effect. The architecture was strange to men, familiar only to the underlings. Pillars of shiny black stone were paired on the sides of the entryways. Images of underlings had been chiseled out of the temple's face everywhere else.

Oran gathered himself and marched right into the largest entrance.

A tunnel burrowed down another hundred feet into a chamber that held two empty pewter thrones and nothing else. Oran clenched his fists.

Do they take those thrones everywhere? We are leagues from the Underland. Why did they bring them here?

From out of the darkness beyond the illumination of the underlight, a stern underling voice spoke.

"Kneel."

Not this again. If there was ever a reason to leave the Underland, this would be it.

He dropped onto one knee and bowed his head, keeping still in the silence that followed. One minute passed by, then two. His back ached, and his knees and thighs burned. It went on like this for maybe an hour. The dangerous minds in the room could not be seen, but they were probing at his thoughts. Eating at his brain. Verbard and Catten were making their presence known in a very quiet and unpleasant way.

Sweat beaded on Oran's forehead, and his body trembled.

Hold it together. Don't give in to them. Weakness only invites trouble.

As the moments lengthened, his body—which was soft by underling standards—quavered from head to toe. Muscles he didn't even know he had were throbbing. His jaw muscles clenched, and a puddle of sweat formed alongside his knee.

Oh how I hate Catten and Verbard.

Still counting the moments in his head, Oran realized the torture had gone on for more than two hours. Time wasn't as precious for underlings as it was for others. They lived hundreds of years. The lords Verbard and Catten were well known for playing these tormenting games all day. It meant nothing to them.

Oh, how I hate them!

Panting for breath with the salt of his own sweat running into his mouth, he shook like a leaf. He'd reached the threshold. Now was the time to tell them what he thought once and for all.

Bish on the Underland! I'll die before I grovel another moment longer!

Grinding his teeth, he gathered his courage.

"Rise, Oran, rise."

Oran's tight jaw hung.

I can't.

His leg muscles were so tight that he felt frozen to the ground. He scooted his foot forward, scraping his sandal over the gritty floor and switching out his knees. He tumbled over, catching himself just before his face hit the ground. Lying face down on the ground, he gasped for breath.

The cave chamber filled with delighted, cruel cackles.

Shamefaced, Oran pushed himself and managed to fight his way onto his feet again. The blood rushing through his legs burned. Keeping his composure, he pulled his narrow shoulders back and searched for his tormentors.

Catten and Verbard were seated on their thrones, Catten with eyes of gold on Oran's left and the silver-eyed Verbard on the right. Their robes were pitch black and traced in faint arcane lines of silver. The magi lords were big for underlings. In their seats, they towered over him with a dark presence that filled the room.

Catten tapped his long fingernails on the metal arm of his chair and leaned away from his brother with a boorish look on his face. The underling lord said, "Have you slain the Darkslayer?"

Oran cleared his throat. "I have not been able to confirm his disposal as of yet." It was a lie layered in the truth. This was what underlings did from the moment they were born: Lie. Lie. Lie. It didn't matter to them how much one lied so long as it got results. It was the underling way. Tolerated to the point of failure.

Verbard shifted in his chair and leaned forward, the personification of concentration, known to be far less understanding and patient than his brother. "And what is the whereabouts of this scaled warrior you have summoned? Has he failed?"

"His unfamiliarity with the terrain has hindered his pursuit, but the scent of the Darkslayer is now his. I assure you, he closes in," Oran replied.

"Oran, you are such a horrible liar. You always were," Catten said. "I know urchlings that are more convincing. Tell us what has happened with this demon of yours."

Clasping his hands behind his back, Oran replied, "I've told you, he is in deep pursuit of our enemy, but it takes time. It has not been so long since we departed on our mission. It will take time to eradicate this slayer. But we shall have his head before long."

"There are dozens of our brethren dead," Verbard said. "How many dozens more shall die? We need to have this vermin taken down. We can't have the Royals receiving a glimmer of hope. We need to take over all of their outposts." Silver fire flashed in his eyes. "Eradicate them!"

"He is one against many," Oran said. "With our earnest pursuit, soon the walls will close in on this overzealous man."

"Have him eradicated soon, Oran," Verbard warned. "Or I shall personally eradicate you."

CHAPTER 12

ENIR PROVED TO BE AS crafty a ranger as he was a fighter. He followed after the gnoll for several miles, getting so close to the rear column that Nath could smell the pack of man hunters moving west. Nath and Venir broke off their trail and headed northeast until they slipped away from the dense jungle onto easier terrain.

With the first sun of the day shining in his face, Nath asked, "Will Chongo be safe?"

Venir climbed up a rock steppe, still coated up to his chin in the grime and mud of the marsh. "Safer than the birds of the sky."

Nath found sure footing on the slippery moss-covered stones jutting up from the blue-green grasses. He moved from one stone to the other in a game of sorts. "And I suppose he'll be able to pick up this wondrous scent you've so willingly soaked us in."

"This grime is good. It covers our scent from many dangerous pursuers. As for Chongo, there's no need to worry about him. He will find us. He can find anybody once he has their scent."

"He sounds like a special dog."

"He's a dwarven setter, the best." Venir started into a jog.

They ran on and off through the day without saying anything until Venir stopped and sucked some water from a skin. "You don't tire easily, do you."

Hands on his knees, Nath looked up at the suns. "I could run for days in my world. But this is different." Nath thumbed a drop of sweat from his brow. "The suns aren't so friendly here, are they."

"This? Ha." Venir spread his arms out toward the surrounding greenery. It was not as thick and heavy as it had been farther south. The grass thinned, and patches of rock and dirt were more commonplace. "Wait until we make it to the Outland." He tossed Nath the water skin. "Drink."

By midday, they approached a village resting in the bowels of a huge sunken meadow. Nath marveled at what was beyond. Miles deep and miles wide, a forest of tall trees with the most colorful leaves he'd ever seen dwarfed the modest manmade establishment it now shielded from the suns. Its trees were so big that the trees in the jungles looked like branches. The tree tops were filled with red, blue, gold, and violet leaves. Birds, speckled and bright, swooped in and out of the tops of the trees.

Nath swallowed. "What is that?"

"That's the Red Clay Forest."

A breeze picked up, stirring Nath's long red hair. He brushed it from his eyes, which were fixed on the strange forest. The trees swayed in the wind, gently shifting from side to side in a harmony of their own. The leaves were of many different sorts and shapes. The forest was welcoming, yet at the same time it seemed dangerous.

Tearing his gaze away, Nath said to Venir, "And this village?"

"The Red Clay Village, of course. Good people thrive here."

Upon their approach, the men working the fields waved their hats and hands. Venir waved back and smiled. The village was made up of small log homes and clay huts with straw for rooftops. The women wore long cotton dresses covering them from neck to toe, and the hardy men wore trousers and loose-fitting cotton shirts. It was an ordinary place just outside an extraordinary forest. It reminded Nath of Ben's village.

"We should find them here," Venir said of his comrades.

From out of nowhere, a fat little boy with more locks of curly brown hair than he had head wrapped himself around Venir's leg.

Still walking with the boy latched to his leg, Venir rubbed his head and said, "Ah, Georgio, I see you're still expanding as fast as ever. Have you been drinking out of the butter churns again?"

"Uh-huh," the boy eagerly nodded. "I'm so glad you're back, Vee. You have to come. I've been chopping wood like you said. I've filled up an entire shed. Come, come, let me show you!"

"Certainly, Georgio, certainly." Venir squeezed the boy's shoulders. "Ah, I see it's thickening your inner girth. Good. Georgio, meet my comrade. His name is Nath."

Georgio glanced at Nath and did a double take. Unfastening himself from Venir's leg, he pointed his chubby finger at Nath. "Your eyes are gold!"

Nath took a knee. "Why yes they are." He extended his hand.

Georgio looked at it and screamed, "Aaaaaaaaaaaaah!"

The entire village stopped moving. People stared.

Nath lowered his hand and gave Venir a look and said, as Georgio continued to scream, "Well, this is a first."

CHAPTER 13

"SO VENIR HAD YOU TAKE a bath in the murk, did he?" Billip said to Nath.

All of the men—Venir, Nath, Melegal, Billip, and Mikkel—were reunited now that Georgio had settled down. It had been his screaming that led the men out of one of the cabins. Now they were all crammed inside another stuffy little cabin that was hotter than it needed to be. Venir was digging a wooden spoon into a clay bowl, devouring some venison stew and potatoes.

Nath was enjoying the same. "He says it will bring a healthy glow to my scaly skin."

Mikkel erupted in laughter.

Georgio, now sitting by Nath, giggled. Now that the boy had settled down, he clung to Nath and kept poking his arm, saying, "I wish I had scales. Are you part lizard, or part fish? Were you born like this?" He stood on Nath's legs and stared into his eyes. "I've never seen golden eyes before."

Venir grabbed Georgio by the back of his pants and pulled him away. "Georgio, how about fetching us some more water? Fresh from the stream."

The boy pulled his shoulders back and beamed a smile. "Anything for you, Vee."

Sitting on a stool in the corner of the room, Melegal added a comment. "Chunk of boy, find some wine too."

The boy balled his meaty hands up and fired back, "My name is Georgio."

Leaning forward with a narrowing stare and a razor-sharp thumb knife in hand, Melegal replied, "Listen to me, you oversized piglet.

Return with wine and I'll say your name, but if you don't, I'll have you squealing mine."

Eyes widening, Georgio swallowed and scrambled out of the cabin.

"Will you leave the child alone?" Venir said.

Melegal eased back into the corner. "If he returns with wine, I will."

"You know they don't have any wine here," Mikkel said.

"Then it is my hope the child won't return at all." Melegal's thumb knife flashed between his fingers and vanished into his clothes. "Now that we're all reunited, Venir, it's time to take me back to Bone. I'm ready."

"Please take him to Bone." Billip wiped a morsel of stew from his goatee. "He hasn't stopped complaining since you left. It's taken all I have to not cut off my own ears."

"I agree with that," Mikkel said, shaking his head at Melegal.

In an agitated but satisfied tone, Venir said, "We'll depart in the morning then. We'll even take a shortcut through Red Clay."

Melegal sat up fast. "No! You said we wouldn't have to pass through there. You said it would be all in the open, dusty land. I'm not going into that spook hole."

"Why, are you afraid you'll never come out?" Billip said.

"As a matter of fact, I am. Too many have gone in and never come back out again," Melegal argued.

"Those are just tales to keep the children out of the woods." Mikkel snorted a laugh. His eyes darted from face to face. "But I'm with Melegal. I'd rather stay in the open. I like the suns where I can see them."

Venir set his bowl down on the table. "So Melegal isn't the only frightened baby, then." He wiped his mouth. "I only suggested it so we could avoid our pursuers in case they doubled back this way. I've no problem avoiding it myself, but no one with ill intent will chase us in there."

"What is so bad about the Red Clay Forest?" Nath asked. "It looks incredible to me. I'm curious to see more of what's in there."

"The forest likes who it likes and hates who it hates. Not all are welcome," Venir said. "So they say."

"But you've traveled through there before?" Nath asked.

"Aye. And I was tickled to get out of there every time." Venir's voice trailed off. "And it hasn't been many times."

Nath turned his attention to the other men. "Tell me what you know about this gnoll pursuing me."

Billip cracked his knuckles. "He was a big one. Carried a bag of jewels. He showed us a ruby he didn't acquire from these parts. No, he's working for the Royals, I suspect."

"Why would they want me?" Nath said. "These *Royals* you speak of don't know I'm here."

"No, but the underlings sicced you on me," Venir replied. "I've discovered many of them with different treasures, but this is odd. If the underlings wanted you, I think they'd be the ones to seek you out. It's another squad of man hunters instead. Their kind won't give up. And I've heard of Collo. He was the brigand king before Jarla became the brigand queen."

"I never heard that," Billip said.

"No, but he was mentioned once before when I was there. I heard some of the brigands talking. The one with the big mouth was found dead two days later." Venir sneered while he picked up his axe and thumbed the blade. "Jarla got an edge on him. That's how she became queen. He was the top nasty before that."

Nath wiped the grit from his eyes. He needed a bath. "You say there's a stream nearby?"

"East," Venir replied.

Nath started to get up but stopped. He didn't feel like he was getting any closer to the answers he needed to get home than he was before. These men didn't have any more of an idea of how to get him home than he did. Perhaps it would be best if he just went it all alone. As soon as that thought occurred to him, he could hear Brenwar screaming in his ear, "You aren't going anywhere alone! It's nothing but trouble when you do!" Nath got up. "For what it's worth, men, I appreciate all the help."

CHAPTER 14

SITTING UP, MELEGAL SWUNG HIS leg over the side of his cot and yawned. No one else was inside the cabin but him. To the song of the morning birds, he grabbed his trousers and slipped in one leg after the other.

I have the place all to myself. Almost makes me happy. Now if I only had some coffee.

He buckled his belt, put on his vest, and gave himself a quick patdown, making sure all of his materials were there.

Coins. Dagger. Lock-picking tools. Dagger. Coins. Thumb blade. Coins. Dagger.

He did some quick calisthenics and breathed in the fresh air. That was one thing he agreed with about a small village like this: he slept better. There wasn't any banging on the walls or late-night carousing. Just peace and quiet. It had been a long time since he'd had such a good sleep. He fished a small box out of a vest pocket, flipped the lid, and took a little snort of snuff.

Bish on the flowers. I like this better.

Crossing the room, he pushed open the door and ventured outside. Red Clay Village was alive with activity. Everyone had obviously been up at least two hours before him. A pair of men carried boards of lumber toward the nearest barn. Women carried wicker baskets on their arms and on their heads. As they passed, he gave them a bow. They giggled as they walked by.

Farm girls. So easily humored. Strong backed too. Too bad they have teeth as long as a donkey's. Oh, how I miss Bone, but today is the day. It had better be.

He sniffed the air. A strong fragrance of coffee filled his nostrils—

and his feet, as if they had a will of their own, led him right to the source. It was a yurt with a stone fireplace in the back. Several metal pots sat on a large coal-burning stove. He eyeballed the steaming baskets of food laid out on the bar. His stomach growled.

A burly villager, more oaf than man, slathered heaps of butter on his biscuits and gobbled three of them down one by one. Dusting off his hands, the man nodded at Melegal and sauntered off.

Enjoy your time baking in the sun all day after some biscuits, plow boy.

Melegal snagged a couple of strips of bacon and filled his hand with a warm mug of coffee that was sitting out.

Come to the city, and we'll shock the disease of farming right out of you.

Sipping his coffee, he managed the slightest smile.

Mmm…best coffee I've had in months.

"Melegal! Melegal! Over here!"

He spied the boy Georgio waving at him. The boy's face was flushed, and he was all excited.

Why must he flap about like he's drowning in water?

Georgio ran up to Melegal, and with his hands on his knees and panting for breath, the fat boy said, "Venir told me to come and find you. I've been looking all over for you." He huffed and fanned himself, staring blankly at Melegal.

"I've been inside the cabin up until moments ago. How could you have lost me?" Melegal took a sip. "Forget I asked that."

"I was at the cabin, but then I got hungry and left and went back and you were gone. I thought something happened."

"Yes, a tragic thing did happen: you found me." Melegal didn't see Venir or the others anywhere. He glared. "So, where is the lout?"

Georgio's face screwed up. "What's a lout?"

"It's a man with too much lard in his brains."

"I stuck lard in my ear once," Georgio replied.

Melegal slapped him in the back of the head. "Just take me to Venir!"

"Ow!" Rubbing the back of his head, Georgio said, "Fine. Come on then!" He marched just outside of the village, where the southern face of the Red Clay Forest loomed.

Venir, Billip, and Mikkel stood in the distance, just outside of the dense forest's edge. They were like insects waiting by the woodland to be eaten.

What are they doing way out there?

Georgio broke into a run toward the men. The boy kept going and going, diminishing the farther he went, until he was in the presence of the men. It seemed to take a long time for the boy to get there.

Continuing his easy stride, Melegal's limber and lengthy limbs stiffened the closer he came to the forest.

I don't like this. I don't like this at all.

By the time he arrived, his feet burned in his boots. He kept his attention fixed on the eyes of the men, ignoring the forest behind them. He just wanted to pretend it wasn't there.

"What's going on, Venir?" he said, not hiding his disappointed tone.

"There's no sign of Nath," Venir replied.

"And that matters why?"

Venir's expression was one of concern. "It matters because we need to go after him."

"After him?" Melegal said. "No, no, no, Venir. You are taking me back to Bone. This man Nath, aside from his attempts to kill you, is quite capable of taking care of himself."

Oh, if I could strangle the life out of you I would, lout!

"He doesn't need our help."

"What's the matter, Melegal?" Georgio said, hiding behind Venir's legs. "Are you afraid the bugs will eat you in there?"

Melegal drew a knife and said with a threatening tone, "Not if I skin you up and feed you to them first. They'll be able to feed off you for days."

"Vee," Georgio whined.

"That's enough, Me. Just leave the boy alone."

"I'm not going into that forest, Venir. We agreed last night. Here's what I think. You and little butter churner can go in there and look for the stranger, since you're so fond of him. How does that sound?"

"It won't be that big a problem," Venir said.

"You gave me your word, Venir. Keep it!"

Venir's lips tightened. He took a glance at the forest and shook his head. "You're right."

Melegal put away his dagger. "Good. You know, you'd fare much better in life if you saw things my way more often."

"Listen, Venir," Billip said, shooting a look at Melegal, "if it matters so much to you, then I can escort this woman back to Bone."

"You had better mind your tongue, archer," Melegal warned. "Or you're going to be staring at the inside of your eyelids forever."

Mikkel stepped between Billip and Melegal. "I think they're going to need a peacekeeper."

Venir gave a huff and shook his head, swinging his axe up onto his shoulder. "I'd rather go in there alone than travel with a bunch of cackling hens." He gave Georgio a hug, frowned at his friends, and headed into the exotic woods.

As his friend vanished, Melegal said to his comrades, "It's good to know the two of you have at least half as much sense as me." He frowned at the boy. "A shame there's no hope for you, son."

CHAPTER 15

V ENIR VENTURED DEEP INTO THE leafy folds of the Red Clay Forest. The exotic woodland was colored with mosses that sprawled out over the packed red clay ground and climbed the tree trunks like coats of fur. Little vermin darted across his path. Their pelts were spotted like deer, and they had raccoon eyes and stubby tails. They stopped, twisted their heads around, and made shrill little cackles then scattered.

Sweat dripped from Venir's chin and splashed on the toe of his boot. Red Clay, despite its inviting foliage of splendid colors and the aromatic bouquet of the flowers, was just as bad as the jungle heat.

I don't remember it feeling so unpleasant before.

One step at a time, he made his way through the forest, eyes searching for Nath. He didn't owe the man anything. He didn't need the man. But for some reason, Venir felt compelled to help him. The man was a stranger in Bish and now a stranger in the Red Clay Forest. The place didn't take well to strangers. Only the bizarre thrived here. Few men. Few beasts. It was a place that liked its pleasantries uninterrupted.

Taking a knee, he studied a faint impression in a mustard-yellow patch of moss. It was the edge of a heel.

Someone's going to a lot of trouble not to be followed.

Venir's nostrils twitched. His nose was keen, at least when it came to flushing out the underlings. Men who didn't smell like orcs or ogres were a little more difficult to track down. He had to rely on the terrain. If he hadn't told Chongo to stay back and guard Melegal, it would have been a different story. He scratched the stubble growing around his jaw.

Why did Nath leave us? He's nothing but a babe in the woods on this world.

Resuming his journey in lengthy strides, Venir pondered the man's reasoning. Perhaps there wasn't anything Venir had to offer. After all, aside from the armament, he knew very little about magic. What Nath needed was something far beyond his comprehension. But he was curious. There was a kindred feeling he had with the scaly-armed man who walked with his entire world on his shoulders. Perhaps the stranger just didn't want to endanger anyone else. Perhaps he just wanted to walk the walk alone. Venir could relate to that.

But this is Bish. I have the armament, but an ordinary man doesn't have a chance alone here.

Venir took a fork in the natural path he was on and tiptoed over a field of rocks jutting through the clay. A stream cut through the red clay and woodland. Its mild waters burbled over the flat stones of the waterbed and twisted out of sight. Venir bent over and scooped up a handful of water. It was icy cold. He dashed it into his face and drank more handfuls down.

"Ah! Now that's something!" He was refilling his water skin when the soothing song of a female voice prickled the hair on the nape of his neck. He froze.

Downstream on the other side, a beautiful woman with hair like a bouquet of flowers kneeled in the waters, filling up a hollowed-out gourd. Clothed in teal-green layers of gossamer, her body swayed from side to side.

The hard lines on Venir's jaw went slack. Music filled his ears, but the woman's mouth did not move, only her alluring body. The water skin dropped from his hand and floated away down the stream right past the woman's eyes.

She glanced up and locked her eyes with his. She extended the gourd of water and beckoned Venir with it.

Shoulders slumped, and with his feet moving with a will of their own, he sloshed across the waters with his arms outstretched. He was so thirsty. His desires were enflamed. This enchantress in the forest was more compelling than any other woman he'd ever seen. Her skin was tan and buttery. Her lips looked as soft as a rose. Everything about her was inviting. Pleasing.

"You look thirsty, warrior," she said in a honey-filled voice that ignited his desires even further. "Come and drink from my vessel. It will satisfy you forever."

Reaching for the gourd, he said, "I thirst more for your lips than for the water within."

"Drink first, warrior." She blew him a kiss, and a smoky mist came out. "My lips can wait until later."

Venir drew in the vapors. The mist was strong, like the squeezed leaves of a eucalyptus plant. Seeing dancing girls rubbing oil over their bodies, Venir felt his sagging jaw turn up into a smile.

The voiceless singing became louder.

Without warning, the vapors seized his throat.

Clutching at it, he tried to cough out the unseen assailant paralyzing his lungs. Wide-eyed, he stared at the woman's green eyes.

She had turned from seductress to devil. Her body had lost its pleasing form and was morphing into something far less comely and shapely. A woodland hag replaced the vibrant woman. Her cackle was shrill and painful.

Venir dropped to his knees, and his hands splashed the water.

I can't breathe!

CHAPTER 16

ACK ON THE BARGE, ORAN sat in the middle with a deep frown around his chin, gliding over the Current with his robes rustling at his sides. He was not alone. His fingers scraped at the wooden bench he sat on, digging and digging.

I hate Verbard. I hate Catten.

The underling lords had left him with a token of appreciation. At least, that was what they called it. In reality, it was anything but. They said the assistants would help him meet his goal. He didn't believe a word of it. He despised company, and they knew it, so they had 'granted him' the worst company of all.

I hate urchlings.

The barge was filled with the rank little bodies of the nastiest underlings of all. The small creatures were crammed at the fore and aft of the craft. They were shorter than Oran but thick in muscle. Their eyes were large and black, their expressions primordial. Hunched over, they sniffed and snorted at one another. Their brutish bodies had shoulders big enough to swallow their necks. Long armed with oversized hands, their fingers were more claw than flesh. They were underlings of a cursed ilk. Spawn which only communicated when it was time to eat or kill.

An urchling with long, pointed ears peeled around the back of his bald head bumped into Oran.

Oran's hand flared up with a crimson light. He jammed it into the urchling's side, sizzling its skin. "Keep away from me!"

The barefoot urchling vaulted to the fore of the craft, crashing into his brothers. They wailed on him with their hammer-like fists in a flurry of savage blows.

"Enough!" Oran yelled.

The urchlings pushed as far away from Oran as they could, huddled together. Their heavy panting eased, and they glanced over at Oran from time to time.

Without looking at them, Oran let his shoulders slump. The urchlings were like dogs: fearful of their master yet always seeking his attention. Dogs, however, weren't nearly as stupid.

After several minutes of floating quietly through the Current, the urchlings, like schoolchildren forced to sit too long, were clambering over each other, rocking the craft. Water splashed over the rim and soaked his feet.

I hate Verbard. I hate Catten. I hate urchlings.

CHAPTER 16

HEAD COVERED IN A TAUPE hood, Melegal followed after Billip and Mikkel. The durable warriors were moving at a brisk pace miles west of the Red Clay Forest's western edge. The soft ground and green grasses had changed into a different terrain. It was sand, cacti, and rocks as far as his eyes could see. Mirages popped up and disappeared mile after mile.

"How are you doing back there, Melegal?" Mikkel moved in a long but fluid gait with his hands swinging like paddles at his sides. "My pace isn't too fast for you, is it?"

"It's not my pace you should be concerned about." Melegal licked the sandy grit from his teeth and spat it out. "I'm not short legged like Billip. He's the one struggling."

"Struggle, my arse." With an arrow in his hand, Billip turned to walk backward and point it at Melegal. "We'll see how you fare as soon as the suns peak again and it gets so hot you can't even breathe. Let's see how those girlie legs you boast about are doing then."

"I've made this trek plenty of times before," Melegal said. *And I swear it gets hotter every time.* "But if you have no concern for me, then I have no concern for you. You should be thanking me for giving you a reason to stay out of that forest. You know you didn't want to go in there any more than I did."

Mikkel stopped and kicked some dirt back at him. "We're just escorting you as a favor to Vee. I'd just as soon stay in the south. As a matter of fact, you need to pay us, the same as you'd pay the merchants if you joined up with one of their trains. You could have done that weeks ago. You'd be just as safe with them as you are with us."

"I'm taking you where you need to be." Melegal swatted the dirt from his trousers. "Bone is best for everybody."

"Says you," Billip replied. "You just like all those pockets for your picking. You won't last much longer if you keep that craft up. I know your game, Melegal. You're just dragging us along to have some muscle around when you need it."

"You're delusional, Billip."

Shaking his arrow at Melegal, the archer said, "You might fool Venir, but you don't fool us. I know how you manipulate him. It just astounds me he's not privy to it."

"Yeah," Mikkel agreed. "He's pretty savvy about most things." He squinted at eye at Melegal. "But why not you?"

"Are you jesting? Wait, stop. First, I deny your accusations about my character. Second, Venir, savvy?" Melegal laughed. "Savvy about what? Women like the brigand queen? Drinking more ale than a drunken ogre? Mixing it up with every fiend he crosses? That's not savvy. That's stupid. Even moths avoid those types of flames."

"You sure are a lousy friend, Melegal." Mikkel turned his back and marched on at a quicker and heavier pace.

"I've never claimed to be a friend to anyone but myself. I can't help it if your brutish ilk find such charming comfort in my presence." Getting into step with Mikkel, Melegal half skipped forward. "If anything, I'm your mentor."

"Do you really believe all of the manure you spout?" Billip said. "You make me want to jam this arrow between my ears."

Melegal glowered at Billip. "What are you waiting for?"

"That's it!" Billip loaded an arrow into his bow and aimed at Melegal. "One more word! One more, and this arrow goes through you!"

Mikkel turned and stopped. With his fists on his hips, he narrowed his brows at Melegal.

Uh oh.

Usually when Melegal picked at Billip, Mikkel reveled in it as much as him, but not this time.

Perhaps I've taken it too far.

The crease between Billip's own eyes said it all. At point-blank range, one of the most dangerous archers in the south was ready to shoot him.

Facing Billip, Melegal lowered his hood. He chose his next words carefully. "Ten silvers says you miss."

Billip released.

Twang!

CHAPTER 17

VENIR FOUGHT FOR HIS BREATH. His constricted lungs would have none of it. He was suffocating. With his face turning from red to purple, he lifted his head. The woodland hag's shrill cackles were poison in his ears.

The old woman had warts and splotches all over her skin, rough like the bark of a tree. Her hair was grimy and coiled up with small vines for ribbon. Long necklaces of bones and colored stones dangled over her chest. The gossamer layers of green clothing were gone. She wore robes like something a traveler would have lost decades ago.

She pointed at him with a long yellow fingernail. "You will feed my forest when you die. A large one like you will be good for the soil."

Venir lunged at her and took a swipe at her legs.

She skipped out of the way, cackling.

He collapsed into the water. Fully submerged, he fought to keep his head above the rim of the icy deep. Unable to breathe and battling to control his limbs, he thrashed about, trying to keep from drowning. The suffocating feeling struck terror in his heart. It triggered the worst of his worst memories. He spied the evil eyes of the old woman. They gleamed with the knowledge that she was winning.

No! Not like this! No!

He had sworn to himself long ago that he would die fighting. Even with his face turning blue from lack of air, Venir scooped a handful of mud from the bottom of the stream and flung it into the face of the woodland hag.

A rock little bigger than his knuckle smote her on the bridge of her nose.

She staggered back and fell.

Lungs ready to burst, he climbed up the bank toward the woman.

Her enlarged eyes filled with his angry image. Crawling back on her elbows, she said, "You are a meal! You will be dead! Stop, youngster. Stop!"

Venir wanted to yell at her. Scream at her. Didn't the old hag realize he was not her enemy? The underlings were.

Remove this spell from me!

But with no air, he was unable to speak.

She wiped the blood from the gash the rock had opened up on the bridge of her nose. Staring at the blood, she started to chant.

No!

Venir lunged for the hag at an agonizingly slow pace. Speckles and spots blinded his eyes. His strength fled from his legs. Lording over the prone and chanting witch, he swayed. He saw his mark, but he couldn't move anymore.

The woodland hag's eyes rolled up into her head until only their whites showed. Her words were quick and fierce. She spat them out like venom.

Venir's heart beat like slow thunder. Gawping for air, he stumbled, blacked out, and fell.

Air seeped back into Venir's lungs. It startled him from his slumber. Weak from lack of breath, he stretched out his arms and tried to push himself up off the ground. He discovered a body crushed beneath him and rolled off it.

It was a woman, but not the old hag who had taken his breath. It was the younger woman, splendid and divine. His numb limbs tingled from his fingertips to his elbows. Shaking his hands, he studied the woman. A spot of blood rose on the bridge of her nose. He took a deep breath and gave her a shove.

Her light body wriggled. Her face tightened into a grimace.

He clamped his fingers around her wrist, holding her fast. "The witch lives, I see."

The long lashes on her pretty eyes fluttered, and she let out a groan.

Her chin rolled in his direction, and her eyelids popped open. She jerked and kicked and let out a piercing scream. "Ahhhhg!"

"Be still, witch, or I'll snap your wrist like a twig."

Holding her ribs with her free hand, she said, "Go ahead. You bruised my ribs when you fell on me, so why not the rest of me?"

He tightened his grip on her wrist. "Good idea."

"Ah!" she moaned. Her eyes watered, and her mouth widened into an 'O.' She gritted her teeth. "If you hurt me, invader, this forest will avenge me one hundred fold."

Venir took a gander at their surroundings. Everything was as exotic and beautiful as she was. Engaging. Tempting. His eyes ran over her body and face. He wasn't sure what to make of her. "This forest doesn't give a slat about you."

She sank back. Her face turned into a long frown, and in a sad voice she said, "It does too."

"No, it tolerates you. It doesn't really like anybody." He lifted her to her feet. "What's your name?"

Scoffing, she replied, "What's yours?"

"Venir."

"A brutish name. Let me guess, as a child you were one of those laborers who milk goats for the Royals."

"True."

She sneered up at him. "You should be dead. I can only assume you're too stupid to die."

Venir dragged her into the stream.

"What are you doing?"

He fished Brool out of the water and held it before her eyes.

"So you're going to slay me now?"

"It's only fair. You just tried to slay me. And you did so without provocation."

"I was protecting my trees from the edge of your axe."

"Does this look like a woodsman's axe?"

"An axe is an axe."

Venir wasn't sure what to do with the woman. She'd almost killed him, but he wasn't certain she meant to. If anything, she was deranged. Beautiful on the outside and dangerous on the inside. The last thing he needed was to have her take his wind again. "I'm not here to cut trees. I'm looking for a lost friend."

"Probably some innocent man the Royals paid you to kill. I know a hunter when I see one. Men." She spat in the water. "You're all so vile and violent. Destroyers of the world. It's devastated because of the likes of you."

He should have corrected her, but all thoughts of the underlings fled his mind at the sight of her beauty so animated by anger. "We're men. We like to conquer things. Especially women."

She closed her eyes and pulled her shoulders back. "Fine, savage. Take me then."

Venir let go of her wrist, and she stumbled backward into the water. "Perhaps I would if I hadn't seen a glimpse of what truly lies within you." He secured Brool between his shoulders and walked away.

CHAPTER 18

BILLIP FIRED. THE ARROW WHIZZED by Melegal's face. Its feathers dusted his cheek.

He didn't blink. "I told you you'd miss. I'll just keep the ten silver of yours I currently have in my possession."

Billip looked so mad he might break his short bow. He scowled. "One of these days I'll put a hole clear through you."

"Yes, but not today." Melegal walked by Billip and Mikkel. "Perhaps I should lead." He increased his distance from the men about a hundred paces. There was nothing but sun and sand, and within moments he lost all sense of the direction he was going. He swallowed down the lump building in his throat.

I miss the city.

Noting the tiny dust devils dancing over the hot ground, he took a glance back.

Mikkel and Billip were talking to each other below the sound of the wind. It was a serious conversation. Quiet but argumentative. Even though his keen ears could not pick up what they were saying, his keen eyes made out every word on their lips.

Oh, Bish. They're going to leave me. I might have pushed the durable louts too far—and I need them. A little longer, anyway.

His relationship with Billip and Mikkel was not the same as the one he had with Venir. Melegal had been with Venir since they were both urchins living in the Royal castles and working as slaves. The two boys had developed a strong kinship with one another. He'd learned he could count on Venir. Even though the man didn't always do things when Melegal wanted to do them, he'd eventually get around to it.

This is Venir's fault. If he were here, we wouldn't have this problem.

Mikkel dropped his hand on Billip's shoulder, and the pair of men went separate ways. Billip headed south, and Mikkel came right at Melegal with a frown on his face.

Not good. Mikkel always smiles, even the slightest on the worst of days.

"Eh, Mikkel, is there a problem?"

"You." The brooding man didn't stop. He kept on going north.

Without another glance back, Melegal caught up with Mikkel. "Billip should have thicker skin than that. You know, his pride is the devil."

"His pride?" Mikkel stopped and drew up on Melegal. "It's your pride! We do what we do for Venir, not you! We'd be perfectly fine back where we came from and not heading to the nasty streets of Bone." He stormed off.

"There is nowhere in the south for you to go."

"No, there's nowhere in the south for *you* to go!" Mikkel yelled.

Over the next few hours, not a word was spoken. Mikkel set a brisk pace with extra-long strides. Melegal jogged and trotted on and off until all of his sweat-drenched body turned dry. By the time the glowering suns were sinking, his legs ached, his feet burned, his mouth was parched, and it felt like his tongue was coated in sand.

Going down into the south had been much easier than coming back up north to Bone was now. He and Venir had traveled with a merchant train. There had been plenty of supplies, and he'd always ridden in a wagon.

Mikkel stopped in front of a barrel cactus with a knife. He cut the top out, flung it at Melegal's feet, and reached inside. He drew forth watery pulps, stuck them in his mouth, and chewed. He ate one after another for a few more moments and said to Melegal, "Help yourself."

Rising up on his toes, Melegal looked inside the cactus. The pulps were leathery, with fine hairs all over them. "You eat the pulp?"

"It fills the belly. We still have a long way to go today. Eat."

"I'm thirsty, not hungry." But after Mikkel glared at him, Melegal rolled up his sleeve, reached inside the cactus, and drained the liquid into his mouth. Its waters were milky and bland. "Yuck."

"What did you think it was going to taste like, wine?"

"I was hoping." He walked away.

"Drink another."

"No thanks, I'm full."

Mikkel replied with a heavy stare, "I'm not asking."

The thief grabbed another and squished the water from the pulp into his mouth. He nibbled off a piece of the pulp and swallowed. "There. Are you happy?"

Mikkel's eyes were huge and glossy. He swayed in the stiff wind like a tree about to fall.

"What's happening, Mikkel?"

Something black scurried across the ground. It was a scorpion bigger than his foot.

Melegal felt spiders crawling over his shoulders. Dancing around and swatting at his clothes and legs, he scanned the ground. He didn't see any more of the giant insects, just the one, and it burrowed back into the ground. "Mikkel? Mikkel?"

A foamy drool spittled from the warrior's lips.

The man weighed a ton, but Melegal caught him as he fell. Back straining, he lowered his friend to the ground and then started slapping his face. "Wake up, Mikkel. Wake up!"

CHAPTER 19

ORAN WANDERED OUT OF THE cave mouth with the pack of urchlings on his heels. He smacked at them. "Give me some space! Give me some space!"

Some of the urchlings scattered, but a few others took the abuse like loyal pets.

Oran rolled his violet eyes. "You're like ticks, just not as smart." He made his way farther into the jungle until he found a clearing more suitable for his needs. Even though he preferred the comforts within caves, it was nice to be outside in a breeze. He shoved a pair of urchlings aside. "You maggots are making me claustrophobic. Go somewhere. Do something!"

The pack began eating flowers and leaves and spitting them out. They climbed the trees and hung from the vines. They poked, prodded, and bit at everything. Their sweaty nostrils flared, and their large, pointed ears peeled back.

A deer wandered into the glen.

Saliva dripped from the jutting lower jaws of the urchlings' mouths. Their eyes were glued on the deer and its rack of antlers.

Oran gave the order with a sharp-sounding chit.

The deer bolted.

The urchlings tore through the jungle in a silent but deadly chase.

Oran felt the muscles in his back ease, and he took a seat on the ground. "That should keep them busy awhile." He rubbed his temples with the tips of his fingers. "Finally, I can think again."

He crossed his legs and meditated. He needed to find the gnoll, Collo. Certainly the man hunter would have something for him by now.

A spell of location should do the trick.

He murmured, and his magic swelled within his chest and fed him with power.

A racket in the nearby thicket broke off his concentration, and he cursed.

An urchling emerged. It lay a broken and bloodied antler at his feet.

CHAPTER 20

VENIR RESUMED HIS SEARCH FOR Nath, but he wasn't alone. The woman whose name he did not know was tagging along. She moved with the silence of a fawn, and her bare feet left no marks on the ground. Everywhere he went, she went too—with a spring in her step.

"Who are you looking for, Venir?" She was leaning against a fuzzy white-moss-covered tree, looking as enticing as ever.

He walked right by her, scanning the ground for any signs of passage. Even though Red Clay was a dangerous area, it was never without new company. The treasures in its growth were highly prized by the world of men. The vast variety of leaves and countless blooms of flowers were known to have intoxicating powers and healing effects, but even more so, merchants laden with treasure had often ventured inside, never to leave again.

Something small and white that had been smooshed into the clay path caught his eye. He squatted down and picked it out.

The druid draped her warm body over his broad back, crossed her feet over his waist, and said in his ear, "What is it you've spied, Venir?"

Between his thumb and finger, he rubbed the clay grit from the object. It was a tooth. A man's as far as he could tell, and it had a dab of blood on it. He flicked it away. "Go figure it out yourself."

"You have a lot of muscles," she said with her lips brushing against the back of his ear. "I like them. I like the straw color of your hair too." She made a sound that resembled a cat's purr. "I bet you're an animal."

"Will you let go of me, woman?"

"No."

"I wasn't asking." Venir rose up and moved on with her clinging to his back like a monkey. He passed over a patch of ferns crushed beneath a tree whose plum colored apple-shaped fruit hung from its branches.

The druid plucked one and pressed it to his lips. "You should eat. These are quite delicious."

"Then you eat it."

Right outside his ear, she crunched into the fruit. "Mmmm, it is so good. Sweet, like my lips."

Venir hip-tossed her off his back to the ground.

She let out a squeal, bounced off the ground, and sprang back to her feet. "Eeee! I'm trying to help you, fool! I'll make you pay for that!" She chucked the fruit at his chest.

He snatched it out of the air and threw it back.

She turned. The fruit smacked right into her back. "Ow!" she cried. "You really are a fool to cross me. And I was going to help you, too!"

"I don't need your help." Venir ran his thumb over a notch in the bark of one of the trees. The dead trail had come to life for him. Spot after spot, he picked up more signs. Torn leaves lay on the ground, which was odd. Red Clay's trees didn't lose their leaves. In a mysterious way, the forest was always tidy.

I'll find you now, Nath.

Picking his way through the woodland, he came across a discernable trail looped around several huge mounds covered in bushes. They weren't like anything he'd seen before, and each of them was big enough to hold a host of men.

The woman crept up along his side and grabbed him by the arm. "You don't want to venture there, Venir." She tried to pull him away. "Come. Come. You're asking for trouble."

"It's not your concern." He considered asking her questions, but he didn't trust her answers. "Go away."

She slapped her hands onto his cheeks and held his face. "I am Laiyn. You have my name, you have my word now. I will help you."

He pushed her hands away. "I don't need your help." He started to move on.

Laiyn blocked his path. "No, you must listen to me. If they have your friend, then I'm certain he is dead. You'll be dead too if you don't leave."

A breeze picked up.

Venir covered his nose. "What is that odor?"

"Death," she said to him. She pinched her nostrils. "We need to go. They'll find us."

Venir's stomach gurgled. He felt a little sick. He let Laiyn lead him away until the stench died down and the flowery bouquets took over again. Looking down at the spritely beauty who wasn't even half as big as him, he said, "Tell me what you know."

"Kiss me first." Laiyn puckered up her lips and rose on her toes.

As tempting as it was, he couldn't get the vision of the hag she'd turned into out of his mind. He'd woken up with some ugly women before, orcesses even, but he didn't ever want to wake up with something as ugly as that.

He covered her face with his hand. "Just spit it out, Laiyn."

She unlocked her face from his palm and pouted. "If you wish, but you'll regret it when I'm gone." She lightly stroked his hand with her fingers. "You have hands like a hairless ape."

"Out with it."

She kept massaging his hand.

He pulled it away. "Now."

"Fine. Those mounds are where the forest magi roost."

"The what?"

"An enclave of dirty men and women who move through the woodland without using their feet. They prey on trespassers." Her olive eyes drifted off into a world he couldn't see. "They take over their minds. Their bodies. Their bones. They make magic with the remains and cast gruesome spells. You won't flush them out of those holes, and it's fruitless for you to enter." She glanced up into his eyes. "If they have your friend, then I assure you he's as dead as the dirt beneath my toes."

CHAPTER 21

P OISON. THERE WERE MANY KINDS. Some paralyzed. Others filled the head with illusions. Judging by the bump growing on Mikkel's leg, this poison killed. The black man was starting to pale, and his body trembled.

Slapping the man's face, Melegal pushed back his eyelids. "Mikkel! Mikkel!"

Only the whites of his eyes were there.

He slapped him harder. "Mikkel!" Melegal whipped out his thumb knife and crawled down to Mikkel's leg, eyeing the black and bleeding spot where the scorpion's stinger must have struck. "If you survive this, you owe me." He made two slices in an X on the site of the mark. Blood ran and dripped to the ground. "You really owe me big."

He put his lips on the wound and sucked. His face soured. He spat the tongue-burning venom out.

I hate the Outlands!

He sucked and spat until he could no longer taste the noxious venom then held his head and swayed. His tongue became thick inside the walls of his mouth, and the desert was spinning. He clutched at his stomach and retched.

Oh, I'm not going to make it. I'm not going to make it at all.

He felt cold under the hot suns, and his limbs had become noodles. He slid belly first into the dust and dirt. His fingers clawed and flinched in the sand.

Please, someone come and kill me. Finish me off or stop Bish from spinning.

Melegal lay there until the suns fell and the moons rose. He managed to roll over onto his back and stare up into the sky. The moons hung in a velvet blanket of black like a pair of red blisters. He scowled at them.

Why don't you two idiots just drop from the sky on me?

At long last, the spinning sky slowed, and he felt the strength returning to the tips of his fingers. Filling his nostrils full of air, he managed to sit up again. His stomach churned. Bile built in his throat. He spat.

My, that was odious.

He scooted over to Mikkel. The knot on the man's calf was still as big as his fist. The rise and fall of the man's chest was uneven, and he shivered in the hot night like a man freezing. Melegal placed his hand on Mikkel's forehead. He was burning up with fever, but his skin was dry as a bone.

He's not dead, but he soon will be.

Keeping watch for anything that might scurry over the sand, he crawled over to the cactus and stood up. With a grunt, he found his way to his feet and reached inside. Many of the pulps had dried, but there were a couple left. He shuffled over to Mikkel and filled his mouth with the milky water.

"I hope you're as tough as you are stupid, because this is going to have to do."

Melegal sat with his arms wrapped around his knees and his head lowered between them. The suns had risen, but Mikkel hadn't moved.

Another long, hot, miserable day in the Outlands. If I ever see Venir again, I'm going to stick a hole in him.

The only companion he had left was down. Now it was just him and the elements. He'd done all he could for the man, too. He'd opened another cactus, eaten his fill, soaked Mikkel's lips with the pulp, and even given him what was left in his water skin. He turned his head, glancing in the direction where he thought the City of Bone might be.

I can go it alone, can't I? He said it was only one more day's walk from here, two at the most.

Conflicted, he wiped the dried lips on his sleeve. The form of Mikkel lay prone in the suns, baking like a potato. Melegal had covered the man's face from the glaring heat. He liked Mikkel. The man had humor in the gravest of situations, laughing and smiling at just about anything, good or ill. Melegal found it annoying sometimes, but today, he missed the man's smile. He nudged the man with his boot.

"If you wake up, I won't be so unpleasant to you anymore. Fair?"

Doubt crept deep into the crevices between Melegal's shoulder blades. Perhaps he'd taken his clever manipulations too far. Mikkel was formidable, and Melegal had him aggravated and off his game. Mikkel had walked the hot sands a thousand times before. He would have noticed something like a scorpion in his sleep, but yesterday he'd completely missed it.

"And now I'm stuck here, caught in the suns like a moth burning in the flame."

An inner struggle emerged, one the thief rarely had occasion to wrestle with. Would he stay by Mikkel or go it alone?

Surely I can make it. So what if the suns don't rise and fall in the same places?

He heard Venir's voice say in his head, "Trust the land."

He licked his teeth.

I don't know squat about the land. I'm a man of the streets.

He stood up and stretched out like an X in the suns. It was so hot, he didn't want to move, but he knew he had to. He caught a scurry out of the corner of his eye. In a cracked voice, he said, "You!"

The foot-long scorpion had squared off on him. It was a coal-black, nasty thing with a long tail curled over the white spots on its back.

"So, you've come to claim your prize or finish me off too. We'll see, you little troublemaker." Melegal backed up and stepped over to Mikkel's heavy crossbow. "You might have snuck up on my comrade, but no one sneaks up on me." He reached down and picked the crossbow up. "Lords of the High Castle, this thing is heavy."

The scorpion darted forward on eight fast little legs.

Melegal braced the weapon against his shoulder, took aim, and fired.

Clatch-Zip!

The bolt skewered the scorpion to the sand.

Shoulders aching ever the slightest, Melegal dropped the wooden crossbow to the sandy ground. He said to the sleeping Mikkel, "It takes a special man to lug this thing around. Too much tree in it, but nevertheless effective."

Melegal hung around for the rest of the long day, contemplating leaving Mikkel every second. He'd been told plenty of times that staying in one spot was dangerous. Enemies lurked about, and if they saw you before you saw them, they'd close in for the kill. Carrying Mikkel was out of the question. Not even dragging him was possible. He waited it out through the night without sleeping a wink. With eyelids more heavy than logs and the toasty warmth of the rising suns on his face, he fell asleep sitting up.

Something shifted through his dreams. His eyes snapped open. The dawn had become late day, and he found himself face to face with hard eyes staring right at him.

CHAPTER 22

PERCHED IN THE CURLED BRANCHES of a tree, Venir spied on the mounds, the homes of the forest magi. He'd been moving about for the last day, angling to find a trace of some activity involving Nath. He hadn't seen a thing.

Laiyn reached down from a branch above his and toyed with his hair. "He's dead, Venir," she said in a whisper. "Come with me and I'll take the sorrow from your shoulders."

"He's not dead."

"How do you know?"

It was instinct, nothing more, but Venir had seen the man in action. He wouldn't be an easy kill for anybody. "I know. Tell me more about these forest fiends."

Scratching his back, she said, "They worship magic. Lust for its secrets. They have little need for anything else. They dabble with the plants and bathe themselves in the soil of the land. They are quite strange, creepy."

"Says the woman who turns into seven shades of withered hag."

"You didn't find my guardian visage alluring?" Staring down at him, her face shifted to the hideous form of the hag. She winked and restored her comely self. "I'm like any other animal that does what it does to protect itself."

"An animal is one thing, a hag is another."

"Humph."

Venir had hung in the tree for another hour when one of the brush-covered mounds came to life. The vegetation parted into a vertical mouth. Covered in robes that looked like a patchwork of rags sewn together, a form resembling a man squeezed out of the hole. He glided down the side of the mound and hovered above the forest floor.

The hairs on Venir's arms stiffened, leaving an icy tingling feeling. The stifling smell returned with a renewed breeze. He glanced up at Laiyn, who had pinched her nose and squinted her eyes. He returned his focus to the strange mage.

What kind of men are these?

The man's head was covered with a hood. The long sleeves and hem of his robe covered his hands and feet. Tiny bones rattled a little when he moved, woven into the fabric in an arcane manner. Then the mage made his rounds, floating and weaving in and out of all the mounds. Venir lost sight of the man several times, only to see him return again.

Stepping in front of the mound he had appeared from, the forest mage twisted his head around a couple of times, then lifted his hands up to his face. The sleeves slid down his arms, revealing bony hands that looked diseased and rotted.

Venir swallowed the foul taste in his mouth.

Disgusting.

The forest mage made a whistling sound that was part hoot and part howl. It silenced the sound of the critters who thrived in the forest. All of a sudden, the foliage of the other mounds spread open like cave mouths. More of the odd men squeezed out of the holes like vermin. They popped out one by one, and within seconds, there were dozens of them, robed and gangly. With the sound of stirring brush, the holes in the mounds closed again.

Venir's skin crawled. Strange for something as beautiful as the Red Clay Forest to be a haven for people like this. Contrary to the gorgeous multicolored plant life, these magi were like a poison living beneath the forest's skin.

Above him, Laiyn was shaking her head. Her eyes were wide as she clung tighter to her branch.

The magi formed several ranks like a military unit. The hems of their robes flapped over the ground as, with a whoosh of foul air, all of the magi floated away in a solitary unit, rounding the mounds and plunging into the woods, out of sight.

"Now what?" Laiyn asked.

"I'm going in." Venir climbed down out of the tree, and on cat's feet, he crept toward the mounds.

She was right on his heels. "Are you mad? Tell me you aren't going to crawl into one of those dirty hives."

"I am." He found the one the first mage had come out of and started climbing into its nest of foliage and vines. Halfway up the mound, he began pushing aside the vegetation that covered the entrance.

Standing at the bottom with her hands on her hips, she said to him, "You'll find nothing but death in there."

"How do you know? Have you ever been inside one before?"

"No, but I assure you your friend is dead, and I fear you will be too."

"It's nice to know you care." Venir kept peeling brush away from the hole, only to see it replenish itself. "Bish. The mound lives." The roots and vines started tangling up his feet. He ripped his boots off. "This place is cursed."

Laiyn called up to him, "You need to come down from there before the forest devours you the same as your friend."

"No forest is going to eat me." He unhitched his axe from his back and swung.

"No, wait, what are you doing?" she said with her hands outstretched. "Do not strike the vines. Do not strike."

Venir brought the axe down. Chopping like a wild lumberjack, he sent Brool's keen edge to cut the brush away, revealing an opening big enough to swallow an ordinary man whole.

At the bottom of the mound, Laiyn was on her knees with her hands stuffed in the brush, crying.

Covering his nose, Venir slung his axe over his shoulder. "What are you crying for?"

"Just go, you fool! Go! Only my apology can save you."

Venir shrugged. Peering down the hole—which smelled like an ogre's armpit—he saw nothing but black. The gap was barely big enough for his huge frame and rucksack to squeeze into. Tossing Brool to the ground beside Laiyn with a "Keep an eye on this," he crawled in, smugly aware that he still had the mystical sack and could summon Brool to him.

She doesn't need to know that. Let's see if I can trust her.

Elbow after elbow, he plunged deeper into a black hole that smelled as bad as a sewage tunnel. He'd crawled in holes before, chasing after the underlings, so this wasn't the first time he'd done such a thing, but every time, it chilled the marrow inside his bones. He stopped, huffing for breath. Memories of being buried alive by the underlings got his heart thundering in his chest.

Don't think about that day, Venir. Don't think about it at all.

Taking more quick breaths, he squirmed through the dirt like a worm in a wormhole. He wasn't sure what drove him to find Nath, but something compelling urged him on. He kept going and going, spitting dirt from his mouth and rubbing it from his eyes. The tunnel got tighter and tighter the farther he went. He got stuck.

No!

CHAPTER 23

MELEGAL SPRANG BACKWARD AND DREW one of his blades. "I'm deadly with this thing!" His keen mind was just coming out of its slumber when he realized it was Mikkel. The warrior was on all fours. His eyes were watery and puffy, and his breathing didn't come easy. "You live?"

"I don't know if I'd call it that," Mikkel replied in a gravelly voice. "What in Bish happened to me?"

Putting away his dagger, Melegal found the bolt with the scorpion pinned to it. He held it before Mikkel's eyes. "Have no fear, I avenged you."

With a sour face, Mikkel said, "Yuck. Get that thing out of my face." He shook his bull head. "Royals, that's a big one. It struck me."

"Like lightning hitting a tree." Melegal flung the dead thing away. "What do you remember?"

"Nothing." Mikkel locked his fingers behind his head. "Son of a Bish, my head hurts. Everything hurts. How long have I been out?"

"Not long, just a night and a day, which isn't surprising for such a formidable man. I don't think many would survive the sting of a scorpion such as that one."

With a grunt, Mikkel pulled his wounded leg up to his face and fixated on the wound. It was still a ball of black and purple, and his foot and leg had swollen up too. He twisted the ankle from side to side. "Did you cut me?"

Melegal lifted his narrow shoulders up and down.

Fingering the wound with a grimace, Mikkel added, "You sucked out the poison, didn't you."

"I'm not admitting to anything."

Mikkel's broad white smile returned to his face, "Aw, you do care, don't you, Me. You saved me!"

Looking away, Melegal replied, "Again, I don't know what you're talking about."

"Help me up," Mikkel said, extending his hand.

"You should rest."

"No, I think I've had plenty of that." Mikkel beckoned Melegal with his fingers. "Come on, come on."

Melegal reached down and took him by the hand. Mikkel seized him in a grip of iron and pulled him to the ground. He crushed Melegal like a mighty bear, saying, "You're good with me! Good with me!" He knuckled Melegal's head. "Thank you, rogue, thank you!"

"Oh, get off me!" Melegal squirmed out of his grasp. "We aren't out of this yet, but what we are out of is water."

Mikkel forced himself up to his feet, slung his crossbow over his back, and leaned on his club like a cane. "Where there's cactus, there's water."

"And I don't see any more cactus. That's the problem."

"Let's start walking. We're bound to find something." Leaning on his club, Mikkel checked the sky and then hobbled forward, grunting a little with every step.

"How far do you think you can make it like this?" Melegal said. "If you haven't figured it out yet, I can't carry you."

"You couldn't even carry a half of you." Mikkel hopped along. "I'll make it. We'll make it. We have to."

"And you're certain you know where you're going? Your head is clear?"

"No, my head isn't clear, but I know where I'm going." Mikkel pointed ahead. "I'm going that way."

Moving at a pace half as slow as they had been traveling before, the odd pair shuffled on hour after hour. The unforgiving landscape changed even less the farther they went. The harsh wind stung Melegal's eyes, and he wondered if they were making any kind of progress at all. Still, Mikkel moved onward, slow and steady. He was a rock against the wind. A fortress of will. They were going somewhere, but Melegal just wouldn't know where until he got there.

CHAPTER 24

WEDGED INSIDE THE TUNNEL WITH blood rushing through his ears, Venir wanted to scream. He wriggled with all his might and power. He clawed at the dirt with his fingertips. Doubt crept into his mind. What if this was all a trap and he was forever stuck in this hole? With a renewed surge of energy, he threw his shoulders from side to side. Finally, the packed dirt gave way, and he burst free.

He moved on until a faint source of light caught his eye. At first, he thought it was his imagination and rubbed his eyes. The light was still there, and the farther he crawled, the brighter it became.

Yes!

His sluggish pace quickened. He emerged on the floor of a chamber illuminated by the glowing green jelly of night bugs. The eerie glowing sap from their tails had been scooped out into odd glass sconces hanging on the walls. There was nothing inside the chamber. Not a chair nor a table. The only permanent thing was the foul smell.

How do they live like this?

Venir rose to his full height. The mound was much bigger on the inside than it looked from outside. It had been dug out deeper than he ever imagined, too. It was a world within a world. Something like insects would build, but big enough for many people.

He meandered around for a bit and noticed a shallow pit in the floor. It was outlined with natural stones. Clay jars were inside. He plucked one up and opened it. A finger-sized bug with many legs crawled out. He crammed the cork back in, stuck the clay jar back in the pit, and backed away.

Venir was putting things together in his mind. The magi were some weird bug-eating sort who kept no material possessions at all. Laiyn must have been telling the truth when she said they were obsessed by magic and that only magic mattered to them.

It didn't explain the stink, however.

He picked his way around the chamber a little bit longer until he came across two other holes like the one he'd came in through. A thought struck him and he didn't like it.

These mounds are connected together. Bone. Nath could be in any one of them.

A man's head popped out of one of the tunnels adjacent to where Venir was standing. His hair was long and shaggy. With his thoughts elsewhere, he crawled out of the hole, but when he started to stand, his sunken eyes widened on Venir. Quick as a rabbit, he scurried back into the hole.

"Bish!" Venir jumped across the room and dove for the hole. He jammed his long arms inside with his fingers grasping at anything he could get ahold of. His thumb and finger clamped around the man's ankle and jerked him back out of the hole.

"You're not getting away from me, you dirty little fish!"

Dangling in Venir's grip, the man kicked and clawed at him. His cracked and dirty nails ripped at Venir's skin.

Holding the man by the ankle with one powerful arm, Venir slapped his free hand against the man's face with a resounding smack.

The mage's body went limp.

Shaking the man's leg, Venir drew his knife. "Listen to me, you two-legged rodent. I'm looking for a man with red hair, and you are going to tell me where he is."

Upside down with his hair dragging on the ground, the mage clamped his lips shut.

"Ah, I see we understand each other. That's the first half of the battle." Venir dropped the man on the floor. "Where is he?"

The raggedy figure was almost as much robes as he was man. His fingers were bony and his cheekbones almost pointy. He was young, maybe twenty seasons, and he glared back at Venir.

"You really don't want to test me. I don't have the best temperament, especially in a confined space."

"You're all the same," the mage said.

"So he speaks." Venir squatted down and held the tip of his knife to the mage's eye. "Keep speaking."

In a defiant tone and with a twist in his jaw, the young man said, "Is violence the only tactic your kind has? Threats! Beatings! You can beat me all you want. I'll tell you nothing."

"What do you mean by my kind? You're a man same as me."

The mage sneered. "Hardly. I am mound people now. A mage in waiting. I have rejected the violent life your violent breed holds so dear. I serve the land now, not you people."

Venir looked around and said, "What people are you talking about? We're the only two here."

Drawing his knees up to his chest, the man said, "You are nothing but a thug of the Royals. All men are."

"You seem awfully displaced to know so much about the business of the Royals." Venir grabbed the man's arm and pushed up his sleeve. There was a blotted mark over what might have been a tattoo, just below the elbow. "Ah, I see."

The man tried to push his sleeve down with no effect. "You see nothing. You only see what they want you to see."

"Uh-huh." Venir's jaws clenched. Grabbing the young Royal by the jaw and the nape of his neck, he hoisted him off the ground and shoved him into the wall. "I'll tell you what I see. A little worm. A spoiled little wretch who abandoned his family. Oh, I know about the likes of you. A crying, lying, spoiled little baby!" He shoved him further up the wall. "Self-righteous and arrogant. You cower in the mud, thinking this dirt hole makes you a man! What did you pay for it? What did you give?"

"Nothing! I've abandoned all of my possessions!" the young man cried. "I am a mound dweller! I am my own man!"

"You are another spoiled little Royal who will return home with his tail between his legs sooner or later. I've seen your kind before." Venir got nose to nose with the young man. "I bet one of these mounds is full of possessions and another one has my friend. Now you listen to me. You're a liar! A robber! And worst of all, you are a Royal. I hate Royals!" He squeezed the man's head until his eyes bulged. "Whatever wrong your family inflicted on you is nothing compared to what they inflicted on me. Now tell me with a blink, are you going to take me to my friend or not?"

The man blinked repeatedly.

Venir dropped him to the ground.

The mage landed on his knees in a fit of coughing and gagging. It took him several moments to regain his composure. Wheezing, he finally said, "You hate the Royals too?"

Venir glared at him.

"Sorry." The young man raised is hands. "Your friend is near, but not here. They moved out, to sacrifice him on the morrow."

"Sacrifice?"

CHAPTER 25

THE STIFF, HOT WINDS TORE at Melegal's clothes and face. Even with a cowl covering his head from the nose down, it took every ounce of concentration to keep his eyes fixed on Mikkel. The sand crusted over his face was like tiny shards of glass. He wiped it off constantly, only to have it build up again.

"Does it always storm so much?" he yelled up at Mikkel.

"Just keep moving."

With the wind howling by his ears, he shouted back, "How can you see where you're going?"

"I can't." Mikkel surged onward. "But if we don't keep moving, we'll be buried alive. Do you want to lead?"

"No," Melegal said, but he didn't figure Mikkel heard him. The wind was so loud, he could barely hear himself think. One burning step after the other, he traversed the sun-cracked, will-swallowing landscape until the suns dropped out of the sky and the moons appeared again.

The winds died down.

Mikkel swayed and collapsed into a sitting position. Melegal sat down and leaned against the man, back to back. He said something he rarely ever said: "I'm thirsty."

Mikkel's body rumbled with light laughter.

"It wasn't a jest," Melegal added. He wiped the corners of his eyes and dusted his clothes off. "I don't think even the dead in the ground are so dry."

Shoulders bouncing up and down, Mikkel continued his chuckles.

Great. He's delirious. I bet we're even farther away than we were before. "Do we even know where we are?"

Still rumbling, Mikkel reached over, clipped his fingers under Melegal's chin, and twisted the thief's head around.

In the distance, standing alone in the vast wasteland silhouetted against the blackening sky, he could make out the stark outline of the humongous walls of a great city.

"Bone!" Melegal exclaimed. He moved his body alongside Mikkel's. "Tell me this isn't a mirage I see."

"It isn't."

"I'm home." Using Mikkel's body for support, he managed his way back up to his feet. Ignoring the fire and aching inside his boots, he stumbled onward. "Oh, thank the Lords of Wine. I'm home!"

CHAPTER 26

A N ORC LAY DEAD AND smoking on the ground. The urchlings were picking at its flesh. Collo the gnoll's stomach churned. He thought he'd seen the worst of everything Bish had to offer, but there was nothing to compare with the urchling. Black, carnal, and savage, the spoiled offspring of the underlings were terror.

"Explain to me what happened again." Oran the underling cleric stood on a rock, eye to eye with him. His violet gemstone eyes burned with a deep, evil fire. The snarl on his face was cruel. His fingertips glowed with a fire of their own.

Collo pulled at the collar on his neck, glanced back at his orcs, who were staring at their comrade's corpse, and refaced Oran. "We followed the man's trail through the jungle into the edge of the Outland and lost it again just outside the great forest of Bish. I doubled back and found a second trail, and it led me here." He took a glimpse at Oran's fingers and swallowed. "The trail is still fresh and leads into the Red Clay Forest. There are witnesses."

"And yet you dally here." Oran laid his hands on Collo's shoulders. His hands glowed with new life. The metal armor on the gnoll's shoulders turned furnace-hot red. "Are you wasting my time, Collo? I was of the impression you were a formidable hunter. One of the best. You don't desire more treasure, do you? What did you do, squander it on trollops and greasy man food?"

Face dripping with sweat and armor searing his skin, Collo maintained his poise. "I have it all. Not one stone spent. Not even on supplies, underling lord."

Oran lifted his hands. The metal armor cooled. "You have the discipline of a loyal dog. Fortunately for you, that's still useful. Tell me more."

Collo nodded at one of his orcs. Behind him was the backdrop of the Red Clay Village. Most of the huts and cabins were burning, and the villagers were in a scramble to put the fires out.

Grappled in his arms, the orc had a man, one of the villagers. He stood the man beside Collo.

Knees shaking, the villager stared at the ground.

"Tell us what you saw," Collo said to the man.

The man's jaw trembled, and no words came out.

Collo bent the man's ear and lifted him onto the tips of his toes. "Tell us!"

"Five! Five men! The one with the hair of flame and scales of a black fish ventured into the forest. The yellow hair, Venir we call him, went after him. The other three journey the Outlands to Bone."

"Interesting." Oran rubbed the stubble between his bottom lip and chin. "And you are certain of this? Remember, oh man of the top, your life and the life of your village depend on it."

"I swear it! I swear it!" The man's stare was fixed on the urchlings, who were tearing into the orc. He shook uncontrollably. He tried to speak again, but his teeth clattered too much.

"Let him go try to douse the fires of his home." Oran shoed the man away with a flip of his wrist. "Go, human. Go, and remember an underling showed you mercy today."

Collo let go of the man's collar.

The man backpedaled, fell, and took off toward the village at a brisk trot.

"Mercy, eh?" Collo said.

Oran made a *chit* sound.

The urchlings' heads popped up out of their feeding frenzy.

He pointed at the man running away on wobbly legs. "Chit-Chit!"

Two urchlings sprang away from the orcen prey. On all fours, they ran with the speed of wild cats.

The running man looked back just in time to let out one final scream.

The urchlings pounced. The high grasses became wet with blood.

Oran let out a little chuckle. "Mercy, heh. Mercy from me, maybe, but no mercy from the urchlings."

"So you are convinced then?" Collo was feeling confident about his accomplishment. They had lost the trail, yes, but he'd been wise enough to double back where he'd last closed in on them. It hadn't taken long for the dogs to pick up the new trail. "Shall we finish off this village or renew our pursuit?"

With the flames reflecting in his eyes, Oran said, "I don't want to waste any time. The village will be the prize when we have captured our prey. They aren't going anywhere. The fires will keep them busy."

Collo nodded and turned his back. "Rally up, orcs! It's time to take our hunt into the forest!"

"Take us to the place where your dogs found the scent."

Near the forest edge, the dogs and their orc handlers waited in the dimness of the night. The handlers pulled the dogs away when the urchlings arrived. With their wet noses pressed to the ground, they sniffed and snorted.

"They have the scent," Oran said with a nod. "It shouldn't be long now. When you finish, bring the enemy back to me."

"Are you not coming?" Collo said.

"Into Red Clay?" Oran took a look up into the great branches and shook his head. "I'm a full-blooded underling. I dare not. These urchlings are now your charges, Collo. Find those men and bring them back to me. If you fail, remember I have many more urchlings. Now go."

"As you say." Collo dug his heels into his horse and headed into the forest. "Turn loose the dogs."

Unleashed, the dogs took off at a sprint. The urchlings were right behind them.

CHAPTER 27

"WHO IS THIS, VENIR?" LAIYN'S eyes were on the young mound dweller.

Both Venir and the young man had snaked their way out of the mound holes and were back outside again.

"A lost little wretch I found squirming around in that pile." Venir had the young man sitting on the ground and was tying his hands behind his back. "He says he knows where my friend is, and he's going to take me right to him." He tapped the fellow on the head with his knuckle. "Aren't you."

"I will. I will." The young man couldn't stop staring at Laiyn. "Who are you?"

Laiyn held Brool in her hands. "I am your slayer. I've come to kill all the fiends who live in those holes." She poked the spike at him. "I think I'll start with your lusty eyes. You are not worthy to see me."

The young man pushed back into Venir.

Securing the man's bonds, Venir took his axe from Laiyn. "You'd make an excellent lumberjack. Maybe later I'll show you how to put your back into a swing." He yanked the young man up to his feet. "Lead."

Following the path in the direction the forest magi had gone earlier, the young man led the way, saying to Venir, "I am Gannon. Listen, warrior. If it's not too late and your friend lives, I wish to depart from this forest with you."

"Why is that?" Venir said. "Do you miss your home?"

Gannon walked backward and said with a skip to his trot, "You and I have something in common. We hate the Royals. We could team up together. We could go back to Bone and stick it to them."

Venir shoved him around. "The only one going to get stuck is you. Now keep quiet."

The man sealed his lips and kept on moving. Venir kept a close eye on him and the woman. He didn't trust either of them. They were strange. The kind of strange where they deserved one another. Weaving through the trees, Venir tried to spot signs of the forest magi's passage. He didn't see a thing. Their ability to float gave them a stealthy advantage, so as much as he hated to admit it, he'd have to rely on Gannon. For now.

"Can you float like the others?" Laiyn asked.

"I cannot." Gannon shrugged his brows at her. "But I feel more as if I'm floating the longer I soak in your beauty."

"Oh, how sweet." She caught up to Gannon and patted his back. "Tell me more?"

"Certainly."

Without even looking, Venir waited for the scream.

"Yah!" Gannon cried out. He backpedaled and smacked into a tree. Watching Laiyn, struggling in his bonds, and yelling, he said to Venir, "Watch out, stranger! A woodland witch is upon us! She's—it's horrifying!"

Venir caught Laiyn's face just as it shifted back to normal. "She looks fine to me." He picked Gannon up by the armpits. "Keep moving."

Huffing for breath, Gannon did a double take at Laiyn. Finally, he averted his eyes in what Venir took to be a permanent effort to never look her way again.

After moving on for an hour, Gannon again broke his silence. "Venir, is it? Venir, if you take me from this place, I'll pay you well."

"What are you talking about?"

With a long face, Gannon continued. "I can't leave. They won't let me. And I've failed to learn their skills. I can't float or summon any magic. I'm nothing but a slave in their dirty little world." He sighed. "I want to return to Bone."

"Then you're going to have to man up and do it on your own, so judging by the looks of you, you'll be living in the dirt forever." Venir plucked a bug from his back and flicked it away. "Once I see my friend, I suggest that if you want to go, then you need to scurry out of here on your own."

"I can't leave. I've tried. They'll find me. That's why I need you. I believe you're here to rescue me."

Laiyn let out a little laugh. "This one is truly sad. I can't believe the forest hasn't spit him out. The sound of his voice makes me want to vomit."

Moving on, the three of them picked their way through some new terrain where boulders popped up among the trees. The forest became quiet.

Gannon came to a stop. "We're close."

"How close?"

Pointing with his chin, Gannon said, "Where the ground rises through this pass, it quickly falls again, creating a ravine that dead ends on the other side. It's a special place to them. A grove of ceremonies. There's a creature too. They aim to feed your friend to it."

"What kind of creature?"

"I don't know. I haven't seen it, but it's one of many they worship."

"If it has fur," Laiyn said to Venir, "then you had better not harm it."

Venir took off his rucksack, withdrew his mystic sack, and jammed Helm on his head. "As long as it doesn't try to harm me or my friend, it should be fine."

Gannon's eyes were wide as saucers and frozen on Venir's face. "Who in Bish are you?"

"Get up the hill."

Without hesitation, Gannon scrambled up the hill.

Like he had said, on the other side of the rocks at the top, a steep ravine went down. Voices caught Venir's ears, moaning and hooting similar to what he had heard before.

Laiyn took ahold of his arm. Goosebumps covered her arms up to her elbows. "I fear," she said.

Venir made his way down into the ravine, leaving the pair of them behind. He was halfway down in the depths when the ravine floor opened up below.

The forest magi were at the bottom. Formed in a half circle facing the other side of the grove, they swayed like trees bending in a powerful breeze, holding hands and moaning in a deep trance. In front of them, a prone figure was rising from the ground. It was Nath. He hovered higher and higher, parallel to the ground and not moving. His long red hair waved beneath his head.

On the backside of the ravine, something Venir couldn't see moved among the trees. It shook the branches and leaves. His blood froze.

The biggest spider he ever saw squeezed through the trees. Venom dripped from its maw. Its many eyes were red stones of evil.

Venir buckled his chinstrap.

Fight or die.

CHAPTER 28

Venir hit the bottom of the ravine, making a rustle. Several of the forest magi turned and let out howls. In an instant, they swooped after him. Sharpened twigs shot out from the sleeves of their robes, flying through the air with lives of their own. He jerked his shield up. The strange darts clattered onto his shield and stuck. He tilted it over and peeked at the twigs. They'd turned into green and yellow caterpillars as big as his fingers. They had sharp little teeth and crawled fast.

"Bone!" he roared.

More caterpillars burst from the ground like a bed of new grass, clinging to his boots and chewing at them. This brought to the warrior the kind of fear that would choke a normal man to death. That would gnaw his will away, bit by bit, until he was nothing but bone. But a warrior didn't have time to be scared. He only had time to act.

With the little monsters crawling up to his knees, Venir focused on the magi responsible. He yelled at them, "You might take me bit by bit, but I'm going to take you limb by limb."

The forest magi who had been floating tall a moment ago drifted away. They muttered. Their hands flailed.

It was too late.

Venir came upon them with his axe. With one mighty swing after the other, he turned the closest mage into fertilizer. Brool ripped through its entire body.

"Let your bugs feast on you, then!"

He bore down on one right after the other. His axe bit into one's neck with a loud, life-ending chop. Razor-sharp steel became a tornado of death. Venir spiked one through the chest. With a lightning-quick back swing, he decapitated another.

Their bodies didn't fall to the ground. Instead, they kept floating.

Blood dripping from his blade, he hunted after the next one.

Some of the magi were scrambling for their escape. Like a frightened heard of cattle, they floated up and out of the ravine's steep climb.

It left Venir alone in the hulking shadow of the giant tarantula-like spider.

The thing towered at least twenty feet high. Its eyes were fixed on Nath, but its spinnerets were busy encasing Nath.

Venir flung himself at the monster. He chopped the first leg out from under it.

The spider made an angry screech and squared off on him, spitting tiny balls of acid from its mouth. "Eeeeee!"

Venir covered up with his shield and screamed, "Geeeeaaaaah!"

The acid was eating into the flesh on his arms.

It was the point of no return. With a white-knuckled grip on his axe and a jaw set in stone, Venir slung away his shield and attacked the monster with long and powerful two-handed swings into its legs.

Chop! Chop! Chop!

The hard exoskeleton of the spider's spiny legs gave in to the whistling steel. The monster teetered to its side. Screeching and flailing, it clawed and spat acid at Venir.

Moving like a hungry jungle cat going for the kill, Venir climbed up the bulk of the spider's body and hacked at it like a berserk lumberjack chopping wood. It was one devastating swing after the other. Hands over head. Up and down.

Chop! Chop! Chop! Chop!

Right through the hard shell, he carved a canoe into its body and started sinking into its collapsing flesh.

The spider twitched and convulsed. It was fighting, but without control of its own body.

Venir waded through the goo on its back and sank Brool's spike into the back of its head.

Glitch!

It twitched no more.

Venir hopped off of the insect's husk, laboring for breath. Something was biting his arms. It was the caterpillars.

"Slat!"

He started picking them off his skin and flicking them away.

"Let me help," someone said.

He whirled. It was Laiyn, with Gannon running right behind her. Their faces were lit up with astonishment. Somewhere along the line, she had untied Gannon's bonds. He was going to have to have a word with her. Later.

Whispering unintelligible words, she combed her hands over his body.

The bugs fell away.

"You'll be fine now," she said to him. "You should spend some time in the stream to get the goo off."

Venir checked himself. Bug guts and blood were splattered all over him.

Gannon gawked at the spider's head, which was as tall as him. "I-I can't believe you killed it. I thought for certain I was going to witness your death. Huh. I actually felt sorry for the spider in the end."

Scanning the area, Venir noticed none of the magi were still around. "Are there any more?"

"The only one who wasn't terrified enough to run was this one," Gannon replied from somewhere on the other side of the spider. "Come look."

Giving Laiyn a stern look, Venir made his way around to the other side of the spider.

The charred skeleton of what Venir presumed to be a forest mage was just outside the brush that edged the rim of the grove—on its knees with fingers locked around Nath's neck.

Nath's sword was stuck tip first in the ground.

"What happened to him?" Laiyn said.

"That sword doesn't like certain people. It's hot as fire to the touch of most who are not its owner. I've seen it burn men but never kill them."

Gannon fell to his knees and spread his arms out around the great blade. "Ah, it's magic. No wonder he wouldn't release it. This ground dweller felt the powerful magic, and his obsession would not let him let go." He stretched out his finger and touched one of the dragon crossguards. "Ouch!" He blew on his finger. "It sizzles."

"Find something to wrap it up with," Venir ordered. He headed over to Nath, who had taken a hard landing and lay flat-backed on the ground. His eyes were closed, but he was breathing. Taking a knee, he gave Nath a firm shake on the shoulder. "Wake up, man. It's time to go."

Nath remained as still as a stone. His creaseless face was almost serene.

Venir slapped his cheek with the backside of his hand.

Nath didn't flinch.

Venir looked up at Laiyn, who'd kneeled on the other side of Nath. "He sleeps like the dead."

Tracing the black scales on Nath's arms with her fingers, she said, "He's so magnificent. I've never seen such a man before. Where's your friend from?"

He picked Nath up in his arms and threw him over his shoulder in a fireman's carry. "Another world. Goodbye."

CHAPTER 29

Venir didn't have any luck convincing Laiyn and Gannon to stay behind. They walked after him like a pair of puppies, wide-eyed and asking too many questions. Laiyn was practically skipping, and she couldn't stay away from Nath.

"What do you mean, 'another world'?" She ran her fingers through Nath's long, silky red locks. "Are they all so marvelous in his world? Where is it? Is it beyond the Mist?"

Helm off and remaining silent, Venir resumed his trek, huffing up one hill and down another in the weird forest until his calves ached. Nath was heavy, like two men in one. Cresting the next hill, he shoulder-tossed Nath onto the ground and leaned him against a tree, then wiped the sweat from his own eyes with his forearm. "They must make them out of lead where he comes from. Carrying him is like carrying a bag of iron." He took a long drink from his water skin. "Ah."

"Why does he sleep?" Laiyn had snuggled beside Nath and was hugging his arm. "Are they heavy sleepers where he's from?"

"I have no idea." Venir turned his attention to Gannon. The young mound dweller had the sword wrapped up in a dead forest mage's robes and held it in his arms like a log. "Is this something your brood did?"

"There are some toxins they use, but not any to make one sleep. Not to this effect." Gannon grimaced. "Can I set this down? It doesn't burn, but it's still hot."

Venir shrugged.

Gannon dropped the sword and rubbed his arms. "Thanks!"

"So if you don't know this man so well," Laiyn asked, "then why have you gone to so much trouble to find him? Does he owe you money?"

Arms crossed over his chest, Gannon piped in. "Yeah, it's about money, isn't it. He owes you a debt or he has a treasure. Hah!" He slapped his head. "I knew it. I should have known by this sword. The man's wealthy, obviously, and there's a reward for him. And you're some sort of man hunter, aren't you."

With all eyes on him, Venir said, "That's right." He walked up on Gannon's toes, looked down at him, and said, "Is there a problem with that?"

Gannon swallowed, shrank away, and said, "No."

Moving away, Venir shook Nath again.

Laiyn slapped his hands away. "Don't do that. He's resting."

"He needs to wake up. I'm tired of carrying him." Venir could see that Gannon and Laiyn had formed an odd alliance against him. In some bizarre sort of way, they had decided they were going to protect Nath from him. "Why does this always happen?"

"Why does what always happen?" Laiyn asked.

"Nothing." Venir took another drink and capped his skin off. He slung it over his back. "Before the two of you dirt urchins decide to try something against me, this man is no Royal, and he has no treasure. He's lost, and I'm all he's got. I don't know why I'm helping him, but I am. I can't explain why."

"Sounds like a lie to me," Gannon said under his breath.

"What?" Venir replied.

Biting his nails, Gannon said, "Nothing."

Venir picked up the sword draped in old robes. Gannon wasn't lying. It actually was very warm to the touch. He took the sword and set it down beside Nath, then opened up Nath's palm and eased the sword grip toward it.

"What are you doing? Are you trying to burn him?" Laiyn said.

Venir rolled his eyes. "It's his sword. Perhaps it can wake him."

"That is the most ignorant thing I ever heard!" Gannon yelled.

Irritated, Venir said, "Why are you yelling?"

"It's appropriate." Gannon eased back and averted his eyes. "He's defenseless."

"Listen to me," Venir growled. "If either of you interfere with anything I do again, I'm going to pin you to a tree." He looked where Brool lay nearby and right back at them. "I mean it."

Pulling her hands back and brushing the hair out of Nath's eyes, Laiyn said, "Just be careful. I don't want you to hurt him."

Venir placed Fang's grip in the palm of Nath's hand.

Gannon and Laiyn crowded in.

He hoped the sword would give Nath a spark of life. A jolt. After all, he'd seen Fang do some incredible things. Venir folded the man's fingers around the grip and held them there in a tight fist. He let go. Nath's fingers held their place.

Drumming on Venir's shoulders, Gannon was jumping up and down like a little kid. "He holds it! He holds it!"

Venir cast a glance back at the young man.

He stuck his hands behind his back. "Sorry."

Nath's fingers fell back open.

"So much for that," Venir said. "Gannon, those ground dwellers, will they be coming after us?"

"After the show you put on? I'd say not unless they want the magic in the sword that bad. Seeing how it turned one of them to ashes, I just don't think they'd trifle with it again, but one never knows with them. They are strong in numbers, but for the most part, they are cowards. Bullies, so to speak."

"Ah, well, being a Royal yourself, I'm sure you fit in quite well."

"I'm of a good house," Gannon said with a frown.

"Then why did you leave?" Laiyn asked.

Picking at some leaves hanging from a tree with a guilty look, Gannon said, "I had my reasons."

Venir picked Nath up and slung him over his shoulder again, saying to Gannon, "Now who's the liar."

"What do you mean? I didn't lie about anything."

"Didn't you just say you came from a good Royal house?" Venir said.

"Yes."

"There's no such thing as a good Royal house." Venir resumed his trek.

Right on his heels, Laiyn said back at Gannon, "I agree with him."

After another mile of travel, Venir had a question for Gannon. "I'm curious. You say the magi are cowards. This man I carry is formidable. How did they capture him?"

Gannon had a crooked smile on his lips. "They didn't. He was lying there asleep, the same way we just found him. But you should have heard them boast about it." He got Venir's attention on Laiyn. She was on her knees in a deep trance, with her fingers dug in the ground. Her eyes were up in her head. "What is she doing?"

Venir shrugged

All of a sudden, Laiyn's lips parted, and she said, "Danger is coming."

CHAPTER 30

WITH NATH STILL HANGING OVER his shoulder, Venir managed to jam Helm back onto his head, where it pulsated. His senses went on high alert. He could see a vision of dark creatures racing through the forest. They weren't underlings but something like underlings. He didn't think underlings could come into the Red Clay Forest. It was a sanctuary away from them.

"Something is indeed coming. I can feel it. It's closing in but still far away." Venir had a decent knowledge of the terrain, but it wasn't the best, as he'd only been in Red Clay a few times before. They needed sanctuary, a little deeper inside its zone. He shook Laiyn. She snapped out of her trance. Despite Helm urging him to stay and battle, he said, "We need to hide."

She was shaking her head. "There are many invaders. Very many. You've brought nothing but trouble to this forest." She raced over to Venir and held Nath's face. "But we must protect this man. Come."

Venir followed her. The lithe woman cut through the woodland with the grace of a young deer, splitting through the trees and snaking through the brush. Chasing after her fleet feet, Venir matched her stride for stride, but the man on his back was getting heavier with every step. His lungs started to burn just as they reached a steep climb.

"Hurry, hurry!" she said back to Venir. She had doubled back, and she took him by the arm.

The hill was filled with an assortment of trees in thicket after thicket. She tried to avoid the thickets. Her frame was small, making it easy for her to pass unnoticed. But moving so fast, and with a man on his back, Venir threw his natural caution aside. He crashed through the brush when it couldn't be avoided and surged up to the high ground. It left a trail a blind halfling could follow, but time was more important.

Nearing the top, he found Laiyn waiting just outside the mouth of a cave burrowed behind the trees, well concealed by ferns and moss-covered rocks. Venir ducked down and stepped inside. The cave stretched back into the darkness.

"What is this?" he said to her.

"There are caves like this all over. It's the safest spot I could recall. A great one lived here once before. He'll not bother us if we don't bother him."

Setting Nath down, Venir asked, "A great what?"

"Yes, a great what?" Gannon said with eyes the size of the moons.

"Just a grizzly." She sniffed. "He sleeps deep if he sleeps at all."

Venir buckled Helm onto his head and readied Brool, saying to Laiyn and Gannon, "Stay with him. I'll be back."

Huddled over Nath, Laiyn said, "But there are so many. I saw them. And those things. Those things are so evil. I felt them. The forest feels them. It doesn't like them. They're dangerous. Be careful."

Without a glance back, Venir spun his axe handle in his hands and left the cave. Heading back down the hill with his boots digging into the dirt, he let Helm guide him where he needed to go. The farther he went, the more energy he felt coursing through his veins. With the setting suns' light creeping through the leaves above him, he came to a stop just outside the daylight, hunkered down, and waited.

Something was coming. He could feel it. Hear it. Less than a hundred yards away, the hunters stalked along the trail Venir and company had left. There were dogs panting. The gear on the horses made soft jangles, and there was a nicker from time to time. Huddled in the brush with Helm on his head hungering for a fight, Venir put it together.

Collo the gnoll had caught up with him, and he had help now. Underling help. It made Venir sick to his stomach. No matter how undesirable some of the races might be, none of them should ever work with the underlings. The black fiends never showed mercy to anyone, not even gnolls or orcs. But of late, the underlings were working more with the races. He'd seen it before, with Jarla the Brigand Queen. Now even more were selling out to the underlings. What had Bish come to? He squeezed the haft of his axe.

Side with underlings, then you are an underling. No one will be spared.

The metal panther began his hunt. Breaking free of the brush, with the aid of the armament, he moved ahead on silent feet. Trusting Helm's directions, he crept up behind a dark figure huddled in the forest. The creature was bare chested and corded in sinew. It had the natural build of a savage predator. It held its head low, and its ears were pinned down as it sniffed and snorted the ground. It was an underling. What kind of underling Venir didn't know. But it was alone. A scout.

Let's find out how you bleed.

Venir waded into the backside of the monster and ran his axe spike first through its back. The subtle hump in its back straightened and its arms flung outward. It thrashed for a moment and died. He gave it a quick study. The monster had claws like a wolverine and the wide nostrils of a bloodhound. Its skull was smaller than that of most underlings, but its brow protruded.

You can die. You can all die.

Venir left the body where it lay and headed for the next mark. Helm urged him in several different directions, which told him the search party had fanned out. The strange underling monsters were in the lead. He caught sight of one's head popping up among the plants and moved toward it. Lining himself up alongside a tree, Venir grabbed a stick off the ground and tossed it.

The strange little underling pounced to the spot.

Venir snuck behind it and let Brool sing. The blade tore its head from its shoulders. Moving quickly, Venir couldn't pass up the opportunity to taunt the enemy. He took the underling head and hung it in the branches for all to see. He gave it a little push and let it swing.

Let's give those orcs a little something else to think about. Try to put the fear in me, I'll put the fear in you.

Using the forest for cover, he followed Helm's urgings and his own hatred for the underlings to track down another pair. The two of them were spread out by several yards, and he tried the same tactic again. He picked up a stone from the ground and slung it into a tree. It hit with a notable *clok*.

The underlings tore through the foliage, heading for the spot. Venir slipped right in behind them and swung.

Slice!

There was dark blood.

Slice!

There was quick death.

Helm surged a warning, and Venir whirled. Two of them appeared in the brush. One of them let out a shrill howl like a monkey gone mad. The nearest one charged like a lion. All of a sudden the forest came to life. Orcs hollered and horses charged the thickets.

Everyone who hunted Venir was closing in.

CHAPTER 31

WITH A HOWL OF HIS own, Venir took it to them. Running full speed, he ripped an underhanded swing up from the ground and severed the closest one's lashing hand.

It cried out, bleeding, but gave chase.

Not slowing, Venir bore down on the next. Just as he closed in to swing, two more appeared in the clearing. Venir hacked the closest one down and kept running.

His one-handed pursuer jumped onto his back and sank its teeth into the meat on his shoulder.

Venir flung it to the ground and gored it in the chest.

Glitch!

These little underlings were fast. Like wild dogs, they were on his heels in moments.

Venir didn't want to slow. He didn't dare stop. Being flatfooted was the last thing he needed with so many attackers.

No, my tactic is to move. Move fast and use surprise.

An orc on horseback cut into his path and jabbed a spear at him.

Venir knocked the weapon aside with his shield and bull rushed the horse. He lowered his shoulder and hit it like a ram.

The horse reared up and tossed its rider.

Venir kept running, fighting Helm's urgings to stay and fight.

Control it! Control it!

With the branches slapping against him and a pack of what he figured were young underlings on his heels, Venir surged on. Dogs barked. Horses whinnied. Orcs were shouting out commands. The forest had become a fox hunt, and he was the fox. Jettisoning himself between a pair of trees, he happened upon a pair of orcs with their swords drawn.

They turned just as he blindsided them. He cut one across the chest, spinning it to the ground, and kept on running.

Something clipped his heel, tripping him up, and his shoulder collided with a tree. Fighting for balance, he regained his feet and cut at the nearest attacker.

An underling launched itself from the ground with its wide jaw hanging open and claws out.

Venir split its face. Wrenching his blade free, he prepared another swing.

Two fastened themselves to his body.

"Argh!" he screamed.

Claws and teeth tore at him. His flesh burned from lancing pain.

Dropping his shield, he caught one in a headlock and crushed its neck in the crook of his powerful arm.

Eyes bulging from the sockets, it sputtered and spat. Its muscles gave. Its neck snapped.

He dropped the corpse on the forest floor, found a patch of hair on the second one, and ripped its biting mouth from his leg. He pinned the little monster down to the ground with his boot and stuck it again and again with Brool's spike.

Coated in his own blood and sucking for breath, he picked up his shield and trotted away from the oncoming chase. The voices of his enemies were getting louder. More were closing in.

Bone! How many of them are there?

On the prowl, Venir managed to circle back on his pursuers and charge their flank. He hit an unsuspecting orc with everything he had, sending it to the grave in two pieces.

Out of nowhere, a towering figure riding high in the saddle came upon him.

Venir snapped his shield up.

The horse and rider trampled him and flattened him on the ground.

It jarred his bones. Helm rang. But on woozy legs, he managed to make it back to his feet just as the rider wheeled his horse back around.

It was the gnoll, Collo. He was as big a gnoll as Venir had ever seen. Dog headed and packed with muscle, the man hunter drew his bastard sword and spurred his mount into a charge.

Venir ran right at him. "Yaaaaaaaaah!"

The rider's sword came down.

Venir's shield came up.

Metal crashed into metal.

Clang!

Striking like a snake, Venir swatted the horse's red flank with the flat edge of his axe.

The beast reared up, but the rider didn't fall. Instead, the rider pulled the horse around and hit Venir with its backside and knocked him from his feet.

Venir sprang back up. He was surrounded. There were orcs, riders, dogs, and a horde of little underlings. It was more heads than Venir could count.

"You're finished, outlander!" Collo said. "Be wise and surrender." The gnoll tilted his head. His lips curled up over his teeth. "The helmet you wear. It's familiar. You must be the one I heard about. Venir."

Venir's heart raced with the fuel of battle. "Why don't you come and take a closer look?"

"The view is fine from where I am. There is quite a reward for you and the other man. Your bodies will be enough to feed me for a lifetime." Collo led his horse back out of Venir's range. "Before I vanquish you, I want you to know I'm grateful."

"Just to be clear, Collo, the only one of us two getting out of this forest alive is me." Blood dripped from his axe. "Now let's stop talking and get this battle started." Venir rushed the horse and rider.

With a sharp whistle from Collo, the underlings took off after Venir at a dead sprint. They closed the gap in a second and flung their bodies into him.

Venir killed one in midair with his axe. He dropped his shield and drew his knife. With fists full of steel, he carved into the rabid horde.

The fiends were wild fighters. They cut loose like caged and starving animals.

Venir matched their ferocity. Helm fed him. Energy. Speed. He became a boundless pylon of power. A whirling death machine. Venir loosed this havoc on them.

The fearless underlings fell in ones and twos. Their bodies were gashed and broken.

Venir swung and swung until none moved.

Hot eyed, he stared through Helm's dark eyelets at the orcs and the gnoll seated in the saddle. "Who's next?"

From behind him, a pair of orcs tossed a net over him.

Venir chopped halfway through the mess, but it wasn't enough.

Spurred into action by the orcs, the horses bolted and ripped Venir's legs out from under him.

Collo barked out new orders. "Follow the trail up the hill. I want the other one. I want him now. This hunt is over."

Tangled in the net, Venir sawed at his bonds with his knife. Bumped and jostled, he couldn't get free of his entanglement in time. The horses thundered through the forest, getting farther and farther away. He was going to lose Nath again if he didn't do something quick. He sat up in the net, freed Brool, and started hacking.

The ropes split and frayed.

The horses slowed.

The orc riders risked a look. Seeing what Venir was doing, they brought the horses to a halt. Each of them jumped off and readied its spear. Lowering the sharp heads of their weapons, they came in low and fast.

Still muddled in the mess, Venir was stuck with nowhere else to go. He yelled at them. "If you want to stick me like a pig, then have at me, pigs!" He swatted his axe.

They stabbed like boar hunters. The head of a spear bit deep into his leg.

He bled. He bled a lot. "Aarrgh!"

CHAPTER 32

GANNON STOOD JUST INSIDE THE mouth of the cave. His fingers twitched at his sides. Casting a nervous glance back at Laiyn, he said in a low, excited voice, "I hear someone coming. Horses and riders." He scurried back into the cave. "What do we do?"

Petting Nath's face, she said, "We protect him. Stay here." She headed back outside and turned her ear. Her heart raced. The man, Venir, had lost, and now it was up to her. Pursing her lips, she let out a soft whistle. An enlightening sensation spilled over her body as she became one with her surroundings. She sent out a command to the trees, bushes, and vines. There was life in them. Life she could communicate with. Her whistles gave it new purpose.

The vegetation stirred. The bugs in the ground crept and crawled. As the riders and hounds came closer, she concealed her body in a tree nook. Her skin changed to blend in with the bark.

Come, invaders. Come and play.

Two orcs came up the hill with a pair of dogs straining against their leashes. Saliva dripped from their jaws. They crested the hill and stood just yards away from the entrance to the cave.

A hum started in the ground and rose up into the branches. Roots tore loose from the earth and seized both man and beast.

The startled orcs let out howls and tried to chop their heavy blades into the roots that entwined their legs.

I have you!

The orcs yelled. The dogs yelped.

The roots and branches dragged them to the ground.

Fighting with desperate stretches, the orcs thrashed against the unnatural bonds and were ripping themselves free. One orc chopped. The other pulled. It was a tactic working with success.

Curse them!

Laiyn made a bird-like chirp.

Let it rain death on them.

Every bug on legs or with wings fell from the trees above onto the orcs. In seconds, they were covered from head to toe in stings and bites.

The orcs slapped and swatted. They opened their mouths to scream. The insects filled them.

Perfect.

A mountain of a figure thundered up the hill on a horse as big as any she'd seen. It was a gnoll, and as casually as he would on a stroll through a garden, he dismounted with a great sword in his hand.

The roots burst from the ground and grappled his legs.

Using his strength and heavy frame, the gnoll waltzed through them, snapping them like minor nuisances. He would not be stopped. Lips sealed, he ignored the bugs that clung to his powerful frame and waded toward the cave entrance.

No!

Laiyn came out of hiding and rushed at the gnoll. "Stop! You will not go in there!"

The gnoll stopped and turned.

She transformed into the ugliest hag anyone had ever seen and let out a shriek. A jetting puff of white dust spilled from her mouth.

Collo cowered for a moment then backhanded her silly.

She spun to the ground, dizzy and in pain. All she could see was his feet marching into the cave.

I have to stop him. I can't let him hurt that defenseless man!

With everything she had in her, she scrambled on legs like noodles into the cave. She rushed right past the gnoll and dove on top of Nath's body. "Stay away from him! Stay away!"

Gannon cut the gnoll off.

Collo ran him through with his sword and flung him aside. Face covered in bugs, he sneered down at Laiyn. "If you want to live, move. The man on the ground is mine."

"Never!" she screamed.

"No time to waste. I'll skewer the both of you together then and fling your corpse aside." He stepped closer, and with his hands on the grip and the sword tip down, he plunged.

CHAPTER 33

ATTLING WITH HIS AXE SWINGING from side to side, Venir fought on. The orcs were crafty hunters, toying with their prey, waiting for a mistake.

"Come on!" Venir yelled. "Have at me!"

Huffing for breath, he felt his iron strength slipping from his limbs. With all the nearby underlings dead, Helm's hunger was satisfied. It fueled him no more. No more throbbing. No more surge. He was a man wielding ornate metal. It was his strength and skill against those of the brutish orcs.

The orcs made a move. They deviated from a flanking attack and instead positioned themselves in front of him and behind. The one with a sawed off ear took a fierce jab at his chest.

Also changing tactics, Venir leaned to the side and snatched the orc right behind its head and held it fast. He shifted left. Too late.

The orc with more hair on his arms than on his head buried the tip of a spear in the meat of Venir's shoulder. Only his armor stopped the spear tip from going straight through.

Gritting his teeth, he tugged the other orc to the ground and started punching its head. "One of you might get me, but not before I get one of you!" He beat the orc unconscious. The blood he was losing sapped his strength and blurred his vision. Slowly, he twisted around at the waist.

The last orc was poised, about to deliver the death blow.

"Come on, piglet. Finish it."

The orc's yellow eyes filled with victory, and it let out a howl. It cocked its arms back and advanced.

Thwack!

A feathered arrow pinned itself right through the orc's ears.

Thwack!

A second arrow hit the orc in the neck.

Dropping its spear, it grabbed its throat and backpedaled into the woods.

A huge beast pounced right on top of the orc. It was Chongo.

Venir could only hear his breathing. He fought to keep his head up. "That was close."

Billip stepped into full view. Eyes narrowed, he had another arrow nocked on his bow. "Are there more?"

Somehow managing to lift his chin, Venir said, "Up the hill." He was picking at the net that still dangled over him. His numb fingers struggled at the job.

Billip's fingers went to work for him. In seconds, he had Venir freed. "Bish, man. You're leaking, and leaking fast." He started bandaging the wounds on Venir's legs.

"We need to get up there," Venir said, ripping away from his friend.

"You aren't going anywhere."

Venir clutched the clothing on Billip's shoulder and slowly stood. "I am going."

Chongo treaded over and licked Venir's wounds. The pain on the lacerations burned and tingled.

"That's enough, boy. I'm fine." He was on his feet, but he was swaying.

Billip caught him by the waist. "Venir, you need rest. Me and Chongo will take care of it."

Somewhere, a horse nickered.

Venir stood tall and rolled his shoulders back. "Get me a steed."

CHAPTER 34

NATH'S EYELIDS POPPED OPEN TO a bewildering sight. His scaled fingers were clasped around a very long, very sharp blade poised to run him through along with a woman who was latched onto his body and trembling like a leaf. A drop of saliva dripped onto her back. A gnoll with the shaggy face of a dog stood over them with its jaw hanging open. A gnoll with bugs crawling all over it.

"What's going on here?" Nath asked the woman, who was looking at him. "Who are you, and who is he?"

Her beautiful face filled with wild excitement. "I am Laiyn."

The gnoll put his weight into the sword. It did not budge.

"Who is he and why is he trying to kill us?" Nath asked.

"I am Collo," the gnoll said, "and I am *going* to kill you."

Nath's thoughts were hazy, but his senses were revitalized, his strength renewed. He said to Laiyn, "Excuse me."

She rolled off him.

With the gnoll's sword locked in his hand, he rose to his feet.

Collo kept shoving and shoving.

Nath jerked away. With a punch almost too fast for the eye to see, he sent Collo hard into the cave wall.

All of the wind rushed out of the gnoll, and he gasped for breath.

Nath noticed a fragile-looking young man clutching at his belly. His hands were covered in blood. His head rolled from shoulder to shoulder, and he moaned an awful sound.

Rushing to the man's aid, Nath said to the woman, "And him?"

"Gannon. A friend, perhaps."

On an impulse not fully his own, Nath peeled the young man's hands away and pressed on his belly. A warm rush of energy flowed out of his hands into Gannon.

The young man stiffened. His eyes fluttered. And then he was pawing Nath's arms and looking into his face, yelling, "Goodness! Goodness! Goodness! I'm going to live, aren't I!"

"I suppose." Nath extended his hand. "I'm Nath. It's good to meet you, Gannon."

Collo jumped up onto his feet, snatched his sword, shoved Laiyn into Nath, and sprinted out of the cave.

"Perhaps I should go after him," said Nath, with Laiyn in his arms. He reached for his sword.

Laiyn's fingers caressed his hair. "No, stay with me, Nath. There is nothing to fear from him anymore. You have vanquished him. Stay with me."

"I'm not so sure that leaving enemies alive in this world is a good idea." Cradling the woman in his arms, he made his way to the mouth of the cave. An object flew inside. It bounced off the rock floor and rolled to a stop at Nath's feet.

Laiyn gasped.

It was Collo's head.

Two more men stepped into the cave. One was Venir. He was battle marked from head to toe. Splattered in muck and gore. Billip hung beside the man, bow in hand, covered in sweat, but compared to Venir he was as clean as a whistle. Chongo appeared. His tongues hung out of his mouths, and his tail was wagging.

"What are you doing here?" Nath asked.

"Looking for you." Venir took off his helmet, revealing a blond-haired, blue-eyed face that was clean from the eyes up. "Did you enjoy your nap?"

Nath wasn't sure what to think at the moment. The last thing he remembered was walking through the forest and sampling the wonderful aroma coming from its exotic flowers. It reminded him of some of the places in Nalzambor. There had been a white flower with tiger-like striping with a bloom as full as the size of his head. He had sniffed it, and then he must have passed out. "I'm not sure if I should feel indebted to you. Was I in danger?"

"Do spiders spin webs?" Venir replied. Gritting his teeth, he slid down the cave wall onto its stone floor. He lay his axe across his lap.

"You've suffered many nasty wounds." Nath set Laiyn down, walked over, and touched the gash where the urchlings had tried to gnaw off Venir's leg. "Looks painful. Let me see if I can help." He placed his hands on Venir's wounds and summoned his power.

Nothing came forth. No jolt. No fire. Not a lick of his dragon energy.

Venir gave him an uncomfortable look. "Do you mind removing your hands from me?"

"Sorry, I only wanted to help."

"If you want to help, then don't go running off on your own." Venir lay his head back against the wall and closed his eyes. "It's too dangerous."

"I'll be back," Laiyn said to Nath. She kissed him on the cheek. "I can find some herbs that will help. Come on, Gannon."

"What's she kissing you for?" Venir's head was dipping up and down. "I'm the one who saved your arses."

"I can't say," Nath said.

"Well, you can kiss that one all you want." Venir's eyelids lifted for a moment and closed again. "Let me know in the morning what you wake up with."

Nath took note of the awful scrapes and gashes on the warrior's body. The man wore punishment like a second skin. He said to Venir, "You owe me nothing, Venir. You're an honorable warrior. A tad merciless, but honorable nonetheless. I went off on my own because I didn't want my journey to endanger you or your friends. I'm sure you have your own problems to deal with. This world is full of troubles. Even breathing is a trial."

Billip's nostrils flared. He inhaled a long breath and let it out. "That wasn't so difficult."

"I was referring to the ripe smells lingering in your cities. And whatever it was Venir decided to coat himself in that's just as rotten as a dingy marsh." Nath frowned at the hardened goo covering Venir from feet to waist. "It's disgusting."

Without opening his eyes, Venir's chest rumbled with his laugh. "You should have seen the size of the spider. It would have made a meal of you in one bite. Big thing." He lifted up his axe a hair and waggled it a bit before letting it back down. It was clear he was past his limit. "I got it, though."

Gannon and Laiyn reentered the cave. His hands were full of leaves in a variety of colors. There were mosses too, white and the dull color of a plum. Taking his place near Venir, he said, "That wasn't a spider. It was a gargantuan monster. It was taller than some of the trees. Venir turned it into mashed potatoes." His face soured. "It was nasty. I can still see its legs twitching in my mind."

"Oh, be silent," Laiyn said with her eyes caressing Nath, "and let me take care of this man." Pointing at the plum moss, she said to Gannon, "Put this on the spots where the spider venom scarred his flesh. And this—"

Something deep inside the belly of the cave let out a growl. It sounded like ten bears in one.

Venir's eyes popped open. "What was that?"

Laiyn's response was stone cold. "The grizzly."

CHAPTER 35

A BEAR'S HEAD EMERGED OUT OF the darkness into the dimness. It wasn't some ordinary bear. No, it was a monster, with a head three times the size of a normal bear's. As its hulk scuffled out toward them, Nath's mind struggled to figure out how the animal even fit in the cave.

Billip nocked an arrow on his bowstring. "A good shot in the eye should do it."

But Laiyn stepped up into the archer's path. "No, let me handle this."

Nath caught her by the arm. "Are you sure?"

"Move out, but gracefully." She approached the razorback grizzly with her hands fanned out to her sides, singing a gentle song that pleasantly echoed throughout the hollow of the cave.

The grizzly's mouth opened wide. Saliva dripped from its teeth as if it was looking for its first meal in weeks. Its head was marred with deep scars all over its face. Its black and brown fur had traces of silver and was covered in wounds from dozens if not hundreds of hungry battles. The giant bear let out a roar so loud that all of the men covered their ears.

Laiyn's hair billowed from the blast.

The grizzly was the king, and he was letting everyone know it.

"Laiyn." Venir had one arm slung over Billip's shoulder. "Come on, or that beast will eat you alive."

Her soft but powerful voice kept calling out to the bear in unintelligible lyrics.

The bear's head lowered. The black rims of its lips fell down over its teeth.

Nath got himself under Venir's other shoulder and walked him outside without another glance.

With his hands cupped over his ears, Gannon, whose robes looked like they'd fall away in another breeze, said, "Is she going to make it?"

Birds were flying from all directions and filling the branches in the trees overhead. It was quite a spectacle. Varmints from chipmunks to skunks also huddled nearby. From the brush, deer and spotted elk stuck their necks out.

"That's a sight I never saw the likes of before." Bow ready, Billip swiveled from side to side. "Never in my life have I seen hunting so easy." Aiming for a stag, he pulled the bowstring taut.

Nath tapped him on the shoulder. "I don't think you want to disrupt the moment."

Billip looked over at the grizzly and eased the string back. "I see your point."

Several minutes passed before Laiyn came back out again and the song was gone. A thin film of sweat shone above her arched brows. The animals and birds vanished back into the forest. "He certainly is the monarch of the territory, but I got through to him. My thanks for not making this any worse than it needed to be." She let out a deep breath and smiled at Nath. "He's resting now."

"He looked very hungry to me." Billip slung his bow over his shoulder by its strap. "I don't care to be around when he wakes. Let's get down to the horses. Are you going to make it, Vee?"

Venir nodded. It was about all he could do besides bleed.

Nath said to Laiyn, "I suppose this is it, then?"

Her eyes were filled with him when she said, "Oh no, I'm coming with you as far as my legs will take me."

Nath smiled. He had an instant fondness for the woman. Her voice was as alluring as she was. "I'd like that." Casting a glance at Venir and Billip, he said, "If there are no objections?"

"I can look at a pretty face all day," Billip said. "Just help me get Venir on a horse. You can ride, can't you?"

Venir nodded.

A stir erupted from just inside the cave, where the daylight turned to darkness.

"I thought you said the beast slept?" Nath said to Laiyn.

"He snores," she said. She stood there as pretty as a rainbow in the midst of a soft rain. "Perhaps he needs another lullaby."

Billip was taking Venir down the hill, and Nath was still helping.

A barely audible low growl rolled out of the hollow of the cave.

"Laiyn," said Nath, "come with us. The bear will be fine."

She glanced back at the cave and blew a kiss inside, saying, "Sweet dreams, great one." She faced Nath and walked his way. "And your dreams are about to have a new beginning."

The razorback grizzly burst out of the cave. In a single motion, its clawed paws wrapped up Laiyn's body and stuffed her into its massive jaws as it pulled her out of sight into the cave.

There was a desperate scream, followed by a crunch.

"Laiyn!" Nath yelled. He started for the cave.

Venir's iron grip held him fast. "It's over," Venir managed to say. "Welcome to Bish."

CHAPTER 36

NATH'S HEAD HUNG DOWN. HIS heart was empty. The only life he felt in his limbs was the horse beneath him as they made their trek out of the Red Clay Forest. The beautiful place seemed more haunting now, an exotic world filled with uncertainty and savagery.

On the horses they had rounded up from the man hunters, Nath rode in the rear of the column, with Venir in the middle. The expansive back of Venir was slouched over, and his body rocked slowly in the saddle. The man hadn't said a word in hours. Billip led from the front. His restless eyes scanned the woodland all the time. His bow was ready. Gannon rode just behind him, quiet. But as far as Nath could tell, it was Chongo who led them out of the forest. At least he hoped so, but part of him didn't care.

I can't believe she's gone.

Nath couldn't stop thinking about Laiyn and her horrible end. So savage. So quick. One moment she'd been there, enticing him, and the next she'd been gobbled up in a cruel twist of fate. There was no saving her. She was dead, and with little persuasion, he and the rest of the men had left. There was nothing to be done about it. It was over. The end. Nath didn't even put up an argument.

She at least deserved a burial, but how do you bury somebody who was eaten? We should have sent that bear to the grave.

But deep down he knew the bear wasn't to blame. It was an animal. A predator. It was they who had invaded its space. Still, the guilt weighed heavy on his heart. Nath wasn't used to seeing his comrades die, and even though he'd only known her for a moment, he felt as if he knew her quite well.

He followed, buried in his thoughts, until Billip spoke up. "I see moonlight. I see the Outlands."

They rode out of the forest and crossed over into a barren wasteland of sand dunes and rock. The moons were pearls in the black sky, hovering just above thin layers of clouds. It was quite a contrast from what Nath had become accustomed to in the south. The lush and sweltering greenery was replaced by a harsh and unforgiving land.

Surprisingly, Venir sat tall in the saddle again. "There's not much to look at, but there's not much that's going to cross our path. And the weather looks good for now. We'll keep riding, if you're up to it."

"You aren't going to hear me say I'd rather sleep among the sidewinders and scorpions." Billip guffawed. "I'm ready to ride as far from this skeeter-filled forest as I can."

"We ride then," said Venir. The brisk desert wind appeared to rejuvenate the wounded warrior. The fire was back in his blue eyes when he said to Nath, "To Bone."

"Lead the way," Nath replied.

Gannon rode alongside Nath. With a perplexed look on his face, the young man looked back over his shoulder, gave the forest a long stare, and said to Nath, "I can't believe I'm leaving. I can't believe I'm going back."

Nath gave his reins a flick and followed Billip, Chongo, and Venir. It didn't take long for him to figure out they were in the midst of a long and lonely land like he'd never experienced before. There were some variations in the landscape, but other than that, it was always the same. The boredom of the ride left him contemplating again the jarring death of Laiyn. He decided he couldn't dwell on it and took up a conversation with Gannon.

The young forest mage recruit was a little fish-eyed, but he carried an air about him. His cheekbones were high and his mannerisms polished. With piercing eyes, he sometimes allowed a deeper character to show from beneath the dirt covering his face.

"Why is it you can't believe you're going back?" Nath asked. "Is this City of Bones that bad?"

Gannon laughed. "It's the City of Bone. Not Bones."

Eyebrow perched, Nath asked a question he was not certain he wanted the answer to. "Is it made of bone?"

"It's made of miserable. You'll see." The smile in Gannon's eyes took him to a different place. "And to answer the rest of your question, I can't believe I'm going back because I didn't think I'd ever escape my former mentors. I almost feel like I'm in a dream. I'm going back home. I just never thought it would happen."

Nath nodded. He empathized with what the young man was saying. He just wished he was going home, too. "So, why did you leave?"

"I had a disagreement with my parents."

"Ah," Nath said. It didn't take long for him to reflect on his early days, back when he was barely a hundred years old. He and his father had never had a disagreement, or at least he had never questioned his father's authority, but there'd been too many times when Nath had nodded in agreement and done what he wanted to anyway. It never worked out in his favor. "There's always a price when one ignores the wisdom of his father. Or mother, for that matter. What was the disagreement over? Will you be able to reconcile?"

Gannon's chin sank into his robes. "I don't know, but I think living among the swine would be better now than where I just came from." He shivered. "Those magi are demented. I don't expect forgiveness from my family for what I did. They are a hard lot. But I've come to realize I'd rather be an outcast inside those walls than out."

"So, what did you do that was so bad?" Nath asked.

"They wanted me to wed a woman I didn't like."

"I see. An arranged marriage. The races have those where I'm from." Nath grinned. "And I've seen many grooms and brides shudder from disappointment when their betrothed was not what they expected."

"Or they're just arse-end ugly," Gannon replied.

"That too."

CHAPTER 37

AFTER RIDING THROUGH THE NIGHT, into the dawn, and just past the beginning of daybreak, they came to a stop. Leaning on his saddle with his eyes to the north, Venir said, "There it is."

"That's the City of Bone?"

Nath didn't get an answer.

Instead, his eyes were filled with an uncanny expectation. After Two-Ten City, he'd thought the City of Bone would be more ordinary. When the men had spoken of its walls, he'd imagined something similar to his world's Quintuklen, whose white stone walls were ten feet high and formed a simple maze. Bone was vastly different.

Nath said the next word as if it was an understatement. "Incredible."

The City of Bone sat alone in the rugged plains, a powerful monolith which defied nature. Its walls were monstrous blocks of stone that stretched east and west for miles. The height of the walls was almost incomprehensible. The humongous cut stones were staggered atop each other. A great iron gate gaped open like a mouth of metal on the southern wall of the city, which bustled with activity. Next to those walls, the people looked insect small.

Inside the walls, Nath noted the high, colorful spires and turrets of castles that appeared to hover in midair. "This is not what I expected."

"And what did you expect?" Venir said with a smile as broad as the distant walls.

"Something much smaller."

"Are there no cities so big where you come from?" Venir asked.

"Yes, but different." He combed his hair out of his eyes. "This is unexpected. So, do you think we can find answers to what I seek in there?"

"I know this. It will be a better place to start than Two-Ten City. And the odor is far better. None of the other races are in there, just men." Spurring his horse, Venir took the lead. He was moving east, away from the main entrance.

"Are we going in another way?" Nath said to Gannon, who'd remained at his side.

The young man shrugged. "You know, I've never seen the city from outside its walls. When I left, I never looked back. I don't know if I should be delighted or frightened."

Venir came to a stop. He twisted around in the saddle and gave Nath an up-and-down glance. Then he fixed his eyes on Gannon. With a nod, he said to Billip, "Why don't you take him through the main gate with all of the other pedestrians? Take our horses too. Use them for barter if you have to." He dismounted and handed over his reins.

Billip nodded. "Aye. Let's go, ragged one. It will be interesting to see if they let you in."

"But I want to stay with you, Venir. I owe you a debt," Gannon argued.

With a hard look, Venir replied, "And you can pay it by leaving my sight."

"But—" Gannon started.

The look Venir gave him cut off Gannon's speech with an audible *gulp*.

With pleading eyes, Gannon looked to Nath. "Help me."

Nath got off of his horse and gave the reins to Gannon. He reached out and gave the young man a handshake.

Eyes marveling, Gannon gave Nath's scales one long last look. With a firm shake, he said, "I wish you well on your quest, but selfishly, I hope we meet again."

Billip took Gannon's reins and led the horse and rider away. "Come on, then. The time for long, sappy goodbyes is over." He gave Venir a nod. "See you on the other side, Venir."

As soon as Billip and Gannon were beyond earshot, Venir said, "Let's go, then."

"Forgive me for being a little confused, but why aren't we moving toward the gate?" Nath asked. "I was looking forward to the experience."

"You don't want to go through that gate with arms like that." Venir walked at a brisk pace with a notable limp. "You'll need to conceal them. No, we'll take my way. A better way."

"And they couldn't come with?"

"No. Gannon, he's a Royal. You can't trust the likes of him."

"He seems harmless."

"That's only because you don't know the Royals."

Chongo led them a little farther out than where they'd been. When they caught up with the big dog, his tail was wagging and his tongues were hanging out. An outcropping of rocks and leafless brush partially covered a cave opening.

"In there?" Nath's thoughts fell once more on Laiyn. "Aren't you tired of caves?"

"No. But I am tired." Venir and Chongo vanished into the black, leaving Nath standing all alone.

Nath sighed.

Is there anywhere I can go in this world without feeling swallowed?

CHAPTER 38

NATH'S GOLDEN EYES HAD NO trouble tracing the outline of the pitch-black tunnel they traveled through. The cave had a metal door concealed in the back, and Venir procured a key that let them inside. They had walked for several long minutes, sloping gently downward, before taking a stop over a heavy metal grate. Deep below the surface, dozens of feet, water rushed through a channel. The cool mist tickled Nath's nose. The water was fresh. At that point, the tunnel began its ascent, and after they walked the same length and distance, another door appeared, this one made of wood.

Venir worked at some levers and mechanisms, and the door flipped up, revealing the straw-filled inside of a stable. He closed the secret passage door. The mechanisms locked into place. He walked over to the stable gate, peeked over the rim, and gave his dog a nod. "Stay, Chongo."

The giant dog curled up in the straw as if he'd come home, which Nath supposed he had.

Venir then gave Fang a look. "You should leave that iron here. It will draw too much attention." He took out his mystic sack and put his own armament in it. As always, the sack remained the same size, and he stuffed it back into his rucksack, all the while talking. "Don't worry. Chongo won't let anything happen to it."

"I'd rather not be gone too long from Fang, but yes, he does tend to draw attention, just a bit. And I trust Chongo."

Both of the dog's large heads licked in Nath's direction.

Nath concealed the blade in the straw and scrubbed the dog behind the ears. "Thanks, boy."

Venir swung the gate open. "Welcome to Bone."

Nath exited first while Venir closed the gate behind him. "You're right, it does smell better than Two-Ten."

The barn was huge. It was a hundred yards long, with long rows of stables on each side. The rafters held hundreds of pigeons that flew in and out of the oversized skylights at the top. There were cobwebs high up in the ceiling's corners.

Nath sniffed. The strong scent of manure and hay was in the air, but it was old, more of a musty smell. He expected to hear the nickers and whinnies of horses, but there was nothing. The stable was abandoned.

Venir's stride lengthened as he took off toward the far end, walking and talking. "We need to get you covered up. You'll stand out like a walking fire with those scales and that hair."

As they neared the far exit, an old codger on rickety limbs wandered over. His eyes were as smoky as his shoulder-long hair, but he squinted. "Sire, what can I do for you?"

Venir stuck some coins in his hand. "Feed my dog daily and find me a long cloak." He pressed the money deep into the man's hand. "Quickly."

"Dog or cloak first, sire?"

"Cloak."

With a clacking of his remaining teeth, the old man moved at a brisk but teetering gait.

When Nath lost sight of him, he climbed up onto the hayloft, which offered a view outside. The grand city greeted him like a tempting mistress. It beckoned for his attention. Standing just inside the sunshine that cast an early shadow into the barn, he gazed beyond.

The City of Bone confused Nath. Pretty carriages clattered over its cobblestone streets right beside crude wagons and ill-clad men, women, and children who bustled by on foot with dreary energy. Their long faces told a story of endless toil being necessary for survival. Yet in the backdrop, there were elaborate castles, where cheerful banners waved in streams of color.

Leaning against a post, he said to Venir, "I take it those castles are where the Royals live?"

"That is where the Royals rule." Venir placed more gear in his rucksack and slung it over one shoulder. He still looked like death warmed over but happy to be here. "They're the home of great plots and schemes."

"And those towers are filled with magi who can help me get home?"

"Help?" Venir clucked a laugh. "Not unless their lives depend on it. No, but there will be others who have answers. We'll just have to track them down, assuming you don't vanish on me again."

"I can't repay you."

"I don't expect you to, but I'll help where I can, the best I can, until you figure out a better option for yourself." Venir patted the knife on his hip. "Who knows, maybe you'll find a better ally than me."

"That wouldn't be easy to do." Nath resumed his stare into the skyline of the massive city. Its roads crisscrossed. Bridges traversed the rooftops. Everywhere, there were people, people, people. "Where do we start?"

"Where the Royals aren't." Venir took Nath by the chin and guided his gaze in another direction. There lay a far less appealing section of the city, offering a dreary display. The bright banners were gone, replaced by busted shutters and broken windows. There were no flowers on the ledges or balconies. Tattered curtains and drying laundry waved in the breeze. "This is the part of town where a man goes who doesn't want to be noticed. It's where my kind belongs."

"In slums?"

"Its offerings are a far cry better than what you suffered in Two-Ten. The women have more skin on their backs than hair." He gave Nath a shoulder shake. "You'll like it."

"Sire. Sire." The old man stood at the bottom of the ladder that led into the loft. He held a cloak too heavy for his arms. It looked like it had been buried in the hay for centuries. "Will this do?"

Taking the cloak and holding it out to Nath, Venir patted the old man on the back. "It's perfect."

CHAPTER 39

NATH WAS DISAPPOINTED. HIS CLOAK itched, and he didn't care to have his head covered. The city was hot. The air wasn't fresh. It had the smell of many things, mostly bad. Odor wafted up through the sewer grates in the street. In addition to pitching their garbage out the windows, the people fought, bickered, and hollered. Children dressed in nothing but rags plucked at his robes and clawed fingers, which he kept balled up and hidden.

"Get away, urchins!" Venir said a dozen times, scattering the bold wee ones away. And then he told Nath, "They'll get used to you after a while, but right now they sense the newness of you. That's why they come after you. Don't give them anything. Not even the tiniest scrap of food."

"Don't they have parents or schools?"

"Schools?" Venir let out a robust laugh. "Those are for the Royals. For everyone else, it's the school of 'every man for himself.' This way."

They cut into an alley where the cats lurked on the ledges of the apartments above. Rats could be heard scuffling in the creases where the buildings met the streets.

Nath heard something being heaved out of one of the windows and hop-skipped forward. A bucket of sludge splattered on the ground where he'd just been. He glared up at the occupant of the window, a bald man with flabby arms who had a cigar puffing in his mouth. He got Nath's hot stare and replied with what Nath assumed to be a foul gesture.

"Do we stay here long?" Nath kept his eyes on the small portals in the walls above. "I can't imagine staying here long."

"I was raised here, but I can only stand it for so long." Venir cut into another alley even narrower than the last. "I prefer the Outland. I was born and bred there."

The city twisted and turned. It was a jungle of brick-and-mortar catacombs that didn't seem to serve any purpose other than to get one person lost from another. Nath kept checking details in his mind, but if he had to return to the barn from where he was now, it would pose a challenge for even his keen mind.

"It'll take some getting used to."

"It's the star city of the world. The black gem at the center. The people relish it. Citizens of other cities ship themselves here and boast of it all over the world." Venir took two tight corners, zigzagging left and right. "The funny thing is, they don't go anywhere once they're here. They just shoot their mouths off to the newer wayfarers. Here we are."

A wooden sign that hung on a pair of chains read "the Drunken Octopus." A pair of double doors stood open inward, and the carousing within could be heard in the streets. The building itself was several stories tall, made from large bricks. Clay mortar had squeezed out of the seams. A smoke filament drifted from the inside of the establishment out into the street.

Venir gave Nath a nod and went inside. The floor creaked under their feet, but not a single head turned. Most of the tables were empty, but the place was still lively. The men and women playing cards and whooping or groaning looked to be a sordid lot. Stacks of tiny coins were piled up by their elbows.

Pieces of clothing hung from the crude iron chandeliers. An elderly woman stood on a ladder replacing the chandelier candles and removing the clothes. A boy with a mop of brown hair scrubbed at the floors. As Venir ventured to the bar, where the oak stools were butted up one against the other, a woman with bouncing curls of black down to her neck jumped into the huge warrior's arms.

"Venir!"

She was comely, with painted eyes and long lashes. She wore an amber dress which clung to the generous curves of her body. "I've missed you." She started to kiss his neck but stopped. Her nostrils flared. "You need to bathe. You're filthy. What have you been into?"

"I've been neck deep in spiders and fiends, Amber," said Venir with a broad smile. He pounded his fist on the bar. "Send me a barrel and a tankard, barkeep! If I bathe, I bathe in ale!"

"You are so full of it, Venir Teller of Tales," Amber fanned her nose. "Master of strange smells." She patted the purse hanging from his belt. "Sounds like enough for a bath. I'll have it prepared."

The barkeep placed down a tankard and a small barrel. His face was full of wrinkles, and he had a sullen look in his eyes. Smoking a cigar, he rolled up his white sleeves over his hairy arms and poured, then shoved the froth-covered tankard to Venir. "Do you want some grub to go with that, Venir?"

"Of course, Sam." Venir gulped the drink down. "Ah. Another. I'll pour it myself."

"What about your friend?" Sam asked, staring at Nath.

"I could use some fresh water," Nath replied.

The barkeep's brows lifted ever the slightest. "We mop the floors and scrub the dishes with water." He shook his head, grabbed another tankard from under the shelf, and clomped behind the bar in front of Venir. "Teach your friend some manners."

With a sliver of a smile, Venir poured more ale from the cask and handed it to Nath.

Taking the brew in hand, Nath said, "Manners? Here?"

Venir clanked his own goblet into Nath's. "Blend in."

Nath sampled the brew. It was stout with a creamy texture to it. It went down smooth and filled the gullet. "Not bad."

"It's much better than the orc swill in Two-Ten, isn't it?"

Nath drank some more. "Several times." He lowered the hood of his cloak off his head.

"I wouldn't do that just yet," Venir warned. "Lie low a little longer. Get a feel for the place before it gets a feel for you."

Nath put his hood back up just in time to see Amber return with a smile as warm as the suns. She draped Venir's arm over her shoulders in a move which seemed to swallow her whole. "It's time to get you cleaned up, stinky."

Venir hefted the cask of ale onto his free shoulder and gave Nath a wink. "Lie low." He jutted his chin to the other side of the tavern. "Like him."

Nuzzled in the darkest corner of the tavern, a scarecrow of a man sat in a chair that leaned back against the wall. A stone fireplace with the orange glow of its last coals hemmed the man in, giving him ample privacy. His legs were on the table. Eyes closed, his head was leaned against the wall. He was snoring.

Melegal.

Nath was glad to see the man. Despite the rogue's unforgiving and complaining demeanor, he liked him. He had salt. And when you could get him talking, he was good for conversation. He stood at the table and contemplated whether to disturb the rogue or not.

He probably wants to be woken up anyway.

No sooner had Nath bent over to whisper hello than a dagger appeared at his throat.

Eyes still closed and with a chill in his voice, Melegal said, "Did you come here to bleed to death, bub?"

Nath's Adam's apple rolled.

Gads! I didn't even see that!

CHAPTER 40

"MELEGAL, IT'S ME, NATH DRAGON."

Eyes still closed, Melegal said, "Nath *what?*"

"Never mind. It's Nath."

One of the rogue's eyes popped open and into Nath's hood, finding his face. "Ah, I see you two idiots made it back. Congratulations." In a flicker of steel that flashed before Nath's eyes, he hid the blade away. His open eyelid shut. "Now go away."

Nath pulled up a chair. "So you knew we were here?"

"There isn't a tavern Venir goes to where you don't hear him as soon as he walks in. His mouth's too big for his head—and his head's big enough as it is." Melegal brought all four chair legs down to the floor. He lifted a rose-colored wine bottle and gave it a little shake. A small amount of liquid rattled within. "Time for a new bottle. Time for a new day."

They spent the next couple of hours catching one man's tales up with the other's. The card players cleared out after the first hour, practically giving the men the entire room. Nath removed his hood but still kept his back to everyone.

"So Mikkel is well then?"

"He sleeps above. He'll be back down after a while and try to take over the tavern." Melegal filled up his goblet again. He'd been drinking since Nath sat down. His second bottle was empty and he was on his third. "He'll have competition from Venir, though, and now with you in the mix there will be even more competition."

Nath got up and stoked the coals of the fire. Adding some kindling, he created a small blaze. "What do you mean? And why do you people build fires when it's already hot in here?"

"We just like to play with fire, I guess. As for competition, well, once the women get a load of you, they'll latch on to you like ticks. Oh, the cat fights that'll break out." Shooting a quick finger at Nath, he said, "You might not want to be here when it gets busy."

A black animal that looked like a bobcat hopped up on the table. It was a short-haired feline with the muscular prowess of a panther and somewhat scraggly fur. It had a predator's nasty streak in its smoky eyes. Its paws were the biggest Nath had ever seen on what must be a house cat, and it had eight claws on each paw. It lay down on Nath's hand, purring like a tiny thunderstorm that gently shook the table.

"See what I mean?" Melegal scratched just above the cat's ears. "Octopus doesn't like anyone in this tavern but me. He hates people, but he likes you. Remarkable."

"Octopus?" Nath petted the cat. "Very clever. I've never seen a cat with so many claws. Thirty-two in all. That's pretty nasty."

"You should see what he can do to the rats and dogs. They haven't seen a rat in here in years."

"I can imagine." Nath continued petting the cat. "Do you think you or Venir can assist me with my dilemma?"

"I don't know. I know Venir will try, but what you're talking about is beyond my comprehension. If the underlings brought you here, I'd think it would take the underlings to get you back. It's said they have the most powerful magic." Melegal shrugged his narrow shoulders. "Doesn't mean someone else might not know something useful. I don't, but I know the castles have their wizards. You just can't trust them. And Venir, he's seen more than I. Where does one start? That's the problem."

Melegal certainly wasn't the ray of light Nath was looking for. But ironically, the thief was honest. Getting home wouldn't be easy. He didn't even know if it was possible. Corzan's plan to vanquish him had been a powerful one indeed. It had worked.

Brenwar must be beside himself without me. He'll blame himself and take it out on everyone else. Guzan, I need to get home.

He gave more thought to what Melegal had said about the underlings. If they were the only way back, it would be a sad thing. He couldn't possibly trust them. No, his father had always said there was always more than one way to do anything. Anything was possible. He had to have faith in that. He picked up Octopus and held the brutish cat before his eyes. "If cats have nine lives, I wonder how many lives dragons have."

Melegal fired back, saying, "Why would you want more lives to live? Isn't this life bad enough as it is?"

Oran stood in the tall grass fifty yards away from the Red Clay Forest. He'd been waiting and waiting, a shadow in the day, a terror in the night. The villagers all had eyes on him, but they didn't dare come near. No, they worked to rebuild what the gnoll and the man hunters had so effortlessly destroyed days earlier. He could hear their whispers. Feel their fear. The people knew their days were numbered, but rather than flee, they dug in.

Humans are so foolish. Even the animals are smarter.

With a small metal file, he shaved his black fingernails into perfect little points. He noted the stress cracks on a couple of them.

Strange. I'm not yet old. Missions like this invade my true passions.

An urchling limped out of the woods and came right to him like a wounded dog. Its entire arm was missing. It snorted for its breath and collapsed on its back at Oran's feet.

"They're all dead, aren't they?"

The bloodied and battered urchling let out a ragged chit sound and gave a feeble nod.

Oran balled up his fists so tight that blood dripped from them. Through clenched jaws, he said, "I hate this mission!"

His violet eyes glowed with an angry fire. In the village, he caught sight of a man digging with a shovel. With his hands outstretched and a single thought, the shovel was ripped free of the man's grip and sailed across the plain and into his grasp. With his arms raised over his head, he brought the shovel down on the urchling with wroth force again and again until the handle snapped in two.

The urchling still breathed.

Oran's hands flared up with fire and burned the little monster into a roasted corpse. He turned his attention to the village. He would make them suffer for this failure. He started toward them but then came to a stop and let his energies diminish.

I'm better than this. Leave the animals to the animals.

EPILOGUE

A COUPLE OF DAYS HAD PASSED, and Nath had begun to get acclimated to the City of Bone. With the assistance of Venir, Mikkel, and Melegal, he'd found more suitable attire and even managed to prowl the streets a little more in the day and night without drawing attention to himself. He'd just come in from exploring and was at the top level of the Drunken Octopus in the apartment Venir and Melegal shared. He was alone.

The smell of freshly roasted coffee brewing filled his nose. He poured it out of the pot into a clay mug and took a seat in a wooden chair that had a view out a small window. An alley passed below, and more often than there needed to be, there was a racket of one sort or another.

He took a sip of the coffee and wondered what he could learn in Bish that might be helpful in Nalzambor. Some of the contraptions he'd come across here were fascinating.

I hope they find Billip soon.

The archer had yet to arrive, and Venir and Mikkel had set out to track him down.

As Nath finished up his coffee, the door to the apartment opened. Venir came in first with a furrowed brow. Mikkel was next, and Billip clung to his side. The archer's face was swollen and bloodied.

Nath shot up out of his chair. "What happened?"

Venir slammed the door behind them and locked it up tight. "I'll tell you what happened," he growled. "Royal Gannon happened. He betrayed you. He betrayed us all. That's gratitude for you."

"What do you mean? I don't understand," Nath said. "Billip, what happened?"

Mikkel helped Billip into the seat Nath had been sitting in.

The archer looked up at Nath through his blackened and swelling eyes. "From the moment we parted, he couldn't stop talking about your scales. He kept asking where you would go, but I wouldn't say." Clutching at his ribs, he winced. "He said he'd pay plenty of money. I said no. As soon as we hit the gate, he said something to the city watch. They seized the horses and apprehended me. Took me to some dungeon and beat the Bish out of me." He huffed a laugh. "Well, partly. Did you see that redhead down in the tavern?" He looked up at Mikkel. "Have her bring me some tea, will you?"

Nath's heart constricted. Again, innocent people were getting hurt because of him. "What do they want with me?"

"The Royals think everything special that comes into this city is theirs for the taking. One like you would be a prized slave. A prized possession." Venir gave him an angry look. "But don't worry, we won't let them get you."

"Don't make promises you can't keep, Venir." Billip pulled a tooth out. "Lords of the Suns, not another one!" He eyeballed Nath. "The Royals want you. Before long, your image will be plastered all over this city, and what the Royals want, they get."

BOOK THREE

HEROES TO THE BITTER END

CHAPTER 1

I N THE WORLD OF UNDERLINGS, he was known as Oran the Outcast. At one time, the underling cleric was held in high regard among his evil kindred. Raised in the upper hierarchies of the Underland, he had the dark world laid out before his feet. Then the fall came, and Oran's curiosity about the world above got the better of him. He was shunned because of his experiments with the other races on the surface world of Bish. He was labeled and rejected. Ultimately, his crass methods had him banished from his home in the Underland.

Riding on a small wooden barge in the underground river of foul-smelling waters called the Current, Oran sighed. As the small watercraft glided over the water in the pitch-black tunnels below the surface world, a gentle breeze stirred his dusty robes. The craft, propelled by underling magic, moved at a brisk speed over the underground river, where small, white, glowing minnows swam beneath them. Oran sat on the bench at the far end of the craft, his violet eyes fixed ahead into the enveloping darkness.

I hate Verbard. I hate Catten. His sharp black nails dug into his palms. The underling brothers, Verbard and Catten, had usurped his station when he had been rejected by his people. At one time, Oran was one of the right hands of the all-powerful underling leader, Master Sinway. Now, Verbard and Catten held that station but only because they had tricked Oran and duped Sinway. They were clever, very clever.

I serve them. They should be serving me. Oran reached into the pocket of his robes. He pulled forth a pair of eyeball-sized rubies that burned with a dim fire within. He rolled them in a palm. They had a faint pulse like a living heartbeat.

My time will come. Yes, Master Sidebor, our time will come. Vengeance shall be ours.

Decades before, when Oran thrived in the Underland, his ambition grew as fast as his ego. With underlings and humans sworn mortal enemies, he sought to destroy the men from within. Instead of fighting the surface-dwelling humans outright, he chose to use more subversive tactics. He began making allegiances with the ruling humans, called Royals, who could benefit from underling services. Communication with men of any sort was forbidden, but Oran, confident in his successes, pushed his agenda forward. He shared his inner workings with Verbard and Catten. The gold- and silver-eyed underlings urged him forward, throwing their full support behind his efforts, privately. Oran pressed on, making allegiances with the Royals while at the same time violating the underlings' strictest law.

He stared at the gemstones in his gray palm, shook his head, and put them away. *I was such a fool.*

For the day came when he decided to reveal his secret workings to Master Sinway. The iron-eyed underling overlord didn't take it well. Verbard and Catten denied all knowledge of everything Oran had shared with them. In the inevitable end, Oran was spared but banished. Verbard and Catten took over his station and were charged to keep tabs on his activities. At the same time, Oran continued his meddling with the surface world. His experiments resumed, all with Verbard's and Catten's full knowledge. He had become their stooge.

The small craft butted up against a sandy bank. Oran grabbed a bottle of underling port out of a blanket he had stowed inside. He rose from his seat and hopped out of the barge and onto the bank. He stood in a tremendous cavern, where massive stalactites and stalagmites merged from top to bottom into one. Water dripped from a small formation above as he scuttered through the darkness. A broad stairway made from natural stone met the upper base of the sandy back of the cave. At the top, several flights up and mounted in a bracket beside a centuries-old iron door, a lone torch burned. Oran stopped on the bottom steps.

The things I do for my people. One day I'll be honored for it, I swear it.

Verbard and Catten had given Oran the charge of summoning a hunter who would destroy the Darkslayer. The brothers knew full well that that hunter was not summoned by underlings but by another kind of magic acquired through men. It was through his own research into the surface world above that he acquired the Decanter of Summoning. It came with the help of Royal mages. The creature he had summoned from another world, a flame-haired man with black dragon scales covering his arms, had broken away from Oran and allied himself with the man known as the Darkslayer. It had become a firestorm. Now, Oran had to fix it.

Slowly, with his robes dragging and bottle in hand, he took the steps upward one at a time.

He'd lost Collo the gnoll and the urchlings to the Red Clay Forest. But he'd learned that some of the men he pursued had headed to the City of Bone. It was the last place on Bish one would find an underling, yet there he was, below one of their mighty castles and on the very threshold of the enemy that he was sworn to destroy. He would need their help to find the man whom he sought, Nath. He needed to capture him once again and return him to Verbard and Catten—and at the same time, he had to find a way to destroy the Darkslayer.

At the top of the steps, he stood on the platform and knocked on the metal door. The sound of metal on knuckle echoed through the cavern. Oran stepped back and waited. Finally, after minutes that seemed much longer, he heard the sound of shod feet on the other side. Metal scraped against metal on the other side of the door, followed by a distinct *clack*. Groaning on the metal hinges, the iron door swung outward.

Two towering men, wearing full suits of platemail armor, stepped out onto the platform. Their hard stares fell on Oran. Hands covered in metal gauntlets gripped the pommels of their longswords. A woman in a dark-red dress came down the steps on the other side of the door. Her chestnut hair was braided on the top of her head. Her piercing green eyes, with the smallest crow's feet on each side, locked with Oran's. With her bare shoulders back and chin held high, there was an air about her as she stood between the royal knights. A thin smile formed on her perfect maroon lips. "Welcome, Oran. What a pleasure it is to see you again so soon."

Stroking his neck with his fingers, he said with a sneer in his voice, "I cannot say the same, Lorda Aleta. I come for business." He offered her the bottle of underling port. "Let's get this over with."

She took the bottle, cracked a thin smile, stepped aside, and gestured toward the steps. Caressing the labelless black bottle of port, she said, "Welcome to Castle Vansung."

CHAPTER 2

ORAN STOOD INSIDE A PRIVATE chamber in the dungeon level of Castle Vansung. Much like his own lair, it was a dingy, torchlit room, with wooden shelves filled with many tomes. Among the books were strange blown-glass decorations shaped like wild animals, plants, and flowers that gave the otherwise dreary room some splash. Three work tables were half covered in scrolls, a variety of jars, and vials filled with swirling liquids. Lorda Aleta sat across from him in a plush burgundy chair. Her knights, each sporting a flowing moustache, stood to either side of her. They continued to look at Oran intently with disgust.

Lorda Aleta, a very attractive woman by human standards, sipped the underling port from a pewter wine goblet. "Oran, this port makes all of our dealings worthwhile. It's icing on the cake, as we like to say."

Holding his own goblet of port in his hands, Oran replied, "There is more to be had, Lorda Aleta. It's just a part of doing business. How much you enjoy it matters little to me. I have needs. You can help fulfill them. Let's converse without the unnecessary flattery. You make my skin crawl. No amount of port could quench the sickening feeling that you give me."

The knights rustled inside their armor as they each advanced a full step forward. Their swords came halfway out of their sheaths.

"At ease," Aleta said to her knights. "He is my guest, and barring anything defaming, he is free to speak as he pleases." She set her goblet down on the arm of a round mahogany table beside her chair. A smile played on her lips. She locked her fingers together, put her elbows on her knees, and leaned forward. "So, let's get down to business, shall we? I gave you the Decanter of Summoning, and now you return? Is there a problem with the demon that you summoned?"

"I could make the argument that the demon that I summoned was in fact no demon at all but, rather, a man."

Arching an eyebrow, Aleta leaned back in her chair. "A man. What sort of man?"

"One very much like you. One that I could not control. He was anything but the otherworldly demon that I expected," Oran replied. He moved beside one of the worktables and set his pewter goblet down. He leafed through an open tome on the table. "The spell was spoiled from the onset."

"What are you implying, Oran? The decanter is not some mystical bauble that illuminates a room with rainbows at night." Aleta's voice tensed. "It's a precious artifact, a gift acquired from the wizard towers in the City of Three. Tell me, are you seeking reimbursement for what I am going to assume was your failure?"

"Failure?" Without looking at her, the powerful underling calmly leafed through the pages of the tome. "I am not here to make an accusation. I fully understand the unpredictable consequences of the mystic arts. Underlings are the masters of them."

"Yet, you came to me?" she asked.

"Your kind dabbles in the arcane with a very curious nature. I only sought to build a relationship and try something new," he said as he closed the book. "It was a gesture of goodwill. As for that, I am not here to seek reimbursement of my more-than-ample compensation."

"No?" she asked. "Then what are you seeking?"

"This demon, man, or creature from whatever world he or it comes from has slipped my grasp." He turned and faced her. "I need him back."

Aleta nodded. "Let me guess. You tracked the demon here."

"Yes."

The woman's dark eyes brightened. She grabbed her goblet and took another swig. She crossed her legs. "So, we have a demon roaming the streets of the City of Bone."

"Again, he's not a demon but, rather, a man with a head of flowing flame-red hair and black scales like a dragon's armor for arms. He also came with a sword that stands taller than his waist."

The knights exchanged a glance. Even without the flowing moustaches, they would have looked very much alike.

She raised her eyebrows. "A sword?"

"Yes. What sort of demon summoned from the depths of the arcane shows up with a sword?" Oran sneered at her. "I've summoned worldly creatures far and near from the rocks of this world, but never did they come with equipment. This one, I tell you, is odd. It's vital that I find him soon."

"And when you find this red-haired demon, what will you do with him?"

In a sharp response, Oran replied, "That is my concern, not yours. Just capture him, and bring the man to me. You will be compensated."

"I want triple what you paid me for the Decanter of Summoning," she replied.

"You are being shrewd, Aleta. But I'll indulge your greed and pay you double the last fee."

"Deal," she replied. "I'll send a signal within the coming weeks."

"No, it will be within the coming days," Oran warned.

She tossed him a marble that appeared to be made of stained glass. "See you soon, Oran."

Without a word, Aleta and the knights escorted Oran back into the caves below. Guided by the knights' torchlight, he entered the watercraft. He held up the marble and said to Aleta, "Make it quick." Without a word, he sailed away into the pitch-black tunnels of the Current, leaving them all alone on the bank.

Lorda Aleta covered her nose with the back of her hand. The knights were doing the same. One of the twin knights asked, "Do your sewers run through these waters, Lorda?"

"No, Quint. This is the Current. Only death rides its waves." She marched back up the stairs and entered the sublevel of the castle, not stopping as the knights closed the door behind her. They caught up with her in her private chamber, where she practiced and studied her arcane crafts. As she took another swig of her port, a tingle went up and down her spine. The demon Oran had summoned had her full attention. And she was one step ahead of the underling already. She addressed the knights. "Quint and Luther, fetch my once-forsaken son Gannon and bring him straight to me."

CHAPTER 3

I NSIDE CASTLE VANSUNG'S BATHING CHAMBERS, Gannon was partially submerged in a cast-iron tub of steaming water. It had been over a week since he'd entered the City of Bone. He'd been bathing every day ever since. A pretty house maiden scrubbed his scrawny body down with a soapy washcloth. He had the distinguished features of a Royal with high cheekbones and a narrow but angular jaw. His good looks were noticeable. More so since he'd been cleaned up after years covered in grime. He just wasn't as well-built as his kin. Eyes closed, he breathed in the eucalyptus and ginger that scented the waters. Sighing, he said, "I swear, I'll never live beyond one hundred feet of a hot, steaming bath again. What was I thinking?"

The house maiden rubbed the soapy rag into his chest in a slow, circular motion. She worked her way down to his abdomen.

"Yes, what was I thinking," Gannon said again.

He'd spent years with the forest magi in open rebellion against his overbearing family. Young and headstrong, Gannon figured he knew what was best for himself. His experience among the forest magi and their strange way of living had been humbling, to say the least. At least he survived, and now, he was free.

As the ample young servant rubbed all over him, he kissed her on the side of the forehead and said, "Why don't you join me? There is plenty of room for two."

The rosy-cheeked young maiden, who was ample of chest and full in the hips, giggled. She pulled her dripping-wet arm from the water, set the rag down, and began slipping off her blouse.

The door to the bathing chambers slammed hard into the wall.

The house maiden screeched. Gannon half jumped out of the tub. The hot, soapy water surged over the cast-iron tub's rim.

Two knights in platemail armor marched inside. They were Lorda Aleta's personal guards, Quint and Luther. Though the strapping men were twins, Quint was the heavier of the two. Both of the men kept their brown eyebrows knitted together.

"What do you two hounds think you are doing, barging in here in the middle of my bath?" Gannon said.

Quint grabbed Gannon by the scruff of hair on the top of his head and pulled him up out of the water.

"Unhand me, hound!"

In a gruff voice, Luther said to the house maiden, "Get a robe on him, girl."

Quint pulled Gannon all of the way out of the tub like he was a child while the maiden covered him up in his robes. "Get a move on. Your mother is waiting."

Tying the belt on his sage-green terry-cloth robe while the maiden dried his feet with a towel, Gannon said, "You hounds should know better than to manhandle me like this. I'm a Royal. You are not."

Quint shoved the much smaller Gannon hard in the back. "The Lorda awaits. Move it."

Scoffing, Gannon stormed out of the room and down the hall. He hated Quint and Luther. He had despised them since he was a boy. It was the overbearing likes of them and his mother that had driven him away from Castle Vansung in the first place. The twin knights had been raised from childhood to be the sworn protectors of the Lorda. She'd been with them all of her life, and often the well-polished goons meted out discipline on her behalf. They'd given Gannon his share of whippings.

Glancing back at the hard-eyed men, Gannon said under his breath, "One day you will awaken to bugs eating your faces off if you ever cross me again."

"What was that?" Luther demanded.

Gannon sighed. "Where is Mother? Does she reside in her quarters, or is she down in her snake pit?"

Quint shoved Gannon in the back again, almost knocking him to the floor. "Below, whelp."

Down in the castle's subterranean levels, Gannon led the way through the narrow passages. He entered his mother's private chambers and found her sitting in her leather chair. The knights closed him inside and guarded the door. Gannon took a knee at the foot of her chair and kissed her awaiting hand. "You look beautiful, mother. A star in the gloom."

Aleta stroked his cheek with the back of her hand and said, "You always did have a way with words. I've missed them."

"Given my many brothers and sisters, I'm surprised that you noticed."

"Out of all of them, you were the most like me," she said. "I've been meaning to spend more time with you since you returned. We've hardly had time to talk. You understand castle business."

"Nothing has changed since I departed, but now that I have returned, I have more appreciation for it. The time I spent in the Red Clay Forest truly changed me for the better. Now, may I ask, why have you summoned me?"

Aleta leaned back in her chair and said, "Tell me more about the man with black scales."

Gannon pulled a leather footstool over and sat before his mother. "His name is Nath. He saved me, and I saved him. For all I know, he is a good man who fought like the devil against some bestial sort of underling. He is truly unique."

She tilted her head to one side and studied Gannon's face. "How so?"

"Nath is striking in looks, more so than the finest Royals. His hair is silky, long, and flowing, and red unlike anything I've ever seen." Gannon's fingers massaged the air. "But those scales on his arms made him so magnificent. Beautiful. Each a perfect diamond with its own inner shine. They were smooth as snakeskin but hard as metal." He pointed at her. "I told you that he is something that you did not want to miss."

Aleta sat quietly, considering his words. Finally, she spoke. "Did he seem like a demon?"

"On the contrary, I sensed only good in the stranger. If anything, he is a demon slayer. I tried to impress this man's uniqueness upon you the moment that I arrived. You did not seem interested. Why the interest now?"

"I assumed that you were being overzealous from your journey beyond the wall. I wanted you to settle your thoughts. So, you kept a man prisoner as a helper?" she asked.

"Yes. His name was Billip. I had him arrested and tormented in an effort to figure out where they took Nath. As a Royal and a Forest Magi, I don't think I earned their full trust."

Aleta nodded. "And did you find out where these men huddle?"

"Billip didn't share a word. After two days and no interest from you, I let him go."

Aleta's eyes blazed with fury. "You did what?" she yelled. She backhanded Gannon in the face, knocking him from his stool. "Foolish son! Why did you do that?"

With his shaking arms covering his face, Gannon said in a broken voice, "Forgive me, Mother. I'll find them. I swear, I'll find them. I have—"

"Silence!" Aleta smacked Gannon again. She crossed the room and stood before Quint and Luther. "Use whatever resources you need and bring this man called Nath to me." With a quick nod, the older knights departed.

"Mother," Gannon pleaded, "let me help. I know them. I can help find them."

With a wave of her hand, the door to her chamber slammed shut. Her hands glowed with orange fire as she faced her son. Her eyes glowed in the same way.

Eyes wide open, Gannon crawled back into her chair, trembling from head to toe. "No, Mother, no! Listen to me! You must listen. No!"

CHAPTER 4

I T WAS EARLY IN THE day in the City of Bone. Inside the Drunken Octopus tavern, Nath had joined Venir and Melegal at their usual spot near the fireplace. Mikkel sat away from them at the end of the bar nearest the front door. Even though it was early, the tavern still had several people scattered among the tables, rubbing red eyes and eating huge helpings of eggs and biscuits for breakfast. The coals in the fireplace were dim, and the room was smoky.

Melegal sat with his back to the corner wall, petting the eight-clawed cat, Octopus, that sat on the table. Venir had refilled his third mug of coffee, and Nath had just come down the stairs and sat. He'd checked on Billip, who was still resting but doing better, recovering from the whipping he'd taken days before. Nath's hair was tied back in a ponytail. His arms were covered in a full-sleeved jerkin, and he was uncomfortably warm.

"Friends, I can't sit here all day in hopes of finding a way home," Nath said. Venir and Billip had been stressing to him the need for patience, but he felt like time was running out. "I have to act."

Scratching the big black cat behind the ears, Melegal said, "Have you ever considered that there might not be a way home and that you might be stuck here, just like the rest of us?"

Sitting upright, Nath replied, "I have. But so long as I am here, finding home will be my purpose. My world needs me. I have friends and a family."

Melegal chuckled. "Perhaps you have a wife and litter of children that need feeding. Maybe you are better off not being tied down with them, eh?"

"Ease off, Me," Venir said. He pulled up his plate of eggs, biscuits, and sausage and dug his fork into them. "Our friend is homesick. It's good to have a place such as that to miss." He chewed a mouthful of eggs and biscuit. "Nath, if it is at all possible, we shall find a way. Of course, these are sorcerous dealings, which really isn't in our wheelhouse, but in the City of Bone, you can always find someone that knows something. You just have to pay the price for it."

"I don't have any money," Nath said.

"We can always steal money," Melegal replied. His steely eyes locked on Nath's hair. "Or you can trade and barter. If we hacked those locks from your skull, I'm sure there are Royal women that would pay a fortune for them. Those strands of yours would be a wigmaker's delight."

Nath tucked his braided ponytail into the back of his shirt. "Will you leave my hair out of this?"

"You need to shave it off," Melegal replied. "You stand out too much. It hinders us. Even being out in the open here is foolish. People talk. Be wise and skin yourself down before that mane of yours gets you got."

"Don't pay him any mind, Nath," Venir said. He tapped his broad chest with a fist and belched. "Melegal is paranoid and probably jealous. Perhaps he wants your hair for himself, seeing how he's gray as a goose already and not even thirty seasons old. Besides, the Royals don't navigate these slums. There is sanctuary in the grime, stink, and filth. And people from here don't talk to the Royals. They shun the City Watch as well."

Nath liked Venir's confidence. The young man with a lifetime of battle scars to show for himself seemed ready to meet the new challenge. His blue eyes looked like smoldering fires underneath a heavy brow. Like a panther ready to spring, he was ready for anything. Venir reminded Nath of a younger version of himself from over a hundred years ago. Back when Nath was young, he felt as if he could do anything. Venir was very much the same. It had taken a long time for Nath to learn the lessons in life that made him wiser and stronger. He suffered for it greatly. Venir seemed to be on a course to do the same. "As much as you might feel at ease, I just don't have the same inclination."

Smoothing his floppy cap over the side of his head, Melegal agreed. "And you are smart to feel that way. Venir puts trust in people. These slum-strutters will sell out when paid, the same as anyone. I think it would be best if you moved."

"To a hideout?" Nath asked.

Melegal nodded.

Nath shook his head. "That's the same as being here. I need to roam. I need a feel for the streets."

"Then you need to dye your hair and put gauntlets over those hands of yours. That's not going to go unnoticed," Melegal added.

Nath's hands flexed on the table. They were covered in black scales that at first glance weren't that noticeable, but the yellow-gold, clawlike fingernails were another matter. With one nail, he finished carving an insignia of a dragon head and a sword into the table. It was the image from the breastplate he had received when he'd dealt with the Black Hand over a century before. Nodding, he said to Melegal, "I see what you mean."

"Of course, we could paint your nails," Melegal suggested.

Leaning on the back legs of his chair, Venir said to Nath, "If you cover up, we'll take a stroll." Nath sat up. Venir lifted a finger. "And if you keep quiet and let me do the talking, we can go sniffing around. I have a few contacts that I need to track down who might guide us to some rogue mages that might be able to help."

"Don't tease, Venir. I'm ready to leave now," Nath said.

"Cover up, and we shall go." Venir glanced at Melegal. "Are you coming?"

"No. Take Mikkel with you. I'll head out later. I'd rather not be seen with three louts. My presence with Stupid will only arouse suspicion." Melegal moved his mouth into a parchment-thin smile. "I have a reputation."

Venir tossed back his head and let out a thunderous laugh. When he finished, he slapped Nath on the shoulder. "Let's go. The rogue dreams of being a Royal again."

CHAPTER 5

WITH VENIR, NATH, AND MIKKEL gone, Melegal practically had the tavern floor to himself. He liked it that way. He ordered a bottle of purple wine and immediately filled his goblet. "Splendid moments, how I delight in them."

Octopus slipped off of the table and disappeared behind the bar and through a doorway into the kitchen.

"Even better," Melegal said. He twisted a cork into his bottle and flicked the glass. He took a slug of wine. "Ah, plenty of sour and plenty of fermentation. Just how I like it." He leaned his chair back against the wall, propped his legs on the table, pulled his cap down over his eyes, and drank. "Perfect."

It wasn't that Melegal didn't like or want to help Nath, but he'd waited long enough to get back to the City of Bone. Now that he was home, he wasn't about to let anyone or anything spoil it. Besides, if he were to guess, the man named Nath was doomed, at least for as long as he relied on Venir. Venir knew as much about magic as he did about weaving a blanket, and Melegal wondered how on Bish was he going to get Nath from one world to another. Sure, there were many sects of magic users and the like in the City of Bone, but they were almost all under Royal control, and Royals were the last people that Melegal ever wanted anything to do with. The same went for Venir. The Royals had tormented both of them when they were young servants. At the same time, their mutual suffering had helped to form an unlikely but strong bond between the warrior and the thief.

I've been stuck with the lout ever since. Amid his moment of relaxation, Melegal, for as much as he tried, couldn't shake thinking about Nath's dilemma. There was no telling what stones Venir might turn over that might garner them some help, but he found the whole scenario unlikely. At the same time, he knew he could cover ground five times faster than the others. It was early, and he wasn't motivated, but Melegal would get around to it eventually.

Take a breather, Melegal. You deserve it.

Melegal refilled his goblet twice over the next hour. His keen senses were amply attuned to the scuffling of the people who came and went. Many quiet conversations carried to his ears, but he didn't hear anything interesting. As the morning dragged on, he settled into his homey climate, thankful to be at peace. With no worries in mind, another hour passed, and he momentarily dozed off.

Melegal woke to the fine hairs on the back of his hands raised on end. Without stirring, he breathed easily, the same as he always did, his scrawny chest rising and falling. At the same time, he could feel an unseen presence that crept up and hung over him like a shadow. With his eyes still closed, Melegal set his empty goblet on the table. Without looking, he refilled it and pushed it away from himself. He said, "Sit and have a drink, why don't you?"

Not a word was exchanged. Still, Melegal could feel a dreary presence lording over top of him. With two fingers, he pushed his cap away from his eyes and cracked them open. A chill ran down his spine. Standing on the other side of the table was a daunting man who wore a black hat with a very wide brim and a black cape draped over his shoulders. He had weasel eyes and a thin moustache, and he smirked. With his heart pounding inside his ears, the normally even-keeled Melegal had one word reverberating loudly inside his racing mind. *Slat!*

The darkly clad man pulled back a chair and sat down. He then began to remove his black leather gauntlets, one at a time. He placed the soft leather gloves on the table without making a sound. With a gesture of a finger, he flagged down the lone waitress who stood behind the bar, running her fingers through her greasy hair. Catching the stranger's eye, she grabbed a wine goblet and hustled over with a noticeable limp. The man took Melegal's wine bottle and filled his goblet. In a polite voice, he said, "It's a tad early for drinking, but since it's a special occasion, I think I'll have a sip."

Melegal's front two chair legs hit the floor. He narrowed his eyes on the man and said, "What is so special about it, McKnight?"

McKnight waggled a finger at Melegal. "*Detective* McKnight." He drank the wine, and immediately his face soured. "You drink this swill? I thought I had taught you better. Of course, I shouldn't expect much from a man who wears a sock for a hat and a moth-ridden vest. Hard times, eh, Melegal?"

"Things couldn't be better," he replied. "So, what brings you into the bowels of Bone? Did another Royal house kick you into the gutter?"

"Hardly." McKnight removed his grand hat and gently set it down on the table. He had jet-black hair and a deeply receding hairline. Much older than Melegal, he moved with the grace of a feline. "As a matter of fact, my services are in as high demand as ever. You, protégé, are missing out."

Melegal and McKnight went all the way back to Melegal's childhood. The so-called detective wasn't a Royal but served them with distinction. He'd taught Melegal a lot about the craft of stealing, picking locks, using guile and persuasion, and multiple other facets of the art of deception. Melegal proved to be a very apt pupil—more apt than McKnight realized because Melegal had learned to hold back and not show much of what he had learned.

Melegal grabbed the wine bottle and refilled his goblet. He took a long drink and said, "Ah, perfectly delicious. So, tell me, why are you here? Are you trying to recruit me for another one of the Royals' twisted missions? Is it another one of those difficult ones that you can't handle by yourself?"

"You know, that sharp tongue of yours is going to get you killed one day." McKnight pulled a dirk from his sword belt and stuck in the table. The point landed right beside the carving that Nath had left. He gave it some study. "Intriguing insignia. And it looks fresh. Maybe that brawler you hide behind has found a knack for doodling to go with his drooling."

Mouth closed, the stone-cold Melegal licked his upper teeth. McKnight's timely arrival couldn't be coincidental. He was searching for Nath. He had to be. And he'd just missed the man from another world by a few hours. *Or had he? Perhaps he'd already seen them go. He's vetting me. Be wary.* "We are too familiar with one another to play games. Who are you working for? What do you—or should I ask, what do *they* want?"

"Fair enough. I'll make it simple. My services have been acquired by a Royal family that is searching for a lost person." McKnight grabbed the dirk by the handle and gingerly poked it in and out of the table. "It is very intriguing how fate would have it that the name of the ogre you hang out with was mentioned. What is his name?"

"Venir. As if you didn't know."

"Yes, well, the description was accurate, and the name did ring a bell. Funny how fortune favors me in such matters. Anyhow, naturally, I immediately thought of you." McKnight twisted the dirk into the table. "So, tell me, is Venir harboring new company?"

"Aside from his nauseating attraction to unsavory wenches, no. There's been no new company," Melegal replied. *He's not going to believe it. I wouldn't believe me either. Besides, McKnight always knows more than he lets on.* "Or course, it might help if you gave a fuller description. Man, woman, sheep? What are you chasing?"

"A man. Of course, I think you know the man who I speak of, and as always, you are trying to be coy with me." McKnight stabbed the dirk deeper into the wood of the table. "Because I've held you in good favor, I am almost pleased to let you know that there is a great fortune to be gained when this man is found. Help me find him, and I'll extend to you one-third of the prize. I'll even throw in a good bottle of wine."

Melegal mulled it over. He could always make new friends, but he rarely had enough money. "Now you are talking a language I can understand. How much are we talking about?"

"More than you've ever had," McKnight replied.

"That's pretty vague." Melegal's gaze slid toward the door. A pair of large soldiers with swords buckled on their hips entered. They weren't the City Watch, but men in full armor covered in cloaks. Their big hands were on their longsword pommels, and they carried an air of superiority about them. A table of men who sat and ate breakfast a few tables over from Melegal grew wide eyes. They slunk away from their spot and headed up stairs. "So, how much are we talking about?"

"Your share would be fifty pieces of gold," McKnight replied. He tipped his head in the direction of the two men who had entered. "There won't be any cut for them, of course. But they will cut down any that stand in our way, including you and Venir. Those knights don't play games."

"Fifty gold coins is quite a hoard." Melegal made a quick smile. "I'd be a fool to turn it down. But I'd hate to take money that I couldn't give an account for."

"You're a thief. You don't care about that."

"No, but I don't want any part of dealing with the Royals either. You know that," Melegal said. Out of the corner of his eye, he saw another soldier, who carried a crossbow, block off the kitchen door behind the bar. It was the only other exit out of the main level. Tapping the table with his finger, he added, "It doesn't look like I'm going to have much of a choice in the matter. If that's the case, I'll take the gold in advance."

McKnight laughed. "Heh. Where is this man?" He eyeballed the steps leading up into the rooms. "I know he is near." He stabbed the table again. "I can sense it. Is he within these walls or beyond?"

The two soldiers in front moved deeper into the room as three more barricaded the front door. The muscles between Melegal's shoulder blades knotted. *Slat! The mire thickens.* Lifting his hands up, Melegal said, "Alright, McKnight. I see that you mean business. Show me the gold, and I'll give you the answer that you seek. Besides, I don't want my favorite tavern spoiled on account of me."

McKnight nodded. Narrowing an eye on Melegal, he said, "Naturally, I haven't been paid for my services yet, but in good faith, I will make a deposit from my own stash." He left his dirk in the table and reached for the coin purse on his belt to untie the strings.

As soon as McKnight's fingers disappeared underneath the table, Melegal shoved the table into the man's chest. McKnight tipped over in his chair and hit the floor. Melegal snagged the dirk out of the table and said, "Kiss my arse, McKnight!"

CHAPTER 6

Venir, Nath, and Mikkel sauntered through the streets of Bone at an easy pace. The massive city, which had over a million residents closed inside its massive walls, was a hive of activity. Dirty little children clothed in rags zigzagged through the streets and alleys. Many of them were being chased. Nath dared a look at a boy and a girl. In one moment, they rushed him, their grubby hands clinging to his fingers as they said, "Coin. Please. Hungry. Give us coin, master."

Venir scooped the boy up from under his armpits, held the child up, and tossed him away. "Go away, urchins!" The boy landed in a heap of garbage, and the girl sprinted into the alley.

"You are harsh on the little ones," Nath commented. He covered his nose as he spoke, as the stench of the refuse was overwhelming.

"They are little pickpockets, and if you had rings on your fingers, they'd be gone by now," Venir replied with a glance at Nath's fingers. "You didn't have any rings, did you?"

"No," Nath replied.

Mikkel strutted alongside Nath, wearing a broad smile on his face. "Venir is right, Nath. Those urchins would rob you of your fingernails if they were worth money. That's one of the reasons I hate Bone. I've lost every ring I ever had on my fingers, and I love to decorate myself. I'll tell you, if I had those scales, eyes, and hair like you, I'd be showing them off." He gave Nath a hearty slap on the back. "But that's just me."

"You would do well in my world. I think you would enjoy its splendor." Nath smiled. "I have to admit that I'm prone to showing them off. It seems a shame to hide them."

Bobbing his head, Mikkel said, "Tell us more about your world."

"Nalzambor is rich in greenery with flourishing forests and snow-capped mountain peaks. The ground is softer than a bed, unlike the cracked soil of this harsh world, and the rivers are plenty."

"Sounds nice." Mikkel carried his studded war club like a cane, and it clacked on the pavestones as he walked. "Tell me, what are the women like?"

"There are women with faces as radiant at the shining moon and skin as soft as flower petals. In most cases, the elven women are poetry in motion. They have bright and beautiful eyes and the most elegant features. Their words alone will soothe you."

Staring off as if he were in another world, Mikkel said, "Mmm, I'd like to see those women. And you call them elves?"

"Yes, they are like humans but lithe, slighter in build, and with pointed ears and sharper features."

Venir grunted. "Sounds like underlings."

"If anything, they are the opposite," Nath replied.

"I see." Venir picked up the pace and led the way. They hustled past the storefronts and merchants' carts, avoiding the fuss the salesmen made as they passed. They came to the end of the smaller street and ran into one at least ten wagons wide and paved with gray cobblestones. Carriages rumbled by. Dozens of men patrolled the streets, wearing brown hats with black bills and wearing navy-blue tunics over chainmail vests.

"Those are the City Watch," Venir said. "They are the Royals' henchmen. It's best to avoid them altogether. They'll jail you for a cross look or even sneezing."

"I see," Nath said as he scanned the crowd. Unlike the sordid women he met up with in Two-Ten City and inside the Drunken Octopus, the ones waltzing through the streets were fashionably dressed in colorful and sometimes revealing attire as they exited their carriages and moved from store to store. "I see many fetching figures."

"Aye," Mikkel muttered. He was hanging over Nath's shoulder. "But avoid those women at all costs. They are Royals. Real pit vipers. But boy, oh boy, do they glisten like honey."

"Keep your tongue in your mouth, Mikkel, or the City Watch will cut it off," Venir said. "We need to cross to the northwest district. So keep a low profile, and don't come within ten feet of a Royal, and no eyeballs on the watchmen. They're always looking for trouble."

Mikkel nudged Nath. "See, this is what I hate about Bone. The Royals hassle everyone who isn't a Royal and who's out of the slums. What's the plan, Vee? Why do we need to move to the northwest district? That's real uppity territory."

"The only mage I know lives there," he replied.

Mikkel's brows buckled. "Really? You know a mage? That's the first I've ever heard about it."

"I live here most of the time. You don't. Now, come on." Once there was a break in traffic, Venir started across the Royal Roadway.

Nath could see from one end of the road to the other. The stretch of road they were on ran north and south. He could see massive stone archways on the opposing ends. The massive iron portcullises were closed. People streamed inside underneath the pedestrian barbicans that ran in and out of the city. They were almost across the roadway when a carriage sped down the road. The carriage driver had slumped over in his seat, and the horses were uncontrolled and galloping wildly. A woman inside screamed for help out of the open window, and Nath made a move forward to help her.

Venir spun around and gripped Nath's arm. "It's not our business."

Nath slipped away from the warrior's grasp. Before he could think twice, he was running at full speed, chasing after the carriage. He took an angle that allowed him to cut off the horses then jumped on the last horse's back. From there, as the carriage recklessly tore down the street, he moved onto the pole that hitched the horses together. Walking up the pole with the wind tearing at his face, he made his way to the front. He grabbed the lead horse by the bridle and pulled the team to a stop.

A gorgeous woman wearing a tightly fitting black dress emerged from the carriage. She was stunning with looks rivaling the elves of Elome. Her lustrous black hair hung down to her shoulders, and she had a bewitching face and a voluptuous figure. Nath was working his way out of the horse hitch when she caught him by the arm. She looked deeply into his eyes, seemingly transfixed, and asked, "Who are you?"

Captivated by her natural charm, Nath had started to introduce himself when a well-built and handsome young man with thick brown hair and a sneer on his face cut in between them. He pushed Nath backward with a large hand to the chest.

"Whoa, what are you doing? I was only trying to help."

The young man shoved Nath again. "Don't you ever question a Royal."

"Tonio, mind yourself!" the woman said. She wedged herself in between the two men.

As she did, a host of Royal soldiers raced to catch up then surrounded them. All of them were fully armored in chainmail and tunics, and they brandished spears.

"Back off," she ordered the soldiers. She faced Nath and said, "You'll have to forgive my son. He is very protective of his mother, aren't you, Tonio?" The hot-eyed young man gave a stiff nod. She extended a welcoming hand to Nath and said, "I am Lorda Almen. I am grateful for your bravery." It seemed as if Lorda Almen couldn't take her eyes off of Nath's. "Your eyes are a wonder to behold. I've never seen the likes of them before."

Nath swallowed. The captivating woman was reeling him in with an alluring power the likes of which he'd never experienced in Bish. As she reached for his hands, he clasped them behind his back. "Um... it's a pleasure, Lorda. But it was nothing, really. I must, er, be going."

There was a commotion on the bench in front of the carriage. One of the Royal soldiers huddled over the carriage driver, waved his hand, and called, "Lorda Almen and Lord Tonio, this driver foams at the mouth. And I found this." The soldier held up a dart pinched between his leather gauntlets. "I found this in his neck."

Tonio grabbed his mother by the elbow. "We must go, Mother!"

With blazing-blue eyes, Lorda Almen jerked her arm away. "Unhand me, child!"

In a shocked, whiny voice, Tonio retorted, "But Mother, your safety is of the utmost importance. Assassins could be afoot!" He wrapped his arms around her slender waist and lifted her from the ground. "Forgive me, Mother." He hauled her back into the carriage. "Soldiers, take us back to the castle."

From inside the carriage, Lorda Almen stuck her head out of the window, pointed at Nath, and yelled at the top of her lungs, "Soldiers! Seize that man! I want him brought home with us!"

In military fashion, two soldiers took over the carriage. With a flick of his wrist, one of them snapped the reins, and the carriage lunged ahead. It did a full U-turn and rumbled down the road in the direction from whence it came.

Five Royal soldiers accompanied by a half dozen City Watchmen surrounded Nath. He raised his hands peacefully and said, "I don't want any trouble. I just wanted to help by stopping the carriage."

The leader of the Royal soldiers, a puffy-eyed veteran with broad shoulders, came forward and said, "It doesn't matter what you want. The only thing that matters is what they want. Come along now, nice and easy. I'm pretty sure she wants you alive."

Nath's eyes swept the streets. He caught Venir and Mikkel standing on a street corner, shaking their heads. Mikkel was mouthing the words, "Run, Nath. Run!" Nath nodded, looked at the lead soldier, and said, "Tell Lorda Almen I appreciate the invitation, but I must go now." He leapt over the soldiers in a single bound. At full speed, he raced down the road with the stunned soldiers chasing after him.

CHAPTER 7

ASOLDIER WHO HELD A CROSSBOW and guarded the kitchen door took aim at Melegal. With a flick of his wrist, Melegal threw the dirk at the man's face. The soldier ducked, discharging his bolt at the same time. The dirk stuck in the shelving behind the man, but the move gave Melegal just enough time to get up the stairs and vanish into the second-level stairwell. He raced up the steps, not stopping until he made it all the way to the top floor. He entered the hallway just as the sound of the pursuing soldiers entered the stairwell.

They can't know what floor I'm on or what room I'm in. It should buy me some time.

He ran to his apartment, quickly unlocked the door, slid inside, and secured the door. With his back pressed to the door, he swept his eyes across the small room. There was a small black stove, a cupboard, a small, circular wooden table, and three chairs. Two cots and two bedrolls were on the floor.

Billip lay in one of the cots. He sat up, rubbed his bleary eyes, and asked, "What did Venir do now?"

Melegal crossed the room and opened a small window. "Believe it or not, we can't blame Venir this time. Royal soldiers are here. They're coming after Nath."

Grunting, the stout black-haired archer ambled quickly to his bow and quiver of arrows. He moved toward the window and started to climb out, but Melegal hooked his arm. Billip looked at him like he was crazy and said, "What are you doing?"

"Not that way."

"What did you open the window for?" Billip asked.

"Just follow me. I want to make it look like we fled in a hurry." Melegal hustled back to the front door, put his ear to it, and closed his eyes. A moment later, he said, "Come on." He opened the door and slipped into the hall with Billip right behind him.

As if on cats' feet, Billip and Melegal moved down the hallway. The sounds of shod boots storming up the stairwell and fists hammering on doors carried through the halls. Melegal fished a key out of his pocket. He unlocked the door to an apartment three doors down and across the hall. He slipped inside, pulled Billip inside with him, and closed the door.

Incredulous, Billip said, "What are you doing? They're searching every room in the building. They won't miss us here." He cast his stare to an old man who sat on a rocking chair in the middle of the room with his back was to the wall. He had a woolen blanket on his lap and the huge black cat, Octopus, on his lap.

In a raspy voice, the old man said, "Is that you, Melegal?"

"Me and a friend."

The old man's eyes were smoky-white, just like the cat's. He gave a toothless smile. "Is it a pretty woman?" He sniffed the air. "I imagine pretty."

"Sorry, Clyvel, not a woman. Just a friend of the masculine persuasion." Melegal listened at the door.

"A shame," Clyvel said. The old man had little hair and a big dowager's hump. "I miss women, but I don't think they miss me." He shook his head. "What's happening? Who'd you piss off this time?"

"Hush, Clyvel. Hush."

Inside Melegal and Venir's apartment, McKnight took a quick assessment. There were two cots and two bedrolls. He could account for Venir, Melegal, and Nath, so he made the assumption that the other man was Billip. It was Billip whom Gannon Vansung had in custody before. Taking a knee, he noted blood caked on one of the blankets.

McKnight had been the first to arrive in the wide-open room. He looked out the window. An open alley led to the main streets. A soldier who appeared to have exited from the kitchen's back door stood in the alley. At the far end, two more soldiers waited. McKnight had sealed off the alley, but somehow Melegal had slipped by the soldiers. He looked up to the ledge of the roof and said, "Bone."

The scuff of hard-soled boots entering the room was followed by a strong and authoritative voice. "Is there any sign of him?"

McKnight pulled his head and shoulders back inside the room. Lorda Aleta Vansung's personal knights, Quint and Luther, stood side by side. Their hard gazes swept through the small room. McKnight said, "It seems he ran right by your soldiers. Either that or he vanished. But no doubt, he knows something."

Quint, the thicker of the twins, shoved passed McKnight and stuck his head out the window. He shouted at the soldiers, "Any signs of anyone passing?"

"No, sire!" the soldiers in the alley said.

Although he was in full armor, the knight somehow shoved his big frame through the window. McKnight gaped when he saw the man's ankles and feet standing on the window ledge. There was a noticeable grunt as the knight hauled himself upward. McKnight stuck his head and shoulders back outside. Quint had grabbed hold of a drainage pipe and started the short climb onto the roof. His body disappeared over the rim.

"I'll be." McKnight climbed after the man.

Quint made his way over the tavern's roof and looked out across the surrounding rooftops. He shook his head and punched the chimney. "We had him. We almost had him!" His hot glare locked on McKnight. "Detective, you have failed on your mission. The Lorda won't be pleased, which means that I am not pleased."

"How have I failed? This is clearly where our target is staying. I led you right to him. If anyone has failed, it is you." McKnight turned at the sound of more scuffles. The other twin, Luther, was climbing onto the roof. McKnight couldn't hide his expression. *They climb like squirrels in that armor.* "I told you that the roof should have been covered. But I'm not worried. We came this close." He held up a hand and separated his thumb and forefinger by a small amount. "They won't be able to hide for long."

"Brother," Luther said as he marched toward McKnight and Quint. "What has happened? Did we lose our man? We never lose our man."

Pointing down at McKnight, Luther said, "This man blames us, the Lorda's most precious hounds. I say if it is anyone's fault, it is his. He frightened the man like a rabbit when he should have trapped him instead. I am not pleased."

McKnight looked between the two formidable men. He wasn't short by any stretch, but the knights towered at least a head above him. The twins were abnormally tall and built like athletes, and they were bullish in their platemail armor. They were seasoned veterans of many campaigns, with strength behind their eyes that was clearly echoed in their commanding voices. With them, failure was never an option. McKnight, never one to cower or grovel, stood his ground and said, "This is not even a setback. We are even further ahead than I planned. You hired me because I, too, always get my man. If I didn't, you wouldn't have acquired my services, as my reputation among the Royals precedes me." He squeezed out from in between them. "So relax. Go groom your moustaches or something."

Luther's hand shot out. His powerful fingers locked around McKnight's throat in a mighty grip. With one hand, he lifted the detective's feet off of the ground and hoisted him up over his head. He walked him back toward the ledge of the building and dangled him over the side. "Don't confuse your lowly station with ours, detective. Keep your jests to yourself... or die."

With his face reddening like a ripening tomato, McKnight managed an uncomfortable nod. Luther dropped him on the roof. He landed on his feet but bottomed out onto his knees, clasping his throat while gasping for breath. To his complete surprise, he'd completely underestimated the twins. *What are these men made of?*

"We'll post two soldiers here at the tavern," Luther suggested. "In case they return, we'll be ready. Now, detective, resume the lead back into the streets and pray that you can quickly find these vermin."

CHAPTER 8

With Venir and Mikkel waving him on, Nath ran like a deer and shot past them. He had no idea where he was going. All he wanted to do was stretch the lead between himself and the soldiers. He weaved his way through the people who milled in the streets, darting through the trees. He heard Venir's booming voice shout, "Slow down!" He skidded to a halt.

Venir and Mikkel were half a block behind him. The pursuing soldiers were a half a block behind them, working their way through the crowd. Venir finally caught up and said, "Slow your arse down and follow me." He sprinted down a smaller street then barreled into a narrow alley that led to a network of others. The malodorous and filth-ridden passages formed their own catacombs.

Pinching his nose while running, Nath said, "Are there any alleys that don't smell?"

"No," Mikkel said.

They half ran and half trotted for many minutes before Venir finally slowed to a stop and rested against the wall with his hands on his knees. Sweat dripped from his chin. Mikkel's brown face was covered in heavy drops of perspiration as he struggled to take a full breath.

Clutching his side, Mikkel said, "Bish, I haven't run that hard or that far in a long time. Ugh, my side is burning." He eyeballed Nath. "Look at you. You aren't even breathing heavy or sweating. What in the Bish are you make of?"

Nath shrugged. "Do you think we lost them?"

"Aye," Venir replied. He wiped his meaty forearm across his head. "But we need to keep moving. The districts are big and busy, but those soldiers aren't capable of patrolling everything." He gave Nath a disappointed glance. "What were you thinking?"

"What do you mean?" Nath said.

"I told you to lay low and not draw attention to yourself. Now, more people are looking for us than ever. Well, you, anyway."

Scratching his temple, Nath said, "Those passengers inside the carriage were in danger. They could have been killed. I couldn't let that happen. That woman was in trouble."

Venir slowly shook his head. "They were Royals. Believe me when I say that you should have stayed out of the way and let them die. It will come back to haunt you. Bone, it might even come back to haunt me."

Mikkel huffed a laugh. "I know that's right. That's why I don't hang around here so much anymore." He spat. "This city is ill!"

"So, did they get a good look at you?" Venir said.

With a sheepish grin, Nath said, "I'd say so. I found myself captivated by the woman. She would be fetching in my world. She has natural beauty that rivals the elven."

"Great. Just great," Venir said. He stuffed his long hunting knife halfway into his sheath. "Now two Royal families might be looking for you. Listen, Nath, look at what that wretch Gannon did. He betrayed us, even though we saved his life—or brought him back home, anyway. With Royals, well, they just can't help themselves. Men are prizes to them. It's all about power and possessions. They care about nothing else."

"So all Royals are bad?" Nath asked. "I find that hard to believe."

Venir shrugged his brawny shoulders. "They aren't underlings, but they aren't a bunch of cherubim either, though they convince many that they are. If there is good in them, I've not crossed it in my lifetime."

Mikkel nodded. "Me either."

"Come on. Let's go." Venir started down the alley. "We need to get you back home before you wind up a stuffed display in one of their museums."

Mikkel rumbled with laughter.

Nath's stomach turned queasy.

CHAPTER 9

Inside old Clyvel's apartment, Melegal waited inside the door. He could hear the footsteps of the soldiers who paced the outside hallway. There were two soldiers stationed on his apartment, and he didn't hesitate to think there might be more outside, posted in the streets. McKnight was a very careful planner. He said to Billip, "It's time. You need to go out there and provide a distraction."

Billip had been sitting on a stool, staring at the floor and cracking his knuckles. He stopped the cracking and raised his eyes. "Me? Have you forgotten that they've gotten a few licks on me already?"

Keeping his voice low, Melegal said, "I thought those were the City Watch. These men won't know you." He moved away from the door and stood between Billip and old Clyvel. "Take this old buzzard down to the main floor for dinner. Get an eye on things. If anything goes wrong, we'll rendezvous at the fallen castle."

Billip gave him a puzzled look. "The fallen what?"

"The fallen castle. You know."

"No, I don't know. I'm not from this city."

"Well, you should know. It would make things a lot easier if you knew something for a change," Melegal said. He took off his cap and fanned himself. "Just meet me in the barn, then. But don't be followed."

Billip stood up quickly with his bow in hand. "I'm not a lumbering foot soldier." He poked a finger at Melegal's chest. "And you don't tell me what do."

Smacking his lips, old Clyvel said, "I'm looking forward to this dinner. But I can only have soup, with some hot bread to dip." He made a toothless smile and drew a deep breath in through his nostrils. "Ah, I can smell it already. And it's been quite some time since I've been down below. I don't have any money, so you will be paying for this, won't you?"

"Don't worry about it," Melegal said. He kept his attention on Billip. "Are you on board with this or not?"

Billip picked up his quiver from the floor and stuffed it against Melegal's chest. "Don't lose a feather." He helped Clyvel out of his chair. "Let's go get you something to eat, old one."

Clyvel shuffled along with his withered hands latched onto Billip's arm. "I used to have arms like this. Solid muscle. Plenty of meat. I would have made you look like a child."

Melegal opened the door for them. Octopus darted outside.

"Slat!" the soldier in the hallway shouted. "Ernest! Ernest! Get a look at this cat. It's bigger than my dog. Never mind. It's gone. Blasted thing moved like a ghost. I guess that explains why I haven't seen a rat in this dung hole."

Billip led the old man out of the apartment and closed the door behind them. Melegal listened to them go. Without a word from the soldiers, he heard Billip and Clyvel make it into the stairwell. Clyvel babbled about eating soup and smelling women. Clyvel even said, "Find a woman to sit on my lap. She doesn't even have to be pretty, just not heavy. My knees can't take it, though I miss the days when they could."

His muttering finally fell silent as they moved out of earshot. Melegal had known Clyvel for years, and the old man had many stories to tell, but most all of them were very hard to believe. Still, he enjoyed the man's company and looked in on him from time to time.

Now, it's time for me to slip out of here.

He slung the quiver over his shoulder, and the arrows rattled inside. He looked at Billip's short bow and tested the string by pulling back on it. It was like pulling a cord made out of steel. He couldn't even draw the bowstring back to his cheek.

How does he fire this thing?

Billip was the oldest out of all of them. He'd been soldiering since early manhood and had become a proven scout and marksman among the ranks of the Royal soldiers. He'd given it up years before and had been doing whatever he wanted since, which involved a lot of gambling. He was a good gambler, just not as good as Melegal.

Melegal moved the stool to a corner of the room and stepped on top of it. Now that Clyvel and Billip were gone, he was free to move without them encumbering him. Other people hindered him. He always moved quicker on his own. He pushed on the slats above his head. They broke free, opening up a crawl space between the ceiling and the roof. Melegal had used the apartment at one time, and he'd created the escape hatch for himself. There was another one in the other apartment too. Only he knew about them, and they were just big enough for him to crawl through. He shoved the quiver and bow into the crawl space, climbed inside, and moved the slats back into place. In the darkness, he crawled on his belly like a snake.

Almost there.

He hadn't moved twenty feet when he twisted onto his backside. His fingers grazed a square slab of stone. He pushed up, and daylight spilled through a narrow crack. He took a long pause to listen but didn't hear anyone on the rooftop. He pushed the stone slab up and quietly moved it aside. He squeezed out of the one-foot-by-one-foot hole. Kneeling, he pulled out the quiver and bow.

Why did I agree to bring this thing? It's a pain in the arse.

With a quick scan of his surroundings, he noticed that he was alone. He moved the slab back into place and skittered across the roof. He looked down at the alley from a spot above his own apartment. The kitchen workers were smoking outside of the back door, but no soldiers were posted there. He moved to the front of the tavern and looked at the streets. The back roads of the City of Bone were steady with traffic and men talking about their days of hard work that they had ended early.

Seems safe enough.

He waited, and less than an hour passed before he saw Billip depart. The wiry man glided into the crowd and vanished up the road. Now, Melegal's issue was getting a signal to Venir. He removed a red handkerchief from his vest pocket and hung it from an old unused flagpole. It was a signal they used whenever the City Watch or anyone else came looking for them from other crossings.

I just hope the lout remembers to look up for it. Hopefully, I can find him first.

Melegal got a running start and jumped from his roof to another. He landed quietly on the other side, scaled down the drain pipe on the building's back side, and jumped the last ten feet to the ground. Making haste, he headed to the stables. He didn't sense the eyes that followed him all the way down.

Watching Melegal from an adjacent rooftop, McKnight fanned himself with his large hat. He twisted the hairs on one end of his moustache and smiled.

CHAPTER 10

T HE STONE BUILDINGS WERE CRAMMED closely together in the northwestern district, and Venir led the way up a set of narrow steps. He, Nath, and Mikkel had to press their large frames against the wall as another group of people came down the stairs with big, glazed-over eyes. They pushed by as if the men weren't even there. They smelled of strong incense and smoke.

Mikkel fanned his nose. "Whew. Where in Bone are you taking us, Venir? Because wherever it is, I don't want to come out smelling like that."

"Agreed," Nath said. He fought the urge to pinch his own nose. "They looked like they were staring into another world."

Mikkel nudged Nath in the chest with his elbow. "Those people were induced. That's how they make their escape to another world, they say. Bone is full of odd pleasures. Whatever freaks like that offer, stay away from it." He directed his attention back to Venir. "And again, I ask. Why would we be wanting any part of this?"

"Because I can't think of another option." Venir marched up the steps. A heavy black curtain was drawn in front of an archway across the landing at the top. He entered.

Nath and Mikkel followed him into a circular room about thirty feet in diameter. Oil lanterns with multicolored glass hung from the ceilings and warmed the room. Its outer benches were padded in soft velvet pillows. Men and women with dreamy eyes were sprawled out across the floor and benches. Many of them were dressed in fine silk and leather. They were of various ages, but most were younger. They smoked out of glass pipes while one young man strummed a lute.

Nath fanned his face. The filmy smoke lingering in the exotic quarters stung his eyes.

Venir stepped over the people on the floor and moved deeper into the cove, where another area was blocked by a curtain. He shoved it open. A beautiful older woman with a head of silky, cotton-white hair sat across from a young man and woman. Their eyes were fixed on a green marble that sat on the table between them. They swayed from side to side. The young man turned to Venir and said, "Go away. It's our time."

"No, it's my time." Venir picked the young man up in his arms like a baby and tossed him out of the room and onto the pillow-covered floor. He did the same with the young woman. "You want advice? You can do better than that guy." He dropped her outside of the room then closed Nath and Mikkel inside the chamber with him. He sat down across the table from the older woman. Nath and Mikkel stood on either side of him. He looked at the woman. "It's been a while."

"You can't help but create a stir when you enter, can you, Venir?" the woman said. Her eyes remained locked with his. She was middle-aged and wrapped up in loose silk clothing that revealed much of her full and fetching figure. She was dark-skinned with haunting eyes and teeth as white as her hair. She offered a warm smile to the men. "I am Laana." She offered her hand to Mikkel, and many bracelets jangled on her wrists.

Mikkel leaned back. "No offense, but the last time I touched a city druid, I woke up in another city." He gave Venir a concerned look. "You know I don't like witches."

"Easy now," Laana said. The smooth-skinned woman's brows knitted together. "I don't come into your house and insult you."

"Witch, you aren't ever coming into my house," Mikkel said. He started to rise. Venir pulled him back down into his chair.

"Mikkel, Laana and I go back to my childhood among the Royals. Like Melegal and me, she made her exodus when she was old enough."

He reached over and grabbed her hand. "We helped one another out, back in the day."

Mikkel looked back and forth between the two. "What are you talking about, Venir? She's old enough to be your mother. Look at those locks. She's ancient."

Laana pointed at Mikkel. "You curse my hair, and I'll curse yours."

Mikkel ran his big palm over his short afro. "You leave my hair alone."

Laana's eyes rolled up into her head. She started chanting in soft, quick words.

Stiffening in his chair, Mikkel said, "What is she doing?"

The candle flames inside the room quavered. Chill bumps rose on Mikkel's arms. Nath felt a cold breeze on his neck.

The chanting stopped. Laana opened up her eyes. "All done."

Mikkel got up, rubbing his arms. "I'm getting out of here. She's giving me the willies." He vanished to the other side of the curtain. Somebody yelped on the other side. "Get out of my way, you bunch of leaf kissers!"

"Sorry about Mikkel's manners. He'd treat you better if he knew you," Venir said to Laana.

"It's not something that I worry myself with. You know that. If my sanctuary makes a man uncomfortable, I'm fine with that. He's better off." Laana reached out and began rubbing Venir's muscular forearm. "And I know that you don't care much for it either. The truth is, I don't like it myself, but it's a better living than being a tavern strumpet, and it's the best I can do outside of being a Royal. You know what I mean."

"I do," he said.

"So, Venir, what brings you by? I was beginning to think I'd never see you again."

Venir patted Nath, who was sitting quietly with his hands down at his sides, on the back. "This is my friend Nath. He's lost and needs help finding home."

Laana slowly turned her head toward Nath and focused on him for the first time. Her head tilted from side to side like a curious child seeing a shiny new object. She leaned closer, staring into his eyes. "My vapors are thick, but I swear this man's eyes are gold."

"They are," Nath said. He leaned forward. "Would you like a closer look?" He wasn't sure what had freaked Mikkel out about the woman, but he didn't sense any danger from her. She was mysterious, odd, and captivating, but aside from aiding the sordid people that Bish was full of, she didn't ruffle his scales.

Laana didn't break the stare. "You are lost? From where?"

"Nalzambor," Nath said.

She cast her glance at Venir and lifted her brows. "Where?"

"Nath, do you want me to explain it, or shall I make the attempt?" Venir asked.

"I'll try." In his lifetime, Nath had encountered powerful magic that could level mountains. He had a much better understanding of it than Venir did. Though he sensed that Laana had some divine, mystic powers, he wasn't fully confident that she would understand. "In my world, I was banished by a wizard named Corzan through a mystic portal. At the same time, the underlings of this world were summoning a demon. Instead, they got me."

"Well, you don't look anything like a demon," Laana said. "Why did they summon a demon in the first place?"

Nath lifted up his black-scale-covered fingers and pointed at Venir. "To kill him."

Marveling at Nath's hands, Laana gasped.

CHAPTER 12

NATH, VENIR, AND LAANA HAD a long conversation about much of what had happened since Nath had arrived in Bish. She wouldn't let go of Nath's hands. She even crawled into his lap at one point and felt his arms and chest. She was fascinated with him and with his story. The more they talked, the more enthralled she became.

"This is the most fascinating thing that has ever happened to me," Laana said as she moved behind Nath and worked on his ponytail. "The wigmakers would kill for these locks. I think that I would too."

"Yes, Melegal has been quick to point that out several times," Nath replied. He reached around his back, pulled her in front of him, and held her cold hands in his. "Can you assist me or not?"

"What you are talking about is well beyond my skill level."

"Laana, I know that," Venir said politely. "I'm not one to consort with the magi circles in this city, but I was thinking that you could give us some direction. You have connections to that upper ring. Do you know anyone who can be *trusted* and will help us?"

Laana moved back to her chair and eased into her seat. "Perhaps. But I have to warn you that whoever brought you here most likely will have to send you back. The sorcery you are talking about is unearthly. In truth, I think that your chances of leaving are little to none. I'm sorry, Nath." She reached out and caressed his hands. "But you can stay with me as long as you like. I'll do what I can do." In a voice more like a purr, she added, "I'd be very interested in bearing your offspring."

"I'm honored, but I'll have to pass." He would never go into details with them about being a dragon. "I'm committed to another," he said of Selene, his love.

She gave him a welcoming smile. "We have a saying. What happens in Bone stays in Bone."

Nath shook his head. "You said that perhaps you can help. What did you mean by that?"

"I can ask around. Tell me, do you have anything else from your world? Something to link you to it, besides yourself?"

"I have a sword," Nath said. "Why?"

"The more links to your world, the better. That's what the magi will ask for. It's possible that they might be able to open a portal elsewhere." She drummed her cherry-red fingernails on the table. "But this is otherworldly. I know that monsters can be summoned from the mystic planes, but I've never seen it done. It's rare and more or less legend and rumor. I could only dream that it was within the scope of my abilities." She fastened her hands on Nath's again. "It would help if I had a lock of your hair or a few drops of your blood."

Nath patted her hand then moved his away. "I'd rather not."

"I didn't come here so that you can dissect the man, Laana," Venir said. "I came to you for some direction. The question is whether you can help or not."

"Oh, Venir, you know that I would do just about anything for you. Can you check back with me in a couple of days?" she said.

"That's a bit longer than I care to wait," Venir said.

"If I learn something sooner, I'll seek you out. Where will you be?" she asked.

"The Octopus."

Laana's pretty expression soured. "Ech. You still frequent that rat den? If I'd known that, I would have scrubbed you down before I let you enter."

"You are more than welcome to scrub me down anytime." Venir stood, and Nath joined him. "Keep this between us. We have enough trouble as it is."

Laana met Venir on his side of the table and gave him a big hug. "Anything for you." She kissed him on the neck. She gave Nath a hug and kissed him too. "Come back. I want to learn more about you and your world."

"See you in a couple of days," Nath said, "unless I find a way home before then."

"For your sake, I hope that you do. Goodbye for now." Laana held the curtain open for them, showed them out, then closed it again.

They found Mikkel waiting for them at the bottom of the stairs, wearing a disgruntled look. "Did that witch offer anything helpful?"

"No, she wants us to come back," Venir said. He moved on toward the streets. "We'll see."

Nath followed him. "We aren't going to go back?"

Venir shook his head. "Like I said, we'll see."

Nath clenched his fists. "We'll see? I'm not seeing anything. What I want to see is results."

Venir pushed deeper into the crowd without a word. He moved at a brisk pace, leaving Nath alone in his thoughts. It seemed as though Venir was tired of talking and was determined to do something else. He wasn't easy for Nath to follow, but he didn't have much of a choice. "At least tell me where we're going."

"We'll go back to the Octopus and wait for word from Laana," Venir said.

"Is that it?" Nath's temper began to boil. "You don't have any other friends that you can check with?"

"No," Venir said. He ducked into an alley and led them into different streets from where they came. "It might be different if I was a Royal, but I'm not."

"Aren't there any good Royals that we can call upon?" Nath asked.

Venir shook his head. "I've told you that Royals can't be trusted. Besides, if there is someone that can help, Laana will know. She doesn't take the lead on much, but I know better. Nath, you just have to work with me. It just can't be that easy to move someone from one world to another. Of course, maybe that isn't the case where you come from. I don't know."

"No, you're right." Nath put his fist over his chest. "I just feel my heart tightening inside of me. It's as if something is telling me that time is running out. It eats at me. I don't think that you would understand even if I could explain it."

Mikkel put his large hand on Nath's shoulder. "We are going to find a way for you, Nath, or die trying. It's a promise."

The iron-jawed Venir nodded at Nath but continued walking. They managed to cross the Royal Roadway at the northern end, far away from the incident earlier in the day. The route back was longer, but they finally made it back to the narrow roads that led to the Drunken Octopus. About one hundred feet from the tavern doorway, Venir casually cast his gaze upward and stopped.

Mikkel bumped into Venir. "What is it?"

Nath followed Venir's stare. There was a red handkerchief dangling from a flag pole, rustling in the wind.

"It seems like Melegal has had some company," Venir said. His gaze scanned the alley. "Let's go."

CHAPTER 13

VENIR AND COMPANY HUSTLED BACK to the stables from whence Nath had originally entered the city. It was there, deep inside a huge, decrepit barn, that they searched for Melegal and Billip. Venir called Chongo, and the big dog ran to him then licked all of the men half to death. Nath managed to break away to check on Fang. The sword was still safely tucked away under a bed of straw. Not entirely comfortable walking through the City of Bone with such a large weapon, he pulled Dragon Claw, the dagger, out of the bottom of the sword's pommel then tucked it into his belt before kneeling to pet Chongo.

"Now what, Venir?" Mikkel asked.

He scratched Chongo behind the ears. "We go to the old castle."

Mikkel gave Nath an unknowing look and said, "Don't feel bad. I've never been there either."

Chongo whimpered.

Rubbing the big dog's neck, Venir said, "What's wrong, boy? You look like you ate too much underling." He checked the dog's bloodshot eyes, which had flecks of silver in them. "I've never seen your eyes look like that before."

Out of nowhere, Chongo let out a long belch.

Venir fell back on his butt and fanned his face. "What was that?"

Mikkel pinned his nose. "Ew! Lords of Two-Ten, that smelled like a cartful of fish. He hasn't eaten any fish, has he?"

"Not that I'm aware of," Venir said, reaching over to pet the dog's belly. "He's eaten some underling and probably licked too much blood. It makes him sick sometimes. But something lurks in his eyes. It's strange."

Nath took a knee beside Chongo. "Perhaps it is my blood that made him sick. He licked me all over when I was wounded after our battle. It's foreign to him. In my world, the tasting of blood is very dangerous. It can have toxic effects. And, because I'm part dragon, magic is mixed in my blood."

Chongo licked Nath's cheek.

"Well, magic blood or not, he's fond of you, Nath. And if you did him harm, he wouldn't touch you. But that smell." Venir's nose crinkled. "I remember it from when I was a boy, and Chongo and I ate the Silver Fish."

Mikkel arched an eyebrow. "The what?"

"I haven't told you that story?"

"Save it. I've heard enough of your two-tailed stories."

Chongo gave Venir one long last look, whimpered, then nestled in the corner of the stable.

"He'll be fine. It's just a bellyache. He and Georgio get them sometimes. Let's go," Venir said.

They left the dog in the stable and quickly made their way out of the barn. The three towering men traveled the busy streets at a brisk pace and quickly made it into another part of Bone, which showed centuries of deterioration. Away from the bustling people were sections of the city that were entirely abandoned. The buildings were empty, and the wooden porches rotted through. Most of the shutters were missing from the windows. Finally, they came upon the foundation of a castle, where a few towers still stood with steps leading upward.

Together, the men traversed the stairs of the most intact tower. When they were halfway up, they heard a sharp whistle. Nath looked down and saw Billip at the foot of the steps, waving at them. They headed back down. Billip's face was still swollen, scraped, and bruised, but he seemed fine otherwise. "Where's Melegal?"

"He's about," Billip said. The archer bumped forearms with Venir and Mikkel. It was a customary thing the men did that Nath had picked up on. "Come on." Billip led them to a set of crumbling stairs that led into the subterranean levels of the old castle. They descended a full flight and moved down a corridor to find a lantern on a table waiting in the darkness. Melegal was leaning back against the wall, cleaning his nails with a knife.

"Glad you see that you finally made it," the steely-eyed rogue said. "You weren't followed, were you?"

Venir shrugged his bullish shoulders. "Not as far as we know. What happened back at the tavern?"

"McKnight showed up"—Melegal pointed at Nath—"looking for him, naturally."

Venir settled into one of the chairs at the table, and the chair creaked loudly. Venir sat still with his arms out, as if he expected to fall. Finally, he put his arms on the table. "McKnight, huh? So, you spoke with him, huh?"

"He offered me a sizable reward for our torch-haired friend." Melegal hid his dagger inside his clothing. "I'm still considering his offer."

Nath started toward Melegal. "You're what?"

"Easy, friend. Melegal is pulling your scales," Venir said. "Just tell us what happened, Melegal."

"I almost died," he answered in a bitter voice. "That's what happened. Is my life worth giving up for Nath's? No. It's not worth giving up for anyone, yet I almost kissed the grave. No thank you. We need to be rid of him, the sooner the better."

"You are cold-blooded, Melegal," Mikkel said. He turned a chair around and sat down. "You disappoint me. Nath is a good man!" His chair broke underneath him, and Mikkel landed hard on his backside with his eyes big as the moons.

All of the men broke out into gusty laughter, including Melegal. Venir held his gut as he guffawed like a drunken sailor.

Mikkel kicked Venir's chair leg, and the rotting chair collapsed underneath the warrior. Mikkel joined in the laughter. He pointed at Melegal and said, "You're still wrong, Melegal."

"Don't be so sappy," the wry thief said. "I wouldn't be here if I wasn't helping." He paused. "While Billip and I were fighting hordes of Royals, what did you fools find? Did the blond-headed ogre find a rainbow bridge leading from one world to the other? Perhaps Chongo can pull Nath to another world on a magic sled."

Venir tossed the broken chair aside and rose. "Laana is looking into it."

Melegal's jaw dropped open. "Are you a complete dunderhead, Venir? All that spooky witch is good for is cocoa rubs."

"Cocoa rubs? You didn't tell me about that, Vee," Mikkel said, massaging his shoulder. "I could use a rub."

Melegal began to pace. "You should know by now that Laana can't be trusted. She means well, but she can't keep her mouth shut about anything. Remember the lycans, Venir? She almost got both of us killed."

Venir rolled his eyes. "Not that again. And you think you are going to die every time you set foot outside of the apartment with me. You overreact. As for Laana, well, she might have a big mouth—"

"And breasts," Mikkel added.

"Yes, and those," Venir continued.

"And hips," Mikkel noted. "Lips."

Venir turned his focus to Mikkel. "I thought you didn't like her."

"Well, I'd wager that a good cocoa rub from her could smooth over my trepidations."

Nath chuckled.

Billip jumped into the conversation. "If anyone needs a cocoa rub, it's me. I'm the one that took a beating." He rubbed his jaw. "Now, who is this Laana, and when do we meet with her again? What does she look like?"

Mikkel pointed at Billip. "You're too scrawny for a woman like that!" He flexed his arms. "She needs a big man."

"You don't know what she likes, and I'm not trying to court her. I just want a massage... from a fetching woman."

Melegal rapped his bony finger against the table. "Can we please get back on topic? We can't help Nath if we are fixated on body rubs. I question Venir's intentions in going to Laana. As far as I know, she's never even cast a spell."

"No, but she does have a spellbinding body," Venir replied.

Melegal's frown grew deeper.

"Well, what do you expect? Back in Two-Ten, half of the woman looked like boars walking on two legs. I'm only human. Besides, I didn't hear you coming up with any better ideas."

"There are many more choices than Laana," Melegal said. He resumed his pacing and rubbed his dimpled chin.

"Is that so? And what would you have done?" Venir asked. "Who would you have gone to?"

"Well, a thief never reveals all of his connections," Melegal replied.

"That's what I thought. You don't have any. At least Laana knows people in those circles. She could give us some names." Venir looked at Nath. "We'll get there. I have no doubt that someone in this city knows something. I swear we will find them."

"In the meantime, we need to find a better place to hide out now that the Octopus is being watched. McKnight and the Royals won't be giving up this hunt anytime soon," Melegal said with a glance at Nath. "He won't stop until he gets his mark."

"You couldn't be more right," a newcomer's voice said.

Quick as a mongoose, Billip notched an arrow on his bowstring and aimed down the hall.

Mikkel cocked his club back for a swing.

Venir held his long dagger in hand, eyes narrowed on the figure that approached from down the hall.

A well-built man approached as quietly as a cat. He wore a black wide-brimmed hat that shadowed most of his face, a long-sleeved gray shirt, and black trousers. His black leather gloves matched his high boots. A belt with poniards and dirks dressed his hips. He looked past all of them and locked eyes with Melegal. "My protégé is right. McKnight always gets his mark. Thank you, Melegal." Removing his hat, he cast his eyes on Nath. "You led us right to him."

CHAPTER 14

ALL OF THE MEN'S EYES narrowed on Melegal.

"Melegal! You betrayed us?" Mikkel said.

Billip kept his aim fixed on McKnight but added to Mikkel's comments. "You sniveling little hound. How much did you score?"

"That's not what he means, you idiots." Melegal shook his head. "I didn't sell out. He must have tracked you, Billip. Well done," he said sarcastically.

"On the contrary, protégé. It was you that led me here. And that's an honest statement." The swarthy man fanned himself with his hat and placed it back on top of his head. "I am Detective McKnight, currently under the employ of Castle Vansung. I've been hired to capture you," he said to Nath. He scanned Nath head to toe. "You are truly a unique specimen, even in the dim light. Nath, consider yourself captured. It's best that you come along peacefully."

Venir closed the gap between himself and McKnight. Looking down on the detective, he said, "You won't be taking him anywhere. You'll have to come through us first."

McKnight didn't bat an eye as he looked beyond Venir and spoke to Melegal. "It's so warming to see that you two worthless urchins have maintained your friendship after all these years. But today, I don't think that your hulking bodyguard is going to do you any good. I have many goons of my own. Royal goons. They await above."

"I'll check it out," Mikkel said. He hustled down the corridor and out of sight.

McKnight had a wry smile on his crooked lips. His eyes were fixed on Nath, and Nath could see the air of confidence deep in the man's eyes. It made it perfectly clear to him that the detective believed that he held a superior advantage. McKnight reminded him of a combination of people that he'd known over the years. Something about McKnight took him way back to the days when he was a century-old youth. It was then that he was deceived by a group of adventurers called the Black Hand, who were led by a swarthy swordsman named Tobias. Nath glowered at McKnight. Now, fully mature in the ways of men and women, it only took him a few moments to sort out whether someone was good or evil, and he knew that McKnight was indeed evil. It caused Nath to wonder more deeply about the history that the detective had with Melegal.

Mikkel returned with the whites of his eyes showing in the dark and the permanent smile wiped from his face. He shook his head. "There's over a score of fully armed Royal soldiers up there. They are armed for war. A half dozen sit on horses. They carry crossbows and spears. No doubt they will shred anything that comes up and out of here."

McKnight produced a coil of silk rope and held it out for all to see. "I'm going to strongly suggest that we make this a very easy exchange. For the sake of your own lives, step aside and let me take Nath to the Royals. Then all of you can go back to drinking sour wine and eating greasy meats until your bellies are as bloated as the slum trollops'."

In a bearish voice, Venir said, "The Royals have no right to take this man as a prisoner!"

"Technically, you are right, but he is not being taken prisoner if he comes of his own free will. The Royals only seek an audience with him," McKnight replied.

"The Royals can kiss my arse. They seek to make a slave out of him, the same as everyone else," Melegal said. The quick-handed thief pulled a concealed dagger from within his garb. "We don't trust Royals or their bum-kissing detectives."

McKnight focused his attention on Nath. "Listen, stranger, all of you stand a better chance if you come along willingly. I cannot say what the Royals have in store for you, but perhaps it will work out in your favor. These men that you have allied yourself with… Well, they are a sordid lot. Whatever they have to offer, the Royals will have far better. Coming willingly is worth the risk." He dangled the coil of rope in front of Nath. "What do you say?"

Nath scanned the hard eyes of his companions. He had no doubt that they would stand with him, but he didn't want them dying on his account. They were good men, and they shouldn't have to die to solve his problem. Besides, perhaps the Royals would have something to offer that would be worth considering. They might know something about magic. "I'll go."

"Are you mad?" Melegal said. "The Royals will torment you!"

Venir took a knee. He unshouldered his pack, opened it up, and took out a stitched-up leather sack. He eyed Nath and said, "You aren't going anywhere without us. We're going to get you out of here. Fight or die."

"Fight or die?" McKnight looked incredulous. "Why, that's the stupidest thing I've ever heard. Perhaps you should change it to 'bleed and die'? That would make more sense because all of you are going to be doing a lot of both if you don't come to your senses."

Melegal, Mikkel, and Billip surrounded McKnight. "Hand over the silk," Melegal said.

McKnight looked surprised. "Have you lost all of your senses? If even one of you harm a Royal soldier or manage to escape, they will not stop hounding you. You'll be found, hung, quartered, and fed to the dogs. Don't be a fool."

Melegal took the rope from McKnight. He bound the man's arms behind his back and said, "'Tis unfortunate for you that you aren't a Royal, because there is nothing to keep us from harming you."

Billip, still aiming at McKnight, pulled his arrow back. "Just say the word, and I'll pin this arrow through his chest."

McKnight swallowed. "Listen, you are going to be slaughtered up there. All of you. Show good sense and walk out of here alive—"

Chok.

Melegal hit McKnight in the back of the head with the butt end of his dagger. The detective went out cold and hit the deck, busting his nose in the process. "He always did talk too much. It's a shame I don't have it in me to kill him." He disarmed McKnight and bound him up tighter. "So what's the play, Venir? Are you going to lead us out of here?"

Venir stood in the dim light like a monster in metal. He had the spiked helmet on his head, and the rectangular eyelets had an eerie, dark burning life in them. With the axe in one powerful arm and his shield ready in the other, he said, "I'll take care of the soldiers. The rest of you get the Bish out of here."

CHAPTER 15

Upon the fallen castle grounds, the Royal soldiers waited for McKnight to emerge. Led by the Lorda Aleta's top men, Quint and Luther, they had many possibilities for cutting off any potential escape. Six men on horseback and who carried crossbows and spears formed the base. Foot soldiers wearing ring mail armor tunics with the red hawk insignia of Castle Vansung embroidered on their leather breastplates made up the rest of the circle. The stout men stood among the rubble with the finest longswords and spears in hand.

Quint and Luther were on foot and appeared much bigger than the rest of the soldiers. The shine from the hot suns reflected from their polished platemail armor. They were the only ones without weapons in hand, their swords sheathed in scabbards. The twins stood silently and stared intently at the opening where McKnight had departed to the subterranean levels of the fallen castle. Neither one of the formidable men said a word. The only sound came from the howl of the stiff wind blowing through the crumbling towers. Quint's moustache twitched. He swatted at fly, smashing it in the palm of his gauntlet.

The wind died down. Some of the horses whinnied and stomped their hooves. Luther tilted his head to one side and nudged Quint, who tilted his head the same way. The sound of heavy footsteps could be heard coming up the stairs that McKnight had descended earlier. A sharp spike on top of a full battle helmet appeared. The helmet was uniquely fashioned and almost entirely covered the face of the tremendous man who wore it.

Quint and Luther exchanged a glance. Luther swallowed. Both men's hands moved to the pommels of their swords, and they stepped back.

Luther had never seen a warrior like the one that he now beheld. The man matched their towering height, but his limbs were thicker and twitched with muscle. White scars showed on his bare arms like badges from wars. The double-bladed axe with a spike to match the top of his helmet was an inhuman thing that, paired with the rest of the muscle-bound warrior, made him appear indestructible. Luther and his brother had fought many campaigns over the years. They'd battled orcs, gnolls, and even hewed down an ogre, but the warrior standing in front of him appeared otherworldly. Luther gathered his courage and said, "Don't take another step. Who are you, warrior?"

"Venir."

Luther cleared his throat. "Venir, I'm not sure what to make of you, but if you are itching for a fight, I'll tell you that you won't last long. I don't care how big your axe is. Look at us. Here are a score of well-armed men. Your fanciful weaponry might frighten lesser men, but not us. We'll destroy you with extreme prejudice."

Venir spun his axe handle inside the palm of his hand. He flashed a battle grin. "This is your last chance to surrender."

Quint huffed a laugh. The rest of the soldiers chuckled nervously. At the same time, Quint and Luther drew their longswords.

"Fine." He looked at his brother. "What do you say, Luther?"

Luther frowned. "Brother Quint, you know what I think. Bark like a dog, die like a dog. Let's have at him, then."

In spite of the armament, Venir had a slim chance of plowing through them before they brought him down. The armament didn't work on men like it did the underlings. A spring of hot energy didn't supernaturally course through him, but his own adrenaline pulsating through his limbs did. His chest heaved. He was ready to fight. But the goal was to create just enough of a distraction for Nath and the others to escape.

Venir quickly measured up the Royal soldiers. The twin towers, men among men, who led the group and did the talking, weren't average by any stretch of the imagination. He'd soldiered before alongside Royals, and it was clear by the fine armor they wore that they had station. Not only were they big men, but they were swordsmen, and a dark confidence lurked deep in their eyes that told him they were killers. His grip tightened on his axe and the straps on his shield. If it was going to be them against him, it was going to be one Bish of a fight.

"How about this, dogs?" Venir said. He poked his axe at them. "I challenge you and you. The rest stay out of the way. I win, my comrades go."

Luther, the leaner of the two twins, said, "We have our orders. To disobey them would bring our death, but I'll grant you the fight. If you prove you're every bit the warrior that you appear to be, you and your men will be spared. But the one we seek will still be a prisoner. At worst, this will make the day interesting." He lifted his arm and called to his men, "No interference. It's us against him. To the death or until one or the other yields."

Venir brandished his axe with two hands. "Let's go, then."

With wary eyes, Luther and Quint circled him then simultaneously sprang in to attack.

CHAPTER 16

NATH AND COMPANY CROWDED INSIDE the stairwell. All of the men's ears were bent as they tried to listen in on the conversation that was taking place between Venir and the Royals. Melegal stood at the top of the steps, peeking outside but keeping himself out of sight of the soldiers.

From the back of the group, Mikkel whispered, "What's he saying?"

Melegal shot him a nasty look and said in his own loud whisper, "Shush. I'm listening."

"Don't shush me," Mikkel said. "Only my mother shushes me."

"Shush," Melegal, Nath, and Billip said as one.

Mikkel rolled his eyes. "Well, that's rude."

Melegal fanned his hand, signaling Mikkel to be quiet.

Nath stood in the back of the group with guilt gnawing inside his gut. He gently shook his head. "Venir doesn't need to be doing this for me," he said quietly. "There are too many of them up there."

"Don't think anything of it," Billip replied. The archer had his bow ready. "Venir likes to show off his big axe. Who knows, maybe it will scare them."

"He's not scaring anybody today," Melegal said. "There are two Royals up there as big as him. Well, not as fat or muscular, but still pretty darn big."

"Let me see," Mikkel said.

"Just stay put!" Melegal thrust his palm out then pointed at Mikkel. "You'll see them soon enough."

"I don't like this," Nath said. "I won't have Venir getting hurt or killed on account of me. Or any of you for that matter."

Melegal looked down at Nath and said, "Listen, Venir might look like a fool and act like a fool sometimes, but he knows what he's doing. He's providing a distraction. Believe it or not, he's actually very good at drawing attention to himself, especially with that getup on. I think a few of those Royals peed themselves a little when they saw him."

Nath moved farther up the steps. "So the plan is to find a crease and run?"

Melegal wagged his finger. "We all run on my signal."

"And what about Venir? How is he supposed to get out of there?" Nath asked.

"He'll have to figure that out. They'll be chasing after you, but once we make the alleys, they aren't going to keep up. At least, not so long as you stick close to me." Melegal smirked. "No one can catch this big rat in the City of Bone. All of you, be ready to run the moment I give the signal."

"What's the signal?" Billip asked.

"Simple. When I start running, you start running. And don't look back."

Nath was just about to ask another question when the roar of a warrior followed by a resounding *clang* of metal on metal caught his ears. The battle was on.

Venir almost didn't catch Luther's longsword clipping at his feet. The lanky warrior shuffled in quickly and thrust with the speed of a striking snake. Venir slammed his shield into the sword, deflecting the fierce jab into the ground.

Bish, he's fast!

At the same time Quint sliced at Venir's head, Venir blocked the sword swing with Brool's double blades. The jarring blow sent vibrations into his shoulders.

Bone, they are strong as oxen too!

In a moment, Venir was lathered up in sweat. His blood coursed through him like a mighty river. All of his skill, muscle, and sinew was being put to the test. On one side of him, Luther hammered away at his shield with two-handed overhead swings. On the other, he blocked every sword swing Quint unloaded on him with Brool. The cruel-looking warriors' eyes were wild with white fury. They were bent on Venir's destruction.

The surrounding soldiers cheered their leaders on wildly. The fear that had startled them when Venir arrived was gone, replaced with rambunctious vigor. The bloodthirsty men hungered to see Venir chopped down by the twin towers.

Venir ducked, twisted away, and dodged to one side. Instinct more than skill was the only thing that kept him in one piece as the brothers rained down on him with what could have been lethal blows.

Clang! Bang! Crash! The twins attacked in a relentless storm. They fought like men possessed, determined to kill Venir with every stroke.

"Yield, you helmeted hound! Yield or die!" Luther yelled, slavering. He chopped into the shield with strike after strike, each as heavy as the one before.

Venir absorbed the punishment. It wasn't long before his arms began to ache and burn. His natural speed and skill was being put to the test, and the slightest misstep could be his end. He was used to being the attacker, but the twins kept him on the defense. All he could muster was just enough to spare himself while moving them farther from the stairwell. He wanted to attack—to chop at their legs and remove hunks of flesh—but that would have left him exposed. He knew that they wanted him to take such a risk and that they would capitalize on it if he did.

"If this is the best that you can do, it's going to be a long day," Venir growled. He parried Quint's underhanded strike and managed a quick poke of Brool's spike at the man's eyes. Quint jumped backward. Venir rushed after him, leaving Luther on the other side swinging at open air. "Didn't see that coming, did you? Hah!"

The twins backed off. Glistening sweat dripped down their faces. Quint changed sword hands and flicked his fingers. He rolled his neck from side to side. "You have a hard shell, Venir. I'll grant you that. But there isn't a shell that we can't crack."

Dripping with sweat, Venir replied, "You both fight well for giant women."

One of the Royal soldiers from somewhere laughed.

The cruel scowl on Luther's face deepened. "I'll feed your tongue first to the dogs once this is over." He jerked his sword in the air. "Let's finish this." Sword point first, he lunged.

Venir rained his axe down onto Luther's blade. Metal rang against metal. He knocked the sword aside, hoping to disarm the knight, but Luther's grip didn't quaver. He thrust as Quint sliced large arcing swings against Venir's armor.

The twins were coming at Venir with a new tactic. They used a flurry of blinding blows and swings, without putting all of their weight behind them.

Bish!

Venir's skills were put to task again. It took all he had to keep up with the speed of the twin warriors' steel. The twins fought with the robust strength of orcs but with greater skill. Quint's sword tip clipped right across his eyelets, shaving the helmet across the bridge. Luther dropped to a knee and swung low, but Venir hopped over the blade that swished right under his feet. He sprang away from both men and dived away from their lethal strokes. He lost his footing on the broken rubble and landed on his backside. "Bone!" he roared.

The twins came on him in a flurry, and the captivated Royal soldiers roared.

CHAPTER 17

With a wave of his hand, Melegal rushed out of the stairway, and Nath stayed on the skinny man's heels. With Billip and Mikkel in tow, they surfaced in the old courtyard of the fallen castle. The Royal soldiers were shouting out cheers and chanting, "Kill! Kill! Kill!" Nath stole a look in the direction of the action. A throng of well-armored soldiers had formed a ring around the engaged fighters. Nath could see steel flashing up and down with heavy-handed strokes. He slowed in his tracks.

Melegal seized him by the wrist and yanked it. "Keep moving." He pointed to an alley that opened up the gateway to freedom just across the street. Not a single soul was watching them. "Nath, we're free. Move it!"

Steel thundered against steel, and more hard blows were exchanged. Through a small gap between the men, Nath could make out Venir, who was down on the ground and fighting for his life against two towering men. They hacked at Venir like lumberjacks. Venir was trapped.

Billip and Mikkel pushed into Nath's back. "Go, go, go, fool!" Billip urged. "We won't get another shot at this."

Nath trotted alongside Melegal, who had not released his wrist. They had a plan. Venir would buy them time, and they would find freedom. It was working, except for one thing: Nath couldn't leave his friend behind. He yanked free of Melegal. "I can't leave him."

"Don't be a fool!" Melegal said.

A soldier on horseback spotted them and let out an alarming cry. It turned a few heads in the crowd of soldiers.

"Time's running out," Melegal said. He looked between the horseman, who loaded his crossbow, and Nath. "We need to go."

The soldier took aim with his crossbow and fired. The bolt zinged right at Melegal's frowning face. Nath snatched the bolt out of the air. He held it suspended in front of Melegal's widened eyes. "Fight or die," he said. "I'm staying."

"Sweet mother of Bish, did you see that?" Mikkel said to Billip. He twirled his massive club. "Fight or die, brothers. Fight or die!"

"Yeah, well, I wouldn't have missed," Billip said. He fired his bow at the soldier, and the shot knocked the man out of the saddle. Smooth as silk, he unloaded another arrow from his quiver and took a knee. "They came for a fight. Let's give them one!" He fired at another crossbowman, who took a shot at them but missed.

Nath and Mikkel rushed up behind the soldiers who were caught up in the other fight.

Melegal stuck his hands into his armpits and cursed.

Barehanded, Nath waded into the rear flank of the men who surrounded Venir and the giant knights. Not wanting to kill, he used another tactic. He slammed two men's heads together then grabbed another by the arm and slung him aside. That's when he heard a loud, painful-sounding groan come from Venir. The big warrior had collapsed onto the ground. His leg was cut open, and blood flowed freely from the wound. Even from a seated position, though, he fought to block the tide of sword blows that rained death down on him.

The Royal soldiers came to life around Nath. As one, they surged against him. They piled onto his arms and legs and drove their hips into him, trying to bear him down to the ground.

"Get off of him!" Billip's mighty arms brought his studded club down on the crown of a soldier's helmet. The soldier's teeth cracked and shattered. Mikkel whipped his club around like a bat, turned his hips into the swing, and busted a soldier in his sword arm. The sword fell from the man's fingers as he howled in pain. Mikkel punched him in the jaw, dropping the man like a bag of sand.

Using his superior strength and speed, Nath punched his way out of the throng that bound him up in their limbs. He rabbit-punched a soldier in the ribs then picked up a smaller soldier, lifted him to chest level, and flung him into the others. It created a gap that cleared the way to Venir. The outland warrior's skin had turned ashen, and the knights continued to break down Venir's guard with their swords. Venir's shoulders sagged. He lifted his shield and axe one last time, but the towering twins knocked them aside. One of them had a clear shot at Venir's head and took it.

CHAPTER 18

ELEGAL TOOK COVER IN THE ruins. Hand-to-hand combat was a far cry from his talents. He was designed to thrive off of a different set of skills and gifts. He prided himself on the ability to avoid damage. He was also very good at complaining.

What a bunch of idiots! Why are they drawn to the grave? Do they love dirt so much that they want to sleep in it?

Billip fired arrows into the group of soldiers on horseback that bore down on Mikkel's exposed position. The archer pulled the feathered shaft along his cheek then fired. The arrow sank into the broad chest of a warhorse. It reared and tossed its rider. Billip let loose another arrow that struck a horse in the neck. The beast's front legs collapsed, and it crashed into the ground.

A third rider carrying a spear like a lance trotted right at Billip's side. The archer turned to fire, but the soldier closed the gap. The rider poked the spear into Billip's chest, forcing him to jump aside. The soldier jabbed the spear into Billip's thigh, and he went down with a loud grunt of pain.

This is why you run instead of fighting!

Melegal took in the battle scene. The Royal soldiers used their sheer numbers in a well-guided effort to annihilate the brave men. Despite their losses, those who remained were still fully armed, and it didn't take them long to regain control. Before Billip could defend himself, three soldiers in chainmail and leather tunics surrounded him. The archer, with an arrow still in one hand, raised his arms over his head. He shook his head then dropped the arrow.

Mikkel stood tall in a wind tunnel of furious activity, swinging his club back and forth and keeping his attackers at bay until two men slipped in behind him and tossed a net over him.

A net, Melegal thought. *Really, he got caught in a net. That's the stupidest thing I've ever seen. How do you get caught in a net?* A scuffle of boots on stone caught his keen ear. He turned just in time to see two soldiers creep in behind him, carrying a net. They threw it over him. *Bone!*

Venir had fought just about every kind of creature that had ever lived, and he'd more than held his own. His failure in the battle came when he tripped and fell. The leaner knight, Luther, had slipped a sword stroke deep into the meat of his thigh. Blood pumped out of the wound. Sitting back on his ankles, Venir had continued to fight with the ferocity of a cornered wolverine. As much as he wanted to get back on his feet, he couldn't. They'd pinned him down. It took all he had to fight them off. He took another blow to the shoulder from a stab by Quint, and it felt as though his laboring arm was on fire.

Fight or die!

The twins' strokes grew harder and harder, and Venir's mighty arms quavered. He'd underestimated the men, and it had been a fatal error. All he could hope was that his comrades had escaped, in which case dying would be worth it. He took the hammering, his shield and axe dipping only to rise again until finally he could lift them no more. His knuckles scraped against the ground as he bled out the last of his strength.

Luther lifted his longsword above his head. The blade caught the sunlight just right.

Venir took a deep breath. *Helm, it's time to find out what you are made of.*

The sword flashed down.

Out of nowhere, a black-scaled hand caught the blade in midair, its strong grip closing around the steel. Luther's fierce expression froze, and his eyes filled with confusion. With a yank, Nath ripped the sword from the man's strong hand.

"Impossible!" Luther shouted.

Quint rushed Nath and released a swing that could have cut a man in half, but Nath blocked it with the armored scales of his forearm. Nath punched Luther in the face. The blow sent the man staggering backward. Before Quint could attempt another swing, Nath held the glowing blade of his dagger, Dragon Claw, against the man's throat. "Drop the sword."

With huge eyes, the knight swallowed and dropped his sword then scanned his surroundings. A smirk started to form in the corners of his mouth. In a dry voice, he said, "Take a look around you. You might have the drop on me, but we have the drop on the rest of you."

Nath pressed Dragon Claw harder against the man's Adam's apple, knowing that the edge of the blade burned the tall knight's skin. "Be silent." It was Nath's turn to look around.

Venir grunted at the sight of Billip, who the soldiers had dragged front and center. The archer's hand was clamped over his bloody shoulder, and he grimaced. Not far behind him, Mikkel was being dragged over the ground by a net, which ensnared him. The powerful fighter fought against his entanglement only to take the butt of a spear to the head. Two more soldiers dragged Melegal over the ground and left him with the group. Venir found Melegal's glowering eyes and laughed weakly.

"This isn't my fault, lout!" the fuming Melegal yelled.

Venir's entire group had been surrounded by the small army. It was apparent that they'd lost, and that hard truth was settling in. In the meantime, Venir was bleeding to death and losing all the fight left in him along with his blood. His helmet, which had once healed him in the presence of underlings, was not responding. Concern grew in Nath's eyes as he cast glances at his friends.

Luther said, "Listen to me, Nath. You can come quietly, and all of you will live. On a whistle from my lips, your small force will be slain. You might avenge them, but vengeance won't bring them back. What will it be?"

"Let them go, and I'll come willingly," Nath said.

"These men are criminals," Luther added. He rubbed the sweat dripping from his brow with his finger. "They assaulted Royals."

"You aren't Royals," Melegal said. "You are Royal hounds, nothing more and nothing less."

The stone-faced Luther glowered at Melegal. "To think that for a moment, I almost considered letting you go. After all, this brute earned my respect. However, I'm bound by duty, and I cannot allow you to go free. Secure them. It's been a long time since the torment chambers of Castle Vansung have tasted fresh blood."

CHAPTER 19

Idiots. Idiots. Idiots. Idiots.

Melegal remained bound up in the net. The soldiers dragged him down the street. The bumpy cobblestones jostled his scrawny limbs and knocked him around in the net. When he could, he looked to see how all of the others were faring. Behind him, Mikkel was being dragged by a horse, as he was too heavy for the men. Ahead were Venir, Nath, and Billip. Their arms were bound behind their backs, except for Venir. He could barely walk. His wounded leg was covered in blood that soaked even the rim of his boot. He extended his long arms over Nath and Billip's shoulders, and his head sagged. Melegal hadn't seen his robust friend in such bad shape for a while. He speculated that the blood loss had been critical and possibly fatal. Venir's sluggish movements suggested that his iron vitality was gone.

Serves him right.

They moved down the streets of Bone, drawing comments and stares from the gawking pedestrians that they passed. People were already hollering about seeing a good hanging. It was commonplace to see the Royals parade criminals down the roads before their fate was settled and they swung by the neck on the gallows. Another fate waited for them, though. Melegal looked farther ahead and saw that the wood-and-iron gates to the glorious Castle Vansung were swung open, waiting to swallow them. He had no desire to go in there.

As the soldiers looked away from him, he slashed at the net with one of the many daggers that he kept concealed in his clothing. His attention was on the soldiers as he sawed away. The soldiers who'd tossed the net over him checked him with hard looks, so Melegal concealed his dagger inside his sleeve. He kept the appearance of being tightly bound in the ropes by coiling his hands and arms up in them. The soldiers looked away. He started cutting again.

"Pssst! Pssst!"

Melegal looked back at Mikkel, who was trying to get his attention. He shook his head and mouthed the words, "Be silent!"

Mikkel gave a terse nod.

Melegal shook his head at him and continued his work on the net. Nets were difficult because one had to figure out which cords to cut. Melegal's keen eyes and deft hands went to work. He cut through the man-made web, undoing the puzzle. He stretched his neck and could see the front ranks, with the twin towers in the lead, start into the castle gates. The soldiers looked back at him, and he shrank inside the net. The alert soldiers made sure that the prisoners were secure before they were taken inside and kept their eyes on him.

Look away, flat-nosed bastards, look away!

Melegal's goal was simple. He needed to make a break for it before the gates closed. He knew it would be ten times harder to escape once he was inside. *I should have just run to begin with.* Time was running out, and he still had a few more cords to cut.

I'm not going to make it. I'm not going to make it. Melegal was being dragged through the gate. *Slat! I'm not going to make it!*

All of a sudden, a commotion started up behind him. Melegal turned to see that Mikkel had managed to stand. Using his great strength, he yanked the net, stopping the horse and turning it around. "I'm not going in there! I'm not going in there!" he screamed.

The soldiers rushed Mikkel and beat him down with the butts of their spears. Melegal returned to the last few strands he needed to cut to be free. The big man crumpled inside the net after the soldiers hit him again. Both men were just inside the gate when Melegal peeled the net away from his body.

"Close the gate!" the soldiers bringing up the rear shouted.

The door began to close.

Melegal caught Mikkel's eyes. The warrior gave him a stiff nod. Mikkel shoved his way into the soldiers.

Melegal slipped free and sprinted toward the diminishing gap between the gates. One foot snagged on the net, and he tripped.

The soldiers who guarded him came at him with swords. "Halt! Halt!" they yelled.

Seeing his foot snagged on one strand of net that kept him from full liberation made him curse loudly. He had only a split second to think. He moved to cut the last strand, and the soldiers came upon him, their swords poised to strike through his body. As he sawed away, in his mind he directed a command at his attackers. The mystic powers of his floppy cap warmed. His mind tingled. *Halt!*

The soldiers froze in their tracks. The gates stopped closing.

Melegal cut through the net and dashed through the crack between the gates. Holding his cap tightly on his head, he dashed across the street and into the alleys, vanishing as his pursuers screamed.

CHAPTER 20

NATH, VENIR, BILLIP, AND MIKKEL were taken to the dungeons below Castle Vansung. All of them were locked in the same cell, which was barely big enough to hold them. Thick steel bars and a heavy keylock sealed them inside. Venir sprawled on a bed of rotting straw. The durable warrior had passed out from blood loss, some of which covered his leg like paint. As soon as the guards locked them in, Billip used his own belt to make a tourniquet around Venir's upper thigh.

"That ought to do it," the archer said. He wiped Venir's sticky blood off of his hands and onto his trousers. "I'm not used to seeing the big fella down. He's even peaked. I'll tell you this, though, that belt isn't going to help him without more attention. If it stays like that for long, he could lose the leg."

With his hands locked on the cell bars, Mikkel pressed his face against the metal and said, "Get us a healer down here! Now!"

The dungeon had many other cells, but all of them were empty. If there were guards inside the room, they were out of sight and not saying anything.

"Save your breath," Billip said. "They don't care if we live or die in here. They are Royals."

"Bish on the Royals!" Mikkel said.

Nath kneeled down by Venir. "This is my fault. I'm sorry, but I think that I can help."

Billip and Mikkel leaned over Nath's shoulder, each shaking their heads as they exchanged doubtful looks with one another.

He laid his hands on Venir's leg and summoned his powers of healing. Great warmth started from his shoulders and moved down into his hands. His fiery healing energy spread quickly through his fingers and into Venir's leg. The deep laceration started to mend and close.

Marveling, Mikkel muttered, "Sweet mother of Bish."

With his golden eyes aglow with inner fire, Nath turned to Billip. The archer stepped away.

Nath said, "Be still. Your shoulder."

Billip stood his ground and let Nath reach up and place his hand where the spear had pierced his shoulder. Billip's eyes popped open, and he gasped. His jaw dropped open, his eyes watered, and tears streamed down his face. "I've never felt such a thing. It's as if light fills me!"

Nath removed his hand. The glow in his eyes faded. "Feel better?"

Billip rolled his shoulder. "That was amazing. Whatever you do, don't let the Royals know that you can do that. They will abuse you."

Mikkel reached over and swiped the tears on Billip's face with his fingers. "You were crying like a baby. Heh heh."

Billip smacked his friend's hands away. "Oh, shut it. You wouldn't understand. I'm just grateful." He offered his hand. "Thank you, Nath. I have no doubt that Venir is in better shape now, after feeling what you just did."

"Well, I'd take it easy on that shoulder. You're mending enough to stop the bleeding, but you're far from fully healed. My power is limited. I just hope it was enough for Venir. He still looks weak."

"He's survived worse. Trust me," Billip said. "You did well by him." He peered through the cell bars. "The question is, what do the Royals have in store for us now? And how did that little rat Melegal escape? His cowardice will only bring more of the Royals' wrath down upon us."

"I've never seen Melegal captured before," Mikkel commented. "So you should be surprised. He's clever, unlike you."

"Hah. If my shoulder wasn't busted, I'm certain that I would have broken out too," Billip said.

"Keep dreaming. Besides, I lent Melegal a hand. Just be glad he's out. It might be up to him to get us out of here."

Billip looked at Mikkel as if Mikkel was a fool. "Are you jesting? Melegal isn't going to risk his neck to mount a rescue mission to get us out of here. We are deep in the belly of a Royal castle. Melegal's probably elbows deep in a vat of wine right now, and I wouldn't blame him."

Nath leaned against the back wall and slid down into a sitting position. He truly felt bad for the men who had fought so hard to help him. The last thing he wanted was for all of them to be locked up in a musty and damp cell with a straw-covered floor that reeked. He gently shook his head.

Mikkel sat down beside him. He took a handful of straw and flicked it at Nath. "You should be used to it by now. Actually, this dungeon isn't as bad as many others that we've frequented."

"If you're trying to make me feel better, I want you to know that I don't think it's going to work," Nath replied. "But I swear, I'll get us all out of here."

"If you're talking about taking us to your world, based on what you said before, that would be very nice," Mikkel replied. He scratched the side of his face. "But it's hard to imagine."

"That's because you don't have any imagination," Billip said.

"I do too!"

Billip laughed. "That's not what the ladies say."

"Ha ha." Mikkel frowned.

Nath put his face down on his knees and began to contemplate his situation. In truth, he'd gotten well enough used to Bish that he felt he could survive on his own. In a sense, it was the others who held him back. Granted, Bish had many dangers, and it was a foreign place, but he hadn't crossed anyone who could match his power—except, perhaps, Venir, who proved to be an exceptional individual, especially with the armament.

The problem for Nath was that he needed to find a way home. The other brave men had sworn to help him, even putting their own lives in peril. A big part of him wanted to cast them aside for their own safety, but deep inside, he knew that it was quite possible that he couldn't get home without them.

I feel selfish.

Nath scratched the top of his head. Out of the corner of his eye, he saw Venir lying flat on his back, breathing deeply. He knew the warrior should be fine unless the Royals did something inhumanely cruel to him or even flat-out killed them—which was a strong possibility. He considered a few things. Busting the men out of the dungeon would be his first course of action. He might be able to bend the bars or even melt them, if he could summon his own dragon fire. He needed to retrieve Dragon Claw too, which proved to be another problem. His mind rummaged through many options. Hour after hour went by, and the men's empty bellies began to growl.

CHAPTER 21

After escaping the clutches of Castle Vansung's soldiers by the skin of his teeth, Melegal took to the alleys and hid. Normally, he would have gone back to the Drunken Octopus to lay low, but now he had no place to go. Worse yet, his friends were at the mercy of the Royals, and that was the last thing he wanted.

Like a cat, he picked his way through the catacombs of narrow passages that made up the alleys in the streets of Bone. He needed to contemplate his next move. He ducked into a different tavern, found a small corner table, ordered some plum-colored wine, and started drinking. The lunch crowd, taking a break from their day of hard labor, talked quietly and kept to themselves. No one paid Melegal any mind at all.

Ah, that's better. I always think best on a sloshy stomach.

Basically, Nath wasn't his problem. Venir wasn't either, but there was loyalty between them that dated back to when they were servants of the Royals as children. Venir had looked out for him then, and against Melegal's natural instinct, he had looked out for Venir.

He took off his cap and fanned himself. *Of all the dungeons to get locked up in, why did it have to be in a Royal castle? I can handle the City Watch's hold, but inside those walls, it's not likely they'll come out alive.*

Melegal twirled his cap on his finger then replaced it back on his noggin and smoothed it over the side of his face. The cap was a curious magical item that had powers he hadn't quite mastered. With it, he could command others by locking thoughts with them. He called it his cap of command. He had stolen it not for the power it gave him but out of a unique fascination that he had for it. Now, it was his, and it had saved his scrawny hind end once again. He finished his first goblet of wine then gave the waitress a frosty look. She quickly hustled back to the bar and came back with another.

The service is far better here than the Octopus. The waitress is much cuter as well.

Three women sat at the bar casting curious glances his way. They all wore cheap black garb, more robes than dresses. All of them had messy black hair. The oldest, who sat on the end, was built more like a man. The woman beside her was a big gal, busty and curvaceous, while the last had long straight hair and was as skinny as Melegal. Sneering, he looked away from them.

What a motley lot. I have standards, even on the worst of my days. I think.

Trying his best to make the most of a sour situation, he sipped his wine slowly. He'd wanted nothing more than to get out of Two-Ten City and return to his dreary life in Bone, but he'd found his life as upside down as it had ever been. When his former mentor, McKnight, showed up, his heart had frozen inside his chest. There would be no shaking McKnight. The swarthy thief was a bloodhound, and it didn't help that he and Melegal had parted ways on a sour note.

Melegal could have been a servant of the Royals much like McKnight, but after his childhood, he wanted no part of their twisted war games, whereas McKnight delighted in being a pawn on their behalf.

I'll never be able to shake the man until this is all over. Or will I?

For the time being, the Royals of Castle Vansung had their man. For all intents and purposes, McKnight's charge should have been satisfied. As for Melegal, he didn't commit a crime, aside from escaping. It was entirely possible that he could drift into the shadows and disappear. After all, he wasn't important, and that was the way he wanted it.

He closed his eyes, leaned his chair against the wall, and propped his feet up on the table. It had been an exhausting morning. He needed a cat nap and dared to take one. It wasn't long before the comforting sounds of heavy conversations, the scraping of utensils on plates, and the scent of bad perfume put him to sleep.

Someone jostled his table, and Melegal's eyelids cracked open. The motley gang of women walked right past. He caught the scrawny, gray-eyed woman's eyes searching his. She turned her sharp chin away and moved on, following the others through the exit door.

Melegal put all four chair legs back on the floor. He wiped the drool from the corner of his mouth, took a deep breath, left some coins on the table, and exited the tavern.

I should lay low. But like a fool, I'm going to do otherwise. Blast me and my bloody conscience. One way or the other, I'm going to have to get their arses out of there.

CHAPTER 22

"MELEGAL, WHAT A PLEASURE IT is to see your frowning face," Laana, the enchantress, said. Melegal met up with her in the plush, pillow-filled chamber that reeked of incense, the same place where Venir, Nath, and Mikkel had talked with her. The white-haired, dark-skinned woman sensually rubbed oil on her arms. The silks she wore barely contained her voluptuous body. Her voice was a purr, matched with a playful smile on her full lips. "And I thought I'd never see you again." She rubbed her hands together quickly. "So what can I do for you? We could talk over an oil rub, just like old times?"

Melegal cleared the knot forming in his throat and said, "You look well, Laana. But as enticing as that sounds, I'll have to pass, though I appreciate the offer."

"Well, it wasn't going to be free." She lifted her hands and wriggled her fingers. "These hands are very valuable, and so is my time. The truth is, by the looks of you, you couldn't afford my services."

"Why would I want to pay? It lacks intimacy, after all, and the best things in this miserable life, I find, are free."

She offered him a toothy white smile. "I miss you and the way you have of saying things. As I've always said, you are meant for great things, Melegal. You never fully valued yourself."

"I'm perfectly fine with my station in life, and I have no intention of becoming some Royal suck-up." He reached across the table and took her soft hand. "I know you met with Venir this morning, and now he and Mikkel and Nath have been taken in by the Royals."

Her eyes widened. "Already. They just left here hours ago. I haven't even left my seat." She eyed the curtains behind him. On the other side was the pillow-filled lobby loaded with spaced-out Royals. "As you can see, I stay busy with my services. But I was going to help. I swear it. Who took them?"

"Castle Vansung," he said.

Laana's nostrils flared. She made a face like she'd swallowed a bug. She put her other hand over Melegal's and slowly shook her head. "I'm so sorry."

"What is that supposed to mean? You make it sound like it's a death sentence."

She gave a serious nod.

Melegal leaned back in his chair. He took off his cap and started to fan himself. "I only know the Vansungs in name, and it seems like you know a great deal more about them than I do. Tell me what you know."

"As you know, I've been dabbling in enchantments for years, and I've dealt with many Royals as a result. One of the Royals, whom I have personally met, is one nasty witch. Her name is Lorda Aleta Vansung, and when it comes to the devices of the arcane, they say that she is one of the greatest. The truth is, if your friend—this Nath—sought to find his home in another world, she would be the one to contact."

Melegal's expression perked up. He tapped his fingertips together. "Really."

"This is not a good thing, Melegal. Aleta will dissect that man if she has her way. If he has power, she will take it and absorb it." Goose bumps popped up on her arms, and she shivered. "Venir is in big trouble."

He narrowed his eyes. "You seem to have a lot of knowledge about the Vansungs, Laana. How intimately do you know them?"

Her back straightened, and she averted her eyes. "I don't know anything." She pulled her hand away from his. "I don't mean to be rude, but I'm very busy. You saw the crowd, and they'll be restless if I don't tend to them." She stood up, moved around the table, and gave Melegal a quick kiss on the cheek. "If I hear anything, I'll let you know. Best to you, Melegal."

Rising from his chair, he sought her eyes. "Wait a moment. You know something, don't you, Laana?" He seized her wrists. "Look at me."

She wouldn't look at him.

"Laana, don't make me do what I don't want to do."

She looked right at him. "You wouldn't dare! I'll curse you if you try."

"Then tell me what you don't want me to know."

She gave her head a stiff shake. "I don't know anything."

"You are lying." He twisted her arm behind her back and pushed her down on the table. "I know your weakness, Laana. This is your last chance. Out with it."

"No," she pleaded. "I swear, I'll curse you—*eep!*"

Melegal's nimble fingers dug into Laana's ribs. She burst out in laughter. Fighting like a wildcat, she tried to escape his clutches. Melegal shoved her down into the pillows and overwhelmed her with an attack of tickles.

"Stop it! Stop it!" she pleaded, only to resume the gleeful laughter that at times became maniacal. "You're going to make me pee on my pillows!"

"Tell me," he urged. "Tell me now!" He wore her out until she couldn't fight anymore. All she could do was buck in the pillows.

Finally, in a lathered fit of laughter, she said, "Fine, just stop!"

Melegal kept her in his clutches as she lay on her back, her chest heaving as she caught her breath. "I hate you," she said.

"I know," he replied. "Now, out with it."

"Fine. Castle Vansung is a client that I offer my services to on a routine basis. I have them on the schedule for later this week," she admitted.

"What kind of services?"

"You know, cocoa rubs and the lot. Nothing to do with my enchantments. I do it because I want Lorda Aleta as a mentor." She let out a long sigh. "Melegal, I care about Venir and you, but I really don't want to cross them." She clasped her hands together. "Please, please, please, don't get me involved with this."

"Laana, you might be the only hope that they have."

With a puzzled look, she said, "But what can I possibly do?"

"It's not so much what you can do." He rolled up his sleeves. "But what your new assistant that you're going to take with you can do."

CHAPTER 23

Venir's eyelid cracked open. He was facing a wall in a place that smelled too familiar with its scent of rotting hay and mold. A dungeon. With his wounded leg aching, his thoughts began to clear. He recalled the fight at the fallen castle. He remembered losing lots of blood as his friends helped him out. Then he lost consciousness. With a grunt, he rolled over. Nath was sitting across from him. The stranger's eyes brightened.

"You're awake," Nath said. He helped Venir into a seated position and propped him against the wall. "I'd offer you some water, but the Royals haven't brought us any. Or food, for that matter."

Venir's throat was parched. "I wouldn't expect any either. The City Watchmen treat their prisoners better than the Royals ever did."

"You sound like someone who has spent a lot of time in prisons."

"Aye, you could say that." Venir peered past Nath, his eyes searching the cell. "Where is everyone else? Another cell?"

"Melegal escaped." Nath frowned. "But the guards came and grabbed Billip and Mikkel again hours later. They were led by those two bruisers that you fought. Nasty men. They said not to expect them to come back anytime soon or in one piece."

Venir rubbed his wounded thigh. "That's bad. Real bad. Those Royal knights—I think they called themselves Quint and Luther—are not ordinary men."

"What do you mean?"

"I've fought many, and not many can match me, even two at a time. Those two had unnatural strength and endurance. They wore me down. I can't explain it. Just be wary of them." He sat up straighter. "With that said, I hope I get another crack at them. I won't hold back the next time."

"That's my fault. You were trying to buy me time. It nearly got you killed." Nath placed a hand on Venir's shoulder. "I'm sorry."

"Don't apologize. You should have just done what you were told to do. I didn't need your help."

"But you might have died."

Venir shook his head. "I'm not going anywhere until the last of the underlings is dead. How long have I been out?"

"A day or so."

Venir sighed. On the one hand, he should have been glad that he was alive. On the other, he wouldn't stay that way for long if the Royals got what they wanted from Nath. If that were the case, the rest of them would be killed. He was certain of it. "We still need to get you out of here."

"We need for all of us to get out of here. Perhaps I can make a deal and have the rest of you spared. You've done all that you can, and I can't ask for any more," Nath said.

"Make a deal with the Royals? Hah! That will be the last deal that you ever make." Venir closed his eyes. His nostrils flared. "Bone, I hate dungeons."

"Listen, Venir, I don't mean to sound arrogant, but I think if we can get you out of here, I can manage without you. I have, well, special skills and abilities that should allow me to see my way through this. I can no longer be the source of your troubles." He looked at Venir's leg. "It's cost you enough."

"Let's see what happens." Venir opened his eyes at the sound of the dungeon entrance door opening. The sound of men in heavy armor dragging bodies over stone caught his ear. He started to get up.

Nath pushed him back down and said, "No, lie down. You don't want them to think you are awake."

"That's not my way."

"Just do it," Nath said.

"No."

Nath shook his head in disappointment and hurried to the door.

"Get back, redhead," one of the twin towers said. The brothers, Quint and Luther, each dragged a man in their arms. One had Mikkel and the other Billip. Both were beaten and bruised and had blood on their clothing. Another smaller guard, accompanied by one who carried a spear, put the key in the cell door lock. The spearman poked the weapon through the bars at Nath. The smaller man opened the door, and the twins dragged Mikkel and Billip inside and dropped them on the floor. The heavy stares of the men landed on Venir, who remained seated but glared up at them.

"You live. Good. Now we can torture you in another manner," Luther said.

"I look forward to it," Venir said.

"Fool." He marched up on Venir and kicked him hard in the gut.

Venir rolled over, groaning.

Luther pointed a finger in Nath's face and said, "You are next, redhead. Let's go." With a hard shove, he shoved Nath out of the cell.

Nath pushed against the man's efforts.

Luther slammed him hard into the cell bars. "You best come along peacefully because if you don't, all of those other men in that cell will be dead."

Reluctantly, Nath departed without a word. The guards locked the others inside and left.

Venir moved to aid Billip and Mikkel. Their faces were bruised and swollen. They had red lash marks all over their bodies and bloodstained clothing. Billip shook like a leaf. Mikkel's breathing was raspy and heavy. "What did they do?" Venir asked.

"All they did was ask questions about Nath and beat the slat out of us," Billip said. He spit blood from his mouth. "I didn't tell them nothing."

"I didn't either," Mikkel said. "Bish, there really wasn't much of anything to say, but they beat on us anyway. I hate those goons. They are nasty. Ogre nasty." He looked at Venir through two swollen eyes. "Venir, if we don't get out of here, all of us are going to die. I know it."

CHAPTER 24

E SCORTED BY A FULL SQUAD of soldiers, Nath walked step for step with Quint and Luther. The brothers didn't even bother to bind his hands, which seemed to be unusual treatment for a prisoner. Apparently, they didn't consider him a flight risk—and they were right, because he didn't want to see his friends hurt. For the time being, they had him at their mercy, and all he had to do was work that to his advantage. He hoped he would get a face-to-face meeting with his hunters.

As he marched through the castle, Nath noted that its magnificent architecture and decorations rivaled the palaces in his world's city of Lutheruklen. The walls and floors were made of sandstone-colored marble. The passages had many archways and murals. Cathedral ceilings allowed light to shine on the elegant living spaces that they passed. The walk was long, as he'd been led up out of the dungeons, through the castle's various courtyards, and into another subterranean level in a building apart from the rest of the castle.

At the bottom, an arched set of double doors was open. Quint and Luther escorted him inside and closed the doors behind them. The twins took their places in front of the door and stood at parade rest with their hands locked in front of them.

A man and woman waited within the elaborately decorated chamber. There were many bookshelves that reached to the ceiling, and study tables with stacked scrolls and tomes were placed throughout the space.

Both the man and woman were seated on pedestal chairs. The woman was older, with braided dark hair piled on top of her head. She was very attractive, in her dark-red off-the-shoulder dress. Beside her was Gannon. The swarthy mage was all cleaned up and wearing fine robes. The lanky man had pushed his chair back and was looking at Nath with uncertainty. Between the two chairs was a small round table. Dragon Claw sat on top of it.

Nath glowered at Gannon. He started to speak, but the woman cut him off.

"So you are the one my son has told me so many wonderful things about," she said with a welcoming smile. "I am Aleta, the Lorda of Castle Vansung. I am very pleased to have you as my guest."

"You have a very strange way of welcoming your guests. Do you normally kidnap them?"

Aleta gave a quick shrug. "Sometimes." She moved out of her seat and approached Nath, who towered over her by at least a head. Her haunting eyes gave him a thorough once-over. "My, you are indeed impressive." She looked over her shoulder at Gannon. "Well done, my son."

"If you wanted to meet me, there are much more polite ways of going about it," Nath said. "Gannon, why would you do this?"

Shamefaced, Gannon looked away.

"Nath, perhaps we overreacted in how we arranged to have you brought in." Aleta traced her finger over the scales on one of his arms. "Fascinating. Are there more like you in your world?"

"What do you mean? What makes you think I'm from another world?"

She gave him a disappointed look. "Gannon has made me fully aware of your uniqueness, Nath. But please don't feel threatened." She touched his face with the palm of her hand and looked into his eyes. "Perhaps I can help you find your home, so long as you are willing to work with me."

Nath found himself surprised by her offer. Judging by his unique surroundings, he thought it was possible that she could help him find his way home. After all, it was very clear that she was a mage, just as Gannon was. Since Nath had been in Bish, nothing had worked out the way that he had planned, but he was hopeful that he might finally catch a break. "Why should I be convinced that you have otherworldly powers that can help me? I've seen your son's handiwork. He can barely bend branches on trees."

Gannon slumped in his chair. "You know better than that."

"Silence, child!" Without looking, Aleta flicked a spark from her fingertip that landed on Gannon's lap. He tried to dust it away but touched it. A loud zap made his hair stand on end. He shook all over, stiffened, then fell out of his seat. "I'm still disappointed by my son's destructive behavior. His departure made me look like a bad mother."

"Perhaps you did that all on your own," Nath said.

"Men like you always have the sharpest tongues. Perhaps I'll show you my collection of all the ones I've had removed." Aleta looked at Gannon, who was crawling back into his chair. She shook her head. "Now, where was I? Oh yes, you mentioned a concern you had in regards to my powers. I'm not sure if your world has magi like this one does, but I'd like to show you a little something." She shooed him with her hands. "Step back."

Nath backed up, and the twins moved up along his sides, pinning him in between them. They held him by the shoulders with heavy hands, and he could feel their mighty grips through the muscles in his shoulders. They were even stronger than they appeared. Regardless, Nath was fully confident that he could handle them if he had to, for he'd faced far bigger foes than them.

Aleta spread her arms out like a cross then lifted her palms and fingers up to the sky. Chin up, she shut her eyes and began to mutter mystical phrases. Her soft, quick words became louder with every syllable. Her body emanated power. The chamber shimmered, scrolls rolled from the tables, and the candles' flames and lantern light quavered. Out of thin air, black doors appeared on each side of her hand. She opened her eyes and smiled.

Two black doorways, more than large enough for a man to pass through, stood like black panes of glass.

"Gannon," she said, "you remember the dimension spell, don't you? Why don't you show our guest how it works?"

Wiping his sweaty palms on his sleeve, Gannon hesitantly rose from his chair.

"Hurry up, you frightened little chicken!" Aleta yelled.

With a nervous look, Gannon walked into the door on the right side of Aleta and vanished. He emerged through the door on his mother's left a moment later. His teeth were chattering. He exhaled, and vapor came out of his mouth as if he was in a very cold place. He rubbed his hands together and glanced at Nath.

"Impressive," Nath commented. "Though I'm not sure how that is going to open a way back to my world."

"Those were only two doorways that you have now seen I have the power to open." With a wave of her hand, the black-dimension doorways closed. "With your assistance and some other help, I am fully confident that I can open a doorway to your world. After all, something had to happen in order for you to come here, did it not? You were summoned, weren't you?"

"How do you know that?"

"I just know. So Nath, tell me, are you willing to work with me or not?"

"I'm not sure what you want from me or my world," he replied.

"Maybe I just want my curiosity satisfied." She extended her hand. "Do you want to work with me or not?"

Nath didn't trust the woman, but she'd shown him the only hope to a doorway home. He took her hand and shook it. A chill ran down his spine. *Great Guzan, what have I done?*

CHAPTER 25

ALETA LED NATH BY THE hand and had him sit down beside her on the pedestal chairs. She kept his hand in her icy grip the entire time. She couldn't tear her stare away from him. "You are indeed a marvel. That hair, those eyes and black scales... please tell me that you are unique in your world. I couldn't imagine a place full of the likes of you. Is that even possible?"

Nath had no desire to tell her anything about Nalzambor, but he still needed to play along. Without getting into all of the details, he said, "There aren't many like me. Most of the people are ordinary folk, just like the ones that you see here."

"Do they have scales on their arms?" she asked.

"No, just skin," Nath said.

Aleta nodded. "So the people of your world are flesh and blood, the same as in this world?"

"The people are not so different. My world is not so barren of life like the Outlands either. It's green as far as the eye can see." His eyes slid over to his dagger, Dragon Claw. "And there are many mages too. But this world is a much harsher reality. The people are mindlessly cruel. It's taken some getting used to."

Aleta looked to Gannon, who absentmindedly leaned against one of the worktables. "Come over here, son. Show me your belly."

Gannon slogged over to her and lifted up his robes, revealing his soft belly, which had a white scar running across it.

Pointing at the wound, she said to Nath, "Gannon tells me that he lay dying in his own blood, but you saved him with your touch. That is very powerful magic. But I am confused. Are you a healer, or are you a slayer?"

Gannon dropped his robes back over his exposed belly.

"I do my best to protect the people in my world," Nath said. "I've fought my own fights and a fair share of battles." As for healing, Nath knew that he healed quickly, but healing others in Bish had been an anomaly that he hadn't done in Nalzambor. He assumed it was part of the inherited powers that he hadn't yet manifested but were somehow thriving in Aleta's world. He was glad of it. "Speaking honestly, I'm a far better fighter than I am a healer."

"And there aren't many healers in your world?" she asked.

"No, there are some in the craft with far greater powers than mine." He squeezed her hand. "Listen, Aleta, I'm willing to answer your questions, but if you want to continue to get answers, I'm going to ask that you free my friends."

She sat up in her chair. "That's a handsome request. You see, your comrades publicly attacked my soldiers. As Royals, we can't tolerate that."

Nath pulled free of her icy grip. "As I understand it, it was you that pursued me. We hadn't violated any laws up to that point, at least not that I know of."

"Royals like to make the rules up as they go along," Gannon quietly commented.

Aleta shot him a fiery look. "Yes, my son did not approve of his station. Hence, he decided to find comfort in a lower one, and he almost died for it."

Nath felt his temper rise as he threw out his hand. "I saved your son. We returned him home safely. And this is the treatment that I receive? Imprisonment? You Royals are not fair-minded people, are you? Instead, you are only guided by your ambitions. It's disappointing. As far as I can see, you have everything."

"There is a price that must be paid to maintain what we have. If we lower our guard, another house will take it," she replied.

"Yes, I'm well aware of your so-called 'Royal games.'" He wanted to spit. "I can only assume that all worlds have them. But you can at least negotiate with me and let my friends go free. They don't need to be casualties as a result of my shortcomings, and they are certainly no sort of threat to you."

Aleta looked at Quint and Luther. "As I understand it, those men you fight for are a threat to anyone they cross. We can't have wild men like them running through our precious city. Raving dogs must be put down. Order must be maintained."

His temper spiked again. "Those men helped save your son's life! Venir and Billip risked their necks to save all of us!"

Aleta tilted her head back and forth. Finally, she said, "It does not matter. It would only matter if they are Royal. Now, Nath, are you going to cooperate or not?"

The woman's profound arrogance had Nath seeing red, and his dragon heart started pumping dragon blood through his veins. Finally, he said, "Let my friends go or suffer my wrath."

"Disappointing, Nath. But so be it, then." She snapped her fingers.

Before Nath could move out of the way, he fell into a dimension door that opened up underneath him. He dropped into the inky blackness, swimming toward the shrinking portal of light above him and screaming soundlessly in the night.

CHAPTER 26

DOWN IN THE DUNGEONS, VENIR and Mikkel had their hands locked on the cell bars. With their biceps bulging inside their massive arms, they heaved against the steel. Venir's sweat-drenched locks hung in his eyes, and he snarled and spit then put his back and legs into it.

Beside him, Mikkel was doing the same thing. Sweat glistened on his dark-skinned face. He let out a roar. "I can bend them! I feel them bending!" His fingers slipped off of the bars, and he stumbled backward, lost his footing, and hit the wall. He sagged down against the wall, huffing for breath and holding his ribs. "I swore I had them."

Venir kept trying to pull the bars apart. The heavy muscles in his back flexed and bulged. The inch-thick steel groaned at the joints, and the metal started to bend.

Wide-eyed, Billip said through his split lips, "He's doing it!"

Out of nowhere, the crack of a whip sounded, and then the leathery end of a bullwhip snapped against Venir's fingers. Growling, he held on, pulling the metal bars farther apart. The whip cracked on his fingers again, but he still didn't let go.

McKnight stepped into full view with the whip in hand.

"Up your arse, McKnight! Get out of here!"

The swarthy detective placed the edge of his dagger against Venir's fingertips. "You're going to need those fingers. It would be a shame if I had to remove them."

Venir finally let go and slung his sweaty hair out of his eyes. "What do you want, bootlicker?"

McKnight eyed the additional gap that Venir had created between the bars. "Impressive. You would have made an excellent farmhand with that brute strength of yours. Anyway, I just wanted to come by and offer my condolences."

Mikkel got up. He and Billip crowded alongside Venir at the bars. "What do you mean 'condolences'? Did something happen to Nath?"

"I don't know. I just came by to get my finder's fee, so no, I haven't seen them. But the Vansung family was kind enough to offer an invitation to watch you flea-ridden goat herders in their tournament of death." McKnight stepped back, fanned himself with his hat, and eyed each of them carefully. "I wanted to get a feel for who I should put my money on." He pointed at Billip. "Not you. I'm pretty sure you don't have a toddler's chance against Mikkel or Venir. But it will still be interesting to see how you die."

With his face pressed against the bars, Venir asked angrily, "What are you talking about?"

McKnight put his hat back on his head. "Oh, well, the Vansung family has a very interesting way of doing things. They inject the combatants with mystical juices that cause them to become mindless things that fight against their own wills." He smiled in a dashing sort of way. "It's quite… savage. A shame that Melegal won't be a participant, but we'll see." With a nod and a short bow, McKnight rolled up the whip and departed.

Venir looked at his bleeding fingers and the blood that dripped onto the floor.

"I don't like the sound of that," Mikkel said.

Cracking his knuckles, Billip shook his head and said, "Fellas, we've got to get the Bone out of here."

CHAPTER 27

GANNON'S HAIRS STOOD ON END the moment Nath disappeared through the floor. He never doubted his mother's power, but now his breath froze inside his chest. A cold sweat broke out on his forehead. His stomach turned inside his belly. She was the woman that he had run from, and now he was back.

What was I thinking?

Aleta looked over the dimension door in the floor with a victorious smile on her crooked lips. With a wave of her fingers, the portal in the floor closed. The pedestal chair where Nath had sat was gone as well. Both objects had vanished forever. She turned her gaze to Gannon, and with a note of concern in her voice, she said, "Are you well, child?"

Gannon combed his fingers through his hair. "Never better. But I'll admit that I'm surprised, Mother. I didn't see that coming." His eyes swept through the room. "Er... where is he?"

Quint and Luther were searching the room as well.

"Come," she said, stretching out her slender fingers to Gannon. He took them. She moved deeper into her chamber, where patriot-blue curtains were drawn over one of the shelves. "Go ahead. Pull them back."

Gannon swallowed. Aleta had a way of testing him that he absolutely hated. He was the only of his siblings with the gift of twisting magic, and she'd been very hard on him through the years. He still thought that he came from a good family, as the Vansungs were generally well-liked among their peers, but his mother could be overbearing and dominating, which kept his siblings away. Fully expecting something to jump out and grab him, he took the curtains by the folds and pulled them back. He found himself staring at a rectangular mirror that was taller than he was. Its face was a black sheet of glass. He took half a step back. "What is it?"

"Look closer," she said softly.

Gannon took a long look at the mirror. The blackness began to quaver. There was depth in the inky blackness on the other side of the mirror, as if it was a space that stretched through time. It looked just like the dimension doors, except the mirror had an ancient bronze frame around it. He noticed something moving in the sea of black. The longer he gazed upon it, the larger the object became. It was Nath swimming for his life in the blackness. His mouth was wide open as if he was yelling, but no sound came out. Gannon fastened his eyes on his mother. Her eyes were black as pits. "Can he get out?"

"He will be there forever, if I like," she said in a haunting tone. "He is imprisoned in the black dimension." She rotated the palm of her hand in front of the mirror. "This, my son, is your inheritance, if you embrace it. Omnipotent power at your fingertips. With this treasure, we can rule the City of Bone, and perhaps other worlds as well."

"It's fascinating, Mother." He reached toward the mirror. "I'll embrace it."

She smacked his hand away and closed the curtain. Her eyes turned back to their normal color. "You should have embraced it years ago. All you've done is waste years of precious time. I could rip your eyes out for it, but we have no choice but to move on. Come, help me give Quint and Luther their treatments."

The twins began removing their breastplate armor. They helped each other unbuckle the leather fasteners on their sides and backs. They wiggled out of their suits then took off their sweat-soaked cotton jerkins. Both were strapping men with broad, bare chests packed with hard muscle. Long in length, they didn't have the mighty frames of the likes of Venir, but they were still well-endowed with muscles. Covering their upper chests and shoulders were black, red, and green tattoos of complicated symbols, with cobra faces clearly inked into the meat of their shoulders. Snake bodies and tails entwined with the ancient symbols.

Aleta led all of the men to the back of the room, where a long, elliptical-shaped stone pedestal stood with a glass aquarium on top of it. Wooden stools sat on each side. The twins planted themselves on them. Even sitting, they were taller than Gannon.

Inside the aquarium were cobras lying in a pool of illuminated pink water and colorful rocks that radiated energy. The cobras were albinos, with white skins, iron striping, and bright-pink eyes. They weren't very big, only a few feet in length. There were many curled up in the corners of the tank and hanging from pieces of driftwood.

Gannon removed the lid from the tank. He'd been helping her give the twins the treatment since he was a boy. As for snakes, he was more than used to the wild vipers in the Red Clay Forest's jungles. It was common for him to wake up with a snake curled up on his sleeping mat.

Aleta stepped up on a smaller stool at the foot of the pedestal and reached inside the aquarium. Two snakes coiled around her wrists like bracelets. Their broad heads fit into the palms of her hands. She stroked the tops of the snakes' heads with her thumbs.

Since Gannon was young, he had seen the bizarre ceremony performed countless times. It was something started long before he was even born. Aleta cast enchantments on the unique snakes that carried their own poisonous magic. They were kept in the special tank to breed among the special stones and mystic waters. Their poison, if a man could survive the bite, would add new strength to his blood. Quint and Luther were very young men who wanted nothing more than to please their Lorda, so they had volunteered for the process the first time and survived the test. Now, every few months, they would be injected with the cobras' poison to renew their enhanced strength. It turned them into awesome warriors who had endurance of iron and uncanny quickness. The cobras' bites made them superhuman—the perfect bodyguards for Lorda Aleta.

Approaching Quint, who sat on the left of the tank, Aleta whispered foreign words to the snake. Its head coiled back, the hood behind its head flared open, and its jaw widened. A milky-pink venom dripped from its sharp fangs.

Quint tilted his head to one side and revealed a series of scarred-over holes in his neck.

Aleta let the snake sink its fangs into his neck. The man's eyes rolled far up into his head, and the whites of his eyes turned pinkish in color. Once finished with Quint, she did the same with Luther. The cobra sank its teeth deep into his flexing neck, and the veins in the man's arms and face pulsated underneath his skin.

When it was over, Aleta returned the snakes to their tank, and Gannon put the lid back on top. The twin towers sat on their stools with their eyes rolled up in their heads and their jaws hanging open, drooling like zombies. Gannon moved away from the swaying knights. Their trancelike state made his skin crawl. He followed Aleta into the main chamber of the room and said, "Mother, you mentioned something earlier about ruling *other worlds*. What did you mean by that?"

She sat down on her chair and wiggled on the cushions. "Perhaps Nath's world is soft and could use a strong ruler like me."

Gannon raised an eyebrow but made sure she didn't see it. His mother never lacked in ambition, but exploring another world sounded ludicrous. It seemed that her drive had only increased since he'd been gone. She was hungry for more. "Do you really think that we can open up a portal to his world?"

"It's been opened before, so I don't see why not." She reached for Nath's dagger, Dragon Claw, which still lay on the small round table. Her fingers stretched out over the shining blade. She closed her eyes and made a sucking sound through her teeth. "I can feel its warmth. It is the link between this world and another." She opened her eyes and fixed her stare on Gannon. "You said there is a sword too, did you not?"

"Yes. One of my fellow forest mages touched it, and the man was turned to dust." He pushed her hand away from the blade. "I don't think I would toy with it. There is no predicting what it might do."

"Where is the sword?"

"I suppose only Nath would know."

She licked her upper teeth. "Nath or his friends. I want to see it, and I think we will need it. Quint and Luther, find the detective, figure out where the sword is, and fetch it. When you return, we will finish off the rest of those miserable men."

Wanting to get a break from his mother, Gannon said, "Mother, shall I go with them?"

"No, I want you to stay with me."

Rats!

CHAPTER 28

Reluctantly, McKnight led Luther and Quint through the streets of Bone. They were going to retrieve Nath's sword, which Gannon had described as a "magnificent weapon." McKnight couldn't wait to see the otherworldly treasure for himself. But he hoped to go it alone. It worked better for him that way, as he liked to keep information to himself.

They took the Royal Roadway, passing by the various storefronts and a variety of fruit-cart vendors. They headed south into the southeast district of the city.

Luther had taken a golden apple from one of the carts without paying and ate the juicy fruit, which dripped into his moustache. "I don't see why we didn't torture the prisoners. If we had, they would have told us where that sword was if they knew."

McKnight rolled his eyes as he pushed through a pair of women passersby. "You already whipped the tar out of two of them. They didn't speak then, and they won't speak now. Men like that don't talk. You would have killed them, but you want to save them for the games. Nath doesn't have many options. I know where they hide."

"You'd better know." Luther threw the apple core, hitting McKnight in the back. "I don't like wasting time."

"Me either," Quint agreed.

The two Royal knights drew cautious stares from everyone they encountered. The citizens quickly hustled out of their path when they saw them. It was like walking with a battering ram. McKnight kept moving. He'd trailed Melegal earlier, from the Drunken Octopus to a set of barns where the Royals and their soldiers stabled their horses. He led the group there. One of the barns, at the eastern end, was in deteriorating condition compared to the rest. They entered the north end. Over a hundred horse stalls were lined up on both sides of the barn. Among the great beams that made up the wooden rafters were several lofts.

McKnight heard footsteps above him in the big loft at the north entrance. He moved to a spot where he could look up. A young stable boy was pitching hay down to the main floor.

"Boy!" McKnight called.

The sandy-haired stable hand turned and looked down. His lazy eyes grew big. "Yes, sire!"

"Get your arse down here!" McKnight shouted.

The boy scurried down the ladder. He kept his eyes on the ground but stole a glance at the knights. He started to shake. "Yes, sires."

McKnight produced a thumb knife out of thin air and pushed it against the boy's throat.

He sniffed.

"Listen, stinky, I'll know if you are lying or not, so you'd better answer me right, or I'll cut you open. I'm looking for the stable of three large men, like these knights, perhaps with a skinny man—like a woman—to boot. They have—"

"I've seen them," the boy blurted out. "They're in a back stall on the right. Twelve up from the rear, where the wood is rotting."

McKnight tucked his knife away as fast as it appeared. "Get your arse out of here."

The boy ran out of the barn and down the road, turned a corner, and was gone from sight.

Leading the way, McKnight took the long stroll to the back end of the barn. The deeper they moved into the barn, the more decrepit it became. The stirrings and whinnies of the few horses kept in the front started to fade. They had the entire barn to themselves. He stopped in front of the oversized stall that the boy had mentioned. It wasn't any different from the others. The plank gate was in decent shape, and he could see over it and inside.

Quint let out a loud sneeze. The pigeons in the rafters scattered and flew out of the massive skylight above.

McKnight gave Quint a perturbed look. The sullen-eyed man glared back at him.

"What in the name of Bone is that?" Luther asked, gaping over the top of the gate.

Fully expecting to see some sort of chained-up beast, McKnight pulled free his dirk. Instead of a beast in the back corner, he saw a very strange hovel attached to the woodwork. The weird hatch had a gooey exterior over a bone-type frame big enough to cover a horse, filling the right side of the stable. McKnight unlatched the gate and entered with his dirk ready. "I've never seen a cocoon the likes of that before." He reached out and touched it with his glove. His finger stuck on the tacky substance, and he pulled away. "Yech."

Luther stepped into the stall. "What is that thing?"

"I don't have any idea," McKnight said. "I thought you would know. Who knows? Maybe it's a guardian of some sort, and a giant spider is about to pop out."

Luther drew his longsword. "I don't like spiders. We should kill it."

"Burn it, I say," Quint suggested as he drew his own steel.

McKnight studied the cocoon. He couldn't see anything inside the odd webbing, and nothing moved. "There is a familiar saying that many consider a key to survival: 'Don't bother it if it isn't bothering you.'"

With his wary eyes fixed on the cocoon, Luther replied, "Just look for the sword."

"What if it's inside that cocoon?" Quint asked. "Perhaps it protects the steel."

McKnight tapped his toe through the straw and bumped up against something hard. "I don't think that will be necessary." He knelt and cleared the straw away. With his eyes growing larger, he said, "Sweet mother of Bish, that is one big sword."

Like monster vultures, the twins looked down over McKnight and grunted.

McKnight's fingers hovered over the blade as he studied the

craftsmanship of the dragonhead cross guards. His heart started to race. "I've never seen anything like it."

Luther reached down with his fingers outstretched.

McKnight smacked his hand away. "Fool. Remember what Gannon said? To touch its steel can bring certain death."

"Ha! The coward Gannon tells tall tales. He only wants the blade for himself," Luther said. He pushed McKnight away. "Clearly, it was meant for an imposing warrior like me." He picked Fang up by the hilt and beheld it. "It is spectacular in length and balance. What hands must have forged it!"

"Let me hold it," Quint demanded.

Luther shoved his brother backward. "No! It's mine!" He chopped the sword back and forth in two-handed swings.

McKnight ducked out of the stall. With the twins, a swinging sword, and a cocoon, the small space could no longer contain them all.

The determined Quint managed to snake his way up to his brother. Standing chest to chest, they grappled over the sword. They shoved each other back and forth, their boots sliding in the straw as they tried to wrench the sword free of the other's hands. The lathered-up brothers' metal gauntlets started to glow red and smoke. "What madness is this?!" Luther shouted. The brothers exchanged a horrified look.

At once, they released the sword. They ran out of the stable to a nearby water trough and plunged their hands into the water, which sizzled and steamed.

McKnight let out a hard laugh but quickly cooled under the glares of the disheveled men. Still chuckling, he said, "I'll fetch a blanket."

CHAPTER 29

MELEGAL ACCOMPANIED LAANA AND TWO other maidens to the pedestrian gate of Castle Vansung. He had disguised himself in light-yellow terry-cloth robes that covered his shoes, the same garb that Laana and the other two attractive maidens wore. All of their heads were wrapped up in sky-blue towels. Melegal pushed a cart loaded with rolled-up towels, jars of rubbing ointments, and incense.

Laana led them underneath the archway, where soldiers in ring mail met her. They thoroughly patted her and the other two women down. When they got to Melegal, the happiness faded from their faces.

The sergeant in charge said, "Eh, Laana, who is this ugly woman? Are you certain that she is with you?"

Laana let out a delightful laugh, accompanied by the other women's giggles. "Sergeant Eric, that is not a woman. This man has the finest fingers in Bone. A special request."

"Very scrawny for a man. His light build had me imagining him to be your grandmother," Sergeant Eric said, drawing laughter from the other soldiers and the women.

Fighting away his natural scowl, Melegal smiled and held up his slender fingers. In a soft voice he said, "If the sergeant would permit me, I could quickly work out that kink in your neck."

Rubbing his neck, Sergeant Eric made a sour look and said, "Er...

you have a good eye for things, but I believe I'll pass. But, if Laana was to offer…"

Laana brushed her body against the sergeant. "If you can find your way to the cove, I'll oblige you." She tugged the whiskers on his chin. "After all, you have always been kind to me."

"I'll be there." The sergeant patted her on the rump. "I'll escort you in. Let's go."

Once inside the main castle, Melegal felt the walls begin to close in. As expansive as the grand halls and living areas were, the place felt cold. A Royal house tended to have families numbering from twenty to one hundred members, and each family had anywhere from one to three servants per person, each of whom worked their fingers to the bone doing menial tasks. The servants included urchins, the children who did most of the cleaning and other dirty work. Melegal was brought up in the servants' quarters of such a castle. It was only his deft hands that had saved him from backbreaking slave labor when he matured enough. He never liked the Royals, not even the best of them. As far as he was concerned, they were all self-absorbed and evil.

Sergeant Eric led them into one of the rooms in the upper chamber. It was a bathing area, with flat, leather-bound massage tables and two cast-iron claw-foot bathtubs on the floor. The servants were filling the tubs with hot water. Sergeant Eric gave Laana a wink. Before he left, he said, "I'll let the Lorda know you are here."

As the group set up their stations, the castle servants finished filling the tubs and departed. Melegal inhaled the sweet fragrances. "I could definitely go for a massage, myself. And I've always wanted to soak in those soapy waters." He opened the door and took a peek outside.

Laana closed it. "Don't think that you are going to slip out of here. I need you."

"They won't notice. You saw how easily he waltzed you up here. I'll be fine. I have to find Venir."

"No, you need to wait," she said. "The Lorda always does a head count, and the last thing I want is to see her upset. She has a stare that will kill you."

"I've seen many of those looks before."

She seized Melegal's wrists. "No, literally, she has a look that can *kill.*"

"If you say so."

"It's best that you finish the job and slip away when we are departing." As the handmaidens unrolled the towels and placed them on the massage tables, Lana started oiling up her dark-skinned arms. She tossed a jar to Melegal. "Lather up. We need to sell it."

"I'm not doing that. My fingers will be slippery, and I'm not comfortable with that."

"Don't play with me. You know that the Royals won't play with us," she said as she grabbed his fingers and started to rub them. "Now, you're oily. Listen, Melegal, don't blow this chance for me. I need it."

"As you wish." He pulled up his sleeves and turned toward the door. He could hear voices approaching on the other side. "They've come."

"Stations, everyone," Lana said. Her maidens took their places by each of the two tables. Melegal stood by one table with one maid, and Laana did the same with the other. They all stood with their hands behind their backs at parade rest.

The door swung open. Sergeant Eric stepped aside. Lorda Aleta, in a casual black gown, entered. The striking woman inspected all four of them. Behind her left shoulder stood a taller, younger man who had the chiseled, swarthy features of a nobleman. He too was dressed in casual Royal garb, which was customary of their brethren. Lorda Aleta looked to Laana, pointed at Melegal, and asked, "Who is this one?"

Laana bowed and kept her eyes averted. "This is Geoff. He is a new hand with the best fingers in all of Bone. I went to great lengths to acquire him."

"Is that so?" Aleta asked with a froward stare as she approached Melegal. "Let me see these fingers."

Avoiding her eyes, he showed her his hands. He felt her icy touch run up to his shoulders as she ran her elegant fingers over his own.

"Your hands are steady. No trembling. I like that," Aleta said. "Your bony hands are soft-skinned. Hmm… Geoff, what is your specialty?"

"I have a particular gift when it comes to dealing with one's feet," he replied.

"I'm long overdue a foot rub." Aleta planted her bottom on one of the tables. "Let's see what you can do."

Melegal pulled over a three-legged stool, sat at her feet, and removed her leather slippers. He oiled up his hands and started massaging the bottoms of her feet by rubbing his thumbs into the arches.

"Ah," Aleta moaned. "That feels wonderful. I could sit here for hours. With hands like that, I might not ever let you leave the castle."

The price I pay for being so good at everything pleasurable. Slat!

CHAPTER 30

ELEGAL WORKED HIS FINGERS ON Lorda Aleta's feet and calves tirelessly for over an hour. She lay facedown on the table, covered in a sheet, as he rubbed down her sensuous ankles. Compared to jobs he'd done for the Royals in the past, it was a delight. There was nothing that he enjoyed more than taking care of the needs of a shapely woman. The problem was that doing too good of a job could garner too much attention. He ground his thumbs deeper into her calf.

Aleta stiffened on the table. "Oh!"

Laana fired a concerned look. She and the other two women were working hard on Gannon, who lay on his chest on the other massage table, half covered in the towels and snoring softly, with drool coming out of the side of his mouth.

"Apologies," Melegal quickly said to Aleta. "There is a deep knot in the meat of your ankle. I'll rub it out gently."

"You'll have a lifetime to get my knots out. No rush," Aleta said.

Melegal glanced Laana's way, but she just shrugged. Somehow, he found himself in a situation that he'd strived for years to avoid. The Royals often kept the ones with the greatest talents for themselves, and refusing their offers could prove fatal. At the least, he'd hoped to get the woman talking about the events in the castle, but she'd kept quiet the entire time, and a servant was never to address a Royal. He was stuck.

A knock came at the door.

"Check it," Lorda Aleta said.

Melegal stopped massaging.

"No, not you," she growled.

Laana opened the door. Sergeant Eric stood outside and said, "Please inform the Lorda that Luther and Quint have returned. They are accompanied by Detective McKnight."

Sonuvabish!

Melegal's thoughts started to race. The last thing he needed was to run across them. His disguise had worked on the soldiers before, but McKnight and the twins definitely wouldn't be fooled.

"Send them up," Lorda Aleta said.

Melegal felt his blood run down into his toes. If McKnight came into the chambers, Melegal would be a dead man.

Lorda Aleta stirred. She rolled over onto her side and extended a hand, allowing Melegal to help her into a seated position. "On second thought, tell them to wait for me in the lower chamber." She stretched her arms over her head and yawned. Running a finger down Melegal's chin, she said, "You did well for a man so gruesomely handsome. Do not leave the castle. I would like for you to tend to me later."

Melegal bowed. "Certainly, Lorda."

Lorda Aleta got dressed. She looked at Gannon. "I'll send for my son later." She departed, leaving the group alone with the young man.

Gannon stirred. Flat-bellied on the table, he opened his watery eyes and let out a satisfied groan. "This feels so good." He saw Melegal folding the blankets on the abandoned table. "Finally, she's gone. I can act awake now."

Laana and Melegal exchanged a glance. She started massaging Gannon's shoulders. Daring to speak she said, "Please, continue to relax, sire."

"Now that Mother is gone, the tension has begun to flee." He yawned. "She gives me a headache. Could you work on my temples?"

"Certainly."

As soon as Gannon closed his eyes, Melegal gave Laana a hand signal to engage in conversation. She shook her head.

He mouthed the words "do it." It was the perfect time to massage information out of him.

As Laana worked the man's temples she said, "It's a pleasure to work on a Vansung that I've not massaged before. I'm honored."

With his mouth on the table, Gannon replied, "I've been gone a very long time. You might find this hard to believe, but for the last several years, I've been living in the Red Clay Forest."

"My!" she whispered excitedly. "Isn't that one of the most dangerous places in the world?"

Gannon chuckled. "More dangerous than the urchin-filled alleys of Bone. I trained as a mage there, living among the snakes and varmints, like a wild thing."

"How impressive," she said. "I feel strength in your frame unlike the others in your family."

"Really?" Gannon's eyes cracked open. "What do you mean?"

"You have muscle in places that most men don't. A rugged exterior. I mean that as a good thing," she added. "A firm body is attractive."

Closing his eyes, Gannon smiled. "So, unlike my kin, you think that it brings me an edge?"

"I think so."

Melegal moved to a window that overlooked one of the courtyards. He saw McKnight and the twins talking to Sergeant Eric. McKnight stole an upward look at the window, and Melegal moved away. *No, no, no, he better not have seen me!* He took a peek out the window. McKnight and the twins were moving into the castle at a casual pace. He moved to the door, cracked it open, and waited. He motioned to Laana with a roll of the wrist to keep on talking.

She shrugged at him and said, "Sire, I don't mean disrespect, but you have captured my curiosity. Can you tell more about the forest and your journey home?"

"Ah, as much as I would like to, Mother is very strict when it comes to keeping our lips sealed," Gannon said. "I've probably said too much already. She's liable to cut my lips off."

"But you've just returned, I'm certain that she is elated to have you back." Laana ran her fingers through his hair. "I'm a good judge of people, and I've worked with your mother before. I feel strongly that you are her favorite. She brought you to me, didn't she?"

Gannon shrugged. "I see your point. But since I've been back, it's been quite busy. She is obsessed with a man I encountered. You know what I mean. It's one of those things I don't like about being a Royal."

Melegal stuck his head out of the door. He could hear voices and footsteps approaching the stairs that led to the chamber. *No, no, no!*

Finally, Sergeant Eric said, "It's best that you do not keep the Lorda waiting, detective. Her personal business is her business. You don't want to draw her ire."

"True," McKnight said. The men moved on, and he heard their footsteps fading down the hall.

Melegal breathed more easily.

Laana and Gannon continued their conversation. She said, "Well, at least you are a Royal, and I'm certain that your mother means well. Especially with her children."

"Yes, but sadly, she can be overprotective. The men who brought me home... Well, I'm ashamed to say they're in a spot. If anything, they should be honored," Gannon said.

Laana met Melegal's eyes. "What sort of spot?" she asked gently. "I can't imagine she would harm them if they befriended you."

"It's my fault. I just wish I could forget about it," Gannon said. "I bragged up the one that helped me. He's, well... Being an adept, you might understand. He's otherworldly. I just wanted her to see him, but now he's a permanent guest. And his friends might be in the dungeons now, but she'll start experimenting on them soon." He sighed. "Whew. There's nothing I can do about it, but I feel relieved for getting that off my chest. Just keep it between us. I'd hate for you or me to be flogged. Most likely, it would be you, Laana."

Little coward. Melegal felt the muscles between his shoulders turn to knots. Laana and her handmaidens paled. He'd dealt very little with Royal mages but knew Royals well enough to know that they experimented with the human condition in their dungeons. He didn't even want to imagine what mages did to people—he would have bet it was ten times worse. At least he'd confirmed that Venir and company were in the dungeons. *Time to go on a rescue mission.* He started out the door.

"Say, where is the man who gives those excellent foot rubs?" Gannon said. "The only way to rid me of this guilt is to work on me from head to toe."

With a frown growing on his face, Melegal quietly closed the door. "Coming." *You rotten little bastard.*

CHAPTER 31

NATH FELL INTO A DIFFERENT space and a different time—at least he thought that he fell. Surrounded by what felt like a pitch-black blanket, he swam futilely in the expanse. There was nothing to touch, feel, or hold. It was just him and the blackness. He screamed. He yelled. He shouted for help, but no sound came out. He couldn't even hear himself breathing. He was all alone except for the sound of his heart thumping in his ears.

In all of his hundreds of years, he'd never felt so destitute. Trying to find his way home, he instead had found himself in a cruel twist of fate. He had been trapped in another world, only to wind up in yet another, even darker one.

Bish stinks!

Finally, Nath gave up his vain efforts and stopped swimming in the sea of blackness when it began to seem stupid. He had dropped into the gap when Aleta had opened the floor underneath him, which left him with a free-falling sensation. He couldn't even tell for sure if he was falling, though, and his senses finally brought him to the conclusion that he wasn't even moving. In the open blackness, he stood, somehow existing in the middle of nowhere.

Certainly, Aleta does not mean to keep me here forever. I'll have to be let out sometime.

Nath closed his eyes. He thought of his home in Nalzambor, and of Brenwar and Selene. He called out to Fang. He had put his hope in a new friend, Venir. Time had started. Time didn't stop. He was trapped in a time and a blackness without end, and the mental torment became slow, dripping agony.

CHAPTER 32

After two more hours of Gannon being pampered by Laana and her handmaidens, Sergeant Eric arrived to announce that Lorda Aleta had summoned her son. The mage's relaxed expression vanished from his face. With drooping shoulders, he trudged out of the chamber without a word.

"It's time for me to see you out," Sergeant Eric said to Laana.

"Certainly," Laana replied as she folded up her blankets and towels. "Just so you know, Sergeant, the Lorda has requested that my cohort, Geoff, remain behind."

Sergeant Eric frowned at Melegal. "Oh, is that so? Well, you'll have to stay put in here. Gather up your gear, and let's head out. There's some festivities brewing, it seems, and the castles guests are being cleared out."

The women quickly gathered up all of their belongings, leaving a small basket of towels and oils for Melegal. Laana and Melegal exchanged nods. Escorted by the soldier, they exited, and Sergeant Eric closed the door, locking it with a key from the other side.

"Oh dear, I've been locked inside the chamber. Pfft. Amateur." Melegal took a knee over the basket and unrolled two of the small unused towels. He found a pair of daggers. Underneath his robe, he strapped the blades in place with his belt. He produced his floppy gray cap from inside the folds of the robe and replaced his head garb with it. He then wrapped the towel over his head again. *Why didn't I think of this earlier?*

Quiet as a fox, he crept over to the door and put his ear to the panels. Not hearing a sound, he took out his lockpicks and went to work on the key latch. With a slender metal tool in each hand, he moved the tumblers and popped the lock open. *I've never met a lock I couldn't pick.*

Melegal had ghosted around enough castles in his life to understand their general layout. There were expansive buildings that had plenty of places to hide in their nooks, alcoves, and crannies. When he was boy—a servant-urchin—he and the others had done their best to avoid the eyes of the Royals. The last thing anyone wanted to do was catch the eye of the Royals, who were known to torment the servants for their own amusement. Even the best of them.

He took the steps down to the courtyard level. Using his keen senses of sight and hearing, Melegal stole down the hallways, hoping to find the entrance to the dungeon. Most of the castles were laid out in the same way, with varying architectural differences inside. The dungeons were usually on the back side of the castle, near the soldiers' quarters and stables. It didn't take him long to make his way there, where he found many uniformed servants working the back kitchens and beginning to set the tables.

Melegal slipped through a kitchen door that opened to the storage barns. Inside the vast barn, he moved to a window with a view of the back courtyard. He identified the soldiers' barracks, a stone facility in the back quadrant of the castle. There were training grounds set up in the small courtyard, where a handful of soldiers trained with different kinds of weapons. Melegal also made out a prisoners' stockade and a guard posted by the doorway to another facility.

Ah-ha! Right place, wrong uniform.

There was no way Melegal would be able to cross the courtyard unnoticed in his current garb. Avoiding the busy help in the kitchen, he found a livery closet. Inside, he found a servant's uniform and changed. Hiding his daggers and tucking his hat in the new clothing, he headed to the kitchen and acted as if he belonged there. With the other servants too busy to notice, he stole a tray, a bowl of water, and a bowl of oatmeal. He moved out the back door and gimped along the buildings and toward the dungeon like a much older man would have.

A burly soldier armed with a spear and wearing a uniform tunic over a suit of ring mail guarded the entrance to the castle prison. Keeping his head down, Melegal feigned a slight tremble and said in a shaky voice, "Food for the prisoners?"

The soldier let out an annoyed sigh, pushed the door open, and stepped aside.

With a quick bow, Melegal teetered into a room where stone steps dropped down to a deeper level. At the bottom, he found himself in a dungeon room. There were many torture devices on the floor, bloodstained stockades, shackles, and harnesses mounted on the torch-bearing walls, and tables with crude instruments meant to inflict pain. The musty smell of rot, filth, and death could knock a man over.

Melegal ventured deeper inside, where he found another soldier slumped over on a stool outside of another prison door.

Perfect.

Melegal shuffled up to the man. "Excuse me?"

The soldier snorted. He opened his eyes and jumped out of his stool. With a hand on his sword, he said, "What do you want?"

"I was just told to take this tray of food to the prisoner or prisoners?" He shook. "I don't know."

The soldier rubbed his mouth, eyeballed Melegal, and said, "Hold on." He yanked the key ring off of his belt and unlocked the door. "Hurry up. Knock when you're finished."

"Yes, right away." Melegal entered. The door slammed shut behind him, and he heard the guard lock it. He stood on a granite half-circle landing three steps from the ground. A quick count revealed three rows that were four cells deep, with each cell sealed by inch-thick steel metal bars. He moved to the cells on the right. All eight were abandoned. The middle row was the same, empty, doors open, with broken cots and rank beds of straw. A pair of rats scurried into the small holes in the back wall of one cell.

Where in Bish are they?

Melegal moved to the last row on the left. All of the cell doors that he passed were abandoned. Approaching the last one, he shook his head.

I can't believe they aren't here.

Finally, he made it to the last cell in the very back. It wasn't empty. Melegal's blood ran cold when he saw McKnight standing inside. "Welcome home, rat," the detective said.

CHAPTER 33

S TRIPPED DOWN TO THEIR TROUSERS, Venir, Mikkel, and Billip were led by soldiers through the castle and into a small arena. The circular space was made up of plank benches that seated roughly five hundred people. A stained-glass skylight illuminated the room from above. Venir was all too familiar with the setting. When he was a boy, he and the others would hide in the dugouts and watch the Royal contests and extravagant ceremonies. It was a place where the servant-urchins were tormented too, as they were used as dummies for young Royals training for battle.

"What in the bloody Bish is this place?" Billip asked as he searched the room with his big brown eyes.

"It's a place of contests," Venir said dryly. "A place of doom." His mouth was parched, and his belly moaned.

Mikkel's stomach rumbled as well. "I don't like the looks of this. Ow! Not so tight, hammerhead!" he said to a soldier that was binding his huge arms around a hitching post behind him.

All three of the prisoners were on their knees with their backs to the ten-foot wall that guarded the stands. In a matter of minutes, the guards had fastened all of their arms to the post.

Venir's bindings were secure, but he wriggled against the leather bonds. The rawhide groaned, but it was both strong as steel and flexible. There was no way he could get out of it without untying the knot or cutting the leather. All three men were exposed and at the mercy of their captors.

A dozen soldiers in tunics and chainmail guarded them, all armed to the teeth with swords, axes, or spears. They talked quietly, looking at the prisoners while musing and chuckling darkly.

"Venir, I have a bad feeling about this," Billip said. "What do you think McKnight meant about them experimenting on us?"

"I don't know." Venir stopped struggling to save his strength. He would have felt much better if the mystic sack or his armament was somehow within reach. He hadn't seen any of the items since he'd been captured. There wasn't any sign of Nath, either. It seemed that the redheaded stranger had been sent away altogether. His own doubts began to creep in.

Mikkel called to the soldiers, "Say, hammerheads! What are we doing in here? Give us an inside idea of what's going on."

A soldier with a sergeant's shield on his tunic strutted over and jammed his spear into Mikkel's gut. The big man doubled over. "You'll find out when you find out, wretch," the soldier said. With the other soldiers guffawing in the background, he spun on a heel and strutted away.

Mikkel spat. "I hate Royals."

"I'm sure if you got to know them, you might not feel the same way," Billip said.

"Shut it, Billip."

Chuckling, Billip changed the subject. "I wonder where those twins are. You'd think they'd have a hand in this."

At the top of the arena, above the seats, the main double doors parted. The twin towers entered and held the doors open. All of the soldiers on the arena floor formed a row, faced them, and stood at attention.

"Speak of the arseholes," Venir said.

An attractive older woman with hair braided with green ribbons on top of her head and magi robes that showed off her figure entered. She was accompanied by a man that Venir recognized as Gannon. The former forest magi was all cleaned up, and he trailed behind his mother like a puppy. He caught Venir's heated gaze and looked away. The twins led them down the aisles and to the steps that descended into the arena. As one, the group approached the bound men.

Billip whistled at Lorda Aleta.

Mikkel eyed the woman. "Well, ain't you something?"

Venir chuckled.

With a firm hand, Luther signaled for the sergeant to join them. The soldier moved behind the men, grabbed a lash off the wall, and smote all three men three times across their backs.

Not one of the stricken men cried out, but their faces beaded with sweat. Venir bit his tongue.

With a rueful smile, she said, "I am Lorda Aleta Vansung. I just wanted to thank you for bringing my son home to me."

"You sure have a funny way of showing that," Venir said. Another lash smote his back with a *wupash!* He snarled. "Be careful with that lash. I just might wind up in your—"

Wupash!

Eyes blazing, Venir shouted out, "Arse!"

The sergeant drew the whip back again.

"That's quite enough," Lorda Aleta said. She kneeled down in front of Venir. "Let them save their strength. It's good for them to have some fight in them. They'll need it to survive the venom." She wiped a drop of sweat off of Venir's chin, rubbed it between her fingers, then tasted it. "The taste of fear is sweet."

"If you want something sweet, come on down here," Billip said. "I've got plenty of fear for you, m'lady!" *Wupash!* "Argh! Bloody Bish, I felt all of that one down to my toes."

"I said *enough*," Lorda Aleta said. She rose. "As for your reward, consider this last service that you are about to provide to the Royals as a blessing." She made a hissing sound. The torches hanging in the brackets flickered. Suddenly, the bright-green ribbons in her braids came to life, revealing them to be snakes. The snakes slithered onto her shoulders and down her arms. She lowered her hands, and three snakes in all twisted around her arms and hands before landing on the floor. One after the other coiled up in front of Venir, Mikkel, and Billip.

Venir's muscles flinched underneath his skin. The snakes' eyes shone like diamonds as they coiled back, revealing their hoods. They appeared transfixed by the men. Black tongues flickered out of their mouths. "That's it." He looked at Gannon, who still wouldn't look at him. "What are they supposed to do?"

Aleta gave them a triumphant look. "Enslave you." She made an evil hiss. On command, one snake followed by the other crawled up the men's bodies and coiled around their necks.

With a green snake tightened around his bull neck like a collar, Mikkel said, "Venir, did I ever tell you how much I hate Royals?"

"No," Venir replied.

"I hate Royals!"

Aleta hissed again. The three snakes each sank their dripping fangs deep into a man's shoulder.

Venir cried out when the sensation of his blood catching fire spread throughout his body. His mighty frame strained against the leather cords that bound him. Arms flexing and veins rising, his fingers twisted behind his back, but he could not move. The venom consumed him.

Aleta turned to Luther and Quint. "They will soon be under your command. You know what to do. Meet me in my chamber when you are through. I'll be interested to see how it goes. Come, Gannon. Let's go make a portal to another world." They departed.

Luther and Quint looked down at Venir, and their eyes rolled before turning into snake eyes.

CHAPTER 34

BACK IN HER UNDERGROUND CHAMBER, Aleta drew back the curtains between the bookshelves to reveal Nath Dragon trapped in the black dimension. His eyes were closed, and his scaly arms, which were hard to see, were folded across his chest. "Our world traveler appears to be getting used to his situation. Interesting. Everyone I've put in the dimension can't help but show a visage locked in sheer terror. It's disappointing yet elating. This man, Nath, knows he must come back out."

"Agreed, Mother," Gannon said absentmindedly. It had always been better to agree with her than to say nothing at all. At the moment, he was busy dealing with some larger snakes that lay in another tank in the corner. The tank sat on the floor and was big enough for large men to lie down in. Among the rocks and deadwood were pythons over twenty-five feet long. Gannon was reeling out a bright-yellow-and-white python like some sort of hose. "Do you think two snakes will do it, or do we need three?"

"I don't want to take any chances, so bring out three. And be gentle. Removing them from their tank upsets them enough, and I haven't fed them in a while. They're probably hungry."

Gannon felt a powerful snake's body constrict around his arm. He'd seen entire persons and wild beasts, including large boars, swallowed whole by monstrous pythons in the Red Clay Forest. The snake wound itself around his body. It was heavy, every bit of one hundred pounds.

He trudged toward Aleta with the snake's tongue flickering in his face. "Where do you want it?"

"Place them near my pedestal chair. That will do it," she said.

He unwound the python from his body and laid it at the foot of the chair. With more effort—and to his mother's amusement—he grabbed the other two and delivered them to the chairs. By the time he was done, his chest was heaving and he was drenched in sweat. He wiped his brow on his sleeve. "Now what, Mother?"

She gave him the stink eye.

"Sorry."

"Now, we will get everything in place, starting with this." She moved to the small table where Dragon Claw lay. Using a piece of heavy cloth, she picked it up. "It is warmer than toast, and I don't think it likes me. I can't imagine why." She turned her attention to a spot about twelve feet across from the pedestal chair, where a solid white-oak coffee table that had ornately carved snakes on the legs contained Nath's sword, Fang. The weapon stood tip first, stuck through the center of the table. She slid the dagger, Dragon Claw, back into the pommel and pointed at Fang. "That is a truly magnificent creation."

The sword, an object out of place in the macabre scene, shone brightly in the dimly lit chamber. It was a shining star among them. Gannon couldn't tear his eyes from it, and for some reason he felt ashamed. Nath and what he'd brought with him was pure good, and it showed, but his mother only wanted it for its power and beauty. "How are you going to use this sword to open a portal to another world?" he asked somewhat breathlessly. "We can't even touch it."

"I have a better understanding of other worlds than you realize. You would know that if you hadn't left." Aleta glided to the wall-to-wall shelving and picked up an ornately painted, foot-high decanter. "As a divining rod leads one to water, so shall the sword lead us to another world. This decanter of summoning will provide the power to open the portal. My magic, your magic, and the one called Nath's magic should do the rest." She handed him the urn. "Of course, we will need the support of the underling Oran, as well. This will be the most powerful incantation I have ever cast."

"Are you not going to turn Nath over to the underling?" Gannon asked as his finger traced over the gold and silver inlaid lines on the decanter. "I don't think we want to make an enemy of him."

"We are already enemies. As for Nath, if I get what I want, then Oran can have him, or at least what is left of him. But one thing is for certain, he will not be taking Nath out of our grasp if he does not agree to help us first."

"But you agreed to turn him over to Oran."

She shot him an angry look. "I swear, one of these days, I might just feed you to my snakes. You can be so annoying. Are you such a fool to believe that the underling can be trusted? He'll break his promise, as we would. No, son, you need to learn." She spread her arms like a great eagle. Small snakes rose from the braids in her hair, and her eyes glowed with the same rosy-pink as the nails on her fingertips. "For this day is going to be a big day, one that will change the destiny of the Vansung family forever."

CHAPTER 35

AS SOON AS MCKNIGHT FINISHED speaking, Melegal kicked the cell door shut. The metal door banged hard inside the frame and closed McKnight inside.

Shaking his head, McKnight puffed out a mocking laugh. "You little fool. There is no lock on this door. You should pay better attention to detail. But the one that you entered… Well now, that one is sealed." He walked to the door and pushed it open.

Melegal held it closed by blocking the door with his boot, still holding the tray of water and oatmeal. "It looks to me like you're sealed inside. Now, back away so that I can feed you."

"You always were a smart-alecky rodent. But don't be a fool, Melegal, or else you'll just wind up like your friends."

"And what would that be?"

"Well, to start—" McKnight snaked a dagger out of his clothing and jabbed it at Melegal's throat from between the bars.

Melegal sprang backward, and McKnight kicked the door open. Melegal tossed the tray of food at the man's chest. He had no way of ducking it, and the tray of food splattered all over McKnight's chest.

"I'll cut your neck for that!" the red-faced McKnight shouted.

Melegal removed his other dagger from his cloak and held one in each hand. As he backed farther away from McKnight, the detective brushed the oatmeal from his chest and flung the food from his fingers.

He wiped his sticky hand on his pants leg and drew another dagger from his scabbard.

Melegal's eyes narrowed. It had been a long time since he had battled with dirks and daggers. To make matters worse, everything he knew, he'd learned from McKnight.

"It's not too late to surrender." McKnight took off his hat and flicked it into the cell, which revealed that his slicked-back black hair was thinning on the top. His mouth twitched as he advanced, and he turned up the corners of his moustache. "How long has it been since you stuck a man, hmm, protégé? For me, it's been barely a few nights. You never had the stomach you needed to draw blood and kill. I always suspected that was why you weren't cut out to work for the Royals." McKnight jabbed as quickly as striking snakes as he stepped forward, trying to stab Melegal with the tips of his dirks.

Melegal stretched his neck backward. He parried one blade while dodging the other. He unleashed a flurry of rapid strikes and stalled McKnight's attack.

"You are so quick but so weak," McKnight said. "You've always had the frame of a vulnerable man." He stabbed, chopped, and sliced in the direction of Melegal's midsection.

Melegal countered with successive parries.

Steel scraped against steel. Wrists and forearms collided from fierce blocks. Back and forth, the two steely men went at it. Melegal fought with icy vigor. McKnight battled with a burning anger. Vengeance brewed in the men's eyes. McKnight was the taller of the two but still lean, with a firmer build than Melegal and catlike quickness for such a lanky man. Though he wasn't a soldier, he was sturdy as any. Melegal knew he was no physical match for his former mentor.

The battle raged on as the men shuffled back and forth in the cellblock. Melegal ducked a swing. McKnight jumped aside from a stabbing blade. Both men twisted and turned in their boots, trying to score the first hit.

McKnight stabbed both blades downward at once. Melegal blocked the strikes, hitting wrist against wrist. McKnight leaned down on him, pointing his daggers at Melegal's eyes. Melegal's back started to bend, and his arms began to shake. The tips of the daggers came dangerously close to his eyes.

Slat! McKnight's strength and experience had started to show. In truth, Melegal avoided fighting at all costs. The last thing he ever wanted was a mark on him. For years, even as an urchin, he managed to evade damage and punishment, but now there was no choice. If he was going to survive, he was going to have to get hurt.

Here goes everything! Melegal shoved backward with all of his strength. At the same time, he twisted his head away from the blades. The small cross guard of McKnight's dirk caught him right across the temple, and bright spots burst in his eyes, followed by pain. He felt himself bleeding right over the temple, then fresh blood flowed over his eye. He stood in a defensive pose, his chest heaving as he struggled for breath.

McKnight backed off. He huffed for breath as well, but a thin smile broke out on his sweating face. He tilted his head. "Ah, first blood. It gives me some satisfaction to see you bleed. I'll feel even better when the last drop runs dry."

"You don't really want to kill me. You just want to humiliate me." Melegal leaned against the wall and felt his lungs burn inside his chest. He was in decent shape, but fighting for one's life took a lot out of a man. "I never understood your obsession with me."

"Every master needs a protégé. I'm doing you a favor." McKnight drew in a long breath through his nose. "And you could use some more mentoring. You are sloppy. The moment Sergeant Eric told me about Laana and gave account of her crew, I knew you were part of it, and then I saw you in the window. But I played along, leading you right into my trap. I needed to show you what an amateur you still are."

"I really don't understand why you care. There are plenty of others that can be your adept. Just leave me out of it."

"But you have the gift, and you are wasting it." Keeping his distance, McKnight flipped his daggers end over end and caught them by the handles. "Instead of abhorring the Royals, you could profit from them like I do."

"No thanks. I'd rather hang out with normal people."

McKnight shook his head. "I can't believe you actually came here to save these men. They are brutes, and brutes like that don't live long.

That muscle will be used and abused. Men like that are good for war and nothing more. Your loyalty for Venir is foolish. It will only get you killed. Forget about them and side with me. You won't regret it."

Melegal reached inside his shirt and grabbed his cap. "Do you mind?" he asked as he dabbed the blood that was leaking down his face. "Plain and simple, McKnight, I like them, and I don't like you or the Royals." He replaced the cap on his head, staunching the flow of blood. "I've seen you torture and kill people. I have no desire to be on either end of that, ever. Unlike you, I have some principles. My mind's made up. I've made my stand."

McKnight shrugged. "Well, I tried. You denied." He flipped his dirks in his hands. "You've wasted your life, Melegal. It could have been a good one."

"It will be once you are dead." *I can't believe I'm saying this.* "Fight or die."

"Pfft, not that again."

Melegal summoned the powers inside his cap. "Drop your weapons."

McKnight casually looked around. "Are you talking to me?"

Realizing that his cap wasn't working, Melegal only had one choice left. He summoned every ounce of anger he had left in him, let out a loud battle cry, and charged.

CHAPTER 36

NATH FOUND HIMSELF RELEASED FROM the suffocating blackness only to wind up in a prison of another sort. But to his relief, he could see his captors. Great yellow-and-white pythons were entwined around his limbs, fastening him to Lorda Aleta's throne-like pedestal chair. The pythons' bodies were hard like flexible iron. He thrust against them, but even his own great strength was no match. "Guh!"

"Please don't strain yourself, Nath. I promise that you aren't going anywhere unless I release you," Lorda Aleta said. They were in the same chamber where he'd been before she'd dropped him into the hellish black dimension. She had a crystal wine glass in her hand, half full of violet wine. Gannon stood beside her, casually leaning against a table and sipping from his own glass. "How did you like your time in the other dimension?" she asked coolly.

"It was void of senseless chatter, and there weren't any ugly snakes to look at," he said.

"My snakes aren't ugly."

"I wasn't talking about them. I was talking about you."

"You certainly aren't lacking in charm, are you?" She set her glass down on the table and moved toward him. She put her hand underneath his chin and tilted his eyes up to meet hers. "I could look into your eyes all day. Perhaps when this is over, we can be partners. I think you would delight in all that I have to offer if you would let your guard down."

"No, I'm not fond of people that slither on their bellies. And I'm talking about you, just in case you weren't sure."

"You are such a tease." She kissed his forehead. Nath frowned. She ran her fingers through his hair and continued talking. "Tell me—and be honest. How do you think the likes of me will fare in your world?"

"What? Why would you want to come to my world?" For as much as Nath had learned to pride himself on keeping his composure, he broke out in a cold sweat. *What would happen if the inhabitants of Bish, the likes of her and the underlings, invaded my world?* He had enough to protect there, and dealing with the likes of Lorda Aleta would bring certain calamity. "You wouldn't fare any better than anyone else. My world is full of the very same dangers, some on much grander scales. You should be satisfied where you are."

"A Royal is never satisfied."

"My, you are overbearing people." Nath knew deep in his gut that he couldn't let their worlds collide, no matter the cost. It was more of an instinct than anything, gnawing away at his gut, and he had to stop it. It was bad enough to have thought that his own world might have been suffering without him. Brenwar could be dead. Days, months, years or decades could have passed. He had no idea what would happen if and when he returned, but he knew he had to go home. Fang, the only hope he had, was mounted in the table in front of him, not glowing but still shiny with what looked like internal light. "How did you acquire my sword?"

She moved away from him. "It wasn't difficult. Your companions took us right to it."

"And where are they?"

She gave him a cold, compassionless glance. "The same place that all men are destined to be. The grave."

Nath fought against his serpentine restraints, and his veins bulged in his neck. "You evil witch!" The snakes constricted around his chest and neck, choking him.

"Tsk, tsk, tsk. Mind your temper and save your energy. You will need it once the spell is enacted, as I am certain it will drain the life out of you—and perhaps out of this sword." Aleta grabbed her wine and finished it off. "I'm very eager to get this process started. Gannon, I'm going to trust that you'll keep an eye on him. Do not let me down. I'm going to summon Oran. Can I trust you, Gannon, or do I need to call for Luther and Quint?"

"No, Mother, I'll see to it that he doesn't go anywhere." He gave her a confident nod. "See you soon."

"Yes. I won't be gone long." Aleta set her glass on the table and left the room.

Nath opened his mouth.

Gannon cut him off. "Listen, Nath, save your breath. I'm not going to help you. I'm thankful that you saved me, I truly am, but deep down, well, I'm a coward."

"That's your mother talking, Gannon. A coward wouldn't run away and join the Forest Magi or defend me when I was down. Now is your time to do the right thing. Free me," Nath said.

Gannon refilled his wine glass. "The snakes are under Mother's command, not mine. I couldn't free you if I tried. Again, I'm sorry, Nath. I really am, but I just can't help you. I suppose it's the Royal in me. That self-serving aspect that I could not stand, in the end, is a large part of me. But know this: no matter what happens, it was never my intent to have you captured. I was bragging about you." He hopped onto the table and averted his eyes. "Too much, perhaps."

Nath shook his head, convinced that Gannon would not help him in any way. His mother's hold on him was far too powerful, and no amount of words could break it, so he tried a new tactic. He had the ability to talk to animals and, though snakes were considered an abomination to the dragon family, it was possible that he could communicate with them. In dragonese, he made his case to the snakes, whose heads were bigger than his hands. With their tongues flickering in his face, the serpents looked right at him.

"What are you doing?" Gannon asked. He slid off of the table. "Stop that. Stop talking like that."

Nath spoke in colorful, melodic words that no human could comprehend. The snakes hissed. Their muscles constricted and cut off his words.

CHAPTER 37

VENIR'S BODY WAS NO LONGER his own. He'd been untied from the post and swayed to the sound of eerie music in his ears. His blood still burned in his body, but his attention hung on the snake-eyed men, Luther and Quint.

Luther waved Venir, Mikkel, and Billip to the middle of the arena. The other soldiers in the arena formed a wide circle around them. Luther separated Mikkel and Billip from Venir and had them face off against one another.

Seeing Billip's eyes fluttering inside his sockets, Venir's mind cried out. He took a step forward.

"Stop, Venir," Quint commanded.

Venir's limbs seized. It was as if he was in a dream, watching his own body follow another's command. He could see what was going on, but his thoughts and actions were blurred. He'd been bewitched by poison. It had something to do with the witch woman Royal, but his mind was not clear. Someone else was thinking for him, but deep down inside his gut, he resisted as his own consciousness tried to claw its way back to the surface. But the bars that imprisoned him could not be bent.

"Billip. Mikkel. Fight one another. Kill!" Luther commanded.

Billip crouched down with his fists up and eyes alert. Mikkel unleashed a haymaker swing. The much smaller man ducked under the swing and popped Mikkel in the ribs. The brawny Mikkel, who had over a hundred pounds on Billip, sent his massive fist crashing into Billip's face. Billip's legs wobbled. He landed on his backside.

Mikkel rushed him.

Billip scooted away, tripping Mikkel and sending the man sprawling face-first into the dirt floor. Billip pounded on the big man's back like a wild animal. He locked his arms around Mikkel's neck and fastened on in a chokehold then cracked the other man's neck back.

With a snarl, Mikkel climbed back up to his feet. With Billip latched onto his back, he jumped a foot off of the ground and thrust backward. He crushed Billip underneath his broad back.

A whoosh of air exploded from Billip's mouth. His chokehold loosened.

Mikkel twisted out of the man's grip, pinned Billip down with a knee to the chest, and started punching away. Billip punched back like a wildcat for the first several seconds with a flurry of stinging blows that bloodied Mikkel's nose. Mikkel slugged Billip hard in the temple. The archer's eyes rolled up in his head, and his body went limp, but Mikkel kept hitting.

Somehow, the desperation lurking in Mikkel's eyes registered with Venir. He yearned to stop the senseless fight but could not move a muscle. The laughter of the soldiers in the background howled in his ears and made him fighting mad. His eyes twitched. His fingers clenched.

Fate saved Billip from breathing his last breath as Luther intervened. "Mikkel. Stop fighting. Stand up."

The big man rose with blood on his knuckles, leaving Billip in a pool of his own blood, breathing raggedly. Mikkel shivered all over as if fighting some unseen force.

Luther and Quint let out a grunt and nodded at one another. "It works well," Luther said, stroking his moustache. "These brutes will make for excellent entertainment. Soldiers, what do you think?" he called to his men. "Do you want to see the big ones fight?"

The soldiers let out loud shouts of support.

"Venir and Mikkel," Luther boomed. "Fight until there is not breath in you."

Venir and Mikkel crossed the small expanse between them and collided with a wooden effort. They began to hammer away at each other with oversized fists. Mikkel's punches hit Venir solidly in the body, jarring him. Fists smacked against hard bone and flesh. Venir felt the impact but didn't slow. It fueled him. As much as he didn't want to fight, his instincts kicked in, and the fighter inside him awakened. He put his shoulder down and drove Mikkel into the ground.

In a tangle of massive limbs, the seasoned fighters wrestled on the floor. The soldiers surrounded them, clapping and jeering wildly. The brutes were knotted up in a ball of muscles, throwing short punches into each other's ribs.

"Break it up!" Luther ordered.

Venir and Mikkel rolled away from one another. Mikkel's nose was broken, and his lip was bleeding. Venir could taste his own blood in his mouth.

Luther dropped his hand. "Fight!"

It wasn't a boxing match. It was a brawl. Both fighters were strong and crafty and launched a wild exchange of punches. It went back and forth for minutes as the men sprayed sweat and saliva and collided in blood and bone. It got ugly.

The soldiers howled with glee.

Finally, Mikkel popped Venir hard in the face, which rocked his head back behind his shoulders. Venir came back at him with a southpaw uppercut that blasted the man in the ribs. Groaning, Mikkel wrapped Venir in a headlock and tightened the hold like a vise. Venir turned his shoulders and flipped Mikkel onto the ground. Mikkel's head cracked hard on the packed dirt that lay over the stone floor.

Venir unleashed hard and heavy punches as Mikkel covered his face, deflecting the blows with the meat on his forearms.

Venir was a punching machine, and he had started to wear Mikkel down. He wanted to stop fighting but couldn't. His fist busted through Mikkel's fading defenses. Mikkel's robust resilience faded, and his arms gave out, falling by his side. With his own arms weighted like anchors, Venir threw more punches. It was all he had left.

"It seems that we have a victor," Quint said to Luther.

"Let's make sure that our victor is a true servant of the serpent," Luther replied. "Venir, put your fingers around Mikkel's neck. Finish it. Choke him to death."

Venir fought against the command with every fiber of his being, but he felt like he was screaming into a vacuum. He locked his fingers around Mikkel's neck and squeezed.

CHAPTER 38

With unorthodox fury, Melegal attacked McKnight. The well-equipped detective froze for a split second, and the hesitation was all Melegal needed. Aiming his daggers straight on, Melegal slipped through McKnight's recovering defenses. Melegal buried his daggers into McKnight's shoulders and kept pushing, driving the detective to the ground and pinning him on the floor.

McKnight let out a painful "Argh! You bastard!"

Sitting on top of the man, Melegal pushed his daggers deeper into McKnight's shoulders. "What did you call me?"

McKnight's face was contorted in anguish. "You heard me!"

"Release those dirks if you don't want to die," Melegal said.

McKnight's hands opened, and the blades fell from his grasp. "You're going to pay for this, rat! You won't get out of this castle alive. Mark my words. It won't happen. You're as good as dead already."

"The only one who is going to be dead is you if you don't stop talking."

"Heh." McKnight smiled crookedly. "You don't have the guts to kill me. That's the weakness in you. You had your shot, but you didn't take it."

There was a ring of truth in the devious detective's words. Melegal could have gone for the kill, but McKnight's dirks were on the inside, not the outside. And in the heat of the moment, he just wanted to hit whatever he hit. The meat in the shoulder would have to do. "Where is everyone else?"

"I'm not telling you anything. There is no point in it. They are dead already."

Melegal twisted one of his daggers in McKnight's left shoulder.

"Aaargh!" McKnight started to spit. "Stop doing that. Have some guts and just kill me."

"No, I like seeing you suffer. You deserve it. Maybe I'm not a killer, but I'm not entirely averse to torture. Not in your case, anyway." He twisted the dagger again.

McKnight's jaws clenched. Sweat beaded on his face.

Melegal knew McKnight well enough to know that he wasn't going to talk. They could go at it for a long time, but Melegal didn't have time. He needed to find his friends. Whether they were dead or alive, he needed to confirm their condition. "Well, time's pressing." He inspected McKnight's shoulders. They were bleeding badly. "Maybe I will kill you. Depends on how much blood you leak."

"What are you talking about?" McKnight asked.

In a swift move, Melegal pulled out his dagger and smote McKnight across the jaw with the bottom. The man went limp. Melegal cleaned his daggers on McKnight's clothing and tucked them away. He grabbed the man by the boots and dragged him into a nearby cell. He made his way through the dungeon and found some shackles and gags. He also fetched McKnight's black hat. He crumpled it up and placed it on his head. Then he bound McKnight up tightly and locked him inside the cell.

McKnight sat slumped against the corner wall with his ruined hat covering his face.

Melegal had an itchy feeling that he should kill him, but he just couldn't do it.

I hope I don't regret this.

Quickly, he searched the room for another avenue of escape but didn't find so much as a sewer grate where the waters washed below. He wiped the blood from his face, grabbed the tray and bowls, and knocked on the door.

The dungeon guard opened up the door. He gave Melegal a curious look.

"All finished," Melegal said matter-of-factly.

The guard scratched his head then took a long look inside, shrugged, and stepped aside.

With quick little steps, Melegal hustled away.

Thank Bish!

CHAPTER 39

A CHILL OVERCAME ALETA'S CHAMBERS THE moment she arrived with Oran the underling. The black-robed underling's violet eyes burned like gemstones. He stood a few inches taller than the woman but was more imposing. His evil countenance landed on Nath. He sucked through his sharp teeth and said, "You have him. I have to admit, Aleta, I had my doubts. But you delivered." He set down a chest. "Here is your fee."

Nath felt the tension in the room increase quickly. Gannon's fingers dug into his robes. He could barely dare to look at Oran. Lorda Aleta raised her chin and swallowed. Nath's own anger built. Oran had put him through a lot. He needed to pay. The only problem was that Oran might have been the only way home.

"About that fee," Aleta said. Her comment drew a quick and disapproving stare from Oran. "There is something that I would like you to consider."

Oran's voice was a powerful hiss. "We made a deal." His black fingernails glowed like burning coals. "Don't dare tell me that you wish to break it."

"I seek to magnify both of our opportunities." The sensuous Aleta moved over to a pedestal where the decanter had been placed. The sword, Nath, and decanter formed a perfect triangle. "I have another Decanter of Summoning. With your power and mine, I believe that we could open a portal to this man's world."

"Why would I wish to do that?" Oran asked.

She gestured to Nath. "Look at him. Certainly, there are more like him. Perhaps other things we can use. I admit, I am vastly curious about where a man such as this comes from. I have a feeling that you share my fascination as well."

Staring at Nath, Oran groaned. "Never speculate about the mind of an underling." He kneaded his glowing fingernails in his palm. "Has he revealed much about his world?"

"Only that there are more like him, in various shapes and forms." Aleta moved closer to Oran. "But I imagine a world without the strength of this one. A world that we could rule for ourselves. Wouldn't that be worth taking a look at?"

Oran rubbed his hand over his mouth. His brows knitted together, and his eyes twitched.

It was apparent to Nath that the underling's wheels were turning. He didn't think the underling would even consider it, but now, the fact that he did amped up his worry. On the one hand, he wanted them to open the portal because it was his best shot at getting home. On the other hand, it might kill him, or worse—his own world could be invaded by underlings.

"What makes you think that you can open a portal to this stranger's world?" Oran asked. "The Decanter of Summoning brings forth demons, but not necessarily from the same place. It seems unlikely."

"Together, we will link our powers and our minds with the decanter, the sword, and the stranger," she said. "I have no doubt that it will tie us to his world. The only concern I have is that it might kill the stranger, but at least you will have his corpse."

Oran nodded. "Dead or alive, I must have his body." His eye slid over to Gannon. "And what will this one do?"

"My son will lend additional strength to ours. We'll need the additional firepower." She extended her hand to Oran. "What do you say, Oran?"

He cast a sneering look at her hand. "Your customs have no meaning to me, but I like your idea. Let's make preparations for this ceremony."

"Excellent!" she said, moving behind the decanter on the pedestal. She cradled the decanter in her hands. "I will ignite the decanter. Oran, if you will, link our powers together. Gannon will focus on holding the portal open. I've not merged my powers with an underling's before. I look forward to the experience."

"It will be an experience that you will never forget." Oran took his place across from her, between the sword and Nath. Gannon moved between the sword in the table and his mother, completing the circle. Oran nodded. "I'm ready."

Aleta started to chant in her dusky voice. The snakes in her braids rose with her voice. She spun a weave of syllables as smooth as silk. Her voice became stronger and stronger. The curtains and flames stirred from a brisk wind that suddenly tore through the room. Aleta removed the decanter's lid. The wind picked up, howling through the bookshelves.

With a jerk of his neck, Nath tossed the hair out of his eyes. If the scales on his arms could have stood up like hairs, they would have. A dark, evil power was being unleashed from the decanter. It spilled out an inky, gray-brown smoke that cascaded to the floor, covering the floor to the top of the knee. Nath's fingertips tingled.

Oran spread his arms. His violet eyes burned brightly as he spit hissing and chittering sounds in Underling. In the wink of an eye, his hands flared with mystic orange fire. Pointing one hand at Nath and the other at the sword, he let loose separate bolts of energy.

Fang's handle sparked as if struck by lightning. Nath felt a dark energy pass through his body. Oran's ropes of energy spread out from Nath and Fang and into Aleta and Gannon. The mystic rope moved on, quavering through them, from mother to son. The circle was completed. The room lit up in a scintillating swirl of colors like an eerie sky in a thunderstorm.

Oran bared his teeth. His shoulders flexed as his robes rustled. His fingers clenched around the ropes that filled his hands. Pulses of energy pumped through the coil.

Nath screamed. The dark magic that passed through his body latched onto his heart and mind. Evil tendrils, cold like snow one moment and hot as fire the next, crawled like worms in his head. His thoughts and memories were invaded. His past life flashed through his thoughts. But he wasn't alone. He shared Oran's, Aleta's, and Gannon's thoughts. Evil and perverse, bent on control and destruction, their wicked thoughts made him scream again.

"It is working!" Aleta cried out. Her face was contorted into a grimace of victory. "I can see his thoughts. I feel his mind. Focus, Oran and Gannon! Open the portal!"

"I will. But it will take much to open a portal this big. I will lend Nath's vibrancy to my own!" Oran yanked on the ropes.

Nath felt a dark claw ripping out the very essence of his being inside him. Oran's tendrils dug deeply, ripping into his heart and tearing out the vibrant strength within. He heard the underling laughing with triumph but realized that the sound was in his own head. Nath's body tremored. He felt his cheekbones sink in. He looked down at his hands. His scales shriveled down to the bone. The hair now dangling in his eyes turned dry and gray. "No! No! What is happening?"

"You are dying, Nath," Aleta said in an augmented voice. "Your years drain as we speak. But before you die, at least you will get to see your home once more. The portal opens. Behold!"

Inside the circle, an image started to from. Like a perfectly painted mural, the bright and colorful skies and landscapes of Nalzambor appeared.

Nath's gaze hung on to the quavering image of his home, which moved over the splendid land. His jaw hung, but from astonishment instead of a lack of strength. *I'm so close to home, but in moments, I'll be dead.*

CHAPTER 40

BACK IN THE OLD BARN, the old stable hand had a boy by the ear—the same boy that had aided McKnight. The rickety-limbed old man in deteriorating garb seemed overmatched by the spry young fellow who stood taller than his stooped posture. The old man tugged the boy deeper into the barn by the ear.

"Ow!" the boy said. "I didn't know."

In a raspy, angry voice, the old man said, "We don't talk to Royals. We don't even look at them. We are friends with any other, but not them." He drove his bony knuckles into the boy's ribs. "Never! I've told you that a hundred times."

"You did not," the boy argued. "Ow!"

"Don't tempt me, boy, or I'll have you shoveling hog slop for the rest of your life. Little fool. If Royals come, you need to run and hide." The old man marched the boy deeper into the stables until they reached the opposite end. "You can be replaced with a hundred other urchins if I like. And that's not saying much for you."

The boy held his mouth open, showing silent pain from the wringing of his ear. "I'm sorry, I didn't see them coming!"

"Oh, shut it." They stopped in front of the gate of the stall that housed Chongo. "Did you see them take anything?"

"No," the boy replied. "I hotfooted it as far away as I could. I should have kept my mouth shut and not told you."

The old man released his ear and smacked him stiffly in the back of the head. "I hope you're looking forward to being knee-deep in manure this evening." He raised up on his toes and looked over the gate into the stall. "I like the salt of certain men," he said, speaking of Venir. "It's something you're too young and stupid to understand yet." His eyes widened. "Sweet Mother of Bish, what is that?"

"What?" the boy asked, taking a peek for himself. "Ew. That's nasty."

The old man's gaze attached to the sticky cocoon in the back corner of the stable. It was unlike anything that he'd ever seen. "Back away."

The boy moved aside as the old man opened the gate. Together, they entered. They approached the cocoon with caution then touched the tacky, somewhat crystalline substance that coated the labyrinth of ribs covered by the odd webbing.

The boy wiped his hands on his pants leg. "I don't like this. What is supposed to be in here? Yuck."

"A dog. A very big dog."

The cocoon shimmied.

The old man and boy jumped backward. The pigeons in the rafters flapped their wings, dropped from their perches, and flew out of the massive roof opening. The man and boy exchanged a glace.

A deep burping sound came from the cocoon and puffed out the webbing. Then it happened again.

"Oh my," the old man said, scratching nervously at the long whiskers under his chin. "I don't know what's happening."

Within the cocoon, a loud growling started. The cocoon began to bulge and bend. The ribs within the webbing began to pop and crack like dried branches.

The boy's fingers clamped around the old man's arm like a vise. He swallowed hard.

A dog's head burst out of the cocoon. It wasn't an ordinary dog's head, but one as big as a horse's. It had the bull face of a mastiff and a big pink tongue hanging out of its mouth and dripping saliva.

The old man stammered as he stuck his shaking hand out, "Uh-uh-uh. Nice doggy."

A second dog head popped out. It was the same as the first, but its teeth were bared, and its ears pointed upward. It growled. Its massive jaws snapped.

The old man jerked his hand back.

The monster-sized, two-headed beast started to shake its body like a dog shedding water. The cocoon broke away from the dog's stout, pony-sized frame. The magnificent beast just stood there. It had a rich coat of chestnut-brown fur, with a layer of darker hair on its belly. Its hackles were up, and bulging knots of muscle heaved along its body. It had powerful legs and feet like a lion's. Two tails wagged stiffly behind its back. It set all four of its eyes on the old man and boy, pinned its ears back, and growled.

"We need to run," the boy said with his eyes squeezed shut.

"I know, but my legs won't move."

"Mine either. I think I peed my britches."

"Me too, not that it matters."

The huge dog started to look around, sniffing the air and snorting. At the same time, the dog let out a loud bark. It reared back on its haunches and sprang over the old man and the boy.

The old man's locked-up limbs went loose. He dragged the boy attached to his arm outside of the stall just in time to see the monstrous two-headed dog sprinting away. It left him scratching his head. "It's gone."

"Really?" The boy slowly opened one eye and let out a long sigh of relief. "Thank goodness. What in the Bish was that thing?"

"I don't know, but don't you dare say a word to anyone about it." He fastened his fingers on the boy's ear. "Got it?"

"Yes." The boy sniffed. "Do you smell fish?"

"Indeed, something fishy lingers in the air." He released the boy and closed the gate. "Let's fetch something to eat. I'm hungry."

CHAPTER 41

ENIR'S STRONG HANDS WERE LOCKED around Mikkel's neck like a vise. The only things keeping Mikkel alive were the hardened, steely muscles in his neck. But the man's eyes began to bulge in their sockets. There was nothing Venir could do about it. His body was not his own. He squeezed harder. Inwardly, he screamed. *Noooo!*

Luther and Quint stood on either side of Venir, looking down on him like hawks. They had their arms crossed over their chests. Gathered around them were the rest of the soldiers, who cheered Venir on.

"'Tis a shame to see a formidable warrior die," Quint commented. "He has a neck like iron."

"Aye, but there will be others," Luther said. He began twisting the end of his moustache with his fingers. "I want to break this blond warrior first. There is much resolve in him. It must be broken." He bent down and spoke in Venir's ear. "Venir, finish this man. Crush his throat like an egg."

Venir's mighty arms started to shake. The cords of muscle in his forearms flexed. His inner voice kept screaming as he looked into Mikkel's eyes. He tried to speak. He wanted to tell Mikkel he was sorry. Yet, with his teeth clenched and tongue cleaved to his mouth, he couldn't. Mikkel, his comrade, was going to die by his own hands, and there was nothing that he could do to stop.

The distinct sound of metal rustling against metal gave him a rush. He knew that sound because it was the sound of his armament rattling inside the mystic. It gave him fire, and a deeper strength rose from within him. His grip froze on the cords of Mikkel's neck. Venir's eyes drifted. He searched for the armament. *But where is it? Or was is something else I heard?*

Luther slapped him hard in the back of the head. "Get on with it, man, or I'll slit his throat myself!"

The stained-glass dome above the arena busted open with a crash. Shards of glass fell like rain, but that wasn't all. Chongo, the two-headed dog, dropped out of the opening and landed near Venir. Like a ram, he charged at Luther and Quint. The twins ran to the interior wall and drew their swords while the other soldiers scrambled for the stands. Chongo bumped Venir with one of his heads, knocking his grip free of Mikkel. The two-headed dog stood over Mikkel protectively, with its hackles up and growling.

Venir shook his head as the hold that Luther and Quint had over him faded. As his mind sharpened, his own consciousness briefly took control. The two-headed dog was the size of a small horse, and he knew in his heart it was Chongo. He couldn't comprehend the beast's metamorphosis, but he could think about it later. There was business he had to attend to.

Chongo let out a loud bark. The soldiers in the stands jumped, and many of them scraped their swords out of their sheaths.

Luther and Quint hung back against the wall but still readied their longswords. Luther pointed at Chongo and shouted a command to the soldiers: "Kill that beast!" He fixed his snake eyes on Venir. "Attack that dog monster!"

Venir's knees wobbled. He drew his fist back to strike as he squared off on Chongo. One dog head stared at him, and the other head panted with its tongue out. Venir's eyes swept the arena until he spied his stitched-up leather sack and the place where Billip was laid out. It wasn't too far away, so he circled toward it. The venom in his blood tried to take his mind again, but his iron will would have none of it. He played along, easing toward the sack.

With bared teeth, Chongo kept his eyes on Venir. Gobs of saliva dripped from his mouths.

Venir kneeled by the sack. He slipped his sinewy arm inside the neck of the bag. When his arm was almost shoulder deep, he found a handle. He pulled his axe free then snagged the helmet. He withdrew it by its eyelets.

"Where did that come from?" Luther said, looking shocked. "I thought you locked it in the armory!"

"I locked it all in the armory. I tossed that sack away," Quint replied. He started to wave down the soldiers, summoning them into the arena. "Get in there, you dogs! Kill them!"

Venir put the helmet on his head and buckled the leather strap underneath the chin. His head pulsated with a new, hungering awareness. His nostrils flared. Hot blood pumped through him like a raging river, so Venir knew an underling was near. He bared his huge double-bladed axe in front of his chest and snarled. "Let's take them, Chongo!"

Two soldiers snatched up spears and rushed Chongo. One spear snapped just below the tip against Chongo's chest. One set of Chongo's jaws clamped down on the shaft of the other spear. He bit the spear in half then pounced on the shocked soldiers and pinned them down with his paws. The soldiers kicked and flailed their arms wildly. Chongo's huge jaws opened wide. Striking as one, they bit the heads from the shoulders of both men with a crunch of teeth on bone. He crushed their skulls and swallowed the heads.

The approaching soldiers looked at the dog with horror. "Get in there! Get in there!" Luther ordered.

Fueled by new fire, Venir went after his attackers with broad, powerful swipes. He moved with startling speed.

Slice! Chop! Glitch! In three strokes, he gored and mutilated three soldiers with hits to the neck, chest, and abdomen. Venir waded into the rest of the fray like a hurricane made of steel. A sword blade snapped against his helmet. He jumped as a sword sliced at his legs.

He made them all pay for it. *Chop! Slice!* He head-butted a soldier with the crown of his helmet. *Smash!*

Chongo's claws ripped the chainmail and tunic from a charging soldier's chest. He bit into the man's arm and slung him away like a ragdoll. Soldiers whacked into Chongo's haunches, but they couldn't get through his thick fur. He ripped into his attackers like a ravenous lion.

There was blood, carnage, and death.

Venir finished off the last soldier by driving the spike of his axe into the man's chest. The soldier gasped his last bloody breath, and Venir pulled his axe free. His burning gaze swept the room. Luther and Quint were gone. "Bone!"

Chongo started licking the blood off of Venir.

"Enough, you big beast." He scratched the dog, who almost stood eye to eye with him, behind the ears. "I don't know what happened, but I'm glad it's you." Venir was still in full battle mode. He felt the underling presence. "I feel underlings, but we need to find Nath. Chongo, take me to him."

Chongo let out a loud bark.

Mikkel sat up, rubbing his neck and groaning.

"You going to make it?" Venir said.

Mikkel gave a thumbs-up. "Go get those vomitus pisswillers." He coughed. "I'll take care of Billip."

Venir grabbed his sack and pulled his shield in front of him. "Go, Chongo, go!"

CHAPTER 42

INSIDE ALETA'S CHAMBERS, THE PORTAL ring started to spin faster. It glowed as brightly as twinkling stars, and more images within it started to blur, move, and reveal new landscapes. It moved over the plush and colorful lands of Nalzambor at alarming speed.

Aleta gasped. "This world is so beautiful. I've never imagined the likes of it!" She clenched a fist. "I will rule there!"

Nath wanted to disagree. He tried to say, "I won't let that happen," but his skin was shrinking and tightening over his face. All of his strength fled his limbs. His power was being sapped. The spell and link to the decanter were feeding off of him, sucking centuries of dragon years out of him. That wasn't all—it fed on Fang's power too. Somehow, he and the sword made a latent connection. He could feel the presence within the weapon's metal. *Fang, we need to get home.*

The portal made an unexpected move. As it hovered parallel to the floor, it slowly started to tilt into a vertical position. It broke free from everyone aside from Nath and Fang. Its wavering tendrils of energy clung to Nath's body.

Nath lost sight of Fang, but he could see the other people. Their eyes were bright.

"There it is," Oran said with sincere excitement. "It is powered by the sword. It feeds it life. It will stay open possibly forever with the sword's energy powering it."

Oran, Aleta, and Gannon stood outside of the portal, gaping at the pictures that it revealed. "We could drive an army though this portal and invade this other world."

Nath wasn't certain, but he felt a twinge of the sensation Fang sent him when he was controlling it. He focused on the moment when Corzan, the goblinlike sorcerer, banished him with the Thunderstones. Weak as he was, fighting through the life-draining pain, he focused on his last moment in Nalzambor. The portal image moved through time and space, and he dived from the sky into a mountainside half covered in trees and shale hillsides.

Aleta and Gannon covered their faces and let out sharp gasps. Aleta's chest heaved in her robes. "I felt as though I was going to crash into the mountainside." She held her stomach. "Where are we now?"

The image in the portal moved to the interior of the mountain, which had been carved from solid stone. The broad hallways and caverns were like that of a castle. The images moved into a great chamber fashioned much like a Royal throne room.

Nath fought to keep his head up. He knew where it was—Corzan's home. *So close. Hang in there, Nath. Hold on.*

The door that led into Aleta's chamber burst open, and Luther and Quint filled the doorway.

"What are you doing in here?!" Aleta screamed. "Get out of here!"

With a quick bow, Luther said, "Lorda, the prisoners run free. A wild beast roams the castle. We only sought to warn you. I fear they come here for him." He looked at Nath. "Perhaps he summoned the two-headed beast."

"What prisoners?" Oran said.

"The men who brought Gannon back from the Red Clay Forest," Luther replied. "The one with the axe. He fights like a demon."

"A double-bladed axe?" Oran said, rubbing his throat.

"Aye!" Luther said.

"It is no matter! Luther, Quint, secure that door, rally the soldiers, and put an end to the man. Go now!" Aleta ordered. She paced across the room, and the twins departed, slamming the door behind them. "I will not be denied this prize. Fear not, underling. My host will take care of those men."

"Fear? An underling does not know the meaning of that word," Oran said.

"Gannon, bar that door," Aleta said.

Her son hustled to the doorway and lowered the wooden bar into the brackets.

She kept her place in front of the portal, staring deeply into it. "Who are those people?"

Fighting to keep his head up, Nath could see Brenwar lying on the ground in front of Corzan's throne at the bottom of the steps. Corzan sat in his grand chair with the Thunderstones slowly swirling around his head. The stones made a bright ring of energy. Both goblin master and dwarf had their backs to Nath, but Corzan's head suddenly turned in Nath's direction. Corzan's face turned into a mask of anger, and Nath's own fury started to swell.

Melegal managed to sneak past the soldiers lingering in the training grounds and back into the storage houses behind the kitchen. He set the tray aside on a table. As soon as he did, a commotion of conversation broke out among the servants. They chattered excitedly. Some of them cowered in the nooks. Others climbed up on tables and peered through the windows over the courtyards.

"It was a monstrous dog with two heads. Big as a horse," a kitchen servant girl said to others that had gathered around her. She shook like a leaf.

"I saw it too! It comes to devour us. Lorda Aleta summoned it. She must have. We disappoint her," a manservant said. "One of the soldiers, a huge man wearing a spiked torture helmet, comes to slay us. It is death. Our rotten cooking has brought death to our quarters!"

A heavyset woman with flour all over her apron said, "That cannot be true! The soldiers search the halls for the man and imaginary beast."

"They will not kill this man or the beast!" the man said. He kept turning his head and looking behind him. "This warrior has an axe bigger than a man. I know. I saw him!"

Venir! Melegal hurried out of his hiding spot and took the man by the elbow. "Where was this man heading, fool? Clearly not here, or he would be here by now."

"Um-um-um… er," the man stammered.

Melegal shoved him away and took off into the castle's main halls.

Venir shouldn't be that hard to find. Just follow the noise.

He picked up the shouts of men and the distinct clanking of armor. Then out of nowhere, he heard a loud "rawoulf!"

Chongo? The dog was big but hardly the monster that the servants described. *Stupid people.*

Melegal slunk through the hallways, chasing after the sound of the dog. It was difficult because the expansive rooms in the castle served as great echo chambers. But he went where the sound was loudest. Crossing a small inner sanctuary, he looked up toward the clamor of armor. On the marble balconies, a group of three soldiers were running for their lives. They rounded the corner at the top of the stairs and came rushing down toward the sanctuary. Melegal's head tilted to one side.

What in Bish would make these stalwart soldiers flee?

From the archway that led onto the balcony, another loud bark sounded. A two-headed mastiff-faced dog the size of a small horse burst through the archway. His four eyes were fixed on the soldiers. Ears bent back behind his head, the dog leapt over the balcony wall. The monster-sized dog flew over Melegal's head. *Chongo!*

Chongo landed right in the midst of the fleeing soldiers. Their armor and bones were crushed under the big dog's bruising weight. He tore into the screaming men.

Melegal caught a shadow over his shoulder. At the last second, he looked up to the balcony. Venir, in full battle raiment, dropped down to his level from the higher landing. The blood-splattered man gave him a nod.

"I'm not surprised by many things, but I have to ask. What in Bish did you feed Chongo?"

Venir shrugged. "There's no telling what he's been into." He looked from side to side. Rushing footsteps were coming from all directions. "We're going after Nath." He spun his axe in his hand. "And I've got a score to settle. You coming or going?"

Melegal drew his daggers. "Lead the way."

"Chongo! Find Nath!" Venir roared.

Chongo bit an arm off of a soldier, chewed, swallowed, and licked the blood from his nose. His moist nostrils flared. "Rawoulf!" He ran.

"Well done, Vee," Melegal said. "Now your dog is even more disgusting."

Like Melegal, Venir had a deep familiarity with castles, a familiarity that he'd rather forget. The Royals, however, always had a way to make sure that didn't happen. But it only served to fuel the fight in him, along with the scent of an underling. He raced down the hallways after Chongo. His long strides were barely enough to keep up. Bewildered castle servants who crossed their path screamed, cowered, or jumped out of the way.

Finally, they reached the northwest end of the castle, where a dozen soldiers guarded a doorway with spears. Chongo slammed into the men in a wave of claws, teeth, and fur. Spear shafts snapped against his body.

Venir waded into the fray of men clad in ring mail. Brool turned life into death.

Slice! Slice! Hack! With his axe and shield in hand, Venir became a blur of limbs and steel. No three men were a match for his relentless power and speed. He slipped under spear thrusts and stuffed his shield edge in men's faces, breaking noses and jaws. The limbs of the dying flailed. Venir suffered from new wounds but shrugged off the pain and fought until the last soldier was dead. He slung the blood from his axe and busted through the door. A broad stone stairway led down into the castle's subterranean levels.

Melegal tiptoed through the field of carnage and caught up to Venir. "More are coming."

"Come on. Nath is down here. I know it. And he's not alone, either." Helm throbbed on his head. It hungered. Brool's handle heated up in his hand. "Stay close. Chongo can handle the soldiers."

They took the steep steps, which were illuminated by torches bracketed on the wall. Chongo backed into the stairwell but faced outward, creating a wall of two-headed dog between them and the rushing soldiers.

At the bottom landing, Luther and Quint guarded a door. They stood shoulder to shoulder, with eyes like snakes, brandishing their longswords.

In a voice that was more of a growl, Venir said, "Get out of the way or die."

The snake-eyed twins let out a gloating chuckle. "The only one that is going to die is the man that hides behind a shield like a woman," Luther said.

Venir sneered and handed the shield to Melegal. "Watch my back."

"I'm not worried about your back. I'm worried about mine." The thief's eyes were on the mayhem of battle swirling at the top of the stairs. "Just get it over with, will you?"

The stairwell made for close quarters to use his big axe in, but Venir had fought in close quarters before. Slowly, he approached the twins, feeling his blood pumping in his temples. There was an underling beyond the door. He was close. "Last chance to yield, lizard kissers."

"Dog, you could not prevail over us before. What makes you think you will conquer the likes of us now?" Quint said.

"I held back before." Venir bent at the knees and sprang. He propelled himself through the air like bolt fire from a ballista with his axe spike forward. He impaled Quint through the chest, pinning the man to the door. He turned his head just in time to catch the full weight of Luther's sword to his face as he released the handle of his axe.

Krang! Bright stars and pain exploded behind Venir's eyes. The special metal of his helmet had saved his skull from being split open. His instincts kicked in. He locked up Luther's sword arm and drove the man back against the wall. He wrenched the sword free. The two men wrestled back and forth like two angry grizzlies. Luther's tireless strength was that of an ogre. His grip locked around Venir's neck like a python. "Urk!"

He dug his fingers into the cords of muscle in Venir's neck. Like hammered iron, they held, for the moment. Venir chopped at Luther's hands then punched the man's hard gut. When Luther's fingers didn't slip, he lifted the bottom of his feet into the man's chest and kicked free of his grip.

Luther crashed into the stairs. He popped back up in time to catch Venir jumping on top of him.

Venir pinned the man's arms back long enough to head-butt him in the face. "How does that feel?!" He did it again and again.

Luther's nose caved, but his fighting spirit did not. He snaked a dagger out of his sheath and stuck it into Venir's leg.

Venir let out a painful growl. Furious, he slugged Luther hard across the chin. He pushed off of the man and staggered back toward the door, where Quint hung still breathing but pinned. He ripped his axe out of the man's chest. Clutching his heart, Quint collapsed. Putting his weight on his good leg, Venir tipped his chin at Luther's sword. "Pick it up. Let's finish this!"

Luther hustled to his sword and snatched it up. He stroked his moustache. "What manner of man are you that breaks the snake's venom and matches my strength?"

Venir held out his axe with one hand. "A very mad one!"

Sword and dagger in hand, Luther charged. He thrust with a fencer's skill and a bull's power. Venir pushed the swings aside with effortless power flowing through his arms. He matched Luther's speed, and Brool smacked against the other man's steel. He snuck a poke into the top of Luther's knee, drawing blood and forcing a limp.

"Now we're even," Venir said. With widening eyes, Luther backed away. His face clenched in a fit of rage. He advanced. As quickly as a striking jungle cat, Venir crouched and swung. Brool's keen edge struck like black lightning, and Luther's leg came off at the knee. "And now, we're not."

Luther stumbled to the ground with his leg spitting blood. He raised his sword.

Venir struck right through the man's blade with an overhead two-handed chop. The sword snapped. Brool split Luther right between his snake-eyes.

The battle was over.

Melegal ambled down the stairs and looked at the gory scene. "Do you always have to make such a mess?"

Venir removed his axe from Luther's face. "Just be glad that you aren't the urchin that has to clean this up."

"True." Melegal stepped over Quint's body and checked the door. "It's locked." He rapped his knuckles on the wood. "Definitely barred on the other side."

Venir held Brool out. "Don't worry, I brought a key. Stand back."

Thud! Thwack! Ker-chunk!

The dull sound of an axe hitting wood blasted through Lorda Aleta's special chambers. Eventually, the keen edge of an axe hacked through, and those in the room got a glimpse. It disappeared and popped through again, sending splinters of hardwood onto the floor.

"Impossible!" Aleta decreed. "Oran, do something!"

Oran picked up his chest. He'd said that he didn't have fear, but that wasn't true. The sight of the axe unnerved him. He knew all about the Darkslayer and how the butcher mutilated his kin. It would have to be another time and another place for him. The mission had failed, and he would have to accept it. He gave Nath and the portal a final glance and shook his head. "So close." He looked at Aleta and Gannon then spit on the ground. "Farewell, fools." He muttered under his breath, then his body shimmered. He buzzed out of the room like a hummingbird.

Lorda Aleta ripped the snakes out of her hair and slung them at the door just as the double-bladed axe chopped through the bar that secured it. Venir kicked the door in, sweeping aside the little snakes and smashing them into the wall.

Nath's heart leapt the moment he saw Venir enter the room. The man looked as though he had fought his way through a war field. At the same time, the swirling portal began to diminish in size. Since Oran had gone, not enough power was fed to it. With a dry throat, he said, "Here, Venir! Get these snakes off of me!"

Venir instantly spied Nath, who was bound to the chair by the huge snakes. The man's hair had lost its fiery luster. His skin was sunken, dried, and cracked—he looked like an old man who had one foot in the grave. A mystical doorway hung in the room like a burning grinding stone. He ran to the man.

Lorda Aleta let out a shriek. "Stop them, my pets! Stop them!"

Snakes of all shapes and sizes slithered out of the nooks and crannies and across the floor. The floor became alive with them.

"Bish!" Venir yelled. There were too many to fight at once. The venomous ones would kill him. "I don't have time for this!" He eyeballed the woman. "Stupid witch. Melegal, shield!"

From the doorway, Melegal flung him the shield. "Heads up, lout!"

Venir caught the shield. In the same motion, he slung the metal disc at Lorda Aleta. The shield hit her square in the face. She crumpled to the ground. "I hate to do that to a woman, evil or not." The snakes didn't back off but instead came at him. Venir had no choice but to wade through them. He chopped a path through the snakes, but several bit him deeply and injected their poison into his legs. "Gah!"

"Hurry, Venir! The portal home fades!" Nath said. He felt selfish saying it.

Venir marched onward, suffering bite after bite. The warrior, with his jaw set as if in stone, bore the pain. The portal, once ten feet wide, had shrunk to eight feet in diameter. With Aleta out cold, it was fading faster.

Nath could see his home. He also saw Corzan turn in his direction. The necromancer's eyes brightened with rekindled fury. Nath could barely keep his head up. "Hurry."

Venir stormed through the last several feet of snakes and stopped at Nath's chair. He used Brool to cut the heads off of the snakes that bound the man. He grabbed Nath by the arm and heaved him out of the chair. He looked into the portal. "Is that home?"

"Yes."

Venir eyed Corzan. "That's the man who did this? What is he?"

"Part man and part goblin, I think. An abominable thing."

"What's a goblin?"

"A lesser version of your underlings, I suppose." Nath ambled toward the portal and nodded. He couldn't hear what Corzan was saying on the other side, but the necromancer's arms and hands gesticulated wildly in the air. It appeared that Corzan was using the Thunderstones that swirled around his body to try to close the portal from his side. At the bottom steps of his throne, Brenwar, the dwarf, stirred. Nath felt his strength renewing as the portal shrank further. With the link broken, it faded faster. He locked arms with Venir. The man's legs were turning purple and blue. "That snake poison will kill you."

"If it could, I'd be dead already. Instead, it just hurts like I'm dying." Venir slammed him hard on the shoulder. "Let's go!"

"What? You can't come! You'll be trapped!"

"Then we better make it quick!" Venir shoved Nath through the portal. He followed right behind. They landed on the ground just below Corzan's feet.

Tall, lanky, and hairy-armed, the goblin-faced necromancer turned on both men, screaming at the top of his lungs, "Impossible! Impossible! I'll turn you and your friend into ash, Nath Dragon!" The Thunderstones lit up with a lightning effect. Tendrils of energy flew from Corzan's fingertips. "Die, Nath! Die!"

Melegal jumped through the portal, carrying the shield. The blast of energy ricocheted off of the shield and knocked him to the ground.

Venir tore the shield from Melegal and handed it to Nath. "It's your fight. Finish it." He gave Brool to Nath. "Fight or die!"

Nath took in a lungful of the Nalzambor air. As it filled him, his boundless strength rushed into his body. Rising to his feet, he charged the throne.

Corzan flung waves of energy right at him, but the shield scattered them. "No! No! No!" Corzan screamed.

In a one-handed swing, Nath brought Brool down with all of his wrath. The great blade whistled through the air.

Slice! Corzan fell into two pieces.

Nath was far from satisfied. With a huff of hot breath, flames spewed out of his mouth. Corzan's flesh turned to ash, leaving the bones flaming in two perfect halves.

"Nath, snap out of it!" Venir roared.

He turned. The portal was no wider than three feet. At the bottom, Melegal waved at him with his cap and jumped through. Nath slung the axe and shield to Venir. "Farewell! And thank you!"

Venir banged his axe on the shield and leapt through the portal.

"Oh no! Fang!" Nath ran for the diminished portal. It was barely one foot wide and was closing fast. He wasn't going to make it in time. "Fang!"

Fang's magnificent blade erupted out of the shrinking portal. A corded, bloody hand and forearm held it by the handle then released it. The big hand gave a thumbs-up then jerked back into the portal a split second before it closed.

Nath picked up his sword. "Whew!"

EPILOGUE

BISH

INSIDE ALETA'S CHAMBERS, GANNON CRIED out, "Get him off! Get him off!"

Venir could hardly stand, but he stood, swaying. The moment the portal had vanished, Aleta awakened and started casting a spell. Chongo bounded into the room and jumped her. The dog knocked her to the floor and mauled her.

Melegal ventured over to the former forest magi and put a dagger up against his gut. "It's over."

Gannon's face turned ashen. "B-B-But he killed my mother. Ew! Is he going to eat her?"

"Chongo, heel!" Venir commanded. The dog moved away, growling at Gannon as he walked by the lesser man. Venir could see that Aleta was dead. Her neck was broken. "Let her snakes eat her. As for you, Gannon? I think you would make fine snake food too."

"No, no, please listen, Venir. I did not want any part of this. I swear it!" Gannon pleaded. "As a Royal, I give my solemn word—*ulp!*"

Melegal poked the man's belly a little harder. "Don't you dare make any Royal promises, bub. That will just get you killed quicker."

"Where's the underling?" Venir asked. He no longer had any sense that an underling was there.

"Underling?" Gannon's eyes started shifting. "How did you know?"

"I know," Venir said.

"He or it fled a moment before you crashed through the door. He's long gone by now," Gannon replied.

Venir grabbed Gannon by the collar. "Where?"

"Er... that way." Gannon pointed to the door in the back of the chamber.

"Venir, do you really think there was an underling in this city?" Melegal asked.

"I sensed it. Stay here. I'll check it out."

Mikkel and Billip entered the chamber, assisting one another as they walked. "I don't know what is going on here," Mikkel said, "but more soldiers are gathering in the courtyards. Other houses are lending arms to this one."

Venir looked at them. "How did you find us?"

Billip cracked his knuckles. "We just followed the trail of blood. Duh! Now let's go!"

"We aren't going to be able to walk out of here. The three of you can barely walk at all," Melegal said. "And I don't want any more Royals on my tail." He put the dagger to Gannon's neck. "Do you have another way out of here?"

Gannon raised his hands. "Aye." He pointed a bookshelf. "That opens into another passage that will take you through the outer wall of the city. Listen, I'm a coward, but I swear I meant no harm. I'll keep your names out of this, and I guess I'll blame this carnage on my mother." He frowned. "She was truly evil. I see that now."

Melegal tucked his dagger away. "Don't let all of the blame fall on your mother. Detective McKnight had a hand in this, right? Put the blame on him. Let him be the source of all your troubles."

Gannon nodded.

Melegal opened the secret passage, stepped aside, and let Chongo lead the way out. Mikkel and Billip hobbled along, then came Venir. "You know, you're nothing but trouble," Melegal said.

Venir smiled and patted him on the head. "And you wouldn't have it any other way."

NALZAMBOR

Brenwar clawed at his beard. "What in the wild world just happened? You were gone, but now you're back." He eyed Nath up and down. "You look like you've been chewed up and spit out by a dragon."

"I feel like it." Nath had sat and was staring into the space where the portal had been. He'd gathered and laid the Thunderstones on the steps by his feet. Fang lay on his lap. He hoped his friends were okay. They'd gone through a lot to save him and get him home. He looked at Brenwar. "Would you believe it if I told you that for the last several months I've been in another world that was far nastier than this?"

"No." Brenwar said. "But I know that you don't lie, so it must be true. And I saw those men. They were not of this world. I could tell by their gear and clothing." He shrugged his eyebrows. "But that axe, Nath, I've seen its mold in the forges below Morgdon. I swear it. Tell me more about this world."

"Its landscape was rugged in some places. Dry as a bone. In other spots, the wilderness sweltered. There was no getting comfortable. It caused a prickly feeling all over." He ran his fingers over his blade. "Two suns and two moons. Mischief and deceit at every turn."

"I like it."

Nath nodded. "I never would have made it back without those men. They were an unlikely source of light in the dark, and they saw me through it. With that said, it's good to be home, Brenwar."

"Aye. Now let's get these stones back where they belong—in Morgdon."

Nath looked at the stones. Each was a rich gemstone color. The Stone of Command. The Stone of Sight. The Stone of Transport. The Stone of Power. The Stone of Thought. It made him think of the underling's eyes. "I think it would be best if we kept them separated. Together, they are far too tempting and dangerous."

They gathered their items and headed out of Corzan's abode.

Brenwar quickly picked up his grumbling. "Pah, it was the elves that fouled it up to begin with. We will take them to Morgdon. It has the safest vaults in the world."

"No doubt, but the high council must decide."

"Argh… With talk like that, I want to shave my beard."

Nath threw his arm over his best friend's shoulder and chuckled.

Nalzambor, it's good to be home. As for Bish, I'm stronger for it, but I don't want to ever go back.

MORE ON THIS SERIES
FROM THE AUTHOR

Friends of Nalzambor and Bish, I really hope you enjoyed this story. I really love telling stories in Bish. I have no idea if you have read the Darkslayer or Nath Dragon book series, or if you just started with Clash. Clash had some people, places and things that are part of the other books' storylines. They might have popped up and left you scratching your head because they didn't play a big part in this story, but they do play large roles in the other stories. Here, I think of them as cameos. Some examples are the Motley Girls and Lorda and Tonio Almen. Big parts in the Darkslayer series one.

There was a huge reveal in this book that the Darkslayer series did not cover: how Chongo got so big and grew two heads. I get this question a lot, but now you have your answer. I'm going to clarify. In book one, *The Darkslayer, Wrath of the Royals*, Venir is young. He almost dies at the hands of the magical Silver Fish. He survives the encounter, and he and Chongo eat the Silver Fish. Again, it's magic and it made Venir grow, but the magic never manifested in Chongo until this story. Chongo licks the blood from Nath's wounds, and Nath's blood is magic. That triggers the Silver Fish magic that still lingers in Chongo's blood and prompts his transformation. Hence, we have a giant-sized two-headed Chongo. Confusing? I hope not, and I hope you find this explanation satisfactory. I didn't want the leave the diehard fans lingering without it.

Again, remember, in this series Venir is young (*Pre Series, The*

Darkslayer, Wrath of the Royals), so Clash works great as an intro to that series. Nath is older (this takes place between *The Chronicles of Dragon*, series one and *Tail of the Dragon*, series two). Nath's story begins in The Odyssey of Nath Dragon, a prequel to the Chronicles of Nath Dragon. Crossovers can be complicated, but I hope I kept it simple enough for you to follow.

OTHER BOOKS AND AUTHOR INFO

Craig Halloran resides with his family outside his hometown of Charleston, West Virginia. When he isn't entertaining mankind, he is seeking adventure, working out, or watching sports. To learn more about him, go to: www.thedarkslayer.com.

FREE BOOKS
The Darkslayer: Brutal Beginnings
Nath Dragon – Quest for the Thunderstone

THE ODYSSEY OF NATH DRAGON SERIES (NEW SERIES) (PREQUEL TO CHRONICLES OF DRAGON)
Exiled
Enslaved
Deadly
Hunted

THE CHRONICLES OF DRAGON SERIES 1 (10 BOOKS)
The Hero, the Sword and the Dragons (Book 1)
Dragon Bones and Tombstones (Book 2)
Terror at the Temple (Book 3)
Clutch of the Cleric (Book 4)
Hunt for the Hero (Book 5)
Siege at the Settlements (Book 6)
Strife in the Sky (Book 7)
Fight and the Fury (Book 8)

War in the Winds (Book 9)
Finale (Book 10)
Boxset 1-5
Boxset 6-10
Collector's Edition 1-10

TAIL OF THE DRAGON, THE CHRONICLES OF DRAGON, SERIES 2 (10 BOOK SERIES)

Tail of the Dragon #1
Claws of the Dragon #2
Battle of the Dragon #3
Eyes of the Dragon #4
Flight of the Dragon #5
Trial of the Dragon #6
Judgement of the Dragon #7
Wrath of the Dragon #8
Power of the Dragon #9
Hour of the Dragon #10
Boxset 1-5
Boxset 6-10
Collector's Edition 1-10

THE DARKSLAYER SERIES 1 – 6 BOOKS

Wrath of the Royals (Book 1)
Blades in the Night (Book 2)
Underling Revenge (Book 3)
Danger and the Druid (Book 4)
Outrage in the Outlands (Book 5)
Chaos at the Castle (Book 6)
Boxset 1-3
Boxset 4-6
Omnibus 1-6

THE DARKSLAYER: BISH AND BONE, SERIES 2 (10 BOOK SERIES)

Bish and Bone (Book 1)

Black Blood (Book 2)
Red Death (Book 3)
Lethal Liaisons (Book 4)
Torment and Terror (Book 5)
Brigands and Badlands (Book 6)
War in the Wasteland (Book 7)
Slaughter in the Streets (Book 8)
Hunt of the Beast (Book 9)
The Battle for Bone (Book 10)
Boxset 1-5
Boxset 6-10
Bish and Bone Omnibus (Books 1-10)

CLASH OF HEROES: NATH DRAGON MEETS THE DARKSLAYER MINI SERIES

Book 1
Book 2
Book 3

THE GAMMA EARTH CYCLE

Escape from the Dominion
Flight from the Dominion
Prison of the Dominion

THE SUPERNATURAL BOUNTY HUNTER FILES (10 BOOK SERIES)

Smoke Rising: Book 1
I Smell Smoke: Book 2
Where There's Smoke: Book 3
Smoke on the Water: Book 4
Smoke and Mirrors: Book 5
Up in Smoke: Book 6
Smoke Signals: Book 7
Holy Smoke: Book 8
Smoke Happens: Book 9
Smoke Out: Book 10

Boxset 1-5
Boxset 6-10
Collector's Edition 1-10

ZOMBIE IMPACT SERIES
Zombie Day Care: Book 1
Zombie Rehab: Book 2
Zombie Warfare: Book 3
Boxset: Books 1-3

OTHER WORKS & NOVELLAS

THE SCARABS CURSE – SWORD & SORCERY NOVELLA
The Scarab's Power
The Scarab's Command
The Scarab's Trick
The Scarab's War

It's not him, It's them (Jerk of All Trades) 1 book - Drama

Gorgon Thunder-Bot Incinerator of Worlds (1 book, childrens)

www.ingramcontent.com/pod-product-compliance
Lightning Source LLC
Chambersburg PA
CBHW070644310726
48982CB00001B/411